MW00944570

**STRANGERS AND PILGRIMS SERIES**
**BOOK #4**

# CAUGHT UP

## Morgan's Son

## Written By

# John and Patty Probst

In memory of "Mother" Maggie Mae Berrier,
one of our greatest fans and a most enthusiastic
reader of our books.
Also, of "Dad" John Albert Probst,
whose pride in what we were doing
was a sustaining encouragement to us.
Their prayers had a profound
impact on our lives and this book.
Both went to be with the Lord before
"Caught Up" was completed. But, their lives and
influence are caught in these pages.


Dedicated with a great sense of love
and appreciation to dear
and trusted friends who have served alongside
us in churches and the
media ministry, ones who have shared
in the struggles and the triumphs.
We treasure the memories of the ones who have
passed on and the friendships of
those still with us. They are un-named on this page
but registered in our hearts.

Also to our pastor, Alvin Alcantara,
whose message one Sunday,
became the inspiration and basis for Caleb's sermon
in the great Concert Crusade.

**John and Patty Probst**

**Strangers and Pilgrims Series**
*The Last of the Wagon Pioneers*
*A Place For Farmer and Emile*
*Janee*
*Caught Up*

# FOREWORD

Behold, I show you a mystery, we shall not all sleep, but we shall all be changed.

In a moment, in the twinkling of an eye, at the last trump: for the trumpet shall sound, and the dead shall be raised incorruptible, and we shall be changed.

I Corinthians 15:51-52

For the Lord Himself shall descend from Heaven with a shout, with the voice of the archangel, and with the trump of God: and the dead in Christ shall rise first:

Then we who are alive and remain shall be **Caught Up** together with them in the clouds, to meet the Lord in the air; and so shall we ever be with the Lord.

I Thessalonians 4:16-17

For two thousand years Christians have held to the belief that one-day millions of believers would disappear from the face of the earth. Such an event is so amazing in size and scope that many found it incredulous. Yet, countless others over the centuries have wondered and hoped - could it possibly be? Will I be one of those **Caught Up**?

# CONTENTS

# Chapter 1

# Arriving in Atlanta

It was a cold, gloomy January morning. The Interstate led Caleb Hillag into Atlanta, Georgia. Oh, how he had prayed for a bright sunny day, at least warmer. Not this!

Icy roads and miserable rain had not only delayed him a whole day driving from Memphis, Tennessee, he was two and a half hours late for what could be the most important meeting of his life.

In his mind, he envisioned the five board members as old, cranky and unsympathetic to his reasons for not being on time. He felt the cards of rejection already stacking against him! Frustration had long ago taken over.

He noted the car battery's "low" light flashing, and breathed a prayer for enough power to get to his destination. Stormy weather shaded his solar panels from sun to keep his batteries up, and that forced three unplanned stops for charges. He missed the days when he owned a gasoline-driven car, but who could afford one now? Not him! Gas stations were as scarce as the gasoline, and no wonder the world had converted to alternate power sources. The least desirable but most inexpensive were the solar chip cars - that's what Caleb owned, and he hated it. He couldn't count the number of times he sat on the side of the road waiting for the sun to come out - or come up!

"Only a few more miles, you heap of plastic," Caleb muttered, as he switched on the geo-tracker. The familiar electronic voice took over the wheel directing toward the programmed-in address.

Caleb had no idea what to expect. His imagination pictured a very old-fashioned two or three-story house that resembled something between a fine southern mansion and a haunted house. Furthermore it was stuck right in the middle of modern downtown high-rises - as if trying to impede the march of change. He felt doomed, as he foresaw a war of words with this board. His mind had already rehearsed all kinds of possible scenarios and conversations, so he was completely shocked to face an ultramodern skyscraper in downtown Atlanta.

Parking security assigned him a space number, which took him down several layers. He located his spot, backed in, and hurriedly slid his charge card into the slot that turned an intense light onto his solar chips. Maybe, just maybe, he would be here long enough for the batteries to recoup.

He ran across the parking area to the elevator. Coming out into the lobby he maneuvered his way through people to the directory. His eye scanned the lists until he found:

Global Missions International - Floor 15 - Room 1517

Caleb crowded into one of the elevators making sure button 15 was lit. Up the elevator zipped, stopping several times before reaching Caleb's floor. He quickly located room 1517 and literally burst through the door going directly to the receptionist.

A very attractive young woman with light brown hair and hazel eyes turned to greet him.

"Welcome to Global Missions. My name is Rona, a Gamma - fourth generation. How may I assist you?"

This robot took Caleb aback. It was a new model and so realistic at first glance he had thought it human.

"I'm Caleb Hillag. I had an eight o'clock appointment. I'm so sorry I'm late - I had weather and battery problems and...." his voice trailed off. Why in the name of common sense was he explaining himself to a robot?

Rona smiled turning back to a computer. She pushed a key.

"Mr. Hillag is here for his eight o'clock appointment. That will be in 9 hours and 6 minutes. Mr. Hillag is early, but he says he is sorry that he is late."

Caleb groaned, waiting for the board's reply.

"Tell Hillag to have a seat, and we will be with him directly," he could hear laughter.

"Please have a seat, Mr. Hillag, the board will see you in a few minutes," Rona said politely.

Caleb found a seat and took a moment to study the room. The reception area was first class with expensive-looking furnishings and plush carpet. It was ultra-modern, not anything Caleb had expected. Rona was a testimony to that.

He glanced at the large atomic clock on a sidewall. It read Thursday, January 5, 2017 - Temperature 76° - Barometric Pressure 30.1 - Humidity 87%. In big numbers was 10:59 a.m., and below that, all time zones were listed. On the very bottom was print too small for Caleb to read, but he knew what it was. "Accurate to within one second every two million years." Caleb doubted the claim, and smiled to think he wouldn't wait around to see it lose or gain a second.

He left his seat to study a world map of Global Missions. He was impressed at the size of their outreach.

"Must be a place for me and my family to serve," Caleb voiced his thoughts out loud.

"We have 248 possible locations," he heard Rona respond from her desk.

Caleb studied the map - silently praying over it for God's will and anointing. He sat again. Eleven eighteen! He got up, looking over some pictures, walked to a table and picked up a magazine, but all he did was thumb through the pages. He was antsy and wanted this interview to start.

"Would you care for coffee?" Rona asked. Caleb hesitated. Could she do that? How?

"Yes - please," Caleb, replied slowly. He was amazed to watch her rise and walk to a coffee maker, but here is where her realism stopped. Her gate was slow and more stiff legged. She opened a cabinet and removed a cup, pouring it full without spillage. Caleb took note that Rona was professionally dressed in a suit skirt and top, nylons and low heels. Who dresses her, he wondered, and suddenly had this impish idea of pushing her over. Would she get up or would her legs and arms keep going in a mechanical walking motion as the robot lay on the floor.

He smiled to himself as the mental picture played in his head. He quickly squashed the impulse and accepted the cup of coffee she offered.

"Thank you, Rona. I too am a fourth generation. Do you know that?"

Rona made no reply, but returned to her desk. He heard her typing something on the keyboard, then the robot placed her finger on the screen, and there was a fast clicking sound. She turned to face Caleb with a smile.

"Yes, I do," she spoke in an expressionless voice.

"Caleb Hillag, born to Joseph and Morgan Hillag in 1977. Morgan Trevor was the second child born to Clifton and Rachel Trevor in 1952. She had a brother, David, deceased in 1994. Clifton Trevor, born to Farmer and Emile Trevor in 1922. Clifton had a brother, Walter, and sister, Leah, all deceased. Four generations."

Caleb sat dumbfounded! He had recently read an article about these robots, but never had seen one in action. They were amazing!

Caleb remained silent as he sipped his coffee. He was growing impatient. He glanced at the clock for the hundredth time - eleven forty-three! His anger was reaching the boiling point!

"Rona, can't you check with the board to see how much longer?" Caleb blurted out.

"I'm not allowed to disturb them, Mr. Hillag, but you are early."

"I'm not early - I'm late!" Caleb raised his voice. "Just let them know that I'm still waiting."

"I'm not allowed to disturb them," Rona repeated her prior response with a smile. Caleb could have sworn she was laughing at him! He threw up his hands in exasperation!

When the clock hit 12:20, Caleb could take no more. "What are they doing in there, Rona?" Caleb's voice was shrill and angry.

"It is lunch time," she spoke without looking up.

"What?" He couldn't believe his ears. Their rudeness was inexcusable!

"Lunch is over at 1:00 p.m.," Rona continued.

Caleb collapsed into a chair. He knew he had to get hold of his anger and calm down or he would be so agitated when he finally walked into that boardroom he'd end up cutting his own throat. He sat still and attempted to pray and settle down. In a moment of panic realization, he wondered if they weren't in there - watching him.

"Rona - can they - see out - here - from - in there?" Caleb stammered over the question.

"They see what I see," Rona remarked as she made entries on her P. C.

"Oh, no," Caleb moaned burying his face in his hands.

It was 1:37 p.m. on the atomic clock when the board-room door clicked - opened - and a man entered, walking to Caleb. Caleb stood to meet him.

# Chapter 2

# The Interview

Caleb was ushered into a sizeable conference room dominated by a massive dark wood table. Matching chairs ringed the table, and the newest blu screen television was mounted on one wall. Beautiful outdoors pictures from various countries filled the other walls. The man who greeted him in the reception area, Gerald Pullman, introduced Caleb to the other board members, "Caleb Hillag, this is Marcus Willabee."

Caleb tried to size up each of the individuals as they were introduced. Marcus, like Gerald, seemed friendly, but Marcus was more business. Hub Crabtree grunted with a firm handshake. Caleb knew immediately this was the obstinate devil's advocate.

Of the two women board members, Nancy Stroder was abrupt and serious. Tiffany Gong was the youngest, bright and bubbly. Caleb felt he had an ally in her.

"We apologize for the delay. We had you scheduled for yesterday, then rescheduled you this morning. We had to fit you in whenever we could, so we are rushed," Marcus explained.

Caleb's heart sunk. Another card stacked against him!

"I'm sorry," he muttered. "Had nasty weather and - car problems. Just thankful to be here," he was groping for a way to turn the conversation more positive. "It has taken nine months of phone calls and letter writing to get this opportunity. Thank you for your patience and time. I hope and pray it will be worth your while."

"Well, yes, let's get to it," Hub directed.

"First of all, we want to play a disc explaining Global's procedures and policies. It will conclude with an overview of our mission work around the world. Please have a seat, Mr. Hillag." Nancy Stroder touched a panel to commence the program as Gerald dimmed the lights.

Caleb watched the presentation carefully; taking notes on the pad of paper he was provided. Deep feelings stirred within him that he had felt for nearly three years. He had watched missionaries among nationals of other countries and knew God's call on his life was strong and clear. Tears filled his eyes and his heart yearned for that call's fulfillment to happen in his life.

"Any questions or comments," Marcus inquired as ending credits came up on the screen.

Caleb thought a moment to give an honest reaction. "That was very well done. I was quite impressed to see the vast extent of your work. I prayed to be sent out by the best, and what I just saw convinces me you are the best!"

Tiffany and Gerald smiled; the others sat stone faced as they opened folders that Marcus had handed them while the presentation was playing. They studied the contents in silence, slowly turning the pages. This went on for some time, and Caleb grew uncomfortable. He could feel the back of his neck get hot against his collar.

Marcus Willabee was the first to lay his folder down. He began the interview.

"Four years Bible College in Asapha, Washington, and three years in their Seminary. You graduated with a 3.8 grade average?"

"Yes, sir."

"The record shows that in 1999 you married Tammy Hutton and divorced in 2001," Nancy Stroder spoke next. "Tell us about that."

Caleb felt his face flush. The board was taking him to a place he did not care to go - but knew he must.

"I met Tammy in college. We fell in love, and married in my senior year."

"Was she pregnant?" Hub asked coldly.

"Does your record there list any children by her?" Caleb snapped. He instantly did not like this man.

"No, but perhaps an unrecorded abortion?" Hub dug a little deeper. This drew a reaction from Gerald and Tiffany. Even Nancy was disgusted!

"I don't think that was necessary, Hub!" she scowled in protest.

"How can we know what kind of a missionary he would be if we don't have a handle about his morals. Was Tammy a virgin on their wedding night?"

The whole board became noisy with objections until Caleb called for silence.

"I'll answer that," he spoke painfully. "No, Hub, she wasn't. Morally, I was weak and selfish, but I am honest, for whatever that's worth."

Tiffany Gong wanted to ease the tension by moving on. "But you married Sarah Crothers in 2007, and you have a daughter Esther and a son, Mark?"

"Yes'm."

"Tell us how you met Sarah?" Gerald asked.

"She was a member of my third pastorate."

"Humph," growled Hub. "Was she also a non-virgin when you married?"

"None of your damned business!" Caleb exploded. "I answered your question about my ex, but now you're talking about my wife!"

"That's enough," Marcus injected. "I see you pastored in three churches from 2003 to 2006. You didn't stay in one church for very long."

"I wasn't up front in disclosing my divorce to my first congregation. When they found out they asked me to leave."

"Can you blame them?" Nancy wanted to see his reaction.

"No, they had a right to be upset."

"I see you were at your second pastorate for three years. Why did you leave there?" Gerald questioned, looking over the top of his folder.

"I felt God's call to Timberdyke. That was also in Washington."

"Humph," Hub shifted in his seat. "Smaller church with LESS money," he growled sarcastically. A look of triumph cast his face as his eyes rolled around the room.

Again, Caleb answered, "Yes, Hub, it was a bigger church with more members and more responsibility. Yes, it was a higher salary, but would you say it was against God's will for me to go there where I met Sarah?"

Hub straightened up and took Caleb's challenge, "Only God and you would know that."

Caleb ignored the remark. He was beginning to seriously doubt whether God ever intended for him to have anything to do with this organization.

All of the members instantly retreated into their folders except Hub who stared at Caleb. Gerald scratched his head as he turned a page in his folder.

Tiffany was the next to speak. She attempted a smile.

"You pastored at Timberdyke for six years and apparently had growth," she was trying to build Caleb up.

"Yes, I accepted that pastorate in 2006. That's when I met Sarah; we got married the next year. Esther and Mark were both born there."

"You resigned in 2012," Tiffany Gong continued.

"Yes."

"Why did you leave a growing church?" Marcus questioned.

"We felt a call to Tennessee," Caleb swallowed hard.

"An elder at Timberdyke told me on the phone they were ready to vote you out," Hub injected.

Caleb's face burned. This interview was a disguised interrogation!

Nancy Stroder sat up and adjusted her glasses. "What was that about?"

Caleb hung his head in thought before he answered. The words about a painful experience did not come easily.

"A small group in the church who were also the major contributors didn't like what I was preaching and wanted to dictate my messages." Caleb took a deep breath. "I refused their advice, and they withheld their giving. The church went into the red within four months, and the congregation got scared. I resigned before the whole thing collapsed."

"You seem long on principle and short on tact," Marcus observed.

"All I know to do is teach and preach the Bible - all I've ever known," Caleb spoke sadly.

Nancy gave a forced laugh. "Not many churches that want that anymore in this day and age."

Caleb wanted to defend the church, but Hub jumped in before he could speak.

"That's why he moved to Tennessee. Thought the so-called Bible Belt would be more Bible," Hub said dryly tapping a pencil on the desk.

All eyes were on Caleb to see his reaction. He felt - frozen - frozen in thought or speech.

"Were they? I mean - more Bible?" Tiffany asked.

"Must not a been," Hub answered her question. "He tried three of them in three years, and hasn't pastored since August of 2015!"

Caleb felt the sting of shame. He was stripped of any pride; his manhood, dignity, confidence demolished. The final blow for him came with the next question. He didn't even know who asked it, but it rang in his ears eating down into his very heart and soul.

"But you are a minister! What have you been doing?"

Tears filled Caleb's eyes and ran hot down his cheeks. He dared not look up; his answer was barely audible.

"I mow grass - and - landscape. Nights - I deliver - pizza, and weekends I – I – try to pick up anything I can. Two Sundays I supply preached for a vacationing pastor."

"Oh, dear!" he heard Tiffany gasp.

She offered him a tissue. Caleb felt like a big baby and was ashamed. He was the boy with all the promise - saved early in life – outspoken, bold, smart, yet what a mess he became! This Board made him face his failures! Still, in this interview he couldn't be the only guilty party. The panel was successful in peeling back layer after layer of his past. But what of their own lives - he knew they undoubtedly were no way squeaky clean. This verbal barrage must stop!!

"You haven't given us much to build a recommendation on, son, have you? We have certain guidelines and requirements we must adhere to," Hub just seemed to be rambling words mechanically, no different than Rona.

Caleb raised his head.

"Why do you want to be a foreign missionary?" Gerald asked.

"Because God called me!" Caleb was very direct.

"Humph, just like you were called to all those other churches," Hub spoke with a smirk.

Caleb stood up!

"What do you know of God's call?" he questioned. "You call yourselves a Christian mission board responsible for the lives of countless people - the missionaries and their families - people in little churches all over the world! We've not prayed over this - not once was prayer even hinted at!"

The board members were surprised at Caleb's sudden outspoken boldness. He forced them on the defensive side.

"Don't you dare question my spirituality, boy! I pray everyday," Hub retorted.

"I do question it, Hub! Listen to you! You haven't spoken one kind word to me since I walked in this room. I'm not your enemy; I'm not here to steal your money. We're supposed to be brothers in the Lord for gosh sakes - lost people treat me better! And whatever happened to people praying together?"

Hub tried to retaliate, but Caleb wouldn't let him.

"Were you not interested in my personal testimony? No one asked about that!"

"That's in your file," Nancy pointed out.

"Yes, but that's on paper and so impersonal. It takes on a life when talked about - even leading people to Christ, Nancy."

"We are short on time, Caleb," Gerald reminded him.

"Is that the problem? You are upset over my lateness?"

"That isn't our problem. We had to fit you in," Marcus raised his voice.

"And I appreciate that - but this is a decision lives and eternal destinies hinge upon and you rush through it? For their sakes, reschedule me!" Caleb was leaning on his hands over the table in the board's faces.

"I think your decision was already made before I ever got here!" Caleb concluded and sat down.

He could tell by the looks on their faces he had agitated some of them and wounded the others. He knew he had blown any chances for an appointment from this missions group. He remained silent.

Hub closed his folder with a smack!

"I believe this interview is over," Marcus followed Hub's lead and also closed his folder.

"Wait, I have a final question for Mr. Hillag," Nancy Stroder spoke up as she too closed her folder. "If we sent you out on a mission field how would you proceed?"

Caleb studied her face as he thought over her question. He saw something in her expression that wasn't there before, but he was unsure of what it meant. He lowered his voice when he answered.

"I'd tell them the Good News that Jesus saves."

"That's it?" she seemed unmoved.

"That's how Jesus instructed to do it."

"What about the ones who come into your church?" Nancy pursued Caleb's train of thought.

"I'll love them, encourage them and teach and feed Christ's sheep from His Word."

"That's your plan of action?" Nancy asked.

"It's what Jesus did. I just follow Him."

"Didn't work on the churches here," Hub muttered.

Marcus smiled and shook his head.

"Let me ask you a question?" Caleb made eye contact with each of the members.

"Let's assume that God has placed a call to be a missionary on me and my family, which reminds me, no one asked about Sarah and what she thinks or feels. She's not even here!"

"That would come in the second interview," Tiffany piped up.

Even Gerald now appeared short-tempered. "You had a question, Caleb?"

"Yes - let's say that God has called me to be a missionary and has led me here to Global Missions, and His Spirit impresses that on your hearts - would you do what God was telling you or would you adhere to your guidelines and policies or your personal feelings toward me?"

"What if you weren't called and led here?" Hub threw a question back on Caleb.

"Oh, I'm clear and definite about the call. God made it that way! But, I am having doubts about Global - no, that's not fair. My doubts are in this room."

"Does that mean you want to withdraw your request?" Hub questioned sitting up to take notice.

"Not unless the Lord tells me to. You have not answered my question."

At that moment, Rona's face came on the P. C. screen. "Reverend Chalkie Bloom and his wife are here for their appointment."

Nancy tapped a key. "Thank you, Rona, someone will be right out."

The board members stood in unison, and Caleb would have sworn they pasted smiles on. It was a routine they had rehearsed and played out a thousand times before. They smiled, shook his hand, thanked him for coming, and acted as though nothing bad ever happened. No disagreements, interrogations or accusations hurled at each other. Amazing! The finale' was even the routine, "We'll be in touch."

# Chapter 3

# Sarah

Sarah was startled out of a restless sleep by her doorbell. At least she thought she heard it chime. She was at that place between sleeping and waking which made it hard to determine if the doorbell had really been rung - or maybe she dreamed it. All she knew was that she lay hushed in bed, and her heart was pounding in her throat!

Could it be Caleb? Had he returned early? He wouldn't ring the doorbell. He had a key!

She glanced at the illuminated clock face - seven minutes after midnight! It was six minutes after when she heard the doorbell! Did that mean anything?

She didn't move, scarcely breathing.

Nothing. Silence. She relaxed, but was uncertain. If only Caleb were here. She hated the times he was away! She prayed for him - for herself and the children. Surely, the doorbell would have awakened them - especially Esther - and she would be rushing through the door. No, it was a dream!

Sarah was jolted out of sleep a second time by the sound of the doorbell. She quickly looked at the clock - six minutes after one! Something was going on!'

Quietly, quickly she slipped into a robe and slippers. She reached for the hall light switch, but retrieved her hand thinking better to keep the house dark. Caleb had taught her that.

"Why turn a light on yourself and make it easy for an intruder. The darkness can be your ally," he instructed. Sarah smiled, remembering his wise words.

Esther and Mark were both sound asleep. Had they not heard? Or was someone playing games? The last time was too real to be a dream! She maneuvered with stealth through the dark shadows of the living room. The beating of her heart was amplified by the eerie silence. She slipped to the front door and peeked through the security window. A dark form stood near a tree in the front yard. Sarah felt her knees wobble and her head grow light!

"I can't panic! Lord, help me! Protect us!" she gasped.

Curiosity got the best of her - she looked again.

"Dear God!" her voice came out in a squeak. "He's still there! Go away in the Name of Jesus!"

She switched on the outside light and looked again out the small peephole. The form was gone! What did he want?

Sarah went for her satellite phone. She hit speed dial for Caleb. It rang - rang again!

"Honey?" she heard a sleepy response.

"Caleb! There's someone in our yard, and he's been ringing our doorbell!"

"Is the alarm system hot?"

"Yes. Caleb, I'm frightened!"

"Did the alarm go off?"

"No," she whispered, "I sense it's demonic, but it was so real! I know I saw a man out in our yard! I prayed against him in Jesus Name."

"I'll hang up. Just to be sure it's not someone trying to break in, call emergency and get the police there. Stay on the phone with them until they arrive. Call me back as soon as you can!"

"Should I dial the anti-terrorist number?"

"No, I don't think so. Why would terrorists bother us? If it were terror-related they would have already blown the house up. Call the other number. I'm praying for you and the children, Sarah. I love you!"

"Oh, Caleb!"

"Be brave! Get the police there!"

Sarah's hand shook as she dialed the emergency number.

"Mommy, what's wrong?" Esther was by her. Sarah held her close, waiting for a response on the phone.

"Emergency."

Two patrol officers were at the door within five minutes. She explained how she heard the doorbell ring twice exactly one hour apart, and then saw the dark form of a man lurking by the tree. The officers searched around the house and looked into neighboring yards. They came inside the house, and reassured Sarah and the children. Mark was up by now and asking questions. One of the officers seemed skeptical.

"We had new snow and ice tonight, Ma'am," he began. "Your doorbell button is frozen tight. I attempted to push it and couldn't. I believe if someone had broken it loose, I would have been able to ring your doorbell now. Also, we made tracks in the light snow, and there were no other tracks near or around your house."

"That's right," the other officer collaborated.

By now, Sarah was certain this was a spiritual attack to un-nerve her. But how could she explain that to the officers? They wouldn't believe her.

"We didn't hear anything!" both Esther and Mark spoke in unison.

Sarah wanted to scalp them, but was too relieved they were safe to be angry. She graciously thanked the officers for their promptness and thorough search.

"Keep your security system armed. You have a good one," the officer touched the brim of his hat.

"My husband - had - it installed," she muttered. She could feel her face get red. She hurriedly shut the door and tucked the children into their beds. Esther wanted to talk.

"Not now, sweetheart. We are safe and warm - it was just my imagination. I have to call your daddy. He will be worried!"

"Sarah, are you and the children all right?" He picked up on the first ring.

"Caleb, I feel like such an idiot!" she unloaded. "Two officers came and searched all around the house. The doorbell button was frozen - there were no tracks in the snow. They think I am a silly, scared-of-my-own-shadow dumb female. But, Caleb, I swear something was going on! The first time I heard it, it was twelve-six. The second time was exactly one hour later at one-o-six. I know. I looked at the clock! And I saw someone, I swear! I was scared, but I know what I saw!"

Caleb was silent for a long time.

"Caleb?" she thought she had lost connection.

"I'm thinking and praying. I know you are right. It's in the spiritual realm. Does it feel like a strong battle is churning in the air? You can't see it, but it's like you can sense its heaviness."

"Yes, Caleb!"

"I feel it too."

"I know your interview didn't go well," Sarah murmured. She went on before he could respond. "You didn't call. When something doesn't - you won't call, so I knew."

"I'm sorry, Sarah, I was so downhearted I just couldn't – the thought of talking. It was the mother of all disasters! It became an interrogation into our personal lives. In the end I told them off. I lost my cool and blew it."

She detected deep sadness in Caleb's voice. She wondered how many more letdowns her man could take - she could take? She wanted to hold and comfort him at that moment - but couldn't. They were miles apart.

"Sarah, why does my mouth always make trouble for us?"

"I love you, Caleb," was all she could say.

"I don't understand why they wouldn't let me bring you. There was another pastor there with his wife. The board said you could come on the second interview."

"Is there going to be a second?"

"Hon, if our life depended on it, I'd say we better pick out a pair of caskets."

Sarah stifled a laugh.

"The weather was too wicked to take secondary roads so I stayed on the interstate. I made Nashville before my batteries crashed - so I'm in Nashville and should be home tomorrow."

They talked on into the night. It was as it had been since they met, they never wanted for conversation. They could go on for hours talking about anything and everything. They finally kissed a long-distance goodnight and clicked off their phones. As she crossed the living room to switch off the lights, she paused to pick up a photo taken of her and Caleb soon after they had met. She smiled as the picture brought back memories. What a strange and unusual circumstance had thrown them together!

Tonight, she came under a demonic attack, and it was a demonic attack eleven years ago that was instrumental in bringing her and Caleb together. It could have happened yesterday. The events still so vivid in her mind, each detail etched clearly in mental pictures. It was also a dark night in January when it happened.

# Chapter 4

# Strange Occurrence

A frantic rapping on Sarah's bedroom door sat her straight up in bed!

"Sarah! Open up!" It was her stepsister Penny in a hushed whisper.

Sarah darted across the carpet to unlock her door. Penny slipped inside quickly, her face white with fear in the dim light.

"Penny, what is it?" Sarah took Penny's trembling hand.

"Shhh! It's Stoner! He's gone crazy! He was trying to get in my room earlier!"

"Oh, no!" Sarah gasped. She locked her door again. "Did you tell Mom and your Dad?"

"You know they don't believe us," Penny shook and began to cry. Sarah held her tight. She knew what Penny said about her brother was true. Three years ago something happened to him, and he changed. He tried to set up situations to be alone with Penny or Sarah. The two girls had stuck together and forcefully resisted him. They even told their parents. Sarah went to her mother, Hannah, who was afraid to disrupt the family's closeness.

"Mom, this kind of closeness is sick!" Sarah protested.

Penny's father, Gary, laughed and attributed Stoner's behavior to his wildness. Neither girl trusted him and kept their bedroom doors locked at night and took precautions to never be alone with him.

"He was pounding on my door and raving to let him in. Dad yelled and told him to go back to bed. Later I heard strange noises and howls coming from his room. I tiptoed to his door and tried to peek under. He has boards with candles all over the floor, and he was groaning and saying weird things. Sarah, he's never been like this!"

"Good Lord!" Sarah covered her mouth.

"Sarah, he has Mitzee and her puppies. They are howling and yelping. I think he is hurting them! The puppies whined like they are in terrible pain - maybe he is torturing them! Sarah, I was so scared I wet my pants!"

"We've got to do something, Penny!" Both girls were whispering frantically.

"Yes, but what?"

"Let's wake up Mom and Dad!"

Sarah unbolted her door and together they ran to the other end of the house. They banged on their parents' door before barging in.

"Mom! Dad! Stoner's got Mitzee and the puppies in his room, and he is hurting them! Something's scary with him! He's acting weird!" Sarah and Penny cried, talking fast and at once.

"What gives you that idea?" Sarah's step-dad grumbled, trying to collect his mind and get his eyes opened.

"I heard them! Oh, Daddy, he's hurting the puppies; I wouldn't lie. Make him stop!" Penny urged pulling at his pajama sleeve. He pulled his arm away.

"Penelope Howser, pull yourself together!" he snapped.

"Mother! Do something!" Sarah pleaded.

"Now, Sarah, I think you girls' imaginations are running away with you."

"Go see for yourselves!" Sarah insisted.

Sarah's step-dad gave her a mean look. He was irritated for their disrupting his sleep, but he got up and proceeded toward Stoner's room with Hannah and the girls trailing behind. He banged twice, loudly on his son's door.

"What's going on in there, Stoner?"

The room was silent. The question was repeated the second time more forcefully. An evil voice came from the room that wasn't Stoner. His dad was shocked - then troubled.

"Stoner! Open this door! Who's in there with you?"

"Go to hell!" the same voice replied.

"What?" Gary Howser exploded! His face grew crimson with rage!

"Open this door Stoner, or I'll rip it open!"

"Rip it open! Rip it open! Try it if you can - haaa - haaa - hahahaha!" the laugh was insidious.

"Open this door!" Gary was pounding with one hand and rattling the knob with the other. Mitzee yelped in pain, which brought pleading cries from the women to stop and open the door!

By now the anger Sarah's step-dad had displayed was replaced by one of confusion. He stepped back from the door and with one giant thrust of his foot kicked the door in! What they saw none was prepared for.

The room was filled with candles and smoke. Mitzee was shivering and whimpering under Stoner's desk. The puppies staggered and fell over like they were drunk! One walked blindly into a wall, and another displayed blood on its back.

But where was Stoner? The women cautiously followed Gary into the room careful not to knock over candles. Suddenly, all the flames pointed toward a figure covered in a blanket. Sarah began coughing from the smoke. A glance at Penny told Sarah her stepsister was near panic stage!

Gary stepped quickly amidst the candles and yanked the blanket from the figure. It was Stoner! No, it wasn't Stoner! His face contorted in an evil sneer.

"Get out!" he hissed. "You are treading in a fearful place! You dare enter my domain? You fool!"

The body was Stoner's, but the voice was not!

"Dear God in Heaven, Stoner, what are you doing?"

"Don't speak of God or Heaven!" Stoner snarled. "There is no God but the one I serve! Heaven is hell!"

They were shocked! Gary gasped in disbelief - Hannah covered her mouth, and Penny shook!

Sarah held her head and cried, "No! No! No!"

"Stop being stupid, Boy" Gary yelled. "This will - stop - now!"

"Go to hell, old decrepit man!"

Gary stepped closer to his son. Stoner recoiled!

"Don't - touch me!" he hissed loudly.

"Don't tell me what to do!" He grabbed Stoner's arm in a strong grip. Instantly, the boy became a vicious animal clawing, kicking, and punching his father wildly. He had superhuman strength that the family had never witnessed before. He grabbed his dad in a hammerlock, then threw him to the floor, scattering candles. Gary wrenched in pain, coughing for breath. Hannah tried to help him, but the wicked laugh from Stoner, and his claw-like fingers sent the women scrambling out the door, screaming for fear of their lives.

"Sarah, lock yourselves in your room, and don't open it!" Hannah shouted as she disappeared into the living room.

Sarah and Penny ran down the hallway! Penny fell at the doorway, and Sarah pulled her in, slamming the door and bolting it behind them. Penny was screaming hysterically, covering her ears! Sarah could hear coarse yells from Gary and that horrible, evil sneering voice and taunting laugh that came from somewhere Sarah did not want to go! She could hear banging on the walls and stomping in the hallway. She fumbled in the dark for her phone and punched in 911. Her heart was racing so rapidly her chest hurt, making speech difficult when an officer picked up her call. She choked out her name! Address? What is my address? She sobbed out what was happening, and the officer assured her she had her mother on another line, and help was on the way.

Soon, Sarah and Penny heard the voices of the police and sounds of a struggle in Stoner's room. They heard Gary talking, but nothing of Stoner. They held each other tight talking into the dead of night. They waited! Would daylight ever come? Would anybody come?

"What shall we do?" Sarah asked the question both had been thinking. "Stoner is possessed!"

"Sarah," Penny spoke into the dark. "I've attended church a couple of times at Timberdyke Calvary. They have a new pastor. He knows the Bible and maybe we should see him!"

# Chapter 5

# The New Pastor

It seemed an eternity before the girls knew what had happened with Stoner. Earlier, Sarah heard her step-dad ranting to the police officers about his demented son. She could hear the officers' firm and aggressive voices as they apparently were taking Stoner down in handcuffs. There was fighting! At one point she could make out her stepbrother's sobs and pleading voice begging to be set free. This voice was one she recognized, not the evil voice she heard coming from a person she did not know. Then all was quiet except for the muffled voices of her mother and stepfather.

Both girls were jolted out of a fitful sleep by a light knock on the bedroom door.

"It's mom," came the voice out in the hallway.

Sarah and Penny leaped for the door, fumbling at the lock, flinging it open, and throwing themselves into Hannah's arms. Forget that Sarah was the sophisticated sophomore in college, and Penny the wannabe grown up high school junior, this incident with Stoner freaked them out to the degree they retreated back to little girls needing their momma!

"It's alright," she soothed them and held them close. "It's alright. It's over now."

"What happened? Where's Stoner?" the girls cried their questions in unison.

"Is Daddy okay?" Penny was concerned, looking down the hallway toward Stoner's doorway.

"The police had to arrest Stoner. He attacked your father. He is right now at Juvenile Hall where he can get some help," Hannah explained.

"What happened to him? He was wicked! He scared me!" Sarah searched her mother's face for answers.

"I near fainted!" Penny added. "Where's Daddy?"

"Your brother hurt him, and we had to go to the hospital emergency. He has cuts and bruises. He is better now, but in bed resting. He was too upset to talk to you girls, but wants to have a family meeting when he gets home from work tomorrow to discuss Stoner's behavior and what we are to do."

Sarah's thoughts drifted in class the next morning to the events of the night before. She had never seen nor experienced anything like that in her life! She had seen TV specials about demon possession, read articles concerning it, heard others speak of its reality – but truly, Sarah pushed it all aside as nonsense. Yet, Stoner's ugly, contorted, evil face kept coming up before her. She wanted to reach out to him, help him, try to understand what had taken place - but she truly was at a loss to know what to do. She shivered at the possibility her stepbrother was demon possessed – or had lost his mind! What a horrible thought! She desperately wanted to talk about the night before, but with whom? She doubted any of her college friends would understand, and the ones who did she wouldn't associate with. Others would probably laugh or scoff, or attempt their amateurish psychoanalysis of her stepbrother's weird behavior. She found herself eager for the family meeting, which her stepfather had called. Maybe there would come some much-needed direction she relentlessly sought all day.

Sarah could hardly wait for her afternoon class at college to start and get over. She absent-mindedly took some notes, but she could not erase Stoner out of her mind. Visual images kept haunting her! Was she the one going crazy? She hoped the professor would not call on her! She might as well have stayed home!

The minute hand on the clock at the rear of the room seemed glued to one spot. The second hand drug its way around the face - would the four o'clock hour never arrive? Sarah kept looking back over her shoulder at the time until her distraction was obvious.

"Miss Crothers, it would seem the class timepiece holds more interest to you than my lecture. Would you care to turn your seat around, the better to see the clock?"

"No, sir," Sarah responded, embarrassed. She dropped her eyes, vowing to herself to pay attention. She sighed relief when the professor dismissed the class.

She hurried to her car in the parking lot. She needed to pick up Penny at her high school, but knew she must stop for gas first.

She saw a station on Timberdyke Drive which advertised regular unleaded at $3.79 per gallon. Most stations were selling at $3.91. So much had changed after the Katrina Hurricane in 2005! Usage from emerging countries continued to rise. She had heard her step-father predict that in a few short years the premium grades of gasoline would be phased out along with the larger gas-guzzlers, and most people would own hybrids. In fact, that is what Sarah drove.

She would only get one gallon. She held her breath when she used her credit card because she knew it was nearly maxed out. She was thankful when the transaction went through, never giving thought to how she would pay for it. Looking past the pump as she waited, she realized she was looking directly at Timberdyke Calvary. She remembered Penny's words of the church having a new pastor. A peak of curiosity caught her attention for a moment, but she shrugged it off. She pictured him a distinguished gentleman with silver hair and deep voice, knowledgeable but unapproachable.

Penny was standing on the sidewalk talking with a group of friends. They were bundled up in heavy coats, hats, gloves and boots. Timberdyke was nestled along the side of the mountains where the timberline formed - low enough to escape the heavy snows of January, but high enough to warrant warm protection from the cold. This winter of 2007 had not been mild, and piles of snow remained in some shaded areas. When Sarah pulled up, Penny slipped her backpack off her shoulder, bidding her friends good-bye.

One of the boys in the group, whom Sarah knew was sweet on her stepsister, was saying something, which she could not make out. This was a goofy kid they called Toe Jam or T. J. for short. He scooped up chunks of packed snow from a heap piled up against the school fence. He plastered Sarah's windshield! She honked her horn, which prompted a barrage of snow and ice chunks pelting the front of her car. She turned on her wipers, which T. J. tried to hold down.

"Stop it, T. J. You'll break my wipers!" Sarah yelled.

"Hands off!" Penny reinforced the order.

The wiper blades cleared the windshield in time for Sarah to see T. J. make a gallant bow. He made some remark to Penny as she opened the door.

"T. J., you are such a nut cake!" Penny laughed.

"All the better for you to eat me!" T. J. came back.

"Shut up!" Now Penny was mad. She slid in beside Sarah and slammed the door.

"What did he say?" Sarah asked.

"He said the better to eat me - he's so stupid!"

"No - no - before that?"

"He said, "Anything you request is my command, my princess. That is so last century!"

By now T. J. had his hands and face up against the window making goofy gestures at Penny.

"Just go! Rip his nose off!" Penny ordered, disgusted. Sarah sped off.

"Toe Jam is a fit name for him," Sarah remarked with a smile.

"No, it should be worse. I don't want to talk about him - I can't seem to get rid of - of - the child!"

"Penelope Howser, you know he likes you!" Sarah teased.

"Then why doesn't he treat me kind - like - well like the new preacher at church?"

"Whoa, girl. Don't go there! You aren't even sixteen!"

"Will be soon enough."

Sarah glanced over at her stepsister. She saw something there she hadn't noticed before. She decided to pursue her instincts.

"Penny, he has a wife and children, and he's too old for you!"

"No, he doesn't! He's divorced!"

"What?"

"He married a girl he knew in college. She divorced him in just two years. I feel sorry for him; he seems so sad when he talks about it, which is almost never."

"I didn't think that's allowed. I mean a - divorced man for a minister."

"I heard there was a lot of debate over whether to have him come as pastor. I can tell some of the church people don't care for him. I don't know much as I've just started attending, but I like his sermons. Besides, he's only 29 or 30, I think."

Sarah laughed out loud! This was incredulous!

"Penelope Howser! You have a teenage crush on the preacher! Ha!"

"Not teenage and not a crush!" Penny shot back, as her face grew red.

"Well, I don't think I'd want any part of a minister who couldn't hold on to a wife more than two years. He probably is such a - a - snobbish bore - he drove her away."

"I don't believe that!" Penny was defensive.

Sarah was amused by her stepsister's apparent interest in the new pastor and would enjoy holding this private knowledge over the younger one's head. She pulled into their driveway.

"Well, Penny, you can have your old preacher. I don't care to see him - or listen to him." Sarah spoke pointedly, relishing the moment.

"Well then, high and mighty Sarah, you'll have to leave the house, because on lunch break today I called him and invited him to come to our family meeting tonight."

"You what? You actually spoke to - him?" Sarah sputtered. This was serious.

"Sure did," Penny beamed.

"He's coming?"

"Said he would be here."

"Does your father - know?"

"No."

"Oh, Penny, I don't think this is such a good idea. Gary will be furious! You should have asked our parents first."

"Sarah, our family needs help. We were a mess last night. We need some direction!"

"But from a preacher - a divorced one at that?"

"Oh, I get it! You think he's a second-class person! Then go sit in your room all night and hide like you are so good at!"

The sting of Penny's words kindled a reaction in Sarah that was totally unlike her! She slapped Penny's mouth!

Penny reacted in kind, and instantly there commenced a flailing of hands, arms and knees. They pulled hair and scratched, filling the car with grunts and angry accusations. Spent, they both were in tears. Penny tried to open her door, but Sarah prevented a hasty exit.

"We can't part, Penny! Not like this! Look at us. We are a fright! I'm sorry! I don't know what got into me - maybe it's - Stoner – and - last night. Please forgive me! I don't want us to be angry - at each other. Not now! Not tonight. Perhaps you are right - this new pastor may help us. If Gary will let him stay!"

## Chapter 6

# Unanticipated Reaction

Penny demonstrated a strength and determination Sarah had never seen in her when she faced her father with the announcement she had invited the new pastor to their house.

"Why in God's Name did you do that?" Gary Howser exploded. "I'll not have someone in here selling books or peddling their damn propaganda!"

"He isn't selling any books, Daddy!" Penny protested.

"We don't need a preacher meddling in our family affairs - which I remind all of you - is private!"

"Maybe he can help us," Sarah offered.

"Stay out of this, Sarah!" Gary thundered.

"Why? Am I no longer a part of this family?"

The man in his rage was taken back by Sarah's penetrating question. He stared at her a moment, then a nervous glance to his wife - Sarah's mother - then back to Sarah.

"I didn't mean that! Of course you are a part of this family. I'm saying we don't need him here."

"Yes, we do!" Penny stood her ground stubbornly. "I need him here!"

Gary looked like a man who had the wind knocked out of him. He searched for what to say to his daughter. He sucked in a deep breath, and the rage returned.

"Girl, are you nuts? Have you lost your mind? We need - counselors - psychologists - therapy! Not some know nothin' preacher!"

"Gary, for goodness sake, calm down!" Hannah had risen from her chair and moved to her husband's side and began stroking his hair. He tried to push her hand away, but she didn't stop. She spoke gently to him.

"What can a preacher stopping by to visit hurt? I can't recall anyone we ever turned from our door. Ministers are counselors, I believe. Let's just listen to what he has to say."

Gary went down grumbling.

"Alright! All right, but one wrong word and he's gone! Everyone into the family room and sit down; we need to talk about last night."

The women found places while Gary turned a wooden chair around backwards and straddled it, propping his arms upon the back. He began what was painful to express.

"I swung by Juvenile Hall today and met with the resident psychologist. She told me that from preliminary observations, Stoner is a case of schizophrenia. It's characterized by delusion and bizarre behavior - that's what - she - said." Gary dropped his head in futility.

"What does that mean?" Penny was bewildered.

"I think it means he hears voices," Sarah speculated.

"It means he is a very sick young man," Hannah added.

"Yes," her husband replied.

The four stared at each other. Thoughts were everywhere, but words would not come. Penny finally expressed the question all of them were thinking - would he get well?

Before the answer came, the doorbell rang. Penny jumped up and ran into the entrance hall to answer it.

Sarah could hear Penny's excited welcome and a man's voice returning her greeting. Soon Penny emerged into the family room accompanied by the pastor.

"This is Pastor Hillag from Timberdyke Calvary Church."

"My congregation mostly call me Pastor Caleb - a few call me other names I won't mention," his smile was warm and charming. Nothing at all like Sarah had imagined! His face was young looking and handsome. His hair was neatly trimmed, medium length. He sported stylish glasses to match his casual slacks and pullover sweater. If he had a jacket, Penny had already taken that and hung it in the entrance hall.

Caleb was well built, however, not a bodybuilder kind of guy. He displayed a confident boldness, yet not too aggressive. He was well mannered, and Sarah was attracted to his gentle strength from the moment he stepped into the room and spoke. She pushed those feelings aside.

When she was introduced to Pastor Hillag, her drab, "Hello," sounded as lifeless as a wet dishrag. She felt self-conscious.

Then she did something totally out of character. She held out her hand! 'Why did I do that?' she wondered.

He smiled and took her hand in both of his. She released her hand and retreated to a seat, flustered. It was a most unanticipated reaction, which she did not like.

# Chapter 7

# Reverend Caleb Hillag

Introductions over and the issuing small talk fast losing its momentum, Pastor Hillag wanted to cut right to the reason for his being in the Howser home.

"Penny tells me you had some difficulty with your son last night?" he addressed Mister Howser.

"Yes, we went to blows," Gary mumbled.

"Must have gotten rough. You look pretty banged up," the pastor observed, peering intently into Howser's face. "Tell me what happened."

"Stoner, my son, became disrespectful. When I tried to discipline him we got in a - scuffle."

"Daddy, Stoner was beating and clawing you!" Penny injected loudly. Howser flashed a displeased look.

"The room was full of candles! All over the floor and everywhere! Penny continued.

"Penny, that has nothing to do with Stoner's problem. You know how...."

"Maybe it does have something to do with the problem," the pastor interrupted. "Was there some sort of design to them?"

"I think there was!" Sarah spoke up. "They appeared to make a circle with - some sort of design in the middle – a pentagram? The rest were scattered around the room. I couldn't make out any kind of pattern - or anything else - with those."

"Where was Stoner? What did he do or how did he act? Pastor Hillag probed thoughtfully.

"He was covered in a - damn blanket standing like a statue!"

"Gary, your language!" Hannah reminded her husband of whom he was speaking to.

"I'm sure he's heard damn before!" Gary protested.

The pastor sidestepped an argument and repeated his question, "How did he act? Penny told me he frightened all of you.

"Not me," Howser smirked. "The psychologist at the Juvenile Hall told me today Stoner has schizophrenia. It's a mental disorder."

"I'm familiar with the term, but I must tell you that I believe Stoner's problem is a spiritual one that can and does affect his mind," the young pastor was not afraid to speak his assessment of the problem.

Gary appeared skeptical.

"What do you think happened to our Stoner?" Hannah asked, she was more open-minded than her husband, "and we cannot forget how the dogs acted."

"Well…" he was choosing his words carefully, "just from what I've heard, somewhere in the past probably, a year or more ago, Stoner began to dabble in the occult. He opened himself up to demon possession. He was holding a ritual, and the dogs were part of it."

Gary Howser threw up his hands! "That's the damn dumbest thing I've ever heard of!" he bellowed. "This isn't some science-fiction movie we have going on here, Preacher!"

Sarah could see the minister's neck redden, but he never wavered. He pulled a small New Testament from his pocket. He began to turn pages. "Let me - read - you - something," he muttered as he continued looking for a passage.

"Here it is in John 8, staring with verse 26. It reads: 'And they arrived at the country of the Gadarenes, which is over Galilee. And when He went forth to land, there met Him out of the city a certain man, which had devils long time, and wore no clothes, neither abode in any house, but in the tombs. When he saw Jesus, he cried out, and fell down before him, and with a loud voice said, 'What have I to do with thee, Jesus, thou Son of God most high? I beseech thee, torment me not.

'(For He had commanded the unclean spirit to come out of the man. For oftentimes it had caught him: and he was kept bound with chains and in fetters; and he breaks the bands, and was driven of the devil into the wilderness.)

'And Jesus asked him saying, 'What is thy name?' And he said, 'Legion:' because many devils were entered into him.

'And they besought Jesus that He would not command them to go out into the deep.

'And there was there a herd of many swine feeding on the mountain; and they besought Him that He would suffer them to enter into them. And he suffered them.

'Then went the devils out of the man, and entered into the swine: and the herd ran violently down a steep place into the lake, and were drowned. When they that fed them saw what was done, they fled, and went and told it in the city and in the country.

'Then they went out to see what was done; and came to Jesus, and found the man, out of whom the devils were departed, sitting at the feet of Jesus, clothed and in his right mind.'"

Caleb closed his New Testament and concluded, "The scripture gives us an incredible glimpse into the spiritual realm with that story."

Gary Howser shook his head in disappointment.

"But it sounds like Stoner," Sarah spoke up. Her step-dad glowered at her!

"What would you say needs to be done for Stoner? I mean to help him," Hannah was at a loss for answers.

"He needs delivered from the demon that possesses him. That's whom you saw and heard last night. When the demon receded and tried to hide its presence, that's when you saw Stoner come back. Am I right, Hannah?"

"Yes - I -."

Gary slammed his fist down on the sofa arm in anger. "Stoner needs therapy, not exorcism!"

"I'm talking about deliverance as Jesus did, not exorcism. Exorcism is a person coaching a demon to leave the possessed man or woman to enter into himself or some animal or object. As a child of God and believer in Jesus Christ, I have the authority to command a demon to come out; I don't have to plead with it!"

"You mean you can do this - cast out demons?"

"Yes, Gary, in the Name of Jesus Christ."

"I doubt Jesus ever existed. His tale is merely a myth."

"Oh, He existed!" the pastor's voice raised. Sarah feared an ugly argument!

"Well, He's been dead and gone for centuries, Preacher."

"No, He's alive! He rose from the dead and is ever present with us."

"How do you know that?"

"I spoke with Him today, Gary."

"You spoke with Him," Howser repeated. He was visibly agitated. "You're as bad off as Stoner! This conversation is over, and so is your visit."

Sarah and Penny raised their voices in objection. A wave of Howser's hand quickly silenced them.

When Howser handed Caleb his coat, both men's eyes locked in defiance. Neither flinched or blinked. They stood toe-to-toe - eye-to-eye. It was in the spiritual the two disagreed, and both were aware of exactly where their differences lie.

Without breaking eye contact, Caleb Hillag took his jacket from Gary Howser.

"You aren't helping your son, Mr. Howser."

"Neither are you! Good bye."

# Chapter 8

# Damage Control

S arah could not sleep that night. She felt terrible over the way her step-dad treated Pastor Caleb. She played the evening's events over and over in her mind. As night wore on into the still hours of the early morning, the focus shifted from her step-dad towards the young man. She could hear his gentle strong voice. Each smile, every expression formed vivid images in her imagination. She wanted to see him again! Was she losing her mind? Was she waging a war with an unruly heart? She didn't have interest in or time for a relationship! By sunrise she was exhausted.

She dragged herself into her morning class and slumped into her chair. A classmate, Ray, seated next to her studied her face. He looked away, running his hands through his hair. Their instructor entered the room, and the immediate shuffle of books and papers began. Ray whispered to her, keeping his eyes straight ahead.

"Sarah, you party last night?"

"Couldn't sleep."

"How 'bout coffee after class?"

"Sorry - can't!"

Ray was disappointed, and Sarah knew he didn't understand, but she could not - would not try to explain to him something she herself did not fully comprehend. All she knew was that she had to be at Timberdyke Calvary Church as soon as she left class!

Session over, Sarah tore out of the class and ran all the way to her car. She peeled out of the parking lot and drove like a maniac the two miles to the church. She had never been inside the building, but her eye caught a small sign pointing to the church office. She treaded down a sidewalk where the sign pointed and came upon the office door. She hesitated, gathering up courage. "God, what if he isn't here!" Sarah caught her breath and swallowed hard. She opened the door and stepped into the office.

"Hello. Welcome to Timberdyke Calvary. May I help you?" the woman seated behind a desk cheerfully greeted her.

"I'm - here -" Sarah choked on her own words! "I'm - here - to see Pastor Ca - I mean Hillag."

The woman eyed Sarah over her glasses for a long moment, as though looking inside Sarah and scrutinizing her intentions. Did she need to protect her young pastor?

"Pastor left about a half hour ago. He didn't inform me where he was going. He has no appointments scheduled until 3:30 this afternoon, if you would care to wait? Or I could give him a message."

Sarah was too restless to sit in the office. She thought to leave a message, but something wouldn't let her leave. She thought to hang around awhile. Perhaps Pastor would return.

"I have - never been here before. Would it be - all right - if I look around? Maybe I'll check back in a few minutes to see if Pastor Hillag has returned. He visited our home last night, and, and, I wanted to speak to him about that." Sarah was calmer with better control.

"Of course," the woman nodded. "I want to invite you and your family to our Sunday morning service."

"I plan to be here." The thought of attending church had not crossed her mind until this moment, but suddenly it seemed so right! There was no decision process - she would come. No pros or cons - she would be in church.

Sarah wandered on the church grounds. She looked in a gym the church utilized for youth activities or sports. She peered inside classrooms along a walkway; two displayed colorful pictures tacked on cork bulletin boards. She curiously peeked into the main sanctuary. She could barely make out a figure in the dim light seated in the front, head bowed. She knew it was – him!

Her first inclination was to quietly close the sanctuary door and run for her car and go home! No, she came with a mission. She could not let the night before go unexplained. Her step-dad did not speak for all of them. She was ashamed of his treatment toward the pastor.

Sarah tiptoed down the aisle to where Pastor Hillag sat, and silently took a seat a few feet from him. He must be praying. The rustle of her clothes and the slight jar of the pew startled the man. He looked up!

Caleb's tear-stained face affected Sarah in a profound way! She didn't know what to say; despite the need she had to tell him she was so sorry for her step-dad's behavior.

Caleb pulled a tissue from a box that was left on the front pew for just such a purpose.

"I'm sorry, tough guys aren't supposed to cry," he apologized, wiping his face.

Sarah studied his every move, his expressions.

"Let's see - you are -?"

"Sarah Crothers," she murmured.

"Oh, Yes. Well, it seems I didn't make much of an impression last night at your house, and certainly was not of any help. All I managed to do was get your dad riled up. Of course, that seems to be the story of my life," he laughed.

Sarah snapped back to the whole purpose of her visit.

"Gary is my step-dad, and I came to apologize for his rudeness to you. He wasn't himself last night. Well, none of us were, but that is no excuse for him to treat - you - our guest, in such a despicable manner. I couldn't let you think - we were such an awful - messed up family. Penny has come to church - she likes you! I don't know you - I mean not very well, but my – er - I felt so embarrassed last night; I thought I would die! I had to make things right. I was ashamed at my step-dad's abruptness and rejection of your advice.

"Miss Crothers, I can assure you that I've faced meaner guys than your step-dad and survived, so you needn't apologize for him, but I am glad you came to talk about it. Penny is a good kid, and when she called me she was frightened out of her wits by her brother. Your mother is kind and a gracious woman. So, tell me about her daughter, Sarah Crothers."

The two of them sat facing each other on the front pew of the church and talked.

Sarah had never felt so comfortable around any man, and she found herself telling the pastor about her life, her thoughts, and her feelings. At one time, she feared getting too personal - even private with him - yet their conversation, Caleb's intent looks that conveyed his interest in what she spoke, her shy glances, the toss of her hair when she laughed at his tease - all this seemed so natural. They seemed to draw from an inexhaustible well stream of lively, engaging communication.

Sarah became aware that the content of their discussions was not silly, shallow, flirty exchanges between a man and woman, but theirs displayed an intellect that was growing, stretching Sarah even in this short time to be a better, stronger person. She felt alive in a way never experienced before! She was sure somehow she was having a similar effect on this pastor.

The conversation never waned; they talked on completely caught up in each other's company. The church secretary walking into the sanctuary interrupted them.

"There you are, Pastor. I've been looking for you," she eyed them suspiciously as she approached in a brisk walk down the aisle. "Your 3:30 appointment is waiting in your office."

"My gosh! Is it that late!" Caleb jumped to his feet, looking at his watch. He turned to Sarah and took her hand.

"You will have to excuse me, Miss Crothers. Thank you for stopping by and sharing. I hope to see you Sunday."

Sarah detected a 'please come' appeal in the pastor's eyes and slight squeeze of her hand.

"Sunday," was all she could get out.

Sarah drove to her house lost in thought. She didn't acknowledge her mother when she passed through the kitchen on the way to her bedroom.

"Sarah," Hannah called out to her daughter.

"Yes," Sarah turned around.

"Where have you been?"

"At the church - talking to the Pastor."

Hannah stepped closer to look in Sarah's eyes and search her face.

"All this time?"

"Yes."

"You have an afternoon class, Sarah. Did you go to class?"

"No."

"You missed your class?"

"Yes."

"Why, Sarah?"

"I was with the Preacher at church."

"Doing what?"

"Talking, Mother, just talking."

"Sarah, are you interested in this young man?" She stepped closer, her gaze searching.

The shock of her mother's probing question jolted Sarah back to reality!

"Don't be silly. We were just talking - trying to make sense of Stoner - and our family. I apologized for how Gary – we treated him last night. One of us had to do it. Anyway, what would I have to do with a preacher? Sounds boring!"

# Chapter 9

# Lots of Advice

A month's worth of Sundays were agreeable for Sarah. She wished to speak with the young pastor, but it seemed every Sunday after services he was flocked about by a bevy of women, her own sister Penny included. Pastor Hillag was cordial to each one; however showed no romantic interest.

Sarah thoroughly enjoyed Pastor's messages and came away each week with what she called little sermon treasure gems. Something was stirring within Sarah besides any interest in Pastor Hillag. It seemed to have nothing to do with him, and Sarah simply dismissed the feeling. She did decide to compliment his sermons by telling him of a little gem she learned each Sunday. She discovered this approach was more engaging to the preacher than the sticky sweet flattery lavished on him by the other admiring females of his flock. She always hoped for a stimulating conversation; however, was short changed with shallow surface niceties.

Sarah began attending mid-week services as soon as her conflicting, February evening class was over. She figured the less formal Bible study would afford her an opportunity to speak more openly with the pastor, but to no avail. He was the same cordial but brief pastor mid-week as he was on Sunday. She finally threw her hands up in exasperation!

"I give up!" she declared. "The only way I can talk to him is to make an appointment."

She felt awkward when she called the church office.

"This is Sarah - Crothers. I'm calling to - make an - appoint - appointment with Pastor Hillag."

She heard the secretary sigh. "Are you having a problem?" she asked.

"No, I just need to see him."

There was a long silence on the phone before the secretary continued.

"Miss Crothers, may I give you some advice."

"Yes...." Sarah hesitated.

"I have a dozen calls every week from women such as yourself, wanting to see Pastor Hillag. Can't say that I blame them; however, there are a couple of things you should be aware of. First, the church has some members who would not be pleased to see the pastor dating. They believe it would distract from his ministerial duties. Second, you are aware he is divorced?"

"Ye - yes," Sarah was shocked by the secretary's brash assumptions.

"Does he look like a man who took that lightly? Does he strike you as a man who has quickly gotten over it?"

"I barely know him. How could I answer that, and I can assure you, I'm not looking for a date!" Sarah felt insulted.

"I can tell you, Miss Crothers, he is a wounded man, and his heart must heal before he will even look at another woman. I suggest you leave him alone, unless you need serious counseling."

That brief telephone conversation sent Sarah into a raging storm! She announced the next morning at the breakfast table her decision to have nothing more to do with church or God. Her step-dad was more than supportive.

"That's good to hear - I'm glad you have finally shown me you have your head on straight."

"Why?" her mother asked.

"The church secretary was rude and insulted me yesterday on the phone."

"You're just upset 'cause the preacher won't pay you attention," Penny smirked.

"No it isn't!" Sarah snapped. She bristled at the very idea of involving the pastor.

"Oh, be honest, Sarah!" Penny retorted. "You act like Mitzee when she's in heat."

"What!" Sarah recoiled at Penny's vulgar accusation.

"That was uncalled for, young lady," Hannah spoke up in Sarah's defense.

Words were beyond Sarah. She retaliated by soundly slapping Penny's face.

Penny howled, holding a stinging cheek. She dug her fingers in the jar of jam, smearing its staining contents on Sarah's blouse. Sarah twisted Penny's wrist!

"Stop it - stop this right now," Gary Howser yelled, standing to his feet. "Both of you - to your rooms!"

Down the hall, Sarah wanted the last word.

"Pastor Hillag thinks of you as just a good KID."

Sarah didn't see her stepsister the rest of the day. She pitied Penny because in her heart she knew Caleb was too old for her, and she really didn't stand a chance with him. Her mother confronted her that morning when she came home from early class.

"Okay, Sarah, what's going on?"

"Nothing, Mother."

"Slapping your sister's face is nothing?"

"She had no right!"

"That isn't what's really bothering you, is it?"

"What do you mean?"

"Are you falling in love with this young man?"

"Of course not! Give me credit for some sense. Why does everyone think that? I have a heavy schedule in college and none of my goals and plans includes a relationship with any man – especially a divorcee. Pleeease!"

"Sarah, I like him too," Hannah ignored her daughter's response. I went to church when you were small, but got away from it. The decision to fall away has nagged my conscience, but I am pleased to see you attend. I have made up my mind to go with you."

Hannah got a far-away look.

"Your father and I were active in church...once. That was before..."

Sarah saw her mother's eyes mist up.

"Don't, Mom, don't go there!"

Hannah wiped her eyes and turned to her daughter. "What's happening between you and Caleb?"

"Oh, Mother, we had such a wonderful talk. I've never felt so comfortable and at ease with any man, but that's all there's been. That one time! At church, he treats me like - everyone else, and that's ok."

"So what happened with the secretary?"

"The secretary told me he isn't over his – divorce, and to leave him alone."

"He's still married?"

"No! No! His heart isn't over it. I was mortified and felt cheap!"

Hannah sat silently thinking, before she offered advice.

"My Grandmother used to tell me that old saying, 'The way to a man's heart is through his stomach.'"

Sarah laughed.

"Oh, please, Mother. That's like this homely girl who's always taking him brownies!"

"Not a bad idea, but that's not what I had in mind. Invite him to lunch or dinner at a nice restaurant."

"On my budget – hah!"

"If he's proud, go dutch."

70

"Mother! I can't believe you would push me into that crowd of desperate women falling all over him. It's disgusting to watch! They are pathetic, and Penny is right in the middle."

"Of course, you'll have to get past the secretary" Hannah smiled.

"You're joking."

"No, I can't imagine you giving up so easy. Remember, all is fair in love and war."

"There is no love and I'm not at war," Sarah snapped. "I have plans, and I know the kind of man I want to marry. Not a preacher, not a divorcee, so there is nothing to give up about! Should I get to know him? Not! Drop it Mother. Penny is the one with the problem. But you are right about one thing, I won't let the secretary keep me from church – or talking to the preacher."

# Chapter 10

# Decisions

Emotions were emerging strongly in Sarah, which she could not understand. They were confusing and unsettling to her and could only be described as a troubling feeling. The uneasiness was to the point of being unbearable, and Sarah could not figure out what was wrong with her. It was disturbing! On one hand she was confident and happy, while on the other, miserable. What was that about? And why?

She decided to talk to Penny about her uneasiness, which Sarah wanted to deal with. An opportune time afforded itself late one Thursday evening. Everyone was supposed to be in bed.

Sarah quietly opened her bedroom door and stepped into the dark hallway. The light in Penny's room outlined her closed door. She shivered as she slipped by Stoner's dark room, and knocked softly on Penny's door. It opened to a surprised Penny - Sarah tapped her finger to her mouth - a signal to be quiet.

"What?" Penny whispered.

"I've got to talk to you," Sarah said in a low voice.

"If it's about Pastor Hillag, I don't want to discuss it!"

"No, it's something else, Penny. I've had this troubling feeling - that something is wrong. I don't know what's bothering me."

A look of surprise broke on Penny.

"You too? I've been - feeling like that for two weeks!"

"You have?"

The girls shushed each other and were still. They thought they heard one of their parents up.

They were about to resume their conversation when the bedroom door opened. Both of them let out a little gasp. It was Hannah.

"What are you two doing?"

"Talking," Penny replied.

Hannah searched Sarah's eyes for the answer. "Come now, you don't just talk this late at night. Can you tell me? Or is it a big secret?"

"No, Mother," Sarah sensed she wanted her mother's wise counsel.

"I've felt - bothered for awhile, and Penny just told me she has felt it too."

"Bothered?"

"You know...troubled...this uneasy feeling that won't go away."

"You know, girls, I've been feeling it also."

"You have?" they said in unison. "What is it?"

"I honestly don't know," Hannah spoke with downcast eyes. "I do know it's getting stronger and more troubling!"

"That's right!" Sarah agreed.

"I believe that God may want us to be baptized," Penny offered. "I've been praying, and it seems to me it's something He wants us to do!"

"That makes sense," Sarah spoke thoughtfully. "I'll ask Caleb tomorrow."

"You'll never get past his bodyguard!" Penny declared hopelessly.

With, "You both get to bed," Hannah gave Sarah a knowing smile.

Next morning early, Sarah showered and eagerly put on makeup and fixed her hair. She carefully chose a dress that displayed her feminine curves yet was not too revealing. She was in her car before the rest of the family made it to the breakfast table. She stopped by a coffee house to pick up two cups of gourmet decaf coffee and a savory looking Danish she hoped would be to his liking.

She noted Caleb's car in the church parking lot. She had overheard a conversation between Pastor Hillag and one of the men of the church that Pastor liked coming in early on Friday to finalize his Sunday sermon. She knew she took a chance by coming early and interrupting his study time of incurring a hurried distracted meeting. It was a chance she was willing to take and gambled her minister would be surprised and give her his attention.

She prayed the office door would be unlocked. It was! She glided noiselessly past the unguarded receptionist's desk, slowly opening Pastor Hillag's door. She gripped tightly the sack containing coffee and Danish. The paper sack made a faint shuffle noise; Sarah caught her breath. He was absorbed in his Bible and notes. She knocked.

"Pastor," she called sweetly.

He looked up - his face lit up.

"I brought you - er - uh, some coffee and Danish. I thought -."

"Sarah Crothers, come on in! What a nice surprise." He cleared a place on his desk and pulled up a chair for her. She could tell he was touched. He told her several times how much he enjoyed the coffee - and loved the Danish. He asked her questions about her family and school. He sat his empty cup on the desk.

"That was very thoughtful of you, Sarah, and a great start to my day," he glanced at his watch as if to conclude the visit.

Sarah was not ready to leave.

"Pastor Hillag, something has been bothering me," she hastened to say.

"Yes."

"I don't know what it is. It is such a mix of feelings. I'm happy and miserable all at once - does that make sense?"

Caleb studied her for a moment. A smile graced his face. He seemed to know the answer.

"My Great grandfather Farmer had a saying he passed on to my Grandfather Clifton who gave it to my Mother. She told it to me. Great grandpa said that folks have a big empty spot inside demanding to be filled up. That demanding is a real troubling feeling, driving many of those folks to try and fill it up with all sorts of things, such as money, drinking, drugs, sex, power, fame. The problem is that what they need is someone, not something. That someone is Jesus Christ. My question to you this morning, Sarah Crothers, is do you know Jesus?"

"Of course!" Sarah was surprised and offended he would ask her such a question.

"Do you really know Him? Is He in your heart - or just in your head?"

"What do you mean?"

Just then the office door opened and closed. The next instant the church secretary stuck her head in Caleb's office. She eyed the two of them as if she had caught them in the act.

"You know Miss Crothers?" the preacher motioned to Sarah, giving a weak smile.

"Yes, I've seen her in church. Do you want your door closed?"

"No, we're finished," Caleb spoke dryly. Obviously, he was annoyed. He turned his attention back to Sarah.

"Sarah, Christianity is not a religion; it is a relationship...a relationship with Jesus Christ who gave His life to redeem you. Ask Him that question, 'Do I really know You or just know about You?' When you find the answer, I believe you'll also understand what has been troubling you. My sermon Sunday should shed some light on it!"

Sarah relayed her conversation with the pastor to her mother and Penny. Nothing more was spoken of it on Saturday; however, all three were in church the next day. Sarah couldn't wait for the message!

After "Praise and Worship," Pastor Hillag walked to the pulpit and opened his Bible.

"This morning," he began, "I am speaking about an event so incredible, so fantastic, so worldwide in its impact that it seems too good to be true. A lost and dying world scoffs at the idea, yet believers embrace it with hope and anticipation.

Our Lord Jesus spoke of that event in Matthew twenty-four beginning in verse thirty-seven."

Pastor Hillag paused to give his congregation time to find the text. He adjusted his glasses and took a sip of water from a glass that was in the pulpit. His gaze took in all those seated before him. He was most serious.

"But as the days of Noah were, so shall also the coming of the Son of man be. For as in the days that were before the flood they were eating and drinking, marrying and giving in marriage until Noah entered into the ark.

"And knew not until the flood came and took them all away; so shall also the coming of the Son of man be.

"Then shall two be in the field; the one shall be taken, and the other left.

"Two women shall be grinding at the mill, the one shall be taken, and the other left.

"Watch therefore: for ye know not what hour your Lord doth come.

"Paul told the church at Thessalonica that Christ would come as a thief in the night.

"I remember as a lad seeing a film by that name at the church we attended. That story scared me so I couldn't sleep for nights. I didn't know whether to believe that one-day thousands - no millions of graves would release their occupants, and Christians all over the world would disappear! I didn't know if it was true, but one thing I did understand even at my young age was if it were to happen right then, my parents would be gone, and I would be left alone. The realization that something was missing in my life started my search for a Savior.

"Somewhere, down through the ages someone tacked the term, 'Rapture' on the event I'm preaching about today. That word is not in scripture, but it indeed stuck. The dictionary defines 'rapture' as the state of being carried away with joy, love, and ecstasy. That's exactly what will happen. The Lord will catch us up in love when He calls. We will be filled with joy and ecstasy!

"Paul describes that incredible event thus in First Thessalonians, chapter four, verses sixteen to eighteen.

"For the Lord Himself shall descend from Heaven with a shout, with the voice of the archangel, and with the trump of God; and the dead in Christ shall rise first: Then we which are alive and remain shall be caught up together with them in the clouds to meet the Lord in the air; and so shall we ever be with the Lord. Wherefore comfort one another with these words."

Sarah's mind was racing in tiny circles so fast she couldn't concentrate. A war was raging in her mind for her soul. She remembered a series of books about the rapture and the anti-christ when she was in junior high. Why hadn't she been interested? Why had she not had any desire to go to church?

By now, she was struggling in prayer with a God who wouldn't let go. She heard no more of pastor's message - until...

"Think of the sorrow in that day. Some husbands and wives separated. One taken the other left. Families will be torn apart. Parents taken, children left or children taken and parents left. Loved ones suddenly gone, others left behind."

Sarah's heart stopped! She could not stand the thought! She was hit with the truth. She knew it was truth! She would surely be left behind - lost - forever. Her mind refused to harbor that horrible possibility a minute more! All the while, her spirit cried within - 'What must I do to be saved? Oh, tell me! Please!'

Caleb's message again broke into her spinning mind. Everything came to a screeching halt - as though time and motion stopped. She held her breath - the words struck deep and awoke something inside she never knew existed!

"You can know today that if the Son of God were to call - right now - you would be with Him," Caleb's words gave insight and hope.

"Jesus told Nicodemus in the third chapter of John, 'Ye must be born again.' The man did not understand that Jesus was explaining to him that every person is born once physically, and must be born anew spiritually. Then He explained how in verses fourteen to sixteen.

"And as Moses lifted up the serpent in the wilderness, even so must the Son of man be lifted up. How is Jesus lifted up? The cross!

"I want you to see Him on the cross, dying for you! He paid the supreme price to buy you back – to rescue you out of a devil's hell. An old hymn tells what Jesus did with our sin on that cross.

"My sin, your sin, not in part but the whole - was nailed to the cross - and we bear it no more! Praise the Lord! Praise the Lord! It is well with our soul.

"For God so loved the world, that He gave His only begotten Son, that whosoever believeth in Him should not perish, but have everlasting life. He calls you now!"

Sarah was praying with all her heart, mind, soul and spirit. She was not a bad person, but right now her sin loomed before her, black, hideous and ugly, the weight of it was crushing her into the pew.

"Just ask Him to forgive you, look to the cross, open your heart and invite Him to come in. He knocks at the door," she heard Caleb's pleas to come to Christ.

Sarah softly sobbed out the words, "Please forgive me, Lord! I never knew. I do want You - to love you - I open my heart -."

Instantly, sweet waters of forgiveness washed over Sarah as the burden of her sins lifted. She was immersed in a river of love! She wept uncontrollably out of pure joy. She felt clean inside! Her eager heart wanted to shout to the world!

Sarah had attended church enough to sit through numerous invitations. However, she never experienced any urge to go forward. Today she couldn't wait! She wanted to run to the altar! The choir began to sing an old hymn that was new to her - as pastor gave the invitation for those who wanted to receive Christ to meet him at the front. Sarah was moved by the words of the hymn.

"Just as I am, without one plea, but that Thy blood was shed for me, and that Thou bidd'st me come to thee."

She stood up and made her way to the aisle on the first verse.

"Just as I am, and waiting not, to rid my soul of one dark blot. To Thee whose blood can cleanse each spot, Oh, Lamb of God, I come, I come."

She was the first one to arrive at the front. As she walked toward Caleb she could hear people around her break into cries of joy. There was a swooshing sound like a burst of wind sweeping into the sanctuary! She was laughing and crying when she took his hands.

"Pastor, I found Jesus! Just now! There, where I was sitting. He came into my heart!"

"Sarah, I am so happy! I rejoice with you!"

Tears were streaming down both their faces. It just seemed natural that they drop their heads and pray. Caleb praised God for saving Sarah, and they both thanked Him for His love. When Sarah opened her eyes, she gasped to see Penny standing also crying, waiting for Pastor Hillag to see her.

"Just as I am," the choir continued the hymn. "Thou wilt receive, wilt welcome, pardon, cleanse, relieve. Because Thy promise I believe, Oh, Lamb of God, I come - I come."

Sarah put her arm around Penny and felt her stepsister lean into her. Penny's body shook as she wept out her confession to a loving Savior. A thrill leaped in Sarah as she witnessed a transformation in Penny's face. She was conscious of a moving of the Spirit of God. Many people surrounded them now. In the crowd assembled before the altar, Sarah saw her mother.

"Aww," she cried out. An older woman was praying with Hannah. Sarah wanted to go to her mother, but remained holding Penny who was shaking. She felt a hand on her shoulder and knew someone was praying for her. She heard a whisper in her ear - it was the church secretary.

"I'm terribly sorry for the awful things I have thought about you. Will you forgive me?" She hugged Sarah.

"What's to forgive?" Sarah whispered back.

Her salvation experience was strong, but not what one would call earthshaking like her mother's. It was obvious to those who observed those Sunday morning decisions that the

Holy Spirit had moved powerfully upon Hannah Howser! She claimed it was because she resisted God so stubbornly.

Sarah was ready when Jesus called. She was broken by her sin and opened her heart to her Savior in a simple child-like surrender. Her coming to Christ was a beautiful event, leaving no doubt in her mind she was born again and God's child. She instantly felt someone living inside her who wasn't there before.

"That's the Holy Spirit who has come to dwell within. Jesus Christ, the Son of God paid the price and shed His blood. It is the Spirit of God who does the convicting, the saving, and changing, who now lives in each of your hearts." Caleb explained later in a new member's class.

"Now, you must grow in the Lord."

Decisions made that Sunday forever changed the destiny and eternal destination for Sarah, her mother Hannah, and stepsister Penny.

Sarah slowly replaced the photo. No, nothing normal about the way she met Caleb. In fact, nothing about her life with Caleb could be described as anything but catastrophic. She never dreamed back then she would one day be his wife!

# Chapter 11

# Confrontation

Caleb closed off his long conversation with Sarah, but held onto his phone. The early morning darkness made Memphis feel far away from his dingy motel on the outskirts of Nashville. He froze her image on the screen and holding his satellite phone helped Sarah's presence to linger.

A smoldering anger mixed with guilt filled him as he pictured his family being harassed and frightened while he slept – in some roach infested motel. This was one time he wanted to curse the darkness instead of shine a light. Hadn't he been spiritually and emotionally stomped flat already? He was less than a threat! Why attack his wife and children? Was this revenge for past encounters? He could only think of one and that was a miserable defeat.

"And I thought I was so ready to take on the devil; the super hero preacher," Caleb shook his head.

He lay down and attempted to go back to sleep. His mind was too revved up. He picked up his Bible – he was too distracted. Events of the evening and pieces of conversation with Sarah took assertive control of his thoughts and refused to be released. There was so much to think about, to review; to analyze, but out of it a growing awareness of the same uneasy feelings he remembered from the first time, a time no one knew about except him, God and one other person. He resisted opening up a closet he was ashamed of, but the events of the evening demanded 'open that door you've left closed. Replay!"

It started with a call for his help from Penny Howser, a high school girl who had begun attending Timberdyke Calvary. From her description of her brother Stoner, Caleb was positive it was demon possession, and he was eager to take the challenge. He had the authority in the Name of Christ to command any demon out of Stoner. Four years of Bible College and three in Seminary had prepared him for this moment. Revival fire could sweep Timberdyke when word got out he had power over demons. Spiritual cowards would fill the church to hear Pastor Caleb Hillag.

Caleb felt hot tears. It was painful to see him self as he was then. He had big plans for Timberdyke Calvary. He had to succeed, to offset a failed marriage and two, lackluster pastorates. Wasn't he the young man with all the promise?

Growing up, everyone I crossed paths with said I was a lad of destiny; I would accomplish great things for the Lord. It was happening, until Tammy, the divorce; when did it all sour? Timberdyke was to be the upturn.

Caleb hardly remembered Sarah the night he went to the Howser residence. She was pretty and displayed a confident unobtrusiveness. He was focused on the upheaval the family endured the previous night and noticed little else, except Sarah's defense of his diagnosis of Stoner's condition.

He was upset when Gary Howser put him out of the house, but even more determined to help Stoner, and make a difference in the community. Two days later he made a visit to the Juvie Hall where Stoner was detained.

"I'm Reverend Caleb Hillag, pastor of Timberdyke Calvary Church. I would like to see Stoner Howser," he spoke to a security officer, who scanned a roster.

"You mean Ralph Stoner Howser?"

"Very possible. I know him as Stoner."

"One moment," the guard called inside.

Directly, a female attendant opened a large door and escorted Caleb through an open room lined with bland metal chairs and tables. Young people were involved in games, TV, some reading, others were in groups talking, joking. The room was noisy!

"Are you a friend of the family?" she asked.

"Yes."

He was led down a long hallway full of doors on both sides. They appeared bedrooms, but were in fact, cells. The attendant paused at one of the doors, glancing at Caleb.

"Ralph?" she unlocked the door.

"Don't call me that," came a cutting order.

"You have a visitor. I'll be in the hall if you need me." She informed Caleb, leaving him alone with Stoner.

Caleb surveyed the room: a stainless steel sink beside a toilet, all in the open; a desk and chair where homework or reading could be done. Caleb made note of several comics of horror stories on the floor. A metal bed was butted into a corner. Stoner wore a black hooded sweatshirt over prison attire. He sat cross-legged on the bed facing away from Caleb, hood over his head!

"Who are you?" Stoner demanded.

Caleb braced up – ready for battle!

"I'm Caleb Hillag, Pastor of Timberdyke Calvary Church. Your sister Penny called me and I met with your family two evenings ago. They are all very concerned about you, Stoner."

Caleb thought he detected a low drawn out sullen, sneering laugh.

"People say we sometimes act like – beasts. What beast are you?"

Caleb was knocked off guard by the question. He had to think a minute.

"A lion. I'm a lion in the pulpit. I wanted to discuss—."

"What beast am I?" Stoner interrupted.

Caleb shrugged his shoulders and thought to play Stoner's ridiculous game.

"You look like a – right side up bat."

"Wrong!" Stoner jumped up and began dancing in circles around Caleb.

"I'm a raptor – a raptor!"

Stoner danced and ran faster and faster, chanting some gibberish. Suddenly, he leaped on Caleb's back clawing at his hair and face. Caleb fought him off and threw him against the desk. The boy stood up and Caleb saw his face. It was handsome and hideous. What evil had possessed this young man?

"I command you demon in the Name—-."

Stoner held up his hand and Caleb's throat closed, while a different voice came from Stoner.

"You fool! You think you are strong enough to face me? I opposed the apostle Paul once. He was ready. You are a weakling! A lion is no match for a raptor."

Caleb had no voice, but called on the name of Jesus Christ in his mind. Stoner squatted down getting closer to his opponents face. Caleb struggled to move – he smelled sulfur.

"What did you say – I mean think?" Stoner sneered. "What a predicament. You have to speak the name but you have no voice. Pity!"

Stoner began a long, low, mocking laugh. Caleb kept saying the Name of Jesus over and over in his mind. He pointed at Stoner who grew silent then thrust his fingers toward Caleb sending a stabbing pain across his stomach. Caleb kicked the wall as hard as he could. The noise brought the attendant into the room. Stoner quickly overpowered her and escaped out the door. Alarms were set off and guards alerted. Stoner fought viciously with four deputies before he was subdued and placed in a padded cell.

In the confusion, Caleb seemed to slip through the cracks. He carried a sense of responsibility for Stoner's attempted escape, still was thankful nothing was mentioned. Otherwise, the Howser family would blame him and never come to his church.

Once again, Caleb closed that closet door feeling again his pride smart. He remembered the great lessons he learned that day.

'I wasn't prayed up, and I wanted the credit and glory. I thought I could use the Name of Jesus like some magic sword. How dumb!" Caleb mused. 'I really underestimated the power of the enemy, and that confrontation taught me to be a better, stronger, more humble soldier.'

.

## Chapter 12

# Pastor's Struggles

Caleb remembered the morning after his confrontation with Stoner. He was late and agitated when he reached the church office.

"Good morning, Pastor, it's a lovely...day..." the church secretary gave a questioning look.

"Yes, Millie, what's my schedule?" he was short with her. He went straight to his desk and absentmindedly rummaged through notes and papers. Soon, the secretary joined him in his office.

"You have a noon lunch appointment, and a 2 PM with the elders. At 4 you have pre-marital counseling with Ricardo and Libby, and at 5, Mrs. Hopper."

"Reschedule lunch and the church elders. I'll keep the 4 and 5 appointments."

"Are you sure you-?"

"Yes!"

"Pastor, are you – well?"

"No, I'm not Millie. The devil clobbered me thoroughly and I'm not fit to see anyone until I get alone with the Lord – and I can tell you it wasn't Him at my breakfast table."

The secretary waited for him to elaborate.

"Did any of the Howser family call this morning?" Caleb inquired wistfully. He could tell by her look she wondered why he should be interested in the Howser family at a time like this.

"Penny Howser did leave a message for you to call. Would you like me to return her call with a message?"

"No, I'll do it. I won't take any calls or visits until I tell you."

"Yes sir!"

"And Millie."

"Yes, Pastor."

"Thank you. I appreciate your hard work and prayers."

"You're welcome," Millie acted startled and closed Caleb's door.

Caleb got Penny's voice mail and left a message. He wrestled over whether to confess his involvement with Stoner at the Juvie Hall or leave it alone. He was concerned how the family would react. He agreed that matters with Gary Howser could not get much worse. He did recognize that their youngest, Penny, harbored a giddy teenage crush on him and he could do little to tarnish his image. He was concerned about Hannah and Sarah. In his spirit, he saw both of them attending Timberdyke with Penny. He knew nothing about Hannah but did not want to lose her respect. Sarah, he felt a trust and friendship. The day after he met with the family, Sarah found him in the sanctuary to apologize how her family had treated him the night before. She caught him grieving in prayer, yet he felt no shame or embarrassment at letting her see his tears. The following conversation with Sarah Crothers completely challenged and engaged him, expanding and stretching him to the point he was oblivious to the time – until Millie's reminder his appointment was waiting in the office – rudely broke the spell.

Then, he fought off guilt, mingled with anger! The secretary's suspicious tone of voice – made him feel like she had caught them in a scandalous impropriety. But they were only talking. Where's the sin? True, it was a deeply satisfying interaction of words reserved for a man and woman to enjoy. It held an element far different than a conversation between two men or women. He would look forward to visiting with Sarah again, but what would church members think? It upset him that he had to always be on guard around any of the women, especially the single ones.

What to do with them? He resented being held up as a trophy to be won, or a fish in a pond to catch! They were so obvious in their actions they embarrassed him and shamed themselves. They were drawn to him after every service, in the mall, at restaurants, anywhere he showed up in public. Penny could be the hardest to handle – even on a phone call. He constantly was forced to scrutinize his every action, attitude, body language; refrain from hugging or touching, and especially, especially the words he spoke!

But Sarah was different! She was not a threat. She made it clear that day in the sanctuary. Ray was her boyfriend, college was her game, graduation her goal. Marriage and a family were so far off in the future, she never discussed it.

The unknown troubled Caleb. If Sarah knew that he was largely responsible for her stepbrother's lock down in a padded cell, would she remain a friend or stop attending church? If he told the family now, would they be forgiving? If he confessed later, would they not? He was deeply torn!

It was clear he was not free to pursue a romance. He feared revolt in the church body if he began seeing someone. He must face life as it was. He was not free to fall in love – with any woman. How could he, when he still loved Tammy?

Caleb slowly rose from his desk and quietly locked the door to his office. Sadness hung on him like black clouds of a spring rain covering the sunshine. What he was about to do, no one must see. He retrieved a key from a secret place and unlocked a small desk drawer. He pulled out a picture of himself and Tammy taken at Seminary. He studied the couple contained in the frame, then tenderly held the photo to his heart. Soon the tears began to fall.

"How long, Oh God, must I grieve?" Caleb cried out his sorrow. "How do I stop loving? I thought the day she re-married love would die. Oh Lord, something died in me, but it wasn't love for Tammy. I'm tormented every time I think of my wife married to another man. I die a slow death when I remember what we had, what I lost. Father, must I continue to agonize over what I cannot change? Please heal my aching heart – have -."

Millie broke in on the intercom. "Penny Howser returning your call."

Caleb wiped his eyes and replaced the picture in its hiding place.

# Chapter 13

# Trial and Error

"Good morning, Miss Howser," Caleb tried to sound up beat.

"Pastor Caleb, I'm sorry for the delay in returning your call. I was in class and had to wait for it to end. I'm calling in between classes."

The noise and Penny's short breaths indicated she was near running down a fully jammed high school hallway.

"Did you know that Stoner tried to escape yesterday? He fought with the guards and they were forced to isolate him in a special cell."

"I heard that."

"You did? How?"

Caleb swallowed to clear a thickening in his throat. "I've tried to check on him."

"Oh, why thank you Pastor. I'm at my next class, bye!"

Caleb hung up the phone feeling even more miserable. He wanted to just tell the family, so why wasn't he honest with Penny? What was holding him back? Perhaps Penny wasn't the one to tell, but who, Mr. Howser? Never! He would view the incident with his son as a declaration of war.

What about the mom? Gary would take that as going behind his back. No, it was either Gary or Sarah, his step-daughter. But, telling her would make him look a coward – afraid to face, the man – the head of the house.

Caleb groaned and beat his forehead in slow "thumps" on the top of his desk. He finally decided to let them initiate any discussion concerning Stoner.

The next Sunday, Sarah attended the worship service with her stepsister, and a week later Hannah joined the girls. Caleb was pleased and did not want the incident with Stoner to discourage the women's presence in church. Therefore, he avoided any lengthy, in depth talks.

Hannah was generally pleasantly brief on her way out the door. Penny, on the other hand always wanted to tease and flirt, as did several other young women, forcing Caleb to quickly turn to the next person coming through the door.

Sarah however, lingered until later. She didn't gush over him like those other women, but complimented his message. She told him how she looked for what she termed, "Little Sermon Treasure Gems," and would share what she learned with Caleb. This approach not only warmed his heart, but also greatly encouraged him to pray for and plant those trea-sure gems when he prepared his message.

After Easter, Sarah became active in the Wednesday services. He sensed by her hanging around she wanted to talk, but he kept the conversations cordial and light hearted. He felt convicted to discuss the incident with Stoner, which drew his immediate hostile opposition. Besides, he didn't want to give any impression there was any interest in Sarah apart from a normal pastor, church member friendship. By distancing himself, he was taking care of both potential prob-lems at once. Millie didn't see it that way!

"Sarah Crothers called to make an appointment," the secretary informed him upon his return to the office.

"Ok, did she indicate a reason?"

"Just to talk. I told her it best to not bother you unless she needed serious counseling. She hung up."

Caleb was horrified! "Millie, you can't do that," he sputtered.

"She is just another female vying for your interest and affection," Millie fumed.

Caleb studied the church secretary for a moment. She was intent on his reaction. When he didn't respond she continued.

"You already have enough to worry about besides having to fend off a host of base minded women."

"Hold on a minute. Miss Crothers has made herself perfectly clear, she has a boy friend and school is her top priority. She is not interested in a romantic relationship with me."

"She is only more subtle than the rest, but believe me, she wants to get her hooks in you and ruin your ministry at Timberdyke. Can't you see what all of them are doing?" Millie was visibly upset and on the verge of tears.

"Millie. . . your job description does not include protecting the pastor. I've been married, and divorced, and around town a few times. I can take care of myself."

Millie reached for her purse and dug around for a tissue.

"I just don't – can't stand the thought of you being hurt – more."

"Millie, listen to me. My office is open to everyone. I don't care if it's Penny Howser with her teen flirts and giggles, or Catherine with a plate of brownies, or whatever else she has cooked - even subtle Sarah – you will set up the appointments. I can take care of myself!"

"People will talk," Millie muttered.

"Millie! I can handle them. Ok?"

Millie braved a smile but avoided eye contact. Then she dropped her head.

"Yes sir. I understand."

# Chapter 14

# Friday Visits

Caleb continued a habit begun in Seminary that served his ministry well. He was awake and in his office by day break every Friday morning. That was a special quiet time with God for a final review of the message he would deliver Sunday. The Lord spoke the words into his heart during the week, but these Friday morning's was when God empowered Caleb to speak to the church.

This Friday in late March, the crisp dawn air stung his face and burned his nose, making him breathe through his mouth, but the walk from his car to the church office was exhilarating. The feel of the sun beginning to top the distant mountain range gave a hint that spring was soon to follow.

Caleb settled into the chair at his desk, opened his Bible, and pulled out his sermon notes. He began praying over the message God had impressed upon his heart. He was fine-tuning his second point in the sermon when he heard a soft knock and, "Pastor."

A visitor that early startled him. It was Sarah Crothers! He thought he should be annoyed; instead, he was glad to see her.

"I brought you- uh, some coffee and Danish." She seemed unsure she should be there. "I thought…"

"Sarah Crothers, come on in! What a nice surprise." He began clearing his desk and found a chair for her.

"I got decaf, I wasn't sure."

"Perfect! I've already had enough regular to hype me up today. Decaf is perfect."

As Caleb looked across his desk at this young woman who had entered his office, he recalled their meeting two months earlier in the sanctuary. She was mysterious, curious, yet he felt natural and comfortable around her. A strange power moved inside him when he was with her that he could not explain. Yet he felt a prick of uncertainty whether she was safe. Did she intend to take him down like a roaring lion – or – was she an angel?

"I hope you like the Danish," she ventured with a smile.

"What's not to like," Caleb laughed, "let's thank God." He started to take her hand but quickly withdrew thinking better of any physical contact. He glanced at his office door making sure it was wide open.

"How is your family Miss Crothers?" he asked after prayer.

She handed him one of the Danish on a napkin.

"My step dad is finally accepting our going to church, even though he continues to fume about it. Maybe some day he will come with us. I know that Stoner is a heavy burden on his shoulders."

"Is Stoner still in lock down?" Caleb sipped his coffee.

"Yes, but we are told he has been compliant and they will return him to his room with the others soon."

"And your mother and Penny?" he didn't want to linger on Stoner.

"Mom feels good being back in church after so long. And Penny? We fight too much," Sarah grew serious, and took a bite of her pastry.

Caleb watched her a moment, "Sarah, the Danish is yummy. What's happening at school?"

"I'm in a new semester and taking a full credit load. When I leave here, I'll drive straight to my first class."

"And your friend – Ray?"

"Ray's a nice guy, a little nerdy, but ok, a friend. He took me to a movie last weekend."

"Sarah, I can't tell you how good this coffee and Danish are. Delicious! Thank you for blessing me with them."

"You're welcome."

"You say Ray's a little nerdy? You know they generally make good husbands."

Sarah laughed with a slight toss of her head.

"I don't see myself married to Ray," she smoothed her long hair and pulled it over a shoulder. Her glance indicated she didn't want to talk about Ray. Caleb sat his empty cup on his desk and thanked her again for coming and bringing the coffee and Danish.

"That was very thoughtful of you Sarah, and a great start to my day," he glanced at his watch.

"Pastor Hillag, something has been bothering me." Sarah's expression shifted.

"Yes."

"I don't know what it is. It is such a mix of feelings. I'm happy and miserable all at once – does that make sense?"

Caleb studied her face. He smiled, as he knew what was going on.

"My great grandfather Farmer Trevor had a saying he passed on to my grandfather Clifton, who taught it to my mother. She told it to me. Great grandpa said that folks have a big empty spot inside, demanding to be filled up. That demanding is a real troubling feeling, driving many of those folks to try and fill it up with all sorts of things, such as money, drinking, drugs, sex, power, and fame. The problem is that what they need is someone, not something. That someone is Jesus Christ. My question to you this morning Sarah Crothers, is do you know Jesus?"

"Of course!" Sarah bristled.

"Do you really know Him? Is He in your heart or just in your head?"

"What do you mean?"

Just then the church office door opened and closed. Millie stuck her head in Caleb's office. She displayed mild shock to see Sarah sitting there as she surveyed the two. Her look indicated she had caught them – doing something. Caleb suddenly felt very uncomfortable.

"You know Miss Crothers," Caleb motioned to his guest, hoping to defuse a rumor mill from grinding out its divisive and destructive tales.

"Yes, I've seen her in church. Do you want your door closed?"

"No, we're finished," Caleb was annoyed. He turned to Sarah.

"Sarah, Christianity is not a religion; it's a relationship… a relationship with Jesus Christ who gave His life to redeem you. Ask Him that question, 'Do I really know You or just know about You?' When you find the answer I believe you'll also understand what's been troubling you. My sermon Sunday should shed some light on it!"

Caleb was thrilled to see Sarah, her half-sister Penny, and her mom find Christ that next Sunday.

Sarah's Friday morning visits continued off and on into the summer. Although, there was concern that church members would get the wrong idea and having contact alone with Sarah was not in the best interest of his ministry and unwise – something inside him welcomed this young woman's visits. His uneasiness was not motivated by guilt of any kind, but by what other people thought and how they viewed it.

He came to admit he did enjoy and looked forward to those casual chats over coffee and what ever breakfast that she surprised him with. He felt safe with her.

He decided not to encourage Sarah Crother's Friday morning visits – but he didn't discourage them either.

# Chapter 15

# Achim's Deli

One Monday in mid July, Caleb sat down to lunch in Achim's Deli, a small hole in the wall Jewish Café. He was surprised to see Sarah wander in the door. She apparently had not noticed him. She went to the counter and peered at the meats and sandwiches through the glass. Caleb watched her give an order before he spoke.

"Sarah?"

She turned, surprised.

"Oh! Pastor Hillag."

"Come join me. Achim's help will bring your lunch to the table."

"I will be honored to serve you myself," the Deli owner responded loudly.

Sarah smiled and took a seat facing Caleb. He leaned forward to whisper in her ear. She leaned into him making him most conscious of their closeness and the smell of her perfume.

"In here it's Rabbi Hillag."

"Oh?" she sat back with a frown.

"It's Jewish," he grinned.

"I didn't know you were Jewish?"

"What else would Hillag be?" Achim laughed good-naturedly setting down a sandwich, heaping full of thin sliced deli meats, and garnished with lettuce, tomato, and pickle. "And one kiwi-strawberry splash for the lovely lady," he winked at Caleb. "Anything else? Rabbi Hillag?"

Caleb had to laugh and waved Achim on.

"Let me bless your lunch, and mine again," he told Sarah. When he finished a brief prayer and looked up, Sarah was eying him thoughtfully.

"I didn't know you were Jewish, you never mentioned it that I recall all the times I've been in your office."

"Well, I'm what you would call a half-breed. My father was a New York Jew. Mother was born in Alaska to a long line of Christians."

"Oh, Pastor – Rabbi, I just realized I know very little about your family and you. Tell me more!"

"Stop! How long have you got?" he glanced at his watch.

"As long as you want," she had a ready answer. She maneuvered her sandwich to take a bite. She waited Caleb's response as she chewed. She swallowed.

"Rabbi?"

Caleb laughed heartily. "That was just a joke. But why, for as long as I have known you, do you still call me Pastor Hillag?"

"That's what you are – to me," Sarah grew serious as she held eye contact.

"I would like to just be – Caleb, today."

"No problem, Caleb." Sarah smiled sweetly before she took a drink.

"I'm glad to lose Rabbi. That seemed – stuffy."

"Well, I'm not known to be all that – exciting."

Sarah's expression changed. It was one he had not seen before, or at least noticed. He was unsure of how to interpret her look. Was it curiosity or something deeper? Her eyes conveyed a message he could not perceive. Was there excitement or sadness? He could not tell, something was different in her eyes, her smile as she ate her lunch and glanced up at him – waiting.

He thought back to when he met Tammy and fell in love. Was this the same kind of look and smile? No. That was different. Caleb was swept away! He didn't desire Sarah as he did Tammy. She had consumed him. He simply enjoyed spending time with Sarah. Besides, he believed he could never love another – like Tammy.

"Where did you go, Caleb?" Sarah asked.

"I was just, I'm sorry, Sarah, that was rude of me, I did time out."

"Tell me."

"Nothing interesting, believe me."

Sarah looked hurt. "I'm interested in everything about you. I know your thoughts about the Lord and your ministry, your frustrations at times with the church, or at least some of it. You have a Jewish father and Christian mother. I've told you many things about myself and some I have not, but you run silent and deep, Caleb," She reached out and touched his hand.

Caleb drew back and pulled away his hand. He tried to decide what to do with this attractive young woman. Sarah sat quietly and pushed her plate away. She seemed to change before his eyes.

"Today is my day off, you know."

"Yes."

"Are you free this afternoon? We could hang out."

"I'd love to!" Sarah's countenance lit up.

"There's this place in the mountains, by a stream, where I go when, would -."

"Yes!" she didn't let him finish.

'Ah, Achim's Deli, what a special time that was for Sarah and me.' Caleb reminiscenced in the darkness of his Nashville motel room, 'But that afternoon was even better.'

## Chapter 16

# Caleb's Church

The drive was pleasant and beautiful. Caleb had been there alone many times, but this was the first time he ever took anyone else. It was his discovery, it was mystical, sacred, peaceful, a refuge from the world. He felt clueless to his reasons for sharing his special place with Sarah - it just seemed right.

Sarah chattered on as they drove. She told how her father left a letter on her mother's pillow one day and one on hers.

"I was five and mother read my letter to me. He said. . ."Sarah paused and Caleb glanced over to see her quickly wipe her cheek. "I'm sorry."

"Sarah, you don't have to."

"I want to tell you! He wrote how much he loved me and was proud of me. He said God had a special plan for my life and I must find it. Then, then, he said he had to go away."

Sarah watched the passing scenery for several miles before she spoke again.

"We never heard from him again. I still have his letter in a little jewelry box. My mother threw hers away, I think."

"But you've got a family now," Caleb hoped to lift her spirit.

"One might say that looking at us, but the truth is life was hard, cruel – I still have nightmares over those days. My mother was so beat down she must have been desperate for someone to take care of her. Gary needed a mother for his two kids and our families found each other. We went from one struggle to a different one." Sarah reflected.

"How do you mean?"

"My step dad is hard and demanding. Some days, I feel he resents me. When I was growing up, he whipped – me." Sarah's voice trailed off.

"He is an angry man. I've called him numerous times since that first and only time I've been in your home. He usually cusses me out or makes threats before he hangs up. He doesn't understand the decision you, your mom and Penny have made for Christ and hates you going to church."

"That's for sure! We have a battle every Sunday."

"Perhaps he will change his mind."

Caleb pulled off the highway onto a logging road. They drove about a mile into timber, parking at a wide spot in the road. Sarah demonstrated no fear of being alone with him, and he respected her.

They walked about two hundred feet through the tress coming out onto a breath taking meadow cut through by a clear, fast running stream. Beams of sunlight cast brightness and shadow in splendor across grass and flowers; dancing in ripples of melodic movements on the water.

"God is here," Sarah spoke in awe.

"This is where I have my church," Caleb answered softly.

He led her to a fallen log that was partially submerged in the creek. They sat down together watching the water tumble beneath their feet. The magnitude of the timber lined mountains rising high in the distance, combined with the solitude of the meadow rendered speech unnecessary. Caleb could only feel the emotion and was sure Sarah felt it too. He chose this place to share his family with her.

"I visited a meadow like this once, with my parents and grandparents," Caleb began. He spoke low, remembering.

"We had gathered in the lumber town of Douglas Landing, Oregon for my Great Grandmother Emile's funeral. My great grandparents helped found what they named The Church in the Woods. Great Grandma Emile was a widow for many years, Great Grandfather Farmer was killed in the early 50's, a year before my mother, Morgan was born. I never knew him, but heard lots of stories of when they homesteaded in Oregon. Great Grandmother Emile lived into the 1980's. I was 6 when she passed away.

"Anyway, The Church in the Woods was packed, people standing outside. My great uncles, Walter and Harold were there along with Auntie Leah and Mom's cousin Janee. She stood up and told how my great grandparents were together again like two deer. What she didn't know is that great grandma had made me promise to ask Janee a question."

Sarah was intent on what Caleb was telling her.

"What question?" she wanted to know.

"I was to ask how long she was going to stay mad at God?"

"Was she?"

"I didn't understand at the time, but she really was angry when she found out I spoke to the news people outside the house."

"News people? At your Great Grandmother Emile's funeral?"

"They weren't there for that, it was to interview movie star Janee Stemper."

"That's your mother's cousin? I've seen some of her movies – she was incredible!"

"Won an Oscar," Caleb smiled; then grew sad.

"I witnessed at age 6 to everyone I saw. I told the whole world about Jesus that day. People said I would go far, but some where . . ." Caleb threw a piece of bark into the water.

"Back to my story, that afternoon some of the family went out on the Trevor homestead. Grandpa Clifton told how they traveled from Texas to Oregon in a chuck wagon when he was little. Great grandpa Farmer dreamed of owning a cattle ranch, and they lived that dream, a few years, until the Great Depression stripped them of their land.

"Now picture this, Sarah, see over there where the grass rises higher on that small hill? That's where neighbors raised the most rustic, strong log house I have ever seen. There was a small barn for their horses, creek by the front door. Splendid setting, I fell in love with it," Caleb got a distant look, still seeing images of the old homestead.

"Who owns it now?" Sarah asked.

"The family bought it back after great grandpa's death . . . No one has ever lived there, it's almost – like it's waiting. Waiting for them to come back. It's the nearest place to heaven on earth, well, besides this spot. That's why this is my church. I talk to God here."

They both sat quietly, listening to a blue jay and the sound of the stream.

"Caleb, tell me about Tammy," Sarah looked up at him wistfully.

That name was like a thunderbolt driven into his soul opening an old wound. The look of anguish on his face was evident!

Sarah covered her mouth as tears welled up in her eyes, "I'm so sorry Caleb, I have no right.'"

"Why," he choked, "would you want to know about her?"

She studied his face intently.

"Because . . ." she seemed to be gathering courage to say what was on her heart.

"Because, I want to know what she meant to you, how she hurt you, so if I ever had the privilege she had, I wouldn't make her mistakes. I would never leave you – I swear it!"

## Chapter 17

# At Last

Caleb felt irritable and short tempered the rest of the week. How could Sarah have feelings for him? He never encouraged anything apart from their friendly visits. What had he done to this young woman? Maybe he was reading something into what he saw in her eyes, her looks, that wasn't really there. But hadn't she indicated with her question about Tammy that she wanted to be his wife? Impossible! Caleb threw his Bible and books into his car and climbed in. When he arrived at church he retreated quietly to his office barely speaking to Millie. He felt himself withdrawing, and he disliked being that way.

In a few minutes Millie stepped into his office.

"Something is troubling you this morning, Pastor, what's wrong?" she questioned.

"Millie, you are always probing – Probing! Why does something always have to be bothering me? If I'm happy, I'm covering up distress! If I'm quiet, I'm brooding; you would be well advised to tend to church business and not my business!"

Millie stood wide-eyed and speechless. She managed an angry, "You are deplorable!" as she left out his door slamming it behind her.

Caleb vented anger to God and the four walls. Sarah Crothers was filling too much of his mind and suddenly driving him to madness. He must eradicate any feelings for her – cut off any romantic intentions she had – this would never do. Sarah was beginning to intrude into Tammy's territory. How could he break his vows and love another woman? A relationship could end his time at Timberdyke, and even if he loved Sarah, would he cower to pressure from the congregation and break it off? Probably! Dear God, she deserved better!

"But there is no relationship with Sarah!" Caleb cried aloud. "Then why am I so crazy to see her?" he moaned.

'My harsh words to Millie drew tears. Harsh! Why? Why am I so upset? I say there's no feeling for Sarah? Ha! I can't wait for Wednesday – not to teach, but to see Sarah! This cannot be!' Caleb buried his head in his arms.

Sarah was in mid-week service seated in the front. Caleb struggled to teach and avoided eye contact with her. When he did look her way he could tell she was bewildered and hurt. When the service concluded he made a hasty exit, not talking with anyone.

By Friday, he was a wreck. He dared not go to his office for early study. He was not prepared to face Sarah and doubted he could trust himself. He got in his car and drove, lost in questions, crying for answers. He ended up at his church where he wrestled with God and a truth he refused to acknowledge.

Saturday, he attempted to go over his sermon, but his heart wasn't there. His mind refused to concentrate. His angry and cutting words built a list of people he would have to apologize to and ask their forgiveness. He was ugly and how could ugly get in the pulpit the next day?

Caleb was thankful, the Lord lifted him out of the mire he was stuck in, or was it relief Sarah wasn't in her usual spot on the front pew? No! That deeply distressed him. He drove her away! How cruel!

When Caleb began his sermon, the Holy Spirit took over and the message flowed in power. Caleb knew it was not his but God's doing. He couldn't wait to get to his office after the service to call Sarah. He was about to hang up when she answered.

"He – hello,"

"Sarah? Pastor Hillag. How are you doing? Your mother said you weren't feeling well."

"No... I'm not," her voice was weak.

"What's the matter? Would you like me to stop by, and a . . . pray for you?"

There was a long pause before her response.

"I'll be, okay."

"I'm praying that you are well soon."

Caleb hung up and sighed. He was not being fair with Sarah. How dare he toy with her feelings. He must break this off before it went any further! This decision pitted him in battle with his heart! He was finally driven on his face before God. He found no peace.

"Dear God, I'm confused and miserable. Please speak to me – show me something, anything, I can't go another week like the last one. I'm wandering in a dry desert!"

Caleb slept late on Monday. He had no appetite. Any structure of his day he thought about didn't fit. The Lord seemed to be persistently calling him to the church sanctuary to pray. At first, Caleb brushed it off. He was prayer exhausted! But the still small voice of the Holy Spirit got louder. Caleb drove off to the church. He prayed he wouldn't see anyone who wanted to talk. He simply sought finalization to his struggles. He longed for peace; to go back to a place he once was, uncomplicated, sensible.

The sanctuary was all that, his hiding place: a cleft in the rock where God covered him with His hand. It was quiet, the mid morning sun strong, illuminating boldly Moses, King David, the Apostles, and Jesus in stained glass. The sound of the sanctuary door closing broke the stillness. Someone's head popped up at the front pew startling Caleb. What was Sarah doing there?

"Oh Caleb!" she exclaimed, running up the aisle to meet him. "I am so glad to see you! I was happy spending the afternoon with you last Monday, but I died Wednesday at church. I felt you were distancing yourself from me, and I was afraid I had made you angry. Then when you weren't in your office Friday, I was sure I must have hurt you, upset you, I should never have said anything about Tammy." Sarah was searching his eyes, trying to look into his thoughts.

"Instinctively, I knew you were at your church. I only wanted to find you – to be there with you, to explain, and tell you I was sorry. As I drove, I tried to recall landmarks: directions, to no avail. I ended up hopelessly lost. I cried all weekend until I was sick. And when you called Sunday, you don't know how much I wanted you to come."

Caleb was afraid to dare – hope! What was Sarah trying to say?

"Caleb," she whispered, "I'm in love with you. I courageously fought it, but it has over powered me! I kept it covered, but my love demanded release-expression, until I can hold it in no longer. I had to tell you."

Caleb's heart soared! He attempted to smile through his tears. He looked deep inside the soul of this woman who had just revealed her love, and anxiously awaited his response. He led her to the front pew and they sat down. This move seemed to sponsor doubt in her.

"Sarah," his voice carried a husky gentleness with it. He was digging through emotions and memories for words.

"In college, I fell in love with Tammy, as hard as any man could fall for a woman. In my dreams, we lived happily ever after, raised a family, ministered together for the Lord, and grew old, only death parting us."

"She worked, and I concentrated on finishing seminary. Something happened and she changed. Should I have seen the red flags? How could I? I was in love; she was my wife. The day she set me down and told me she didn't want to be a pastor's wife . . . and wanted out, I died inside."

"I fought the divorce; that only drove us even farther apart." Caleb wiped his eyes and looked away.

"So she divorced me anyway. My life ripped open at the seams, and a ministry that hadn't even begun seemed doomed to failure. Fresh out of seminary and divorced – church after church turned me down. I decided to cover up my divorce, and a church called me, but it wasn't long before they found out I lied and I was – asked to leave. Then, when I couldn't fall lower into the black hole I was dumped in, the bottom fell out of that too. I was told Tammy was getting married," Caleb's voice trailed off.

"I've never stopped loving her, I keep a picture of her-us in a drawer in my office desk. I was convinced I could never love any woman like that again – ever."

Caleb took her hand as he continued, "Friday, I did go to my church. I couldn't face you that morning. I was so torn! I hadn't encouraged a relationship outside of friendship, and you were involved in school, had goals and a boyfriend. I told myself you weren't interested in me, until, what you said – last Monday. Then, I was forced to face myself and my own feelings."

"At first, it was safe and easy to just be a friend. You weren't even a Christian. Then you came forward trusting Christ. I waited to see if you would follow in baptism – you did. When you came on Friday mornings, I was concerned over what the church would say, plus I had ideas of what a courtship should be, if I ever had one, and what kind of wife I wanted. Your coming seemed out of sync and ill timed! Those were excuses I used to hold you at a safe distance."

Sarah dropped her eyes and grew solemn.

"Sarah, Friday and Saturday, I discovered something deep inside, like a seed planted, taking root to lift a sprout out of the dead ground. My head told me to be fair to you and break off anything that might be between us and let you go on with your life and discover your own dreams. Up root the plant!"

"But, what did your heart tell you Caleb?" tears trickled down Sarah's cheek.

"My heart – told me to let it grow. Believe me, Sarah, I wrestled with God and presented every argument I could dredge up.

"She's too young," I told Him.

"You need a strong young woman by your side where I'm sending you," He answered.

"But she's only a babe in Christ and I'm a seminary graduate," I pointed out.

"She will learn, besides, Sarah is smarter than you think."

I resorted to my last objection, "I could be asked to resign the church."

"Am I the Head of the Church or you?"

"Finally, I begged God to reveal His will. I opened my Bible to read and I swear Sarah, I was looking right at the verses where Joseph was told, 'Do not be afraid to take Mary as your wife.' Oh, Sarah," Caleb began to cry. "I only have a stack of trials and failures to offer, but I love you – I never believed I would love again - Oh God, I've wanted to say that for weeks, I was just too dense . . ."

Sarah never let him finish. She threw her arms around his neck and Caleb kissed her. She eagerly returned his kiss.

How wonderful and fitting it was. Their love confessed to each other before the Lord in the sanctuary of the church. Thus, began an exciting courtship ending months later in a beautiful wedding, condoned enthusiastically by the Timberdyke membership!

Caleb made his way into the bathroom to wash his face. How precious to remember those early days of meeting and falling in love with Sarah. Now, more than ever he was anxious to get out of Nashville and be home with his family.

# Chapter 18

# Homecoming

An evil presence opposed Caleb the instant he pulled into the driveway of his home. He saw no one, nothing to prove that presence, only a sense in his spirit that something or someone from the realm of darkness was near. He knew beyond any doubt that what Sarah saw lurking in the shadows was real - not imaginary.

"Be Gone in the Mighty Name of Jesus Christ!" Caleb ordered.

Its power and resistance confronted him. It challenged his commands, but Caleb fought back until the hellish devil fled before that powerful Name. He felt the evil presence vanish.

Caleb climbed out of the car and opened the trunk to gather his luggage. He dropped those to the ground when he heard Sarah's call. She bounded down the steps, across the snow-covered grass, into his arms. Eager lips found each other in happy kisses mixed with cries of joy from Sarah. Caleb held her tightly for as long as she wanted - needed - until she pulled back. He saw gladness and relief over his return in her expression.

"I'm so thankful you're home," she whispered as she placed her cheek back against his chest and melted into his arms.

"I was scared out of my mind, Caleb. I prayed and prayed that - that monster wouldn't get into the house!"

"I know, Sarah," he lovingly patted her back - her face. "I prayed for you and the children. I am upset I wasn't here!" Caleb felt again that familiar stirring of anger triggered by the knowledge that the devil seemed to choose the times he was away to attack his family.

"Show me where you spied the figure."

"There - by the tree."

Caleb walked to the tree she indicated.

"Ah ha!" he exclaimed. "This proves it! There are tracks all around."

"What?" Sarah came to look, then scooped up a handful of powdery snow to shower Caleb with.

"You are so mean - that's the policeman's tracks."

She kissed him and gave a glance that always sent a thrill through his body. That kind of kiss and look always made his homecoming extra meaningful.

"Let's get inside where it's warm. It's cold out here," she laughed as she grabbed up one of his smaller bags. "We have lots to talk about!"

Soon they were engrossed in deep conversation. Sarah was fixing hot tea.

"I know it was a demon manifestation, my love. Two times I heard the doorbell, but Esther and Mark never did. I saw a dark figure of a man by the tree, but the doorbell was frozen. I know, I tried it and had to break the ice. There were no human tracks in the snow."

"Yes, sweetheart, what you saw was a demon, and it was real. They don't make tracks in the snow unless they choose to - and they don't have to push a doorbell button to make it ring. No, it was here. I sensed its presence when I pulled up."

"Why us?" Sarah questioned. "Did it intend to harm me and the children?"

"Maybe, but you prayed it wouldn't get in the house, and it couldn't. The Lord prevented it. But the part that puzzles me is why you? What are you doing - or the children - to cause the devil to come at you?

"What if it's you he is after, and he is trying to get to you through me - or Esther and Mark?"

"Uh, uh. That doesn't make sense. What am I doing for God to even cause the enemy to raise an eyebrow, or claw, or whatever? The one chance we had to make a difference crashed and burned yesterday."

"Oh, dear, tell me what happened!" She handed him his tea and sat on the sofa. Caleb took a sip before he continued. "Sarah, I fought through ice storms and slick roads! I couldn't get to Atlanta the day of my appointment, so they rescheduled for eight the next morning. The weather hindered every mile, and I didn't arrive until nearly 11:00 that morning. They said they had to fit me in - that took - forever. I waited and waited! Then they must have taken lunch. I lost my cool - then found out they could see through this secretary's eyes - "

"What?"

Caleb took another sip of tea.

"No - no - it was a robot. One of those new Gamma fourth generation models we read about. She – I couldn't believe it was so lifelike!"

They both lifted cups from saucers and sipped tea together. They held their cups a moment as Sarah waited for Caleb to go on.

"Anyway, I was agitated, it was 1:30, they watched me make a fool of myself. It was a landslide into the valley of rejection from there. This one member was mean and cruel.

He asked about Tammy and the divorce. Did we have sex before marriage - were you pregnant - I think he had decided against us before I ever walked in the room. There was no prayer - nothing asked about you or our kids - they pointed out my failures as a pastor - and questioned my calling."

Caleb found the board meeting so distasteful he refused to discuss it further. He stared into his tea for so long it grew cold. When he looked up at his wife, he knew she had left him to his thoughts until he had enough.

"What do we do now?" she asked softly.

"What I've been doing, I guess. I'll put on my uniform and go deliver pizza."

Tears instantly welled up in both their eyes.

"God didn't call you to deliver pizza," Sarah spoke gravely. "Do you remember the first night you went to work? You walked in here with your shirt and pizza hat on and asked how you looked? Mark thought you looked great, but after you went to work, Esther and I cried and cried. We knew God's calling on your life wasn't this!"

"I have to do what I have to do to provide for our family," Caleb raised his voice. "I don't particularly like it, but -" he had difficulty saying the words. "No church wants me."

"Us," Sarah strongly corrected.

"Me! I'm the one they have trouble with. I'm the one that's messed up."

Then the awful truth that Caleb didn't want to face swept across his mind like a raging dust storm. The mission board didn't want him either. With that realization, months of letters, phone calls, and prayers, seemed wadded up along with his application and tossed in the trash. Grieving began in his heart reaching into the very depths of his spirit. He sat his tea down and laid his head on Sarah's bosom and wept like a baby. She said nothing, only smoothed his hair, but Caleb could feel her crying too.

While Sarah was attempting to console her grieving husband, one far greater, the Comforter, was doing a work in both of them. Caleb took heart and felt strengthened. He sat up with new resolve to not give up on his dream.

"I never knew my Great-grandfather Farmer," he began, "but my Great-grandmother Emile told me he had a dream to travel west to start a cattle ranch. He had that dream when he was a young boy. Years went by, and his dream didn't happen. Then he got married and had my Uncle Walter and my Grandfather Clifton. He just kept on doing what he didn't want to do, and even though his dream grew dim, he never lost sight of it. It stayed - tucked away somewhere in his heart. One day, out of the clear blue, it happened. Great-grandma told me, and I recall how her eyes danced, 'that showed us God hadn't forgotten. He was busy getting everything in place. That was the beginning of our wonderful adventure - Farmer and me!' Well, Sarah, I know what God has called us to do. He's just getting everything in place, and one day, He'll start us on a great adventure of our own - I just know He will. Until then, I put on my uniform and deliver pizza. If I leave now, I can make up some of the money I wasted on this trip."

"Oh, Caleb, must you? You've hardly been here, and Esther and Mark will be home from school soon."

"Keep the children up, and we will celebrate my homecoming when I get off work."

# Chapter 19

# An Enlightened One

"DeLamo's Italian Pizzeria," a young woman answered the phone coarsely. Caleb glanced at the large clock hanging near the "To Go" counter. It read 9:52 - eight minutes until his shift was over. He was tired and couldn't wait to get home.

"Caleb, you're up!" the woman belted out the order.

"Eva, Tommy's up next," Caleb replied.

"This one asked for you by name."

"What?"

"Cash order – who uses cash anymore – dig up some change. They said they would make it worth your while."

"Whoa, dude, you been hangin' with some chick?" Tommy kidded.

"Was a man," Eva injected before Caleb could respond.

"Whoa totally! We got a 'bi' preacher," Tommy kidded.

"In your dreams, Tommy," Caleb took the tease but resented the inference. Let me tell you what Jesus says about – "

"Caleb, clam it! You know it is against the law to discuss that. I've warned you - and I will call the police," Eva's voice instantly become a snarl. "Here's the address. When the order is done, get your ass out there and deliver!"

Caleb took the slip without further words. It was apparent the old law Eva referred to was intended to silence Christians and Jews and made it impossible to witness in the workplace. A person had to request the information, and Eva and Tommy had made it clear they had no interest in Caleb's faith.

Tommy snatched the slip from Caleb's hand and looked at the address. He let out a short whistle, shaking his head, "Totally upscale!"

Caleb took the order back and went to an empty table and sat down in disgust. A new girl, Symphony, who had just prepared the pizza and shoved it into an oven, cleared tables while waiting. She came to Caleb's table and wiped it.

"I would like to hear what you believe - I mean about Christ," she whispered. "Eva and Tommy both are hitting on me, and I hate it. The world seems - so - so ugly, but I think I - trust you."

"Symphony, you burn this pizza, I'll take it outa your pay - if you still work here," Eva threatened. Symphony scurried to the oven to check Caleb's order. She placed it in the warmer pac and handed it to Caleb.

The address was not easy to locate. The complex was a sizeable-gated community with plush apartments. He had to be buzzed in at the gate, and when he got no response, he called on his satellite phone.

"Hello," a distinguished voice came on.

"Your pizza is here."

"Reverend Hillag?"

"Yes, sir?"

Caleb heard a click, and the gate began its swing open. He passed what appeared a country club and nearby tennis courts. The apartments were well supplied with lighted walkways and immaculate grounds. He could make out one enclosure that had overhead heaters and hot tubs. Numerous people were seated at tables, and heads were visible in the Jacuzzis. Caleb knew it took money to live here!

He parked in a guest spot and made his way to 306. His curiosity was peaked. He could not imagine who this was, but they undoubtedly knew him. Was this a former church member? He felt it wise to be cautious. He rang the doorbell, there was a clicking and the door slowly opened, but no one was there.

"Hello, pizza," Caleb called into a dimly lit room. The only light he could see was over a built-in range in the kitchen. Near that was a table and chairs with a candle burning near one end.

"Come in. Place the pizza on the table, please." The voice was deep and authoritative. Caleb complied. He could see the shadow of a man in an overstuffed chair in the living room.

"Your pizza comes to $37.99," Caleb called out after removing the box from the heat pac.

"Your pay is by the candle."

Caleb picked up folded bills. At first he thought it was five tens; however, on closer scrutiny in the candlelight, he discovered five one hundred dollar bills. He turned toward the figure.

"I don't have change for this large a bill - sir. Don't you have anything smaller?"

"I don't think small, Caleb Hillag. No change needed."

"I don't - understand," Caleb stammered. "Do I know you?"

"No, but I know you, Reverend Hillag."

"Who are you? What do you want with me?"

"Let's say, I am An Enlightened One, and that I have a proposition to make you."

"For your being enlightened, it's dark - in here. I'd like to see whom I'm talking with. Let me turn on a light."

"No!" the voice thundered. "Stand where you are and listen. I am making you an offer that will change your life."

"What kind of offer?" Caleb was suspicious.

"Before I answer, let's review some things. You attended Bible College and Seminary, Osapha, Washington. During seminary you married Tammy Hutton. That ended in a bitter divorce. Since then you've been rejected by church after church because of it, and other misunderstood mistakes. Now Global Missions has rejected you. What a joke your life!"

"How do you know all this?" Caleb demanded.

"Master knows everything about you."

Caleb was hesitant. "Who is your Master?"

"One who wants to lift you out of your pathetic existence."

"I do okay. God takes care of me," Caleb objected.

"You mow grass, trim bushes, and deliver pizza. You don't have money to fix Esther's teeth, you can't afford the simple request for a new Z Box for Mark, and Sarah divides one can of chili and ten crackers to feed your family. How can you struggle like that and say you're doing okay and God takes care of you? He won't even let you preach! What kind of a God calls you to a work only to grind your efforts into dust?"

A force filled the room so strong, Caleb felt lightheaded. He heard the door close and bolt behind him. He wanted to answer this man's accusations, but his speech was impeded. His mouth could not move! His chest was being crushed!

"You teach and speak one thing but live another. You portray faithfulness to your wife, but tonight when Symphony came to you - you admired her young body. Why live a lie? Admit the truth, and it will set you free. Don't allow your words to conflict with your desires? Admit it, and be free - to do - to live – to breathe! Join ME!"

Caleb tried to speak, but a gurgling was the only sound coming from his mouth. His mind felt like it was being warped by some unseen power so strong he could not fight it. All he could see was a naked Symphony coming to him with wanton eyes and outstretched arms. He shook his head violently to rid himself of the image, but it came back. He tried to cry out to Jesus, but the very name was snatched from his lips. Now all he could think about was the 500-dollars stuffed in his shirt pocket. A voice kept pounding into his brain '5 million - 5 million - 5 million.'

"You preach a message of sin, death, and hell. Do you enjoy making people feel uncomfortable – miserable? Look at you! Even now you are trying to find forgiveness, and for what? Feeling something natural. All you can think about are rules and laws. Where is your passion? Rules just leave you bothered and powerless."

Caleb was on his knees gasping for breath.

"Reverend Hillag with his ideas of missions, and you didn't even have the funds to drive to Atlanta and spend two nights in cheap motels. Your life is a waste, you miserable man. Get on your face before me. I am an Enlightened One!" his voice shook the room,

A force hit Caleb that flattened him to the floor! The man had risen and was standing in the middle of the living room. His face was not visible, but as Caleb turned his head he could see the man's eyes. They glowed blood red in the dark, and Caleb knew he had not the strength or power to combat this evil unless God helped him. He continued to gulp in air, his mouth opening and closing like a fish lying on dry ground.

Master, offers you a part in a movement so expansive in scope, men have only dared to dream of it. Help us build a new world flowing with peace and harmony, a world alive, free of sin and guilt. Spirit guides walking with you to direct your every decision day and night, not a God you pray to who never answers. Master promises you more wealth, respect and fame than you ever imagined. Let me teach you how. You can become An Enlightened One - even greater than I. Master wants you! Follow him and all your dreams will come true."

Caleb's mind wanted to say yes. He was so weary of unanswered prayers and financial struggles. He pictured a beautiful home for Sarah, fancy cars for both of them, private school and nice clothes for the children, freedom from work, travel to wonderful places. Calm came over him as he pictured a new and exciting life being offered to him.

"Surrender to the master and let me show you the way," the man kept repeating.

"No!" Caleb's heart cried out. He remembered the day he believed in Christ as his Savior. He saw Jesus hanging on the cross, bleeding for him. A still small voice whispered from the depths of his heart and spirit.

"Caleb, I love you. I bought you with a great price. I am here. I am that I am, and I am with you."

Caleb began sobbing," Jesus, Jesus, Lord Jesus, help me; help me, I need you - now!"

Suddenly, a power surged into Caleb raising him to his feet! It was not the power he felt in the shadows of the room - this was light and life! It quickened his spirit, his soul and body. He squared off against The Enlightened One.

"I rebuke you in the mighty name of Jesus Christ!" Caleb yelled in a voice that reverberated off the walls. "I'll have none of your deception! You have NO AUTHORITY HERE! You are bound and powerless before Jesus the Christ whom I serve."

"You fool - Christ is dead."

"No, He is not! I just spoke to Him."

"You ignorant, pitiful specimen. You think you can stand against me, An Enlightened One? I am elite!"

"I can't, but the Son of the Living God, Jesus Christ has already defeated your master. The scripture says: 'And they overcame him by the blood of the Lamb, and by the word of their testimony.'

"There is power in the Name of Jesus Christ, the Son of the Most High God. His blood cleanses from all sin – And He has risen from the dead and is alive! Confess Him as Lord – NOW!"

The man shrieked and stopped his ears.

"I know who your master is," Caleb's words shot into the enlightened one. "It is satan, the wicked one, the father of lies, the deceiver of men."

"Fool! Die!" The man pointed in thrusting motion toward Caleb, who instinctively held up his hands as a shield.

Fire and sparks flew from the Enlightened One's fingers, but bounced in a shower from Caleb's hands.

"No weapon formed against me shall stand," Caleb shouted. "Put on the whole armor of God! I stand with the shield of faith and the sword of God's word. He says: 'Neither give place to the devil.' You walk in darkness whoever you are, and I give you no place."

Again, the man hurled a lightning ball at Caleb, and again it bounced from his hands in a shower of sparks. The next time he aimed at Caleb's head, but Caleb deflected that bolt as well. Caleb sensed he had been taken over by the Holy Spirit, and this fight had merged into something like a scary science-fiction movie. Raw power against power, and he and the man were only vessels. He imagined the fire bolts would burn, but they actually felt icy cold when they hit his hands.

The man's face was more visible now. His expression was one of rage and desperation. If he were the leading man in a film, his looks would leave women weak, but Caleb saw him now for what he was - a toothless roaring lion.

"The Bible says: 'Resist the devil, and he will flee from you," Caleb shouted. "Fleeeeeeeeee! In Jesus' Name!"

The man's eyes went wild. He held both hands, palms out, against his chest.

"This is not over. I'm not finished with you. I will make you pay for your stupidity!" the man snarled.

With that The Enlightened One threw both hands out, pushing them toward Caleb. A force like a speeding big rig hurled Caleb into the wall. Everything went black...........

# Chapter 20

# Temptation

"Hang on, buddy, help is on the way."

Caleb's eyes focused on the face of a police officer. He tried to sit up, but pain forced him back down.

"What happened here?" the officer questioned.

Caleb seemed unable to speak. His mind was dazed; he attempted to look around.

"No one on the premise," a female officer reported emerging from another part of the apartment. "What a mess, and this scene makes no sense. Pizza stomped into the plush carpet of an empty apartment, the box in shreds!"

Caleb saw the pizza scattered around the room, and to his shock the apartment was empty - where had all the furniture gone?

"Your manager called in to have us check on you. She got worried when you didn't return. Your wife has also been calling. Are you on something?" the officer near Caleb was puzzled. "You look like you were in one hell of a fight."

Caleb attempted to speak - only his mouth moved. At that moment paramedics arrived. They immediately checked his vital signs, and then asked Caleb questions to determine if he were coherent.

"He can't speak," one medic commented. "His heart and blood pressure are okay. Hummm... Look at this. The palms of his hands are seared, like someone put a hot iron to them."

"And he has burns and cuts on his face and upper body. What could have burned him? The pizza?"

Caleb shook his head no!

"What then?"

Caleb again tried to speak. Only a low, pleading groan came forth.

"He must be high on drugs and beat himself up," one paramedic offered.

"Look in his eyes. He doesn't appear high, and what would he use - the pizza box?"

"Remember, he was called to this address," the police officer injected.

"Whatever, this fellow has experienced trauma!"

Caleb vaguely remembered being loaded into an ambulance. He wanted them to call Sarah. He fumbled for his cell phone to retrieve it from his pants pocket. It was gone. With shaking hand he reached to the medic.

"I think he wants his cell phone," he spoke to the female officer who stood at the rear of the ambulance. She took one look at it. "Man, this is fried," Caleb heard her explain. He fumbled for his wallet.

"The officers already have that," the attending medic sensed what Caleb was trying to do. "They will let your wife know where you are."

Caleb felt the prick of a needle finding his vein. He heard the muffled shrieking of the siren, and the movement of the ambulance made his body shake. He was aware the medic had hooked up an I. V. and was drawing a syringe full of some - whatever it was, Caleb didn't want any.

"This will ease pain and help you sleep."

Caleb didn't feel pain, and he didn't want sleep. He struggled to protest. The medics held him still, and Caleb waited for everything to fade into a drug-induced sleep, but instead of sleep Caleb was injected into a world of vivid dreams. There was the ringing of a doorbell, and the slow opening of the door to apartment 306. Caleb walked into a dimly lit room. Every minute detail stood out clearly in his mind. His attention went first to the table with the candle where he placed the pizza. Then the five hundred dollar bills he picked up. He could barely make out the sofa and the sinister outline of a man seated in an overstuffed matching chair. End tables with unlit lamps, a glass-topped coffee table and a small aquarium that had a tiny night-light in it un-noticed before were now fixed in his mind. He knew this was more than a hallucination.

Then that same commanding, creepy voice, 'Let's review - Let's review - Let's review!'

With each review, Caleb was transported back in time to relive a major failure in his life.

It started when a bully beat him up after an attempt by Caleb to tell him about Jesus.

Next was the one time he brought home an "F" on his report card. He heard again the anger in his father's harsh words, and saw the disappointment in his mother's eyes.

Review after review revealed missed goals and broken dreams. He was taken back to once more experience the pain of screaming fights with Tammy and her stabbing announcement, 'I'm divorcing you, Caleb. You'll never amount to anything but a poor preacher!'

'Nothing but a poor preacher! Nothing but a poor preacher! Nothing but a poor preacher!' The words seemed on automatic replay in his mind, and he couldn't stop them. The voice that started out Tammy's became the man in the apartment, an Enlightened One.

'You are not even a poor preacher,' the words changed into an even more cruel reproach! Then Caleb was transported in this dream just like Scrooge in "The Christmas Carol" when taken by the spirit of Christmas Past to relive every painful memory of failed, doomed, destroyed church relationships and ended pastorates. Caleb wept uncontrollably. Tears were running down the sides of his face and around his nose, but he couldn't move.

The final blow came when he was forced back into that horrible board meeting at Global Missions. A hatred for those people and that ministry seeking a window into his soul burst into a super heated back draft when he opened the door. Something told him to resist those feelings.

There was a long period of silence. The only sound Caleb heard was the hollow emptiness of his failures. When he looked up he was sitting in a comfortable chair in a room with the appearance of a fancy home theatre. He was facing a screen that filled the whole wall. Again he heard that voice!

'Follow master, and this will be your life!'

On the screen began a series of short vignettes, which Caleb was forced to watch. They brought pleasure to all of his senses as he could see, hear, feel and smell with heightened awareness.

A bank statement appeared on the screen. It was his with a balance of less than one hundred dollars. As the camera focused upon the balance and enlarged it, the figure began to rapidly increase. Before his eyes the numbers multiplied. One million and growing when the scene switched to a beautiful home set amongst trees on a large and sprawling estate. The home boasted a four-car garage, and Caleb didn't have to be shown to know the finest cars of choice were parked in each one. His, Sarah's, Esther's and Marks. The inside of the house was the fulfillment of every dream he and Sarah had ever expressed for a home.

And there was Sarah, radiant with beauty, dressed in an evening gown he had longed to buy her on a special occasion but could not afford. He had never seen her so happy. Then Esther came running to spin and show off her gorgeous outfit. Finally, the camera swung to Mark. He was cool, handsome and dressed to kill.

Now, the scene changed to a montage of pictures. Music came up that stirred and inspired him to the depths of emotions. It was pictures of him. He was speaking to groups of thousands. He was on interview talk shows, newscasters praised him, women adored him, his face on a magazine cover, and his picture all over the globe on Internet news. What's this? Merchandise with his name, Grand Marshal in parades, a sought-after speaker at expensive dinner gatherings, a summer villa in Italy, and beach houses for tropical vacations. As the music rose to a grand finale, a figure of light walked off the screen and stood before the young preacher.

'Caleb - Caleb - join a movement sweeping the entire world. You can help complete my mission. Come to a world of excitement, peace and harmony. You can become the minister and leader you were destined to be and fulfill your most cherished hopes and dreams. You will know wealth and power you never dreamed possible. I can make you an Enlightened One. Bow down and worship me – NOW! Such a simple act, and all you have been shown, will be yours, Caleb'

'There is One God, Him only will I worship, and you cannot enter my heart!' Caleb countered.

'Invite me.'

'I cannot. I already invited the Holy Spirit, and He dwells there. He will never leave me, and you cannot occupy the same vessel as He.'

'Alright, He can stay, but I will control your mind.'

'You cannot. I belong to the Good Shepherd, and Him do I follow, and I know His voice. He is Jesus Christ, my Lord!'

The figure of light disappeared, the screen that was looping the scenes went blank, and the room faded from view.

# Chapter 21

# One Phone Call

Everything seemed surreal until the touch of someone's hand filtered into his consciousness. He recognized that touch. It was Sarah! Caleb fought to come out of a heavy fog. His eyes flitted, then opened. Sarah sat beside his bed holding his arm. She was overjoyed to see him wake up! Her face lit up.

"Oh, Caleb, I was worried out of my mind over you! I can't tell you how - oh, thank God - you're awake! You were in a death sleep - and so long! It's two in the afternoon - I've prayed - our children have been afraid and crying. No one knows what happened to you - how you were hurt! Oh, honey, look at your face – I can't even see your hands. Were you beaten and robbed? The doctor told me last night you had cuts - bad burns which he can't understand - and no voice."

Caleb tried to speak. "Errrrkkkk," was his best effort. He struggled for control to raise his head. Sarah helped him and fluffed his pillow. It was then he looked at his bandaged hands. He pulled Sarah close to him and enfolded her in his arms. She lay there against his chest until she wanted to look at him. She smoothed his hair. She covered her mouth with her other hand as bottled-up emotion let loose.

"Caleb, so much has hit us - in such a short time. Last night I lost it. You didn't come home, and your phone went straight to voice mail, the screen was blank. I called Eva, and she told me you went on a late call and maybe were delayed. She was checking. Time passed and more time. When she called, she told me you were in a freaky accident, and an ambulance was on the scene. She didn't know more, but promised to have the police contact me. I was frantic. I couldn't reach Carla to see if she would watch the kids. More time passed, and no one called. I got Esther and Mark up, and we drove to DeLamo's - they were dark. I was on my way to check out the hospitals. That's when a police officer called and told me where they had taken you. I came straight here. The children are in the waiting room. Oh, Caleb! Last night was supposed to be your homecoming! You didn't come home!"

"Well, well, Mister Hillag, aren't you quite the mystery man." The doctor entered the room.

He checked the chart and did a quick once over exam of Caleb's chest, nose, throat and eyes. He sat on a stool and took Caleb's pulse. He studied Caleb's face a moment before he spoke.

"Do you understand me?"

Caleb nodded.

"Good. Did you do a lot of loud screaming last night?"

Again Caleb nodded yes.

The doctor rubbed his thumb on his chin as he thought.

"Your voice mechanism is surely damaged, but that will heal with rest. What I don't understand is your burns. Your face, chest and arms remind me of someone who had hot coals poured on them. You have burn holes in your shirt and pants. And your hands...they look like they were placed on a hot stove. The burns are severe and to keep infection down,

I'm keeping you on anti-biotics. Do you know how you got these burns?"

Caleb shook his head, no, and shrugged his shoulders.

"The police thought you were high and hallucinating. Tests showed no evidence of drugs. Did you take anything last night?"

Caleb shook an emphatic, no!

"The police are anxious to ask you some questions. Are you up to that?" the doctor inquired.

Caleb gave a quick, no, with his head, glancing at Sarah.

"I understand. I'll be back later," the doctor made his exit.

"I must bring the children in Caleb. They have been here so long and not complained - well, Mark has - but they've been good."

Caleb opened his arms as if to say - "Yes!" Sarah ran out to immediately return with two eager children, who bolted across the room and scrambled up on his bed. They hit Caleb with such force pain shot across his chest. He struggled for a moment to regain his breath.

"Daddy, you're hurt!" Esther kept saying. Mark looked him over but said nothing. They both waited for him to answer Esther's barrage of questions.

"Your daddy has no voice," Sarah reminded them.

"Oh, Daddy!" exclaimed Esther. She held Caleb's face in her hands. "You've been cut," she murmured. "And burned!" she added.

Mark brightened up.

"I saw a movie once where this woman lost her voice. She wrote on paper," Mark said as he looked around for something to write on.

"That's a good idea," a police officer entered the hospital room. "I happen to have pad and pen right here." He pulled both out of his pocket.

"I'm Officer Moreno, and I know the doc said wait, but I must get on with this investigation."

Caleb recognized the policeman as the one in the apartment who rescued him.

The officer turned his attention toward Sarah. "You may not want the children here. I need to ask your husband a few questions."

"I should take them home for awhile, then I'll return. Do you have my husband's cell phone so I can call him?"

"Ma'am, his cell was cooked like a fried egg. The inside had parts melted. Why it didn't burn a hole in his leg - I just can't figure…"

Sarah frowned and without further comment took the children out.

Officer Moreno handed the pad to Caleb.

"Do you think you can write?"

Caleb nodded as he awkwardly gripped the pad and pen.

"Okay, do you have any idea who and why anyone would call you to an empty apartment?"

Caleb scribbled, 'The apartment was furnished. A man was in the living room.'

"Huh?" the officer was surprised at Caleb's answer. "Impossible!" He shook his head.

'I was told to set the pizza on the table by the candle,' Caleb wrote.

"Did he give you anything - touch anything - did he pay you?"

'Five one hundred dollar bills were on the table. I put them in my shirt pocket,' he scribbled.

"Five hundred! That's odd - extravagant." The officer went to the closet and pulled Caleb's shirt out. He checked the pocket.

"Not here." He called to Caleb. He commenced to look in his pants' pocket, then poured personal items on the bed stand and went through Caleb's wallet.

"No bills that large that I can find. Either you got stiffed or someone robbed you - or - maybe you imagined it."

'I saw it in the candlelight. I held it in my hand and stuffed it in my shirt pocket, Caleb wrote. ' Maybe a police officer - or medic - or someone here took it,' Caleb turned the pad.

Caleb saw the officer jerk and his neck redden. He knew he touched a raw spot and prayed the officer drop that matter.

"Can you describe this - other person in the room?"

'Man - about 6 foot one - eyes reminded me of - bloodshot - short beard. He wore a black suit and red tie - I think.'

"How did you get - hurt?"

'We fought,' Caleb wrote bluntly. He knew the officer would not understand the rest.

"Describe the fight." The officer clearly was having trouble piecing the crime scene together - if there even was a crime!

'He threw electrical bullets at me, and knocked me out.' Caleb handed the pad over.

The police officer studied Caleb's last comment for a long time.

"What you are asking me to believe is that this - individual hit you with electric pulses, knocked you out - burned and cut you - moved out furniture and then stomped pizza all over the carpet in less than an hour?"

Caleb gave one quick nod. It sounded ridiculous and improbable to hear the officer say it.

"Why in the name of common sense would he want to do that?"

Caleb shrugged his shoulders.

"Do you have any idea who this person was? Have you ever seen him before? Could you identify him?"

Caleb motioned for the pad. He wrote: 'He said he was an Enlightened One.'

The officer's face went pale, and Caleb heard him swallow hard. He stared at the pad of paper for a long time as if trying to decide what to do next. Finally, he took the pen from Caleb and prepared to take his leave. Tugging his cap tightly on his head he turned toward the wounded preacher.

"Mister Hillag, I'll write my report, and if we come up with a suspect you will be contacted. My advice to you; I think you would be better off just forgetting last night ever happened."

Caleb lay in bed and mulled over all the events of the last two days in his mind. Some were so strange and spooky, Caleb wondered if they really took place. Of course, they were - in the spirit realm! But what puzzled Caleb was why this happened to him and Sarah? Had he mistaken for someone else? Or...did satan know something Caleb didn't?

Then he thought about what he had seen on the screen. The appeal and allure of it swept him out to sea with a tide's undertow. Was he only thinking selfishly and not considering his family and their needs? Life had certainly dished Sarah some low blows. How could she be happy? The only new clothes in two years were the children's school clothes. And what about the simple yet important matter of having her hair done? She did her own! He remembered the time she cried of mortification when it turned out horribly. Perhaps he could have the best of both worlds - for the sake of his family!

Sarah returned with the children and paper and pencil. Caleb eagerly wrote of what he had seen in his dream on the screen.

'The Enlightened One promised this,' he wrote at the end.

"That sounds electric, Daddy. I would love a bigger room and pretty clothes," Esther said thoughtfully, "but, Daddy, how could this man do such nice things for us when he hurt you?"

"Cool!" Mark jumped up. "That means I could get that game Cyborg Slaughter I've wanted to kill for. Let's do it, Dad!"

Sarah was openly annoyed with Mark's response. "There's more to life than H. D. games, young man." Then she grew serious as though reflecting. She sat down on the side of the bed and took Caleb's bandaged hand and kissed it.

"Honey," she spoke softly. "Do you remember right after we married when we visited your Grandparents?"

Caleb nodded and wrote, 'Yes. It was just before Grandfather Clifton passed away.'

"One day I sat near him on the sofa. Just the two of us, and he asked me if you had a dream. I told him you did - to pastor a church. He waved me on - you know how he would do - and told me that was just what you were doing at the time, but you had a stronger, bigger, nobler dream buried away somewhere in your heart. He told me, 'When he finds it, don't let him lose sight of it.'

Then he shared a story Great-grandmother Emile told him. This was it, the best that I can recall:

Your Great-grandparents Farmer and Emile were traveling in a chuck wagon with two young boys, Walter and Grandpa Clifton, and Leah on the way. They were almost swept away by a flash flood in New Mexico, Farmer caught the fever and almost died, one horse was hurt by sharp lava rock, they were robbed, and nearly burned up in the desert. In Arizona a large rancher offered to buy their wagon, give Farmer a good-paying job, a doctor for Emile and a house for the family. Great-grandmother told your Grandpa that Farmer was going to accept the proposition for the family

- until Emile reminded him of their dream. Caleb, we have a dream too, and we must not lose sight of it! Will this - this man - whoever he is - keep his promises? I think not, without requiring our very hearts, minds, lives and souls - a high price for what? Things?"

They sat in silent thought for some time.

Caleb wrote, 'You are right, sweetheart. Besides, he didn't even pay for his pizza.'

Everyone laughed heartily.

"Oh!" Sarah sat straight up. "I almost forgot. Hub - uh - some kind of tree - Crabtree - from Global Missions has been trying to call you on your satellite phone. Since he couldn't reach you, he called me. I told him your phone was out, and you were hurt and in the hospital. He gave me a number and wants you to call him."

Caleb groaned in his spirit. He pictured Hub Crabtree and his sour attitude. Right now, this was one phone call he didn't need.

# Chapter 22

# A Work Sealed

S arah's question, "Well, what do you think of all this?"
sent Caleb's mind rushing back over the past week.
What an incredible seven days it had been. He wanted to
think about every detail before he answered Sarah.

Today was Thursday, January 12, 2017, one week to
the day he had been to the office of Global Missions. Seven
days, yet for all the events crammed into that short time it
could have been seven months.

It was Friday morning. Caleb received his wife's frantic
phone call about the unexplained ringing of the doorbell -
not once, but twice, and the elusive prowler in their yard.
Caleb could pinpoint that time as when the great spiritual
onslaught exploded on their lives.

It was late that same night he encountered the mysterious Enlightened One, which the ensuing battle they fought
landed him in the hospital! That's where he was on Saturday
afternoon when he awoke, and the same day Sarah received
the phone call from Hub Crabtree of Global Missions.

Caleb had postponed his return call to Mister Crabtree
for two reasons. One, because he needed some time to recu-
perate and regain his voice. Second, was every bit as strong

as the first, Caleb had only unpleasant memories of his encounter with this spiteful board member. Even the thought of this man sent anger coursing through Caleb's veins. What could they possibly say to each other that would be nice?

Still, the man had called. What did he want? So it was curiosity, which prompted Caleb to make the call to Global Missions as soon as he obtained a new satellite phone.

"What do I think about all this, Sarah?" Caleb repeated her question.

"I want to think Global Missions is going to do something with us. Just think about it. They wanted us here as quickly as possible, and they said they would cover the expense."

"Ha!" Sarah interrupted. "You told them we were broke, and that's the only way they could get us to Atlanta."

"One thing I know for certain. The Hub I spoke to on Tuesday was not the Hub I saw in the board meeting. To request us both here encourages me, and I would hope- this means an assignment."

"I pray so," Sarah murmured as she took one hand from the steering wheel to run her fingers through the hair on the back of his head.

"My Mother told me the story once of my Great-grandparents. She heard it when she was a girl." Caleb paused to look up at the downtown Atlanta buildings.

"She recounted the day Great-grandfather Farmer received the letter from the government in the post office box announcing they had won a lottery for a piece of land in Oregon. Great grandma said he was so excited he was screaming and yelling, driving the horses so fast he nearly turned the wagon over in the barnyard. She said she had never seen him so happy, spinning her around and around! Oh, Sarah! A part of me is excited like that. Imagine how he felt when he opened that letter."

"I am excited! I can't wait! This will be our time now as it was theirs then," Sarah exclaimed with a laugh.

"I'm almost - afraid - to think - wish - hope. We've come so close before, only to have the desire of our hearts dashed away before we could embrace it - know its feel - the thrill - live it. If this blows up, Sarah, I don't know if - "

Sarah shook her head to stop that train of thought.

"We will still have our love, each other, and our children. We will go on, no matter what."

"There it is, "Caleb pointed as the boulevard turned them towards a beautiful building standing amongst the giants of the Atlanta skyline. The western sunset glistened on the glass face reflecting pools of golden light.

"My - how stunning," Sarah, remarked.

The couple retraced the steps Caleb had made one week prior: An assigned slot in parking, elevator ride up to the lobby, then on to the fifteenth floor. What a difference from a week before. They were ahead of time. No cold, grey, icy day - only sunshine. Theirs was the last appointment of the day and not the first.

'Dear Lord, let this be it!' Caleb breathed a prayer and squeezed Sarah's hand. He felt like a pair of kids going on a new adventure! He opened the door marked 1517, took a breath and led Sarah in. They walked up to the receptionist.

"Hello, Rona, Gamma-fourth generation. How are you? Reverend and Mrs. Caleb Hillag to see the board, and we are early," Caleb teased.

Rona was expressionless, and Caleb thought her hesitation was the evaluation of all he had spoken.

"Welcome, Caleb. I remember you, and very pleased to meet you, Sarah. I am well, thank you, for my generation does not tire from a day's work; however, I will be relieved to acquire a charge on my power pac. Yes, you are early, unless your appointment was scheduled for Friday in which case you would be very early, by twenty-four hours. Won't you have a seat, I will notify the board of your timely arrival."

"A robot with a sense of humor, would you believe," Caleb remarked as they seated themselves.

"She is - beautiful," Sarah whispered, "and so realistic."

"Told you," Caleb grinned.

The board conference room door swung open, and Nancy Stroder motioned them in. The other members greeted the Hillags as they entered. Introductions were warm. The board was relaxed, jovial, and casual. Caleb and Sarah felt over-dressed for this meeting.

"Let's get down to business," Gerald Pullman directed everyone to be seated. "Sarah, feel free to take off your jacket if you wish, and Caleb, you can loosen that tie if it bothers you as much as mine does me." Gerald's laugh certainly had a way of putting the group at ease.

Once seated, there was a moment of silence. Caleb looked at each member and waited. For an instant he saw his Great-grandfather opening his letter with trembling hands.

"Son, are you ready to go on a mission field?" Hub Crabtree asked in his gruff way - but this time his mannerism gave way to a rough kindness.

Before Caleb could answer, tears filled his eyes, and his lip began to quiver. The rehearsed words for this possible occasion seem so shallow and meaningless. Instead, his heart spoke in reply as the tears freely flowed. Sarah took his bandaged hand and began to cry also.

Hub seemed pleased. "I take that as a yes, Son?"

Caleb and Sarah both nodded in agreement. Tiffany Gong handed them tissues, and the board waited for their new missionary couple to gain composure. Nancy Stroder spoke next.

"How about you, Sarah? Are you ready to leave your home, this country, to be a missionary and a missionary's wife?"

"Yes," Sarah sniffed, "I think God was talking to me before He did Caleb. He knew I was the harder one to surrender - and I did. I go where my husband goes, and as I am proud to be his wife, so shall I be proud to serve our Lord as a missionary."

"How will your children react?" Tiffany questioned.

Caleb started to respond, but Sarah's touch on his arm and her look said, 'Let me.' He gave her the go-ahead.

"It will be difficult for them, but our children are resilient as we have moved many times in their few years. They will not only adjust, they will adapt and thrive. I know them. We are ready!"

"Yes, with all our hearts and souls we are ready for this work," Caleb agreed.

"Good!" Hub stepped in. "These decisions have been bathed in prayer. Let's join hands around the table, and, Gerald, would you lead us in prayer that the Holy Spirit will anoint, bless and seal this work for the Kingdom of God."

# Chapter 23

# The Assignment

"I know you both are anxious to find out where Global Missions is sending you. Of course," Gerald Pullman added with a sly smile, "you can always refuse this assignment if it's not to your liking." He walked over to a big screen plasma mounted on the wall. "Who wants to tell them about their assignment? Hub?"

"Let me - let me!" Tiffany jumped up. "I've been there and so love it. I'll be the very first to come check on your progress."

Hub motioned for her to proceed. Tiffany Gong was so excited you would have thought she was getting the assignment. Her enthusiasm revved up Caleb's and Sarah's! She quickly made entries on her sat phone. A detailed map displaying the Gulf Coast of Mexico came up on the plasma. Tiffany focused in on one area and enlarged it.

"This is where you will go," she pointed to a spot on the coastline. "Early last century the village of Vera Cielo was established up on the mountainside above the coastal water. It was a small village accessible only by boat, and had little growth. A few years ago some investors discovered the beautiful beach there and bought up several miles of coastline."

"Rumor tells that the money came from mobsters and drug lords. They are the real owners," Hub injected.

"They built a tourist resort and named it, Lugar de Paraiso. It boasts a plush hotel, casino, nightclubs and upscale bars and fine restaurants," Tiffany went on.

"Complete with gambling, drugs and prostitution," Nancy added with disgust.

"But it is such a pretty place," Tiffany smiled.

"Some locals built around the resort to form Lugar de Paraiso into a city with shops and services of all kinds, eating establishments and a growing number of homes," Hub took over. "There is only one small Catholic Church in the whole area, and this is up in Vera Cielo. Global Missions wants to plant a church in Lugar de Paraiso. What do you think so far?"

"I'm overwhelmed," Caleb responded in an ecstatic daze. "I think we would be complete idiots not to like this."

"I fell in love with it the minute I stepped off the plane - you will too!" Tiffany bubbled.

"Lugar de Paraiso has its own airport that enjoys a sizeable number of scheduled commuter flights," Gerald explained. "That is the only way in or out. Well, cruise ships stop there, of course, but they take no passengers to or from the city."

"I have a slide show to let you see right now," Tiffany went on, "then we can take a short break."

The couple was impressed with the charm of the city and the allure of the mountains. They could see the enjoyment their family would obtain from fun in the sun on Lugar de Paraiso's white sand and the warm Gulf water. Sarah at one point whispered in his ear, "Caleb, this will be like a permanent vacation in Hawaii." She gave him a squeeze to show her pleasure.

During break, Hub came to him. "What do you think?" he asked Caleb. Caleb shook his head.

"It's like a dream, Hub. I couldn't have been given a more perfect place. Don't pinch me - I may wake up an' find - "

"That I am indeed the ogre you thought I was, and this is a cruel hoax?" Hub laughed gruffly.

"I must admit I am a bit confused - by the change. I was convinced I had no chance."

"Son, you must know that even after screening out many prospects. We still interview hundreds of wannabe missionaries. Some truly don't have God's call on their lives; others don't have the grit required. It's our task to find out, so we have developed what we call our mean interview. It doesn't take long for masks to come off, and we also find out how much the person can take.

"But I failed in so many churches."

"I wouldn't say you failed the church. I think you probably stood on principle and were unwilling to compromise God's Word. In these days, that to me is an admirable trait. I'd say those churches failed you. Besides, if God were calling you to the mission field, He wasn't going to let you get too comfortable in a church."

"But my divorce?"

"Son, do you think others won't question that? If you had tried to cover it up, I would've been concerned. Besides, you stood up to ol' man Crabtree better than any candidate I've interviewed in a long time. I like your spunk! We need that for Lugar de Paraiso. I do apologize over the remark I made about your wife. It revealed your love and devotion for her, and now that I have met Sarah, I am quite impressed with her. She will make a fine missionary."

"Okay, let's get on with our business so we can take the Hillags to a nice dinner," Gerald ended the break. "Marcus Willabee is our business end and will take you through the nuts and bolts of your preparations to leave for the field."

Marcus handed a sheet of paper with the Hillag's itinerary and an envelope across the table.

"At the top of the paper is one item you folks are interested in, your salary," Marcus smiled. "We believe you will find the amount most generous, as Global Missions' support base insists their missionaries be well taken care of. With the monetary exchange between American dollars and Mexican pesos, you can live extremely comfortably."

Caleb felt faint when he saw the figure. He had never made that much in his life! He heard Sarah gasp when she looked to where his finger pointed.

"Believe me, you will earn every peso of it. Spiritual warfare has been brewing to block your going," Nancy brought up a vital point. "Your family will be on the front-line of an all out war! Relations between the States and Mexico have been sour for several years now. Anger and resentment will impede your progress. You will have to gain their trust."

Caleb and Sarah nodded in agreement.

Marcus stood up. "First things first. Tonight we will treat you to a fine meal, and you have reservations at Atlanta's finest hotel resort. You need to close out all obligations you have in Memphis. Give notice at work and school. Dispose of furniture except for a few items that can be shipped. Do you own your home?"

"No," Caleb answered.

"Two cars?"

"Yes."

"Sell one of them and keep one for travel."

"Travel?" Caleb and Sarah looked surprised.

"Yes. Both of your families live in Washington. Since your tour is four years before a furlough, Global Missions wants you to take a two-week vacation to spend with your families. The envelope contains a generous account card to cover your expenses."

Caleb felt Sarah shake and knew she was crying. He put his arm around her and held her. Seeing family meant more than any words could convey. It had been a long time - now the reality hit them. They were going home to visit.

Marcus realized he needed to wrap up this session.

"To line this out, you need to tie up loose ends and close out everything at Memphis. Take your much-needed vacation and enjoy it to the fullest. Report back here and we will house your family. The orientation will include school for your children, and classes for all of you in local culture and Spanish. The studies are intense and accelerated, but you will progress at your own speed. The faster you master your work and the language, the sooner you will leave Atlanta. When complete, Global Missions staff will give final preparation for the mission field and you will be flown to your assignment."

## Chapter 24

# Memories

To be a foreign missionary means to cast off all your possessions. You leave the country you have loved and embraced all your life, and travel to a strange place with only the clothes you wear, and whatever meets the weight requirement in your luggage. This strange land will become your home, and a different kind of people of an unfamiliar culture and tongue will be your new family and friends. It was one thing for Sarah to think about going on a mission field, now it was an event in their lives that would actually take place.

The next two weeks were a blur of activity. What they couldn't sell was given away. The solar car sold quickly, so they kept the family van for the trip. Caleb seemed to have little trouble saying goodbye to business associates and friends they had made. He used the opportunity to share Christ with the ones who didn't believe, and prayed with most of them. Even Eva allowed Caleb to pray with her. He was excited when he told Sarah.

"I even witnessed to Eva, and she prayed with me."

"Oh, Caleb, she could contact the authorities," Sarah was concerned that nothing delay their trip.

"No! I asked - she agreed. Only Tommy refused. I left him alone. Symphony was crying. I hope she - trusted..."

The hardest part for Sarah was deciding what to keep. Suddenly, everything contained memories and held sentimental value.

"For Heaven's sake, Sarah," Caleb declared in exasperation. "We can't ship the whole house to your folks!"

After much struggle and a few times of weeping quietly alone, Sarah finally made her choices. Keepsakes, pictures and special personal items were carefully packed and mailed to the Howsers for safe storage.

It is said that the heart never fully leaves the home of your childhood. Upon thought of that statement, one might surmise it depended upon who lived there and the events, which took, place - happy or sad.

Traveling home for Sarah always conjured up a mixed bag of emotions - ranging from ecstatic excitement - to downright dread. She couldn't wait to see her mother whom she loved dearly and was close to. Though miles apart they were close in spirit and spoke often face to face on Internet TV.

And her stepsister Penny - the last time they saw each other was at Penny's wedding to T. J. That was 2012, just before the Hillags moved to Tennessee. Penny graduated college that May and married T. J. in July. They even moved their wedding earlier while Sarah and her family were still in Washington. Now, five long years had separated them. As the drive droned on, eagerness grew until she wished the van were a plane.

However, there was her step-dad, Gary. He and Sarah never got along. She grew up feeling ignored and only tolerated by him. When she married Caleb, the split in their relationship shook violently into a bottomless chasm! She believed her step-dad never forgave her for that decision, and he abhorred Caleb's very existence. Only her Mother's presence kept any peace when they were together, and Sarah dreaded Caleb and Gary occupying the same room for more than five minutes.

"Promise not to argue and fight with my Step-dad, Caleb," Sarah requested in earnest.

"He's the one who always picks a fight!" Caleb shot back. His eyes instantly revealed anger, but as his gaze continued, he saw something in her face, her eyes, a pleading look. He softened, dropping his eyes.

"I'll do my - very best - sweetheart," he spoke with a gentle strength, and Sarah knew she could count on him to make this visit peaceful as possible.

But Stoner was the one who left darkness on the horizon of her thoughts producing a sick feeling in the pit of her stomach. More than confrontations with her step-dad, she feared what her stepbrother might do!

Stoner had disappeared the night he was released from Juvenile Hall. He never stayed in his room again, but always seemed to be there, somewhere in the blackness, watching, lurking. On occasion he would call - and just breathe - but they knew who it was. Sometimes he left objects - or notes in obvious locations. On Caleb and Sarah's wedding day when they returned to Caleb's place, they found a blood-splattered note on the bed that read, 'Marriage made in hell!'

"How did he get in here?" Caleb raged.

Sarah was shaken! It definitely marred their wedding night, but she was determined that no one or no thing would destroy their marriage. Caleb felt the same, and he burned the note. He explained to her that God had blessed their marriage, and the devil could not break their bond. They left that night on their honeymoon and changed locks on the doors when they returned.

They lived in a larger home when Esther was born. The day they brought her home from the hospital they discovered a picture showing only the torso of a man that looked like it had been printed off some Internet porn site along with another blood-splotched note suggesting, 'When she's ready!' Both were lying in the baby's crib.

Sarah had never heard Caleb curse before, but he swore an oath that day to protect with his life the daughter he held in his arms. Sarah grabbed the picture and note yanking the blanket and sheet out of the crib, throwing them on the floor. She wanted none of it touching her baby! She shredded the two hideous pieces of paper with her hands - over and over, smaller and smaller, until she had no strength left in her fingers. She kept on relentlessly tearing, tearing, grunting, until Caleb placed his hand over hers.

"What does he want? Why? Why? Can't he just leave us alone? Why is he doing this? How can he just walk through locked doors? Oh, God!" Sarah crumpled into Caleb. The sudden jolt startled Esther, and she began crying loudly.

"Shhh, shhh, shhh," Caleb was trying to quiet them both. "It's alright, shhh; the devil couldn't hurt our marriage, Sarah, and he won't harm our baby!"

That incident was so deeply embedded in their minds, when they were to bring Mark home from the hospital, they arranged for friends to stay in the house and keep watch. Nothing! No Stoner. Not until six months later when Sarah took Esther and Mark shopping for groceries. It was there when she returned – on the doorstep, a dead black cat and another blood-scrawled note. 'Satan's child,' it read. Fear gripped Sarah! She refused to stay in the house for days. They prayed over the baby, but this felt different than with Esther, maybe stronger, Sarah wasn't sure. She just knew she was disturbed in spirit when she thought of it - and of Stoner.

Her thoughts formed words, as they were driving beside a pristine lake high in the Colorado Rockies. This scene resembled a beautiful painting, so peaceful, yet so stark against the frightening memories filling her mind. "It's uncanny. I mean how he knows."

"Who knows?" Caleb looked over at her.

"Stoner."

"Gosh, Love, what brought that up?"

"Do you - think he knows we are coming?"

Caleb prayerfully asked the Lord about Sarah's question.

"Yes," he answered not taking his eyes off the road.

"How can – "Sarah lowered her voice so Esther and Mark would not hear, "we stop his intrusions and threats? When we lived at Timberdyke we prayed against the demons possessing him – changed locks four times, installed safety windows and a security system, even filed police reports, and got a restraining order."

"Little good that did. They could never locate him to serve the papers. But remember, so far his nasty threats have been empty. We will just trust God to protect us."

# Chapter 25

# Home Visit

The visit at the Howser's went unbelievably well. Sarah wondered if her mother hadn't had a little talk with her step-dad like she did with Caleb. True, T. J. liked Caleb, and the two of them palled around which didn't leave much time for Caleb to spend with Gary. Sarah was thankful for that, but when her step-dad did spend time with her husband, she was amazed at the interest and enthusiastic conversation about Lugar de Paraiso. As she would catch bits and pieces of conversation she began to realize her stepfather had an ulterior motive.

'That sly fox is setting things up for a vacation. He's not interested in our work - just the resort where he can gamble, drink and fish,' she thought to herself. 'Wait 'til I tell Mother.'

"I'm sure he is," Hannah responded to that little revelation. "Your Step-father is always interested in a good place to fish."

"And to drink and throw away money at the casino games!" Sarah added, to which Hannah flashed eyes of disapproval.

"I suppose," Hannah sighed, "however, it will be easier and more often for me to see you, Caleb and the grandchildren," she concluded.

Sarah was extremely happy to be home these few days. There were spontaneous lunches and shopping excursions - some with her mother, once with Penny, sometimes a threesome. There was one weekend outing up to the snow line just for play, but Sarah's favorite and most precious of times were the late night talks when Sarah, Hannah and Penny retreated into Sarah's old bedroom while the men visited in the living room.

Penny voiced concern the second night when she looked at her watch.

"It's 12:15! T. J. will be upset it's so late again," she laughed.

"When Gary gets tired, he just gets up and goes to bed," Hannah remarked.

"T. J. was asleep on the couch, and Caleb was watching TV," Sarah added. "I swear my man hardly sleeps. Says he does his best thinking at night! 'Course, television doesn't require much thinking."

They all agreed the men could fend for themselves and went on talking.

Each night was different. There was tenderness, the remembrance of forgotten memories, which often brought tears and hugs. Then Hannah brought out picture albums. The girls roared in wild laughter and rolled on the bed like schoolgirls. Hannah watched - pleased. All three were aware that soon Sarah would depart - and that fact made each moment they spent together even more special.

There was another topic, which had not been mentioned, but it came up when the women were looking at pictures.

"Oh, look!" Penny pointed. "That was at Stoner's birthday party. His last one - at..." her voice trailed off.

"Do you - does anyone ever hear from him?" Sarah asked.

"One time he called me, years ago. He wouldn't tell me where he was. Wanted to know if I had become a Christian and if I were getting married. I don't know how he knew that. I told him, 'Yes.' He called me 'stupid bitch' for both."

"Has he contacted Gary?" Sarah asked her mother.

"No," Hannah dropped her eyes.

"Did he - I mean - write you a card - or - anything when you married, Penny?" Sarah wondered.

"No," Penny gave a questioning look.

With that, Sarah recounted the horrible encounters with Stoner. Hannah and Penny were shocked!

"Stoner has never bothered us. Perhaps he has gotten over his anger and will leave your family alone," Hannah was hopeful.

"Mother, it's not us he hates, it's the God we serve; and unless he is saved the hate will go on."

Sarah became vaguely aware of a commotion in the kitchen the next morning. She glanced at the clock. Time for her step-dad to be gone to work - but that was his voice - and he was getting louder. She sat up in bed. Then she heard Caleb's voice.

"Oh, Lord, don't let them be fighting over some dumb -!" she groaned as she slipped on her robe. Just then Caleb opened the bedroom door and stuck his head in.

"Good! You're awake. You need to come see this."

"Oh, Caleb, I heard you and Gary arguing. You told me - promised…"

"Sarah, we aren't fighting. We had coffee this morning. He discovered - well, you come and see." He opened the front door.

Two police units and officers in the front yard greeted Sarah. As her eyes swept the scene, she immediately saw a huge satanic pentagram spray-painted on the garage door. Then she looked over at their van where the police officers were talking to her step-dad and now Caleb who joined them. Her hand went to her mouth in shock as she walked around their vehicle. All their tires were flat with gaping gashes protruding from the sides. Painted words were all over the van. On one side was written, 'Jesus idiot missionaries.' The hood displayed, 'Losers,' while 'devil boy' was sprayed across the back. On the other side were the words, 'marriage made in hell.' Sarah bravely fought back tears! All prior encounters were heaped into one hideous nightmare!

"Something's written on the top," a neighbor in a second story window yelled down. Gary climbed up on the rear bumper to see.

"Hard to tell, but looks like, 'When she's ready?' What the hell does that mean?"

That pushed Sarah into an outbreak of rage and panic! She fled back into the house.

# Chapter 26

# The Hillags

Caleb wanted to cut their visit with Sarah's family two days short for Sarah's sake, but she wouldn't hear of it. "I want every minute!" she insisted.

Caleb couldn't get all of the black letters from off the van, and where he did, it ruined the van's paint surface.

"It looks wicked," Caleb eyed their vehicle in disgust, "and we have to drive it clear across the country like this? Lord, have mercy!"

Sarah had an idea and went to a discount store and bought paints of bright colors. She selected five brushes from an art store and went to the house to turn their pitiful mini-van into a work of art.

"Sarah, we look like a vanload of hippies I recall seeing in a movie," Caleb declared as he examined Sarah's finished project.

"Well, it's at least better than those bad words that were on it," Esther remarked.

"Cool move, Mom," Mark gave his approval with a hi five! "I like it!"

"Are you attempting a missionary statement, son?" Mr. Hillag commented dryly, walking around the van after arrival greetings at the Hillag home were exchanged.

"It's a long story, Father; I'll explain later," Caleb replied.

The Hillags lived in an affluent bedroom development outside of Seattle. The trip from Timberdyke was a three-hour drive - with bathroom stops.

Joseph Hillag was a stern man, outspoken in a blunt way. Caleb had retained some of his father's mannerisms which reinforced the saying, 'He was his father's son.' Upon observing that Mr. Hillag had put on considerable weight around his midriff, Sarah hoped her husband wouldn't retain that feature as well.

Mr. Hillag was always polite to Sarah and the children - never unkind. He demonstrated a rigid kind of love, awkward to hug or to advance any kind of physical love. Sarah, sometimes, with humor, wondered how they managed to have Caleb but knew why they only had one child - or so she guessed. True to God's chosen people, everything Joseph set his mind to or touched prospered. There were numerous times he had helped Caleb and Sarah with money, and he was generous toward the grandchildren. His stingy early years had softened over time, but his business ways had remained staunch.

In those regards, Caleb was totally unlike his father. He was very affectionate to her and the children. Yes, he could devastate in a hot barrage of searing words, but would turn just as quickly with gentle magnetic warmth that drew people to him. There was no in-between! He was either loved deeply or hated strongly.

And where Joseph collected and saved wealth, Caleb constantly gave his away. Sarah knew these qualities came from Mother Morgan, and Sarah loved her as much as she loved her own mother. Morgan always had a ready answer for any situation. When Joseph asked her what she thought of the children's van she countered him with, "I think it is absolutely wonderful, Joseph. Not another like it on the block!"

"Thank God!" Joseph responded, "But I could have driven it down town for a new paint job."

"Joseph, must you disapprove of our daughter-in-law's creative art work by trying to rubber stamp it with your boring conservative taste?"

"I – I just wanted to restore it to mint condition," Joseph Hillag was taken back.

"And what fun is there in mint? Lighten up, Grandpa, and look to our dear ones and not their van," Morgan laughed and quickly pecked him on the cheek.

There was always energetic and sometimes confrontational conversation in the Hillag home. Joseph asked many technical questions about Global Missions, their reliability and assets. Finally, Caleb threw up his hands and stated he didn't have a financial statement from Global.

Next he questioned about the mission field and the people. He warned of the gambling to be a waste of solid money. Sarah assured him they had no interest in that.

"I know you don't, Sarah, but Caleb can be most impulsive with his money."

Sarah could see that Mr. Hillag held to high standards and expected all of them to measure up. Like Caleb, she realized that feat was impossible and long before had stopped trying to please him in everything. Sarah didn't feel close to him, at least, not how she envisioned a daughter should be with her dad. Maybe he would mellow with age, but for now, they all must be careful of what they did or said when he was around.

One night, however, was extra-special to Sarah. Joseph had retired to bed early, as he faced a busy work schedule the next day. Esther was downloading music on her ipod in a bedroom, and Mark was intergaming on Internet with his friends back in Tennessee. She, Caleb and his mother were talking while the television played.

"Did your Father tell you that we are getting a new Gamma-fourth generation robot?"

"No! Really? How exciting!" Caleb and Sarah both exclaimed.

"Father wanted a servant girl, but I told him to order a nice butler. Those female robots are much too pretty to suit me. I don't want Joseph getting any ideas," Morgan's eyes danced with good-natured humor.

"How much did - he cost?" Caleb asked.

"Very expensive - oh, look! One of my Cousin Janee's old movies is coming on. Oh! It is my favorite - 'A Bowl Of Dust.' She won an Academy Award for Best Actress in 'Street Smart,' and although she was only nominated in, 'A Bowl Of Dust,' I think this film was the best role she ever played. Come, we must view it in the theatre room."

Sarah watched a blonde Hollywood queen play in a depression era movie of a poor dirt farm family. The actor who played the husband was striking, and both graced the screen with dirty faces and worn clothes. Yet the love between Janee and her leading man seemed of more substance than mire acting. Sarah asked Morgan of it.

"Janee told me once, before she died, how she loved Jason Phen, but to her regret, she drove him away."

By the end of the movie all three of them were in tears.

"Wow, I've never seen that one," Sarah sniffed. "Your cousin was magnificent. The story was so sad!"

"Yes, I know," Morgan reached for a tissue, "and I've seen it a dozen times."

"I hate crying at movies;" Caleb was laughing while brushing away tears, "makes me feel like a baby."

"You are, Caleb – a big one," Sarah hit his arm.

"You remember Janee, son, at Grandmother Emile's funeral?"

"I remember all the news people wanting to interview her."

"Yes, and they talked to you on camera."

"I told them that what the world needs now - is love - sweet love," Caleb broke into song to dramatize his brief claim to fame. "And that need is Jesus Christ. That's what I told them."

"That sure wouldn't air today, Reverend Hillag," Sarah laughed.

"They did it then," Morgan took on a faraway look.

"She was mean and hateful when she made up her mind to be that way," Caleb added. "She scared me. I remember everyone was upset with her, but when she talked to the newscasters she was - different.... like she was in her movies."

"That was the actress in her. Acting was her whole life. Janee was a little girl - younger than Mark when she did her first movie."

"Did your cousin ever marry?" Sarah was curious.

"Yes, she married her long time friend and agent, Bernard Swift only a few years before she died of AIDS. Poor Bernard was so lonely after Janee's passing. He was lost, barely worked, representing only one actor, I think, and later he fell in love with Janee's best friend, Paige."

"Ha! He called me to perform the wedding," Caleb injected," I was young and inexperienced, wasn't ordained, so not eligible."

"It seems Janee struggled with so much of life," Sarah murmured.

"I don't think my cousin ever got over our Grandfather's tragic death."

"Your Grandfather Farmer was shot in a hunting accident." Sarah reflected.

"Yes. It happened the year before I was born. I never knew him, but Janee did. She was nine and adored him," Morgan explained. "At the funeral, she and Grandmother

Emile clung to the coffin, and they had to pry Janee's fingers away. It was such a horrible shock - just - just - "Morgan could not finish and turned her head. "That and ..."

"She means about my Uncle David, Aunt Cynthia, Cousin Mary and an Eskimo friend named Kasha who all froze to death in a freak Alaska blizzard."

"The Trevor family has a history of untimely deaths," Morgan murmured. "Grandfather Farmer shot, Janee died of Aids, my Uncle Walter in a plane crash, David and his family in a icy car in the wilderness, some of our relatives in Texas killed in a car accident. Alas, such pain and woe amidst incredible joy and achievement. What a heritage our family has - one we can be proud of and stand tall with clear minds and heads held high. The Trevor's are made of visionaries - like you two. Leaving family and friends - just like your grandfather and his parents before. Leaving all to follow a dream. I couldn't be happier - "Morgan covered her face in her hands. Sarah slipped over next to her mother-in-law and held her. She looked across to her husband and saw his lips quivering, his face wet from tears.

"I miss Grandfather Clifton and Grandmother Rachel," he blurted out as he also buried his face in his hands, "and we'll miss you and Dad."

Morgan was too wrought with emotion to even speak. She just shook her head in agreement. Sarah sensed a feeling of loss that she had not known these people. She wept with Caleb and Morgan, and the three became emotionally welded together. Sarah would not have traded those moments for the world. The story of the Trevor legacy would inspire her to greater accomplishments on the mission field than she could ever have dreamed possible.

On the way out of the theatre room, she stopped briefly to view the picture of Janee Stemper in the battle of Khe Sanh in Viet Nam. Sarah saw the war that had been waged in that place, the rifle Janee drug by the shoulder strap, her dirty, weary, tear-stained face. Sarah studied that face a moment, and it became apparent something deeper was there besides what was noticed in a surface glance. A silent determined courage was found. Sarah wondered if faced with life-threatening challenges, would she handle them as bravely as Janee? Only the Lord knew that answer.

When Sarah awoke in the morning, she wandered sleepy into the kitchen to find coffee. As she poured a cup, she heard Caleb conversing with his father at the table in what must have been a private conversation from the hushed tones. She couldn't hear what Joseph said, nor Caleb's response; however, she did make out the next statement from her father-in-law.

"Son, on your return to Atlanta, it would prove most helpful if you go south through Douglas Landing and check the old Trevor house on Breach Street. Promise you will see to it, and I will give you ample extra expense money."

Caleb's response to his dad was not audible to Sarah, but she knew he had agreed.

## Chapter 27

# Unscheduled Stop

Driving into Douglas Landing, Oregon, was like taking a side trip back three decades, or so Caleb said. This was a new adventure for Sarah and the children, and she was anxious to finally see some of the places she heard Caleb and his mother speak of.

"Do you remember much about this town?" she was taking in the scenery on both sides of the highway.

"Look at the beautiful river," she heard Esther behind her.

"Not much. Great-grandmother Emile's house went to my grandparents. Uncle David was next in line, but he - they - you know - the blizzard - so it passed on to my mother. If the Rapture doesn't come first, it will be ours. I was only six when we came to Great-grandmother's funeral. That's when we went out on their old place, and I saw the log cabin."

"Daddy, can we go there?" Esther leaned forward, excited.

"I don't know if I could find it."

"Do we have to?" Mark grumbled. "I don't do log cabins - I'm a gamer."

"There were two lumber mills in town. My Great-grandfather Farmer worked for one of them. Father said the larger mill rejuvenated with increased demand for lumber and pressboard. They upgraded and are in production again. There it is!" Caleb pointed ahead to the right.

Sarah saw motion and steam billowing from stacks. A large sign on the mill, 'Cascade Mountain,' came into view between trees.

The smaller mill, Pacific Timberline lay still, boarded up, a huge coffin waiting to be put to rest. It had not survived a changing global economy.

On the left side of the road a recharge station with one remaining gas pump. The building also housed a mechanic, which from the cars parked inside and out, indicated a good business. Next to the station was a small café' and both buildings hung on to the 1980's era.

Next block was a convenience store and the Post Office.

"The store used to be owned by a family. Some other family started it I think - Irish - Grandfather Clifton told me - they passed on. The latest owner has remodeled, looks like."

"The Post Office hasn't changed. Hmmm, the bank is vacant."

The Hillags came to Peppertree, turned left and proceeded to the end where the old Trevor house stood. Caleb had called ahead so the occupants were expecting them. A young mother with a small boy and a baby in her arms greeted them at the door. She was polite; however, reserved - not sure why this family of the owners were there.

"I'm Caleb Hillag, my wife Sarah, and our children Esther and Mark."

"I'm Zipper Drake; Zip for short. Taget is working at Cascade. These are our boys, Meele there and the baby is Clapper."

"Meele and Clapper? Those are - unusual," Caleb commented. Sarah raised her eyebrows at him.

"Taget and me, well, we wanted unusual names," Zipper explained nervously. "When Meele was borned Taget said, 'Why he's just a little Meele mouth,' so we named him that, and Clapper was borned clapping his little hands. Zipper ended with a nervous laugh. When no comment was made, she motioned for the visitors to come in.

"Would you like a beer - juice - water?"

"We are fine," Caleb spoke for all of them. "My Father asked me to stop by and see you and check on the house. Is everything okay? Working okay? May we look around?"

Zipper nodded to all Caleb's questions.

Sarah was curious to look through the house. One would never suspect there was so much history within these walls, looking at a kitchen trash can topped with empty beer bottles, the table and sink stacked with dirty dishes. Zipper made no attempt to apologize for a messy house. Sarah felt the young wife carried the attitude - 'You came to inspect the house - take it like you find it.'

"The living room and kitchen are as I remember them - I mean the rooms." He glanced a smile at Sarah, and she knew what he meant.

"This was Leah's room," Caleb opened a door off the hallway to a small bedroom. It looked like a junk room. Caleb opened a second door on the same side. This was the boys' bedroom, cluttered with clothes and toys. Meele came running in past them and turned with a broad grin.

"My room!" he announced.

"I think this was added on after Great-grandmother passed away, because my Grandfather Clifton and his brother Walter had a room off the back porch."

"This was - her and Great-grandfather's bedroom," Caleb flipped on a light in a larger room across the hallway. Sarah saw an unmade bed with clothes scattered across tossed blankets. Shoes and undergarments were randomly thrown on the floor. The bedroom reeked of dirty feet. Sarah covered her nose.

"It stinks in here," Mark muttered.

"Mom, I'm going to throw up!" Esther gagged.

"Get outside - go!" Sarah tried not to breathe. Caleb was right behind them as they scrambled down the hall back into the living room. Sarah walked out onto the back porch. The air was clean and crisp. Drifted snow still remained on the ground, with enough winter left for a few more storms.

The beauty of the forest-covered mountains and the white peaks rising high in the distance captured Sarah.

There was such a peace here, she could understand why the Trevors loved it so - and how it called family back generation after generation. She pictured Farmer and Emile sitting on that porch watching a sunset - Walter, Clifton and Leah playing - riding horses in the field - Janee running across a grassy field. Sarah remembered every story she was ever told about this place.

"Sometimes I feel their presence here," Zipper spoke from the doorway. "I'm told the old lady died in our bedroom."

"Yes," Sarah went to the young woman. "May I hold your baby?"

Zipper gave Clapper to Sarah and stepped out onto the porch, gazing off into the mountains.

"Taget and I fell in love and - well, got together. He was so tired of the crowds in California. He's just an outdoors' guy. When he lost his job, we were outa there. Packed everything we owned - not much - in the car and - ended up here. He got work, and we found this house."

"The people who lived here loved God with all their heart. It's His Spirit's presence you feel."

Zipper got a forlorn look. "When I was eleven I went to a movie about a man named Jesus. He was beaten, then nailed on a cross, and I cried the whole time. My parents whipped me for seeing it. Told me it was too upsetting for a young girl and wait 'til I was old enough to decide for myself about God. I never forgot about Him dying on that cross."

"Are you old enough to decide for yourself now?"

"I don't know.... that was a long time ago and I have been through so much. It's hard to feel anything kind or gentle anymore. This place makes one this way."

"Zipper, you can know Him and His love right now."

"Here? Don't we have to go to a church, or someplace like that?"

"He is anywhere you call out to Him. When you see Him dying on that cross, do you believe -?"

"Hold on! How the hell should I know what I believe about someone I know nothing about. I can tell you this, if I get religion my man would beat it back outa me!"

"There's a law against wife beating," Sarah remarked grimly.

"So is there about forcing your religion on anyone."

"Zipper, I'm not forcing you."

"Just so we have an understanding. You have the right to push your way into the house, but not my life."

"Zipper, you . . ."

The young woman held up her hand to stop.

"You are . . . "

Again she halted Sarah. She retrieved her baby and turned to go inside just as Esther and Mark came out onto the porch.

"It's beautiful!" Esther declared sweeping in the vast scene.

"Did they ever have animals back here?" Mark asked. "Look, the field goes into the trees. Race you, Esther."

Sarah watched the children run through the snow. Her thoughts were troubled by the misunderstanding she had with Zipper. She was pushy! But she sensed the young wife had handed her an open door to discuss the spiritual. She was the one who misread the discussion.

Sarah returned to the kitchen. Caleb was talking to Zipper in the living room. She stood looking at the mess and decided to get busy.

"May I help clean up?" Sarah called out.

"It's still a free country," Zipper answered back.

As Sarah filled the sink, she heard Caleb ask, "When does Taget get off work?"

A few minutes later Caleb joined her.

"She's very resistant to talk about the Lord," he whispered.

"Tell me about it. She got hostile when I mentioned believing in Jesus."

"How about I go to that little store on the highway and see if they have anything we could fix for supper."

"Great idea, Caleb, but we can't offend Zipper."

"She's putting Clapper down for a nap. I'll run it by her before I go."

Sarah was running fresh dishwater when Caleb came back in.

"I'm going to the store," he informed her.

A few minutes later a more subdued Zipper joined her at the sink.

"I have my hands full keeping up with Taget and two scrappy boys. Breakfast becomes dinner fore I know where the day is gone. Chasing Meele all day and changing Clapper's diapers don't leave much for my man. I get down when he doesn't pay me much attention."

Sarah took quick note of Zipper from head to feet. She was dressed in loose jeans with an un-tucked shirt that was probably Taget's. Worn tennis shoes covered, Sarah was sure, dirty feet.

"Zipper, you have to make yourself attractive if you want his attention. You have a pretty face and probably a good figure, but looking at you no one would know. It's all covered up."

Zipper laughed, embarrassed.

"Go get a shower and fix your hair and face. Put on something pretty."

"I don't know, Taget may get mad."

"Nonsense! If he's a red-blooded man, he will take notice, with delight! Go on, I'll listen for Clapper, and Meele is with Esther and Mark."

"Ok," Zipper agreed.

Caleb arrived with groceries for supper, plus some beyond. He helped Sarah prepare the meal, and was just putting on the finishing touches when Zipper reappeared.

"Well, look at you!" Sarah exclaimed.

"You look great, Zipper," Caleb echoed Sarah's reaction.

The young woman had donned a dress, which accented her figure. Her hair hinted of slight curl and fell around her neck. A little makeup highlighted her features, yet kept a natural look.

Zipper couldn't wait for her man to get home. She was nervous and talkative. She fussed in exasperation when Clapper spit up oh her clean dress. Sarah helped her wipe it off and consoled her. Esther took the baby.

Zipper met Taget at the door when he arrived home. He gave her a quick hug, careful not to get her dirty.

"What happened to you?" he queried.

"I wanted to look nice for you?"

"You look nice. Who are these people?"

"They are the Hillag's. You know, they called and said they were coming. Caleb and Sarah and their children, Esther and Mark."

"Hi," he took in the clean kitchen and prepared supper. "What's going on? Our kitchen's never this clean, and you looking sexy. You sporten a boyfriend?"

Sarah saw how that unfounded accusation crushed Zipper.

"Supper's ready," she said coldly, walking into the kitchen.

"I'm glad for that!" Taget growled. "I'm tired, dirty, hungry, and pissed – in that order, so lets get to it."

It became evident at the supper meal, Taget was not interested in religion, nor did he have any use for Christians. He was crude, forcing himself to be hospitable, and Sarah felt they were walking on thin ice with him. Un-easiness hung over the evening.

Sarah feared Taget would go at Caleb when he asked where they got married.

"Hell no, we never married!" Taget bellowed. "Church ceremony sure don't make a marriage, and I damn well don't need a piece of paper to prove we're married. We have two children, damn it – that oughta make us married."

Sarah could tell Caleb was primed to fire back at Taget's argument; however, was not given the chance for rebuttal. Taget stood up from the table.

"You got what you came for to see we ain't trashed your place. Four a.m. comes quick and I need a shower and sleep – in that order. Goodnight!"

Zipper went to the kitchen sink to hide her tears. Sarah felt sorry for this young woman who, less than an hour earlier was so excited and anxious to see her Taget. What circumstances rendered him insensitive and heartless? It wasn't the mountains or hard winters. Not even the long hours of labor. He made himself that way.

"That was so sad!" Esther spoke in hushed tone.

"What a jerk," Mark declared under his breath.

"You have a rough road ahead, Zipper," Caleb told her when she sat back down at the table. "I suggest you find a church for you and your boys."

"He would drag me out in those trees and shoot me" Zipper replied gravely.

"Wasn't there a church your Grandparents attended, Caleb"'" Sarah asked.

"I've heard there is a church near the Shanko River in the trees, but only a few people go there." Zipper answered.

"You must not lose sight of the one you saw on the cross. Reach out to Him; He will be there to take you in with open arms. Then, find a church, be faithful, no matter what," Caleb encouraged.

"Taget don't care bout nothing but work, hunting and fishing. Me and the boys are just damn trophies hanging on a wall for him to look at when he wants," Zipper turned her head, "But it's still his wall."

Caleb took a deep breath, "We want to visit the old ranch our family owns. Do you know where it's located?"

Zipper thought a moment before shaking her head.

"No, I'm not sure where, wait! Down at the end of this street lives a really old lady. She seems to know everthing bout Douglas Landing. She could maybe tell you where it's at."

Sarah stood, "Come on Zipper, let's clean up."

"I'll help," Esther volunteered.

"Is it ok if Meele goes exploring with me before it gets dark?" Mark asked.

Zipper nodded with a smile, "Dress warm."

When it was time to leave, Sarah gave Zipper a long hug.

"I'm shamed how Taget spoke and treated you all."

"That didn't hurt us Zipper, I was mostly embarrassed for you. He broke your spirit tonight, but you must open your heart to Christ at any cost. Find Jesus, and Taget will follow, trust me." Sarah winked at her as she squeezed her hand.

## Chapter 28

# The Old Log House

The Hillags checked on Zipper and her boys the next morning. There was sadness in her eyes, and Sarah didn't have to be told Taget was brutish after they left.

"I won't forget you, and what you told me," Zipper said as she waved goodbye.

"I feel so sorry for her, Caleb," Sarah remarked when they were in the van. "It's like abandoning a child out in the cold to die."

"She won't die, Sarah! God won't allow it!"

"I gave her my cell number, and told her we can be reached anywhere," Sarah murmured. "We must help her…"

"And pray for her, and Taget's salvation," Caleb added.

They drove down the street to the house Zipper pointed out, and parked in front. It was dilapidated and un-kept. The fence was made up of boards nailed to wooden posts. Some boards were warped from the weather, others missing or laying on the ground. Where the posts had rotted off, the fence was leaning. The broken gate hung open.

The house itself was in bad need of repair and paint. On closer examination there was faded evidence of loving care that once embraced it.

Caleb sat analyzing the house. Sarah waited quietly for him to say something.

"What a dump," Mark muttered.

"You're the dump," Esther came back, which started a verbal battle.

"Stop it! Both of you! I expect you to behave yourselves," Sarah yelled at them.

"I won't go in there - catch a disease and die, I would," Mark tried to be cute.

"One less pain in my butt," Esther sneered.

This time Caleb turned around with a look that said, 'Shut up - now!'

Both of them had displayed attitude since they woke up and with dad's look they went silent.

"If it still wasn't so cold, I'd say we stay a couple of days and fix and paint this place," Caleb spoke what he was thinking.

This raised a howl of protest from both Esther and Mark.

"Do you think she is up? It's still early," Sarah wanted to soothe temperaments.

"I think so. I see smoke from the chimney. Let's go see."

After several knocks on the door, an old woman answered. She was surprised to have visitors, but pleased. She insisted on feeding them breakfast. Sarah and Esther helped. At the table she was eager to talk.

"I don't hear too good no more, but my mind is clear, and I don't do bad for 93. My twin sister Jane and I both outlived our husbands, so when widow Ella May Brooks passed on, we bought this house." The old woman paused and grew misty-eyed. "I lost Jane four years ago. Don't get many visitors anymore. Family scattered all over the place, and my friends...all gone on." Then she chuckled. "You live as long as me, to have a visit I would have to go to the cemetery."

"Shirley, you really didn't have to fix us breakfast." Sarah felt they imposed.

"Yes, I did. You see Jane and I made us a promise when we were very young. Times were bad! It was the Great Depression, you see, but we were too little to understand. Only thing we knew was our bellies was hurtin' from hunger. This man came with our father on the day we was so hungry we thought to die. He gave us one of his steers and canned vegetables and things to eat. He came back to make sure we weren't hungry, and made my parents go to church where we all got saved. So you see, Jane and I made us a promise - no one would go hungry in our house. Once we fill stomachs, we give spiritual food. Do you know my Jesus?"

"Yes, we do," Caleb was instant in his reply. "I'm a pastor, and we are to be missionaries! Yes, we love Jesus, Shirley."

"Glory to God!" the old woman shouted. Sarah had never seen such glowing joy in a person. Shirley began to sing an old hymn with a voice that cracked and was off key, but Sarah had never heard such a touching rendition of, "Blessed Be The Tie That Binds." Sarah glanced at her children. Tears were streaming down Esther's cheeks, and she kept wiping them. Mark was trying to stifle a laugh. When Shirley finished singing, Sarah had a question.

"Do you know who the man was - who came to your house?"

"Sure do. Knew his wife too. Farmer and Emile Trevor."

Sarah heard Caleb gasp.

"Dear Lord," she whispered.

"They were my Great-grandparents," Caleb blurted out.

"Merciful God," Shirley exclaimed. "Come close, let me look at you." Caleb moved next to her, and the old woman took his hand in hers and patted his face. "Farmer and Emile had two boys and a girl. You wouldn't -."

"Clifton was my Grandpa," Caleb was so emotional now he could barely speak. "When you get to Heaven, Shirley, please find them and tell them how much I love and miss them, and how the food they gave to you came back around to their Great-grandson."

The visit broke into a time of laughing and praising God. Sarah left Shirley's home feeling like she had been to church. What a great start to a most profound day.

Shirley couldn't remember exactly where the ranch was located, but she directed them to a family who could tell them.

"Go back south on the highway like you was going down to Applegate. A few miles from town you see a bridge crossing the river. Cross over and drive straight into the trees, and the road will turn right. Follow that about, let's see, over three miles, and take a road left. There be four ranches along that road. Go to the third ranch, and they can direct you to Farmer and Emile's old place.

"Has it remained empty all these years?" Sarah asked.

"Don't you know, child. God won't let no one on that place. It's like the promise land the Good Lord gave the children of Israel. No one else can have it. That ranch was given to Farmer and Emile and their children and their children," Shirley's voice trailed off as she looked at Mark and caught her breath. "Just settin' there waiting for one of their own to come and claim it."

They found the bridge and drove carefully on the road. There were patches of ice and snow with slick places. Caleb feared getting stuck, but the van made it to the house of the third ranch. The home was modern and large. They were greeted by a pack of barking dogs, bringing a young man out to quiet the dogs and greet the visitors. A warm smile spread across his face as he looked at the van's license plate. Caleb stepped out of the car and the two men shook hands.

"I tol' my misses, I shore don't know anyone from Tennessee, and it's way too early to be selling something, so dang it they ain't bad lost," the fellow joked. His ways were so disarming Sarah couldn't help but like him.

"I'm Caleb Hillag with my wife Sarah, daughter Esther and son Mark. We are looking for the old Trevor ranch and were told in town you could tell us how to get to it."

"What have you to do with the Trevor place?" the man was curious. He eyed their painted van.

"It was my Great-grandparents' ranch once," Sarah heard Caleb say.

"Well, I declare, if that ain't news to make the day break! Get your family out, and come in. Someone you gotta meet."

Sarah and the children climbed out of the van and joined Caleb. The young man introduced himself and his wife when they were inside the house.

"I'm Donald, and this here is Macy. Macy, this is the Great-grandson of the Trevors. They came lookin' to see the ol' place. They must meet Granny."

"Yes, yes, of course," Macy was delighted. "Come have a seat. I'll get Granny."

Everyone found a seat in the living room. Donald brought coffee for Caleb and Sarah. He poured orange juice for Esther and Mark. After a few moments Macy wheeled in a silver-haired woman in her robe and bundled in a blanket. Her eyes were searching the room.

"Where are they; where are they?" She kept asking.

"Right here, Granny," Macy told her.

"Get me close so I can see them," the old woman instructed.

Macy pushed the wheelchair to where Caleb and Sarah sat. She reached out to touch Caleb's face, squinting to see him better.

"You are Farmer and Emile Trevor's Great-grandson?"

"Yes'm."

"Tell me your Grandpa."

"Clifton Trevor."

"Clifton, hmmm, yes. I had a crush on your Grandpa, but Rachel Baltman had his heart. You must be David's son, hmmm?"

"No, ma'am - Morgan's son."

"Didn't know your mother. A lot of years have passed by dimming my memory. Your Great-grandparents and my parents were dearest of friends. Donald and Beth Parrigan were their names. Donald here is just like his Great granddad - named after him. My father could talk a porcupine out of a tree and fall timber quicker than you could spit!"

"Granny is their daughter, Beverly Ann Parrigan," Macy injected.

"Since you couldn't have Grandpa Clifton, who did you marry?" Sarah teased.

The old woman laughed merrily.

"Clarence and Locust Tree Judd also had a homestead ranch. In fact, my Daddy tolt' me Mr. Judd planned out the building of your Great-grandparents ol' log house, and he built the fireplace." She seemed to lose her train of thought.

"You were tellin' who you married, Granny," Donald reminded her.

"Oh, yes! They couldn't have children so they adopted a boy they found on the mountain highline. Tom Judd, part Indian, part mustang, but he was a man. My man! Kids called him 'Highline.' Lord, I miss him! Like Daddy used to say about Tom, 'A polecat hangs around long enough you forget the smell and think how cute and loveable it is. Then we had Donald's mother, God rest her soul…She – oh, well – anyway, Macy, I think I'm tired out, but you all please don't leave - I want to see you - again…"

Donald took the Hillags in his 4 x 4 biodiesel extended cab to the Trevor ranch.

"It's all overgrown in there. I could never tell you how to find the place unless you follow Cold Creek. You would tear up your van."

"Have you seen the - house?"

"Yes, a couple of times. I get a strange feeling when I go there. Can't really describe it."

"A haunted house?" Mark laughed. The thought of that made Sarah shudder.

They came to a gate that had a chain and padlock. "This is where they went in," Donald pointed.

"You have a key?" Caleb asked.

"No, don't know if one exists after this long. I go on the west line where I can put a piece of the fence down."

Donald drove another mile or so and stopped. He got out and untied a piece of the barbed wire fence and pulled it out of the way.

Travel inside the ranch was slow and difficult. Drifts of frozen snow were heaped up against brush and trees. Patches of ground where the snow had melted were muddy in the warmth of the sun. Several times Sarah was sure they could go no further.

Donald held a grim expression. "If we ever start to spin, my rig will bury itself." Then he laughed. "That happens, we'll just walk home, and we get to keep you all overnight! Ha!"

Donald made careful progress through tall stately pine, skirting patches of buck brush. The fresh air carried a bite that took your breath, but the woodsy odor was invigorating to Sarah. This place held an attraction, and she wished this day could go on and on.

"Hoorah! There's Cold Creek," Donald shouted, pointing out his window. Sarah leaned across Esther and Mark to see.

"Look at that!" Caleb exclaimed from his vantage seat up front with Donald. "The water looks icy cold and – and – so clear."

"Don't get purer than this," Donald laughed again.

Cold Creek tumbled quickly over rocks as it rushed its way to the Shanko River. The snow cover was melted away where the water ran. The setting so struck Sarah she could have watched it for hours. She imagined how a sunset would be reflected on this landscape to display a stunning beauty. She knew instinctively why the Trevors had loved this ranch. It quietly reached in and settled on her heart and soul, never to be forgotten.

"We'll follow Cold Creek best we can - only way I can find the log house. Be careful to watch," Donald instructed.

Sarah's gaze strained into the foliage. All she could make out was the dark shadows of the evergreen trees, offset by bright snow and the deep blue water of the creek. Suddenly, faintly in the trees ahead, the upright trunks were mingled with logs laid sideways.

"There it is!" Esther cried out. Mark put aside his Tech game to look. Donald drove as close to the old house as he could before he shut the engine off.

Sarah surveyed the area as she stepped from the truck. Trees were grown up around the house, obscuring it from view. As she looked, she thought this to be a more open area when the Trevors lived there.

"Over there," Donald pointed beyond the house, "is the remains of the chuck wagon, I was told, they traveled in from Texas, and over there is the old barn and corral, well what's left of it. But the log house is still in pretty good shape - for its age. They did a good job of building in those days."

"And living," Caleb added. He was standing still, just looking at the log house. Mark and Esther started to go ahead to the porch, but Sarah motioned for them to stop. She sensed something was going on inside her husband. He stood reverent a long time. The rest of them waited - for him to speak - or walk inside.

"This is a dream," Caleb spoke in hushed voice.

Mark burst out laughing. "Wow! That's a deep well of thought."

"No! Listen to its call. This was a family's dream. This very place was God's answer - His promise to that dream. Yes, they lost the land, but this old log house stands as a memorial to that dream - and what God did here. Can't you see it?! Friends and neighbors coming to erect this house – my great-grandparents and Donald, your great- grandfather was here. What a sight that must have been!"

Sarah could see it in her mind, and retrieve the sounds - of building - talking - laughing - children playing - yet silent now, but for the rumbling water in Cold Creek. Caleb stepped up on the porch.

"Right here," he motioned to the porch, "they sat on summer nights and listened to the water and birds. They went right there where the creek widens to draw water. My Grandpa fished in that very spot. Their horses were in the corral, and cattle grazed beyond in the open meadows. This was their dream. This log house stands in memory of it."

"A nightmare of a dream, Pops," Mark scowled. "This old house is caving in. No doors or windows. This porch could dump on us any minute."

"Mark, don't be so negative," Sarah snapped. They all walked inside to look around.

Mark was right about no doors or windows. Glass was broken and doors were gone.

"Donald, has anyone lived here since my Great-grand-parents?" Caleb asked.

Donald scratched the back of his head in thought before he answered. "I heard it told that in the late '60's or early '70's some flower hippies drifted in and found this house - perfect to have a love-in, but the weather froze their tails, an' they lit out for warmer places. When I saw your van, I thought, 'We're back,'" he joked.

Being a woman, the inside of the house held special interest for Sarah. She tried to fix an image in her mind as to how the house might have looked and what rooms were the bedrooms. She had no trouble defining the living room. The floor was still intact, although covered with a mixture of twigs, leaves and pine needles and cones. The fireplace remained a grand piece of work, standing proudly against one wall, undaunted by the silent and empty passage of years. It seemed to be calling.

"Oh, Caleb, can we build a fire in it? It - it - seems so cold and lonely."

Caleb looked at Donald, who replied after a brief hesitation, "Sure, we can do that, if we find dry kindling and wood."

Mark and Esther scrambled to gather sticks and pine needles. Donald went outside to locate suitable wood.

There were two rooms, which Sarah assumed were bedrooms. She followed Caleb into the larger of the rooms. She took his hand, and they stood there – silent.

"This must have been - their room," Sarah spoke quietly. Caleb nodded but didn't speak. "Caleb, it's as if a part of them never left. At nights when they were in here and had their private talks - like you and I do - I wonder what they talked about?"

"When I was a young boy we came here after my Great-grandmother's funeral," Caleb spoke softly.

"Do you remember her?"

"Some, but I do recall my mother saying that Aunt Leah was born in one of these rooms. I'm sure they spoke of that - raising their kids - remembering the past - planning for the -."

"It was - in here," Sarah declared, glancing up at Caleb.

"How do you know?" he asked.

"I just do," she murmured.

"Fire's going, but not roaring," Donald called out from the living room. "Wood's wet."

The little band huddled around the fireplace. The warmth seemed so right, and the fire seemed to project a dancing mirth into the room. Sarah believed the old fireplace was laughing for joy, but dismissed that thought as childish imagination. Yet there was something about that old log house. She remembered Donald's words, but knew it wasn't haunted as Mark had suggested. It was poetic melancholy that caused her to be dreamy as she stood by the fire. Why had the structure survived 92 long years? It could have been torn down, or fallen down, even burned to the ground, but here it stood. What purpose did the Lord have for this place? The Trevors were long gone. Who of the family would ever live here? Sarah's roaming thoughts were jolted back to reality by Esther's question.

"Where did they go to the bathroom?"

Donald laughed. "There's a hole out back where a outhouse used to be."

"No!" Caleb objected. "That was used when they first lived here, but later great-grandfather Farmer devised some method of piping water from a higher level of the creek into the house. I know because I remember using it that day we came out after great-grandmother Emile's funeral."

"It still had water running?" Sarah was amazed.

"No, of course not, the bathroom was – let me see, through that door."

Everyone crowded to the doorway, Caleb had indicated. Sure enough, pipes gave evidence of where a sink and tub used to be. Only the toilet remained as a proud reminder this small add-on room was a bathroom with running water.

"Pretty modern for that time, I must admit," Donald declared, as they turned back towards the fireplace.

"What's up there?" Mark pointed.

Shafts of light shown through holes in the shingle roof illuminating some kind of room built into the attic.

"Grandpa told me that he and his brother Walter slept in the loft," Caleb answered. "That was their room."

"Cool!" Mark let out a whistle. "This old log house would make a neato hiding place!"

# Chapter 29

# Lugar de Paraiso

C aleb stepped to the pulpit, opened his Bible and looked into the faces of the congregation awaiting his message. Nine years had slipped by quietly, sunrise - sunset, sunrise - sunset; however, the time was not spent in lazy resort lounging. Eight years on the mission field added up to endless hours of sacrifice of time and energy in ministry to reaching the lost in the resort city of Lugar de Paraiso.

Looking over the small gathering, the fleeting thought, 'What have we accomplished here?' passed across Caleb's mind. He smiled warmly as he surveyed those present, for he had come to dearly love them.

There were Chris and Kay Fowler. He was maintenance man at the Golden Sands Casino. Kay made up rooms at the Sands resort.

Next to Kay was Maybeline Collier. She cleaned homes for the wealthy.

On the back row, Caleb spotted a sullen Mark. A twinge of sorrow darkened his thoughts a second. He was burdened that he and his son had drifted apart.

Near Mark in the rear of the church was Tazada. The members referred to him as drunk Tazada, for they never knew what condition he would be in until he stumbled into the church and sat down. Caleb was relieved he appeared sober and somewhat of sound mind this Sunday.

Nearby, sat Plomo, a casino security guard. Caleb could count on this man to deal with Tazada, if needed.

Also near the back on the other side was a man who rarely attended and was a mystery to them all. The church only knew him as Sierra. The Mexicans called him the 'Gringo from the States'. He never visited in any of their homes and had ignored Caleb's offer to get together for coffee. Where he worked or lived was unknown. Caleb wondered if he was in trouble and hiding out from the authorities.

In front of Sierra sat Hank and Tulipan. Hank was retired and had come to Lugar de Paraiso to find a Mexican wife. All attempts backfired on him until he ventured up the mountain to the village of Vera Cielo and visited the Catholic Mission, Saint Marcos of Vera Cielo. There he met Tulipan who had been waiting on God for a husband. Since they lived in Lugar de Paraiso after marriage, they began attending Global Missionary Christian Church where Hank accepted Christ as his Savior.

Near them were Espolito, a tired widow and her girls, Fina and Carmen.

On the very front seats were Sarah flanked by two young women. Blanca was on her right - a young teen ostracized by her family for her faith in Jesus Christ. Caleb had tried to reason and witness to them, but they drove him away with threats and guns. Blanca stayed with Hank and Tulipan and apart from her family. This Sunday morning her face displayed the usual mixture of brightness clouded with sadness.

And on the other side of Sarah was Bomba. 'Oh, my, Bomba!' Caleb sighed. Bomba was a bar maid at the casino, and a Sunday outfit for her constituted one that gave the appearance she was busting out of the top. Sarah attempted a half smile at Caleb and rolled her eyes as if to say, 'I'll talk to Bomba again.'

Caleb's sweeping gaze spotted a new face. A visitor, but that was not unusual, as the incredible flow of tourists would often yield some vacationing Christians not afraid to join them in worship. This man was young, dark skinned with a striking face. His slacks and camp shirt were casual and colorful - hinting of expensive. Caleb noticed him earlier during 'Praise and Worship' music. The fellow enjoyed the singing, his voice resounding clear and melodic over the small congregation. Caleb was curious about this young man, as he didn't fit the normal tourist mold.

Sadly, one face was missing. Caleb's eyes locked with Sarah's, and for an instant their souls united as one in that sadness. A week ago they returned to Lugar de Paraiso from their second 6-month furlough in the United States. There they said goodbye to Esther, leaving her with Grandma Hannah. She would keep Grandma company for the summer, at which time Grandfather and Grandmother Hillag would take her to Caleb's old alma mater to get her settled in and ready to begin her freshman year in college. Caleb was learning how hard it was to let his daughter go. The week dragged by, and Caleb and Sarah found themselves on the phone constantly with Esther. Caleb wondered if it wasn't more for their own reassurances than Esther's. His throat tightened, and his eyes got misty as his gaze stopped on the empty seat, which was Esther's, and he remembered...

He straightened up, and cleared his throat.

"Welcome to all of you this first Sunday in June, 2026, to Global Missionary Christian Church of Lugar de Paraiso - a 'Place of Paradise'."

# Chapter 30

# Message of Consideration

"Not one of us is here this morning by accident," Caleb began his message.

"We are in this place and this service according to God's Planned Purpose for our lives. By His Holy Spirit may He reveal that purpose to us though His Word. Amen!

"I haven't spoken on this topic for a long time, but lately it has been on my mind - a lot. I speak of an event so out of this world, so incredibly strange and wonderful the human mind cannot conceive of it actually taking place.

"The scripture implies that one day literally thousands - millions of believing Christians will disappear from the face of the earth and be caught up to meet Jesus in the air. Every Christian generation from the time of Christ's ascension until today has dreamed of that moment, looked for its coming, prayed they would be that chosen generation. I believe this well could be the year!"

Caleb could make out Mark's disapproval and sour face peering over the shoulder of Chris. A few of the congregation appeared uneasy and began to shift in their seats.

"I know, I know," Caleb went on with his message, "the Bible tells us not to set dates, but remember, I said could be the year. Hear me out.

"Turn to Matthew 24, verse 36. Jesus said: 'But of that day and hour knoweth no man, no not the angels of Heaven, but my Father only.' In verse 42, He tells us: 'Watch therefore; for ye know not what hour your Lord doth come.' Hear what Chapter 25, verse 13 repeats: 'Watch therefore, for ye know neither the day nor the hour wherein the Son of man cometh. Mark recorded what Jesus said in the 13th Chapter, verse 33. 'But of that day and that hour knoweth no man.' In verse 35, Jesus warned, 'Watch ye therefore; for ye know not when the master of the house cometh, at even, or at midnight, or at the cock crowing, or in the morning.' which indicates a single day. Jesus, several times in scripture, when he discussed the Rapture emphasized day and hour. He did not say, we couldn't know the month or year. Didn't He also tell us in the Word that His children would not be ignorant of the times?

"I have prayed over this message for months while on furlough. In my heart of hearts, I sense this could be the year of the Rapture of the church!"

Mark shook his head!

"I know, the word, 'Rapture', is not found in the Bible - yet, I believe it is descriptive of the most unique phenomenon to happen to the Bride of Christ - the church.

"Why do I think this could be the year? For several reasons. First, let's think about the unfolding of events over the last decade - or since we arrived here in Lugar de Paraiso. Think about our Sat phones."

Caleb pulled his phone from his pocket and held it up.

"We can communicate globally. I can call anyone, anyplace on the planet, and see them. This device is a computer with incredible memory. With it we can watch TV, get on the Internet, text messages, it can analyze our body and make health recommendations, it can even drive our cars. With it you can make and send HD video, and it will play games, music or movies. Hear me now, these phones are modern miracles, which we can't do without, but they are also tracking devices. Someone, somewhere can know exactly where you are at any given moment.

"Second, we live in a cashless world. How long has it been since any of us have actually seen cash or written a check? Espolito, I would venture to say your girls don't know what cash is."

The middle-aged mother nodded, her two daughters looked puzzled.

"And what about all the people who have chip implants with more requesting the procedure everyday. It would be easy for someone to prevent you from market if you don't have the chip. Remember all the other radical economic changes in the global market after the depression of 2010. There were days Sarah and I did without meals to feed our children, jobless rates were sky high, families loosing their homes, some even selling their children, robberies and murders raged unchecked. We thought conditions couldn't get worse – but they have!

"We have been jolted to the extreme so many times by world news events we no longer feel concerned. For two decades, Russia has experienced one of the lowest birth rates on the planet. They dropped to one child per woman. Any nation needs a birth rate of at least two to replace population. Add early deaths, they were loosing three quarter of a million people per year. Their population reached a low of 83 million. So to compensate, one by one they have invaded and occupied many of the countries of the old Soviet Union. These conquered nations have not only bolstered Russia's need for more people but it's given them vast reserves of natural resources. Ironically, it never satisfied their thirst for power, but has thrust that part of the world into episodes of bitter fighting with NATO and the EU. We've lived under the banner of wars, wars and more wars this whole 21$^{st}$ Century.

"Need I mention the Middle East? I read the other day that world population of Muslims now outnumbers Christians three to one. We have fought Islamic extremists wreaking havoc everywhere for thirty years. Their goal is to dominate and impose their beliefs at all costs. Look at how much of the world they already control. Christians martyred number in the millions. Everywhere there are cries for peace - but there is no peace – only wars and death.

"Need we be reminded of the unthinkable loss of lives and devastating destruction in key cities, 2014 in simultaneous WMD attacks, nor the night a missile fired from the ground exploded an E bomb over Washington D.C. showering the whole city with a magnetic mist thrusting the entire city into blackness and chaos? All computer systems shut down instantly! Next went power grids, and then all back up systems failed. Transportation was dead, so were phones and even battery-operated radios. The city as well as the government struggled, paralyzed while the rest of the country watched in disbelief. How could an act that rendered America helpless for weeks be accomplished so easily and unnoticed?

"Then came the horror development of ten ET stations scattered in major cities around the globe, and the founding of the SIC Colony near the dark side of the moon. It was deceitfully promoted as a place to dispose hardened criminals; however, it was soon evident the targets were Pastors and Evangelists who stood their ground to preach God's Word. Many of our strongest Christian leaders became guinea pigs so a hate filled society could fine-tune their Electromagnetic Transporter Stations. How many died an ugly death in that two-year process? At first we deemed the whole idea a Science Fiction fable that was impossible to accomplish, then it became a reality and our worst nightmare! Were we all blind as a people of good will and love in the beginning to think that SIC referred to sick? Perhaps a viable place for hardened criminals to exist leaving our communities safer. What a shock to discover the world meant it as Scum In Christ, and the Christians who made an outcry against atrocities, calling sin for what it was, or openly displaying any Christian symbol or carrying their Bibles in public, were accused of hate crimes or illegal conversions, even subversion and consequentially transported to that desolate colony on the moon, never to be heard from again. In fact, I could be arrested and sent off for even mentioning this matter, let along to speak against it.

"Then when the Transporter Systems worked and amazingly people could be transported to the moon through an electromagnetic process, Freedom Colony was founded. What a slap in our faces! Freedom Colony veered quickly from its original concept of an ultra modern model society to become the ultimate Sin City for pleasure seekers! No law, no rules, no restraints, no clothes, no sin for those with the money to transport there.

"Think! How many times the last four years in this peaceful resort town have local authorities raided our services, confiscated literature, scoured my message notes, books, all our private affairs, and sat in on our services to monitor what I preach. A sad day they forced us to remove the cross from the mission and burned it. Our opposition landed five of us in jail over a weekend and they padlocked the building. Only by Global Missions paying a heavy fine, was our release obtained. Yes, the world wants to silence our voice, once and for all.

"Furthermore, there is no sanctity of marriage anymore. It has become a trivial matter - a joke - an institution no longer worthy of consideration. Moral values have disintegrated. Drug addiction is widespread and acceptable. Parties and drinking are vital to having fun, sex is recreational, and abortions worldwide outnumber births. What's worse, a powerful spirit of lawlessness roams the streets of this world's cities. They call good - evil, and evil – good, as the Bible said would happen.

"Satan is manifesting his power through his followers more openly with signs and wonders. His army appears massive and indestructible. In 2017, I faced an Enlightened One in spiritual battle. The power then was strong, and only by the Name of Jesus Christ and by His blood did I have victory - but with a price. I was beaten and burned!"

Caleb shuddered as he even now could feel that force.

"Now, Enlightened Ones are numerous across the face of the earth with huge followings, challenging any Christians brave enough to face them. Satan worship with sacrifices is practiced openly - unopposed. Even here in the jungle of Lugar de Paraiso, missing children and young women never seen again end up on an altar of a bloodthirsty devil!

"If all this is not a sign of the end, consider the worsening condition of the earth! Continents are ravaged by hurricanes and typhoons that make Katrina of 2005 a mere thunderstorm. Tornados! They have increased in staggering numbers and not just tornados - killer tornados with baseball-sized hail. The day will come when 100-pound hailstones will fall. What car or building could withstand that? What person? And earthquakes, tsunamis and rogue waves have increasingly brought death and destruction everywhere.

"The Bible additionally predicts that one of the end times' signs is uncontrollable disease. Well, dear friends, we've had that! Bird flu pandemics so far have killed millions. Remember also, renewed outbreaks of bubonic plague - the Black Death revived. It wiped out that whole community in the Southwest. In addition to cancer, AID's and many other diseases I've never heard of before continue to evade cures. And fiber sores! What started twenty years ago as simple lesions with weird fibers growing out of them have become a feared, unstoppable sickness that results in an agonizing death. I have visited people - well, seen them through a glass window only - but the sight was indescribable - like something out of a horror movie."

Caleb shook his head in dismay and took a drink of water.

"But the big one! The Jewish Temple in Jerusalem was completed last year. It stands now as a key element in prophecy, and its beauty is a wonder to behold. I have spoken to a few who have seen it. They say it is magnificent!

"All of these events and conditions I just mentioned would lead us to believe the time of the Rapture is upon us, but there is another most compelling reason.

"The Bible tells us there is coming an anti-christ. Strange word, 'anti.' It means opposed to, against, or hostile to. This person will be against the Lord, Jesus Christ. How will he do this? Because he is possessed by an evil hatred, he will use an odd and devious method. You see, satan is so jealous of Jesus Christ, he not only wants to take his place, he wants to be Christ. How could he possibly do that? By duplicating everything Christ did, only try and do it better. He is a counterfeit, which is an imitation so close it is hard to tell them apart. He will have to counterfeit every part of the Son of God to the letter. Think with me what this means."

The congregation hung on his every word; the Holy Spirit was taking over in powerful waves propelling Caleb on with the message. Thoughts and ideas were coming strong and fast. Words now flowed that weren't his but the Spirit's. Warfare was being waged in the Heavenlies. He could sense it.

"According to historians, Jesus' birth was actually 4 B. C., four years before the turn of the century. That being so, we might assume the child of satan was born somewhere in the world in 1996, four years before the turn of the century.

"Jesus' birth was announced by angels; satan's was proclaimed by astrologers and soothsayers. In 1996, a strange alignment of planets took place.

"John, the Baptist, prepared a path for Jesus; satan's path has been prepared by music, television and movies.

"Jesus grew up quietly in the city of Nazareth; the antichrist has been growing up and preparing, obscured from public notice in a city somewhere.

"So, if the duplication is complete, satan's man must step into the light of world attention when he reaches the same age as Jesus when He began His earthly ministry. That was age 30. This year is age 30 for the anti-christ. Then somewhere along his 33rd year he will be shot and seemingly die. The imitation continues, BUT WAIT! Anti-christ comes alive, and millions are astounded and believe him to be a god.

"There is just one little problem that blocks his coming to power right now! Today! Know what that is? The Bible says that the man of perdition will not be revealed until the Restrainer is taken out of the way. Who is this Restrainer? The Holy Spirit! Where does He live? In the church! The church is in the way of the anti-christ doing his worst; yes, he is held back until the Spirit is taken away, and when the Holy Spirit goes - we go! Isn't that the greatest?"

Caleb was so excited he realized he had elevated his voice and was hopping back and forth at the pulpit. His enthusiasm was contagious and some in the congregation were clapping and shouting, "Amen's" and "Hallelujahs"! Caleb calmed down and stepped behind the pulpit again.

"That's the year," he grinned, "and maybe we can know the month. So far every prophecy has been fulfilled on a Jewish feast day. The feasts give living pictures of major events in human history.

"First was the Passover. This one reminded the Israelites that the blood of the lamb caused the death angel to pass over them. Jesus Christ, the Lamb that was slain was cruci-fied during the Passover Feast to save us from our sins.

"Next was Pentecost. This feast was a picture of the chil-dren of Israel being released into the Promised Land with the strength and blessing of the Lord. The Holy Spirit was given to dwell in believers during that feast. Those Christians burst from the Upper Room in the power of God!

"The next feast, which remains unfulfilled, is the Feast of Trumpets. It was a day for the blowing of the trumpets. In First Thessalonians 4, verses 16 and 17, Paul writes:

"'For the Lord Himself shall descend from Heaven with a shout, with the voice of the archangel, and with the trump of God; and the dead in Christ shall rise first. Then we which are alive and remain shall be caught up together with them in the clouds, to meet the Lord in the air.'"

Caleb paused to take a breath, and then added with deep conviction, "He will call us with the blowing of the trumpet.

"Either in September or October of each year is this feast. Many believe it depicts the Rapture of the church, and the Rapture could occur on one of the feast days. Remember, we don't know the day or hour, but this year, the Feast of Trumpets occurs -"

At that instant, Mark stormed out of the church, slam-ming the door loudly. Caleb tried to bring the church back on track, but the damage had been inflected. He admonished the people of the shortness of time, and the urgency to warn those around the city to come to Christ before it is too late.

He closed the service with a weak prayer, heavy hearted and troubled by the attitude and actions of his son. This disruption could not, nor would it be, tolerated.

The message caused quite a stir and lively conversation from members as they shook Caleb's hand and left for their homes.

Sierra's eyes were penetrating, but he made no comment. Espolito wanted to know more, and Tazada gave a toothless grin on his way out.

"Makes sense," Hank was deep in thought. "I hope it is soon," Tulipan added.

"I loved your message!" Bomba was gushy and gave Caleb a generous hug. "But I did not understand it - maybe - not all."

Chris lingered until last. "You gave me lots to ponder on," he spoke in subdued manner. "Never thought on it like that. I think it scared Kay - you know - because of her family and all. Powerful message, Pastor, powerful to move us!"

He started to leave, then turned back. "By the way, there are hurricanes forming out in the Atlantic - first of the season. They don't look to be any threat here."

# Chapter 31

# Trouble on the Home Front

"You have kilobyte perception in a gigabyte world!" Mark's stinging reaction to his dad's confrontation over the incident in church service took Caleb by surprise and immediately put him on the defensive.

"What do you mean?" he sputtered.

"People - us - disappearing into the sky? Huh? Get real, dim circuit!"

"I'm not a dim circuit! I'm your father!" Caleb snapped back.

"And as piss poor one as you are a missionary. I hate being a M. K."

"What?"

"Look at you. Eight years we've lived here, and who have you converted to your dumb religion?"

Caleb was flabbergasted and speechless.

"Who, Pops? A drunk? An outlaw goes by Sierra? An old man an' his ugly Mexican Senorita?"

"Don't be insulting!"

"I'm just getting started, Pops."

"I'm your father! What has come over you, Mark?"

"I've had it up to- HERE - and tolerated your twisted teaching long enough. I'm speaking out the truth - making you face facts. You have a church full of losers."

"They are our friends," Caleb protested. Only the sadness over his son's vicious words subdued a rising anger.

"Your friends. Eight years here, and you have a hot blonde who only comes to ease her conscience and do penance. Her private life is a laugh. I see her where she works."

"Mark, how do you know?"

"I have my own friends, powerful people who are high end rollers, not nobodies like you have in this church."

Caleb was shocked!

"I know exactly why Global Missions sent you here," Mark continued. "They needed someone too blind to figure it out. You were the perfect candidate."

Caleb shook his head in disbelief at what he was hearing from his son.

"They - all of them – sought a place to come party. They've vacationed here in a steady stream for eight years, Pops, showing interest in the church by day and in the casino and on the beach other times. Hypocrites!"

"You lie! Your mother and I were with them all the time."

"No! I've seen them - gambling - drinking - other things - all of them."

"I don't believe you, and what were you doing at Golden Sands?"

"I live there. Didn't I tell you, I've made powerful friends. One word and I could have you in jail."

"None of this has anything to do with your rudeness in church, young man." Caleb had to recoup and regain his position as parent.

"I'm sick of your Rapture stories."

"It's in the Word - it's true!"

"It's bull crap! Anyone with brains has known for years that Jesus was a fake. He staged the whole thing. He's not coming back - ever - so forget that dream. You make a fool of yourself preaching it! Jesus is no more the Son of God than I am."

"But, Mark, you accepted Christ as your Savior when you were a boy."

"Just to please you, Pops, just to please you. It meant nothing then; it means nothing now."

Caleb looked at his son through eyes of disappointment and grief. All his hopes and dreams for his boy's future imploded into dust. He dropped his head for a few moments. When he looked up again it was with a stubborn resolve.

"Mark, you are sixteen and underage. As long as you live in this house - "

"Don't pull that sh -!"

"Watch your language!"

"Why? It's just a word like crap, feces, manure, bowel movement. Don't go righteous on me here. I know who you are. I've watched you bungle every job you ever took and listened to your empty sermons my whole life. Oh, Pops, the one thing you truly are unique at is your ability to be deceptive with your religious lies. Your Rapture talk today was full of them, and that's why I left, and I'll hear no more."

"As long as you live under my roof -."

"Then I won't live here! I have open doors to me all over this city."

"Mark, your mother would be deeply hurt and ashamed if she was party to this conversation. She would never believe you have voiced these feelings and thoughts if I were to tell her."

"Ha! That's a laugh. Tell her! She's just a dumb broad that believes anything you say and follows you blindly. Tell her!"

Caleb stood frozen until hot anger within him boiled controlling his response. He reacted instantly without thought! Thrusting pointed fingers into Mark's face, Caleb screamed, "I rebuke you in the name of Jesus Christ! Silence!"

Mark rushed Caleb in a rage, both hurtling onto the sofa before falling to the floor. Mark was like a madman throwing blows to Caleb's chest, neck, face, top of his head. Sixteen years of bottled up anger was being liberated through his fists.

Caleb tried to fight back, throwing punches, but his son's youth, and strength were overwhelming so he finally succumbed to feeble attempts at covering himself from the barrage of vicious blows. With each strike given, Mark was bellowing obscenities and accusations. Caleb rolled on his side, and a realization came over him that he honestly did not know who this child was. He now viewed him as a prodigal son and had to admit that somewhere along life's road he lost his hold and influence on his boy. Should he have seen it coming? Were he and Sarah in denial of their son's anger and rebellion? Blind? Where did their failure as parents begin to culminate in today's disaster? A dark sickening sense filled his heart that he was clueless how to heal the damage.

When Mark's anger dissipated, he stood up with a look of scorn. His face red and distorted, he gave Caleb a hard kick into his ribs. The pain was so sharp he could only curl up and groan.

"Don't you ever! Ever! Put a hand on me again, old man! I swear, I'll put you down for good. Today is my last time in church. I'm done with your stupid rules! I'll not listen to your – lies - or take any more crap off you. You ridicule Enlightened Ones because you're too dim circuit to see that's where the power is! They're the ones winning - not Christians. Enlightened Ones have the guts to stand up against fanatics like you who are only preventing a glorious new age from dawning on mankind with the true light. So, don't preach to me - Pops - ever!"

With that final verbal tirade, Mark stomped out of the house, slamming the door behind him. Caleb managed to pull himself up on the couch. He was brokenhearted. He buried his face in his hands to cry out to God in Heaven, interceding for Mark, and pleading for help. That's the way Sarah found him when she arrived home thirty minutes after the fight.

"I'm here," Caleb heard her cheerful voice as she stepped into the tiny entrance, then gasp when she entered the living room. Caleb began sobbing uncontrollably.

"Caleb, what happened, honey? Are you - no - oh, dear God, look at you - your - your clothes - you are hurt! Did someone break in?" She dropped beside him, taking his bloody face in her hands.

"Mark!" Caleb choked out. "We - we - had - a - a - horrible - horrible fight."

Sarah held him and tried to calm him with her words. "Shhh - it's alright - shhh - I love you – tell me what happened...where's Mark?"

"Don't know! Gone! Maybe forever!"

"Oh, Caleb, honey, please calm down. We'll find Mark."

Sarah's soothing voice and manner did calm Caleb, but did nothing for the pain in his heart. By and by he sat up, wiping his face, and for the first time since the fight saw the condition of the living room. End tables, and lamps were scattered across the floor, one lamp shattered near a broken flower vase. The flowers lay in disarray and crushed. Books and magazines flung in all directions, the sofa shoved back against a wall, the coffee table upside down a few feet away. Caleb saw the extent and intensity of the battle was far more extreme than he had realized. Sarah watched him silently, waiting...

"I confronted Mark about his behavior in church this morning. He unloaded on me, Sarah, with harsh words, bringing up angry grievances going back to when he was a boy."

"He'll get over it, he's been angry and upset before."

"I don't know," Caleb shook his head in uncertainty. "He's been hanging out at bars and the Golden Sands."

"What?" Sarah stiffened.

"That's what he told me. He's watched Bomba and made powerful friends at the casino. Said he - he - hated being a missionary kid, and going to church. The message this morning infuriated him, and he won't listen to any more. Threatened to have me thrown in jail!"

Sarah gasped again and covered her mouth. Tears of disbelief filled her eyes.

"He was upset - saying anything."

"No, Sarah, he meant every word. What's worse - "Caleb choked up and couldn't speak for a moment as emotion flooded his heart. He just wanted Mark there with them.

"Sarah, Mark's not a Christian. He did it to please me, and it meant nothing - then or now."

Sarah wept as she reached out to Caleb. The two held on to each other. In their sorrow Caleb relayed more of Mark's angry words.

"He denounced Jesus **and** practically gave allegiance to satan. Called us losers, **and** the Enlightened Ones are his heroes."

"Caleb, how can I believe this?" Sarah pulled back to search his eyes - his face - for any sign of hope for their son.

"That's what started the fight, Sarah! He spoke disrespectful towards you, and accused you of believing anything I told you and blindly following me. That's when I rebuked the demon in him, and we fought! Sarah, it was like the wrath of hell was unleashed on me, I tried to defend myself, but had no will to fight with our boy. Sarah, I've stood against an Enlightened One and done battle with demons, but my command aimed at Mark only infuriated him. I realize now I was not coming against a demon, but our son's anger! My words torched a smoldering buildup of hurts, disappointments and grievances. A rebuke sends a demon fleeing; it explodes anger. Yet I fear his heart is open to..." Caleb couldn't finish.

"Oh, dear God!" Sarah cried out, as she collapsed against Caleb. "What Stoner wrote in blood? Satan's child? Oh, Caleb, could it happen? What shall we do? What must we do? I can't think, Caleb, I fear for Mark!"

"I don't know, Sarah, I really don't. I, too, fear - for our son," Caleb's heartache became a prayer...

"Merciful Father, place a protective shield around Mark! Guard his heart! Speak to him. Open his eyes and mind. Don't let him walk in darkness. Love him; let him know we love him! Help him to know you. Cast away demons, in Jesus Name, who would control him."

"And bring him back to us," Sarah added.

# Chapter 32

# The Prodigal Son

By Friday, Caleb and Sarah were in a state of panic. A parents' worse nightmare was happening to them! Mark had vanished. They both, along with church members and local authorities, thoroughly searched the city of Lugar de Paraiso to no avail. There was no trace of Mark Hillag or the silver gray solar Phantom he drove. If anyone had seen him, they weren't saying. Caleb and Sarah even spent some of Thursday searching the village of Vera Cielo.

"Maybe, he lost his self deep into the jungle," father Junto Angeles offered.

"Can he find his way out?" Caleb asked with distress.

"No, unless he knows the country. I hear of terrible things - in the jungle. Not a safe place."

"Merciful God!" Sarah gasped.

"I will send some of my people to search. We will pray for your boy," father Junto consoled Caleb and Sarah trying to give a thread of hope.

Now it was Friday night, and the missionary couple was no closer to locating Mark than they were the Sunday he disappeared. They sat in their living room, silent for an hour, staring at the floor - a picture on the wall - anything - absent-mindedly - but daring not make eye contact. Their thoughts had driven them to the brink of exhaustion. Caleb broke the heavy silence.

"I need to call Chris and get him to speak Sunday."

"You already missed Wednesday Bible Study," Sarah murmured, looking up.

"I know - I know! Do you expect me to lead a service - with all - with this?"

"No," Sarah retreated, "but the church will be anxious to hear from you. They are worried and concerned as well."

"This isn't the time to prod me to perform!" Caleb snapped.

"I'm not," Sarah shot back. "I'm just telling you."

"How can I help them when I can't even help myself? How can I give something to them when there's nothing to give?"

Caleb got up and headed toward the door.

"Where are you going?" Sarah called after him.

"To the church."

"Caleb, it's nine-thirty."

"I'm going crazy sitting here!" He heard a muffled, "I love you," as he closed the door.

Caleb hoped and prayed to see the church lights on and Mark's car sitting in the parking lot, signifying his wayward son had found his way back to the very place he detested.

But the church was dark, and the small parking lot empty. Caleb sighed, and the disappointment drove his depression deeper. Finally, after lingering in the car for sometime, he got out and went to the church. He unlocked the main door and flipped lights on in the small and familiar sanctuary. He dropped to his knees before the altar, pouring his heart out to a God who wasn't answering. His prayers fell captive within the confines of the church. Discouraged, he stood up and made his way to the tiny room he called his study. There he engaged in a three-way wrestling match with God, the devil, and himself. With God over why he was silent during Caleb's family crisis; with the devil for Mark's release and who would be Lord in his son's life. Eventually, he condemned himself for failure as a father and being so harsh toward everyone around him- especially his love, Sarah.

He conjured up dozens of excuses and justifications, but in the end conceded it was no one's problem but his own. Mark somewhere changed in his early teens, but he was too preoccupied with other things to see it. He felt guilty that he was abandoning his wife, children and congregation when they really needed him. He must call Sarah! Just as he reached in his pocket for his phone, he heard a voice in the sanctuary. Was it Mark? Caleb held his breath - daring only to hope. A few seconds later, Chris Fowler, stuck his head in as he knocked on the doorframe.

"Evening, Pastor. I was on my way home from work and saw the lights and your car, so I stopped."

"Don't you get off at 6?"

"Had a boo-koo of maintenance troubles today – couldn't leave till they got fixed. I am glad I spotted you here cause I sure got a load to talk about. Can we sit a spell?"

Everything inside of Caleb wanted to scream, 'Shouldn't you go home? Kay will worry - she needs you! Besides, I'm tired; I need time to think, and call my wife.' Then remembering the angry words he had over this very issue, he waved Chris on in to have a seat.

"Me and Kay been worried sick over your boy! Any word on him?"

Caleb sadly shook his head. "Locals say he has to be out in the jungle - unless someone is hiding him and his car."

Caleb recalled Mark's hot words, 'I've made powerful friends!'

"Father Junto has some of his people who know the jungle out looking - no word yet," Caleb commented.

"This is first chance I've had to talk with you. What started the ruckus anyhow?" Chris asked. "You said you had a fight when you called us to help look for him."

"You remember how he left the church Sunday? I confronted him about it that afternoon, but what he was really mad at – was me! The message about the Rapture triggered a lot of suppressed anger."

"That message was a big gulp, Pastor. Do you really believe all that - you said?"

Caleb stared intently at Chris before he replied. "Chris, we have known each other for almost eight years. Would you really think me so frivolous about what I preach from a privileged pulpit?"

"Might be a hard theory to swallow - for some folks - musta been for Mark."

"Those thoughts were not a sermon which fell on my head overnight. It's been developing for a long, long time, Chris. The Lord began formalizing these ideas while I was in seminary. Then it really came together in 2006. Do you recall all the fuss about June 6, 2006? 6 - 6 - 06, how everyone was thinking there would be everything from disasters to terrorist attacks. There was even a movie made about an evil child. That energized my theory even more. What if the anti-christ was born under some spectacular circumstances to unusual parents, and this child was born June 6, 1996? Wouldn't that be 666 of sorts? That being, June 6, 2006, was not impending doom - it was a birthday. His birthday! I searched news reports, but couldn't find anything that would hint of the anti-christ child."

"Maybe 'cause it didn't happen, Pastor."

"Perhaps, or possibly it went unnoticed, except for just a few people."

"So what happens if this year passes on and no Rapture? You'll be the butt of lots of jokes."

"We just wait..." Caleb answered quietly, "with eager anticipation, just as man has done for centuries."

"'Nother thing. The young guy who visited in church Sunday? His name is Cory, but didn't get a chance to talk to him more. He's still in Lugar de Paraiso - on vacation. Said your sermon was interesting, and he would be back."

Caleb nodded affirmative.

"Well, guess I best get home to Kay."

Caleb glanced at his watch, realizing it was too late to call Sarah.

"I need to get home also," Caleb muttered, rising to his feet.

The two men turned out lights and locked up the church, and parted in the parking lot. A thrill shot through Caleb as he drove with a simple text message from Sarah, "Mark's home!" When he pulled up to the house he was relieved to spot Mark's car. He rushed into the living room and was about to shout for joy, calling for his son, when he heard voices. The living room was empty; he walked softly down the hallway to the open door of Mark's bedroom. He peeked in, quickly drawing back. Mark was lying on his back, an arm over his eyes. Sarah was sitting on the side of the bed talking to him.

"Your dad will be home any minute, Mark. He will be so glad to see you!"

"I don't want to see him or talk to him. I hate him!"

"Mark, you don't mean that! You can't!"

"I can - and I do! He's a failure and a liar. He's embarrassing; a poor excuse..."

"Mark, that's an awful thing to say!"

"That's right, Mom, I would expect you to defend him."

"He's my husband!" Sarah raised her voice, "And your Father! Where have you been all this time, worrying us sick?"

"With - friends - and I go again if you don't stop given me the whammies!"

There was a dead silence for longer than Caleb felt comfortable. He was ready to make his entrance into the bedroom from his listening post when he thought he heard singing. He listened. Sarah was singing a song she learned when she first found the Lord. He couldn't resist a quick glimpse. Mark had rolled over on his stomach; Sarah sat on the edge of the bed smoothing his hair. Tears were streaming down her face. Sorrow forced the words to cease, and she just hummed. Directly, she sang again - softly.

"I may wonder far and wide with the stars my only guide, but I will find my way - back home.

"I may leave and I may grow, but no matter where I go, I will find my way back home.

"Though I've gone so far away, I'll return again someday. I will find my way back home.

"We will never be apart - please hold us in your heart, I know you'll always find your way - back home."

Caleb realized that Sarah had gently changed the words in the song. He smiled through his own tears. He prayed for Mark to have a receptive heart.

# Chapter 33

# Storm Warning

C aleb was startled by a brilliant light, which filled the bedroom! The brightness was so intense it caused him to sit straight up in bed. He reached over and placed his hand on Sarah's arm. She seemed unmoved by the light or his touch. He tried to peer into the light as visions of his encounter with the Enlightened One years before sent a chill up his spine.

"Is - is - someone there?" Caleb called out. He thought he could make out a figure masked in the light's brilliance. Caleb's heart began to pound.

"Hello?" he gulped.

"Do not be afraid, Caleb Hillag," a strong commanding voice came from the light.

"Do I know you? How do you know my name?" Caleb stammered.

"You must heed this warning. Take your people up the mountain to the place that bears Mark's name."

"My son's name?"

"The writer of scripture."

With those final words the room was dark.

Caleb looked over at Sarah, barely able to see her, and her breathing told him she was sleeping peacefully. He shook her.

"Sarah, did you see that - hear that voice?"

"Whaaa?" Sarah struggled to comprehend what Caleb was telling her.

"Someone was in our room Sarah!"

That statement brought alarm to Sarah, and she sat up, eyes wide in the darkness.

"Caleb, are you sure? You are scaring me!" Sarah whispered. "Are they - gone?" She was shaking and tightly gripped Caleb's arm.

"Didn't you see the light? It was blinding!"

"No."

"You didn't hear me talking?"

"I was asleep, Caleb. Are you sure you weren't dreaming?"

All of a sudden, Caleb wasn't sure. Yet, it seemed so real, so clear, so distinct. Still, Sarah was not that sound a sleeper. His talking was always enough to awaken her. Whether it really happened or just a dream, what did it mean? Take his people up the mountain? Why? It made absolutely no sense, and what place that's called Mark?

He told Sarah about the brilliant light, the form he could make out, and what the voice said. The two of them tried to go back to sleep. Caleb could tell by Sarah's closeness against him that this talk of light, a form of a man, a voice, frightened her. Caleb could not sleep - his mind was ravaged with images and questions.

Around 4 a.m., Caleb felt Sarah relax and grow heavy on his arm. He was thankful for her sleep, but unable to find rest himself - his mind was too active.

Mark had been home a day. Tension was thick when he and Mark occupied the same room. Nothing so far had been said or resolved; at least he was home!

Now, this light and voice invaded to stir up something else. Caleb struggled to dismiss what he had seen as a meaningless dream - but an uncontrollable uneasiness persisted that he could not shake.

Caleb glanced over at the clock and sighed. In a few hours, he must lead the Sunday service. Why couldn't this voice have picked Monday night instead to disrupt his peace? Caleb groaned in his spirit!

He felt wiped out when he stepped to the pulpit and looked out over the congregation. The usual members were there except for Mark and Sierra. The young visitor from the week before was present. Caleb caught Sarah's eyes and smile and was grateful for her reassurance and encouragement. From what she said at the breakfast table, he knew she viewed the night episode as just a dream. They both had determined there was no reason to discuss it further - with anyone.

Caleb experienced trouble delivering the message. His head felt full of peanut butter! Words would not flow, and his tongue worked like it was slogging through paste. He couldn't believe losing a little sleep would drag him down so! He fought it! He prayed for the Holy Spirit to take over, but in the end he practically read his notes and left the church in miserable defeat. He secluded himself in prayer the rest of the afternoon not even seeing Sarah. It seemed his prayers just bounced off the ceiling and went unheard. An empty stomach finally drove him from isolation.

"Are you hungry?" Sarah asked softly when he walked into the room. She was watching television.

"Don't get up. I'll find something. Where is Mark?"

"I don't know. He hasn't been here all afternoon. He didn't get up until 2, and then he left."

"Any news?" he inquired as he rummaged in the fridge.

"Three hurricanes out in the gulf. The first has grown to a category two and will hit the west Florida coast early in the morning. The second one is headed into the gulf and looks like it will make landfall somewhere along the Alabama coast. The storm headed this way just barely made hurricane status and is named Chantal. Sounds dainty," Sarah laughed.

Caleb grunted. "Sure, just like Katrina."

"The meteorologist reported the projected track that puts it way north of here, maybe brushing the tip of Texas. She said that these early first storms of the season have not ever been very strong."

"That's good news. Want me to fix you a sandwich?"

The next two and a half days were filled with keeping peace at home and preparing for the Wednesday evening Bible Study. He gave no time to think about their troubles, and simply deleted the past two weeks' bad memories from his mind. He put his attention to matters at hand.

He was getting ready to meet Hank for lunch when his phone rang. It was Sarah.

"Sweetheart, I just had a call from Kay."

Caleb detected worry in her voice.

"I think you need to come home."

"Sarah, for what reason? I'm meeting Hank for lunch."

"It's Chantal!"

"Who?"

"Chantal, the hurricane. Kay just saw it on the weather channel. It has veered south off course and is picking up strength. Caleb, it's a category two and heading straight for us!"

Caleb pulled the car against a curb and stopped. He was trying to assimilate what Sarah just told him and determine what it meant for their family and friends. He was punching into a weather channel on his phone.

"Caleb, Honey? Did I lose you?"

"No - I'm here. I'm looking at it right now – Umm Ummph." Caleb shook his head in disbelief.

"Sarah, this is not good! This city has never taken a direct hit!"

"On the news, they said the airlines are trying to bring in additional planes to evacuate, but there isn't much time."

"How long?"

"Tomorrow night!"

"Merciful Lord! Sarah, Chris is calling. I'll get back to you.

Chris!"

"You hear about Chantal, Preacher?"

"Just did. What should we do?"

"City Administrators are calling a meeting in the Senior School in two hours. They are driving through the streets on loud speakers."

A low noise outside he had not been conscious of was growing intensely.

"Yes, Chris, I hear them. Oh! It's Hank. Let me call you back!"

"No need, see you at school."

"Hank."

"Caleb, all hell is surely breaking loose. I rushed to the hardware store to get some plywood to board windows. Could only get one sheet - they are nearly out already and this is just starting. There's a mob forming. We can't do lunch!"

"Lands no, Hank. Did you hear about the school meeting?"

"No."

"Two hours. You best be there. Any chance of me getting any plywood there?"

"No! Whoa - a fight just broke out! I've got to get out of here before some crazy tries to steal — my plywood."

Caleb called Sarah.

"I'm on my way. There's a meeting in the school. Be ready to jump in the car!"

Their ride to the school was shadowed by a sense of foreboding danger. In nine years Lugar de Paraiso had never had a hurricane come close enough to produce more than rain and eight-foot surf. The gravity of the situation was settling in on them. Caleb switched on the small local radio station.

"We are in emergency alert," the announcer repeated in English after speaking Spanish. He went on to instruct people to remain calm, and avoid the road to the airport, which was jammed. Word was given again detailing the meeting at the school, and mention was made that supplies of plywood, batteries, water and food staples were still available but being depleted. Everyone who could was urged to evacuate.

"Esther called in, frenzied!" Sarah's voice conveyed worry. "She just heard the news and was watching weather reports! Blanca also text-messaged me asking what she should do, and would there be a service tonight?"

"Dang, I forgot! We need to let our people know. Global Missions called me on the way home to inquire of our condition here. They asked if they should try to get us a flight out. I told them, no!"

Caleb could tell Sarah had a hard time with that decision.

"Where is Mark?" his voice conveyed both concern and anger.

"I don't know!" Sarah cried.

The drive to the school took less time than it did to find parking. Already a sizeable crowd was forming, and Caleb and Sarah merged into a stream of bodies pushing their way into the Senior School's cafeteria. Caleb located space for them at one of the long tables. By meeting time, all tables were packed, the wall space was full, and many more were crowded at the doors.

"This cafeteria doesn't even accommodate a fourth of the town," Sarah observed.

"Some of these people are scared to death," Caleb noted.

The Policia Capitan strode to a makeshift sound system that was set up. He nervously took the microphone and appealed to the citizens for calm. He tried to reassure everyone present that there was a strong possibility Chantal would change course again in the night or downgrade to a category one hurricane.

"And what if it doesn't?" a woman near Sarah shouted out!

"We have a plan for your safety," the Capitan responded instantly.

"Explicacion!" someone against the wall demanded. The crowd grew restless.

The Policia Capitan handed the mic to a woman Caleb recognized as the manager of the Golden Sands Casino and Resort. She introduced herself as Braci Vasquez. She wore a business suit and heels; her pretty face graced a slightly over-weight body. Her hair was obviously dyed, giving her dark hair a reddish copper look. She had the reputation around the casino of, 'Don't push me,' and had the bodyguards to back it up. Her voice today, however, had a soothing effect on the people. They were looking for someone to take charge - give answers.

"Both the Golden Sands and Resort were built to with-stand strong waves and winds. Our ballroom on the second floor of the Sands Casino will be the safest. The windows are high, and we will have cots, food and plenty of water for everyone's comfort. The casino will also remain open for your enjoyment."

The crowd began murmuring their agreement and appreciation, speaking amongst themselves. To Caleb's utter surprise and shock a clear understanding and powerful boldness overcame him. He jumped to his feet and yelled out before he took time to think.

"We must go up the mountain!"

The people were stunned and silent for a moment before anyone spoke.

"You are loco hombre! I stay in my own casa."

"No, listen to me," Caleb implored. "I had a dream…"

"A dream? A dream?" Some began to laugh.

"Listen!" Caleb yelled louder. "A figure of light came in our bedroom and said, 'You must heed this warning.' Take your people up the mountain…"

"Are you sure the voice didn't tell you to go - up the mountain - I want to sleep with your wife."

There was coarse laughter.

"This is no time for stupid jokes!" Caleb retorted. "The warning was real. We must go up the mountain - I know it! The message was clear."

"But Vera Cielo is a place of poor people. They have huts and shacks only. My own house is stronger. Where would we go?" An older woman near Caleb questioned.

Suddenly, the rest of the meaning of the message became clear to Caleb.

"We can go to Saint Marcos of Vera Cielo."

"The Catholic Church," some spoke low.

"That building is over a hundred years old. They have no provisions."

"Take your own," Caleb countered.

Some folks began to argue. Some doubted the church would standup to the storm. Many began to voice their decisions to go to the resort. Caleb climbed up on the table.

"You must listen to me!" he screamed.

"No, you must not! He's lying to you." the familiar voice came from behind. Caleb spun around to see his son standing in the crowd.

"My dad has this obsession to control people and con them to follow him. He gets his power from that. No followers - no power! I've listened to him mislead pathetic dim circuits for years. This is just one more desperate attempt to gain some sort of notoriety. Don't listen to him. He's giving bad advice."

"The lad is correct," a woman wearing a bright-colored blouse and multi-colored long skirt with jet black hair declared loudly, as she pushed her way through the ones crowding a doorway.

"I am Psychic, Destini Polovi. I consulted my spirit guides this morning. They sent me with this message."

At that moment, the woman's eyes rolled up in her head revealing only the whites. Her voice changed dramatically, sounding more like a man's.

"Hear the words of my servant and obey."

The voice left, and the woman Destini became herself.

"All of you will be safe and comfortable throughout the storm at the Golden Sands. Our city of delight will be protected."

"What of this man?" Chris spoke up, "He has a different message."

Psychic Destini walked closer to where Caleb was standing on the table. Her eyes blazed with venom and fire!

"He is a fraud," she pointed.

"I am a minister of the Most High God," Caleb cried out. "I speak the truth and appeal to you. Come to Global Missionary Christian Church in the morning, and we will transport you up the mountain."

"Shut him up!" someone bellowed, then began cursing. Rough hands drug Caleb down from the table. He took a blow to the side of his face. Fighting, yelling, cursing broke out, and Caleb sustained several more jabs to the sides and face. He heard Sarah scream and caught sight of Chris trying to get to him before he was knocked to the floor. He feared he would be trampled when two Policia rescued him and restrained his attackers.

"Out with him!" he heard chanting mingled with Sarah's calls to him. He caught sight of Mark's leering face amongst many faces. Caleb was devastated as they led him to the door.

# Chapter 34

# Getting Ready

A shudder coursed its way through Sarah's body. It was not caused by the cold; it was fright. She feared for their son Mark. Caleb had been out all night trying to locate him, but so far, Mark was nowhere to be found. With each passing hour, the approaching storm grew more ominous, like a black, billowing monster stretched across the entire horizon. It was 8 a.m., and Sarah was frantic! Her satellite phone rang in her hand.

"Oh, thank God, Caleb! Have you found him?"

"No, Sarah!" she could hear the despair in his voice. "I have searched everywhere. I even went knocking on doors where some thought he might be. No one has seen him since after the meeting yesterday. He was in the bar with some girls."

"Girls? Who were they?" Sarah gasped.

"No one knew. They were tourists. I checked the Resort's desk and went to the rooms of possible girls. I struck out, Sarah."

"What can we do, Caleb?"

"Who is there, ready to go up the mountain?"

"No one."

"What? Did you make calls?"

"Yes. Bomba has to work at the Casino. Tazada said he would ride out the storm there also. He didn't say, but I know it's because of the bar, and he can drink."

"Good Lord!" Caleb exclaimed in exasperation.

"Honey, the rest are so torn and frightened. The Casino and Resort seem so solid and comfortable, and the church so uninviting with no provisions. Since we can't find Mark, should we also stay here - for him?"

There was a long pause of silence before Caleb answered. "Maybe we should... I don't know, sweetheart, maybe the whole thing of going up the mountain was just - a dream. Have I made a fool of myself - of us? I'm so unsure - and - and - I can't find - our son."

Sarah knew Caleb was exhausted and her heart broke for him and their son. Finally, he spoke.

"Where are you?"

"In your office at the church. I made calls and told them to meet here, and we would transport them up the mountain in our truck. I brought a few extra clothes, some food, water, and blankets from home. I found our flashlights and grabbed some batteries."

"Good, Sweetheart, but no one's there?"

"Haven't seen anyone."

"Well, I can't see going up the mountain and leaving our son and our people here. Stay there. I'll make the rounds one last time, and then I'm headed to the church. I love you!"

"I love you too; bye."

Sarah sat at Caleb's desk lost in thought. She went over the conversation she just had with her husband. Why was Mark doing this? Where was he? Would he be safe from the storm? Would they all? Hurricane Chantal was out there, spinning toward them like a huge, hideous buzz saw. Sarah brought up the weather channel on her phone.

The storm, which was tracked to parallel the Mexican coast and make landfall near Texas, suddenly veered west as though pushed by a giant hand. This came as a total unexplained surprise to meteorologists at the hurricane center. Sarah listened in horror at the latest report.

"Chantal has picked up strength in the extremely warm waters of the Gulf. It is a high category 3 hurricane with sustained winds of 150 mph, and storm surge of 24 feet.

"Chantal is expected to make landfall approximately 9:30 p.m. this evening, thirty-five miles north of the resort community of Lugar de Paraiso, and the village of Vera Cielo. Both towns are under extreme hurricane warnings. It is estimated that over 500 tourists will be stranded, as the last flight out of the small airport at Lugar de Paraiso will be at 5:20 p.m. The local school and the Casino Resort have been designated as shelters."

Without warning she had a compulsion to go to the sanctuary. She shut down her phone and was startled when she walked through the door to see Sierra standing at the altar.

"Sierra?" she choked on his name.

He slowly looked up at her with penetrating eyes. Sarah felt embarrassed and dropped her eyes. She should have felt afraid, but strangely she was not.

"You must not stay here, Sarah. It is not safe for you and Caleb."

"But what of Mark? We can't find him!"

"Trust God to protect the him."

"And the church members?"

"They will come."

"How - do you - know - Sierra?"

"The Lord will speak to their hearts, and they will believe what Caleb has told them. You will see."

Sierra walked to the main door, turned to smile, and made his exit without further word. Sarah hastened to the door to peer out. She saw a car pull out of the parking lot, but couldn't tell if it were Sierra. She did see Blanca running toward her with a pack slung over a shoulder.

"Buenos Dias," she called out cheerfully. "Hank and Tulipan will come before too long."

Sarah covered her mouth.

"What is matter, Sarah Hillag? Why you sad?"

"I - didn't - think - anyone was - was coming!" Sarah took Blanca in her arms and held her.

"I - I wasn't. Then without reason it seemed to be the right thing to be doing."

"I'm so glad you are here," Sarah held Blanca then took her hand. The two women began laughing.

It wasn't long before Hank and Tulipan arrived. After them came Espolito with her children, Fina and Carmen.

"I packed some food, water and extra clothes," she informed the group.

"Tulipan and I loaded our car also with food and water, although I think we will get plenty of water. Just hold out a bucket," Hank chuckled.

"This no time for joking!" Tulipan hit him.

"We also grabbed some blankets and rain gear," Hank went on, now more serious. "The road up to Vera Cielo is pretty dog-gone rough, but I think the old nag will make it."

"He means car, not me," Tulipan spoke straight-faced, but with a smile in her eyes.

"Seriously now, I would rather have it rained on up there, than under water down here," Hank muttered.

"Senor Hank, you can no be serious," Blanca exclaimed.

The gathering was joined by Maybeline Collier and, to Sarah's surprise; the young man who visited in the church.

"HI, I'm Cory Atkins from Florida. I'm here on vacation; well, I should say extended vacation now. I couldn't get a flight out - along with a few hundred or so other guests. I was going to stay at the Resort when I met this fellow, called himself Sierra and says he goes to church here, and that I should come here - with you all - so here I am."

Sarah introduced Cory to the rest of the church members, then she invited everyone into the sanctuary to pray and visit. Cory got on the piano and played. Everyone began to sing along, and Sarah was grateful that Cory's music and the singing took their minds off the impending danger.

It was 2 p.m. when Caleb arrived without Mark. Sarah thought she would lose her mind and struggled valiantly to keep her sanity! She wanted him there more than her own life! She collapsed in a chair in despair of the hopelessness that caved in on her. She was numb, and not sure she could go up the mountain.

"A plane just took off. There will only be four more flights. People are mobbing the airport, and there have been injuries, but thank God, no life lost. Pray it doesn't get worse," Caleb informed everyone as he looked over the ones present.

"We haven't had much chance to get acquainted," he indicated to Cory, still seated at the piano, "but I heard some beautiful music when I walked in."

"Cory Atkins here," the young man waved hello.

"Well, if this is it, let's get loaded up. The wind is really picking up, and the first band of rain has hit. The storm is stalled over water, which will delay landfall until 11 or 12 o'clock. That can be bad news for us if it slows down, because it will sit on top of us."

"Pastor?" Maybeline had a question. "The weather center says the eye will be coming ashore 35 miles north of here. Won't that be better for us?"

"Hell, no," Hank sputtered in disbelief at Maybeline's thinking that distance would make the storm less violent. "Excuse my French, but that only means we get the south eye wall which carries a strong part of the hurricane - right on top of us!"

"Heaven help us!" Maybeline gasped.

Sarah grew faint! Her tongue was thick in her mouth, and she felt like throwing up. She fought to collect herself. She must be strong!

Caleb and Sarah's truck was being loaded when Plomo pulled up with Bomba.

"I thought the Casino was making you work, Bomba?" Sarah shouted through the wind and rain.

"Plomo told my boss it was unlawful to make me stay if I didn't want to. I wanted to, but they did not know. Plomo tell me to come with him, and I do. Ow, this rain!"

Caleb ordered everyone into the back of the truck and covered them with a tarp. Sarah helped with the tie-downs. By now they were drenched.

"Are you sure you can make it, Hank?" Caleb shouted, rain dripping off his chin.

"If we don't, we'll walk," Hank answered. Tulipan was already sitting in their car.

Caleb turned to Sarah. "Any word from Chris and Kay?"

"No. I saw Sierra. I told you that on the phone, but he didn't say what he was doing. Oh, Caleb, what about...?"

"I couldn't find him, Sarah. God knows I tried! I looked and called. He won't pick up on his phone! I can't find him!"

"I can't go, Caleb! I won't! Not without Mark! You go on, I'll stay!" Sarah was determined.

"You must come, Sarah. I know it's hard. I'm broken-hearted, but I can't risk your life. I'm convinced it won't be safe here. If anyone stays, it will be me! Now, get in the truck."

Sarah fought Caleb; arms, fist, feet, flying, and kicking. Caleb tightened a grip on her arms and wrestled her to the truck. At the same time Chris and Kay pulled up next to Caleb.

"Who's here?" Chris shouted.

Caleb released his hold on Sarah.

"Hank and Tulipan, Blanca, Espolito and her girls, Plomo, Bomba, that Cory fellow and Maybeline. Don't know about Sierra, and we can't find Mark," he yelled.

"Send Hank and Tulipan on up the mountain. She knows Father Angeles. Will you give me thirty minutes? There is someone I must go after. If I'm not back, leave without me. Kay will stay with you."

"Won't leave without you, brother," Caleb spoke with emotion.

Everyone climbed out of the truck and ran for the church. The wind was moaning with driving rain that stung like needles. The sky surrounding them was growing darker, and lightning flashes in the distance illuminated bright spots in the clouds.

Sarah hoped and prayed that Chris went after Mark - that he knew where her son was. She pictured him walking into the church - safe! The thirty minutes seemed like hours. Would Chris make it back? Her heart leaped when she heard Caleb announce, "He's back! Everyone to the truck."

Sarah flew outside into the growing force of wind and sheets of rain hoping to see Mark. Her heart sank when she realized Chris had Tazada with him. All this - for drunk Tazada?

Anger rose in her heart. Tazada wasn't worth risking Mark for. It wasn't a fair trade! Right now she wasn't interested in this worthless, pitiful excuse of a man. She just wanted her son.

# Chapter 35

# Chantal

The church of San Marcos was filled to capacity when Caleb, Sarah and the believers from Global Missionary Christian Church crowded through the large wooden doors. Hank and Tulipan were already inside and Tulipan was speaking to Father Junto Angeles in Spanish. She motioned for Caleb to come near.

"He says the church is full from many people of Vera Cielo who fled their poorly constructed homes. There are also some who have come up the mountain from Lugar de Paraiso."

Sarah immediately began to scan the sanctuary hoping to find Mark among them. She could not see the faces well. The candles at the altar briefly illuminated them. Electricity in the small village was already down.

"Have you seen our son Mark?" Caleb asked the priest.

"No, senor," he shook his head.

"What shall we do Junto?"

The old man ran his fingers through his silver hair. Sarah could tell from the expression on his face that he was concerned for those in his care. As she looked into the frightened faces of men, women and children - lit up in the candle light for a moment when they turned their heads or moved about, she sensed the plight they all were in. If the roof gave way, or the walls should topple, these trusting souls would be crushed. The unbearable humidity booted up by so many bodies made the air stifling. For an instant, she had a powerful urge to rush out of the building into the storm, but then despair gripped her nailing her to the spot where she stood!

"I will not turn you or your people away," Sarah heard Father Angeles tell Caleb.

"Thank you," Caleb replied. "We must stand together in this."

Then the old priest's face brightened - as though he had an idea.

"God has given to us an answer," he spoke with renewed hope. "This we will do. I will place some of my most faithful in the small prayer chapel, and the rest I will take across the garden to my house. Then there is a place for you and your followers."

"Is the chapel room and your house strong enough to withstand this hurricane?" Caleb questioned.

"God in Heaven will protect us - all! You will see."

Father Junto made his way through the people calling forth different ones. He had them wait at the small side door near the altar. Next he cleared several benches in the center of the church on the side away from the storm, for Global Missionary's members. The rest of the people filled in vacant spots and settled in to ride out the fierce blast that was about to hit the mountainside. When Father Angeles was satisfied everyone was safely down, he and his waiting people exited through the small door.

The next two hours were unbelievable! When Sarah thought it couldn't get worse, it did. As the eye wall bore down on them, Caleb alternated use of all the satellite phones available to keep batteries up. They had constant monitoring of news and weather reports. Caleb shouted out reports periodically in Spanish and English so everyone was made aware of Chantal's approach and strength.

"Good news, I think. The hurricane's losing a little of its punch. Winds have dropped to 145 mph as it nears our shore.

"Oh, so instead of getting run over by a freight train we get hit by a semi?" Chris spoke with sarcastic humor.

The church in Vera Cielo was an old but sturdy structure made of brick and stucco. However, as strong as it might be, it was taking a violent beating from Chantal. Without warning, the main doors burst open sending people fleeing a force of wind and water so strong it knocked them down and swept struggling bodies toward the front. All the candles were snuffed out, and amidst the darkness, lit only by a few flashlights, screams of women and children filled the church.

Strongmen fought against the force of the wind to close the doors and barricade them with the heavy altar and benches. There were sighs of relief that they were past the danger, but Chantal retaliated! Candles were re-lit to aid the few flashlights on hand, but the lightning was constant now, lighting the church around edges of the roof and doorframes like a menacing strobe light. The following thunder was instant and maddening. One woman held her ears and began shrieking, setting off others and scaring children. Caleb and other men tried to calm everyone, but hysteria was gripping this crowd. Sarah's phone rang. It was Esther.

"Esther."

"Mom, we all are so worried about you! Where are you? Are you safe? Is Daddy and Mark okay?"

"We are in the Catholic Church in Vera Cielo. We are all right so far, but this storm is horrible. We are frightened out of our minds for Mark. He stayed behind! Esther, I spoke to your Grandparents this morning. You must let them know! Esther?"

Sarah realized she had lost contact and didn't know for sure how much Esther heard. She clicked Esther back, but the call wouldn't go through. She pulled on Caleb's arm.

"Esther called checking on us, but I lost her, and now I can't get through. What's wrong, Caleb?"

Caleb sat down next to her and took her hand. "All the lightning has so much electricity in the air the signal can't go through. I lost the weather channel a short time ago."

"Is the worst past, Caleb? Please tell me it is!"

Caleb gave Sarah a look she had never seen before, and she wasn't quite sure what it meant. It seemed a mixture of love, worry, memories of such intensity it made her afraid. He began rubbing her hand.

"I want you to know how much I love you, Sarah. I couldn't have found a more beautiful, perfect wife."

Sarah's lips began to quiver. "What are you saying, Caleb? You are scaring me!"

"The worst is not over, Sarah. The eye is still out in the Gulf, and the storm has slowed down gaining strength. Last report before loosing signal Chantal reached a low category 4. The eye wall will hit us in about an hour!"

"God have mercy on us!" Sarah cried aloud as she buried her face against Caleb's chest.

"And protect Mark, and all of us, and the ones in Lugar de Paraiso," Caleb added.

The next hours became a fight for survival against a gigantic nightmare storm that lasted until the next morning. Not only did Sarah hear the thunder, wind and rain intensify, she could feel and see it. The walls of the church shuddered, and looking up she saw rafters trying to lift off the building and fly away. Sarah would swear in some of the heavy gusts the walls appeared to sway.

Chantal relentlessly tore at the clay tile of the roof, stripping one after another until flashes of lightning could be clearly seen through holes. Pieces of tile fell onto the floor below, and waterfalls cascaded down giving those underneath a bath. Someone cried out they saw cracks forming in the walls, and many began to panic.

Caleb jumped up and yelled for order. He instructed everyone to take someone's hand in small groups of three or four.

"Now, pray as you have never prayed before! Our lives depend on it, and recall to mind, God's promises. Pray!"

Sarah saw Blanca staring mute in sheer terror. She went to her, grabbing hold of Mabeline at the same time. They held hands and prayed for the storm to weaken and pass over. They begged for morning to hasten!

# Chapter 36

# Aftermath

A shaft of light struck Sarah in the face bringing her out of a fitful sleep. At first she thought someone was shining a flashlight in her eyes. She squinted to see where the light was coming from and realized it was streaming through a hole in the roof.

She listened - fearful - but the monster wind now blew as a stout breeze. Caleb's strong arm had her nestled at his side. She became conscious of families stirring around her.

"Caleb? Honey? Are you awake?" she whispered.

"Yes."

"What is happening?"

"The worst of the hurricane is gone. The wind is still blowing some light rain, but we are all safe, thank God!"

"I am so afraid for Mark."

"I've called his phone but get no response. As quickly as we can go down we will search for him and pray he came through this."

"Caleb, we must call Esther and our parents."

"I already have - early - as soon as I had a signal. They are all relieved but also worried about Mark."

Sarah sat up and attempted to stretch.

"Oh, this bench was so hard. I feel every part of my body - that can hurt." She looked at her husband. His hair was plastered to his head where he had been rained on. Dirt smears darkened his hands and face. She felt of her own hair and tried to fluff it.

"I must look a sight," she murmured.

"Sarah, we just weathered possibly the strongest hurricane to ever hit this coast. We survived by God's grace. After being hit that hard, I wouldn't expect us to look like we were dressed for a ball," Caleb spoke seriously. "Besides, you are a beautiful sight to me."

Sarah laughed. "Where is Blanca? I was holding her."

"She got up and went to Hank and Tulipan. Espolito had a terrible time with her girls. They were freaking out!"

"Poor things," Sarah murmured.

"Tazada was asking if anyone had something to drink. I told him to cut it and to..." Caleb stopped what he was saying. A sudden calm in the wind placed a silence over everyone in the church. As if on cue, a break in the clouds let bright sunshine beam through the holes in the ceiling tile. The beauty and meaning of the moment so struck Sarah she wanted to sing. As if reading her thoughts, Cory Atkins began to sing an early American melody in a strong, commanding voice.

"There is a fountain filled with blood. Drawn from Immanuel's veins;"

Sarah instantly recognized the hymn and started singing. Caleb joined in.

"And sinners, plunged beneath that flood, lose all their guilty stains."

One by one Global Missionary members added their voices.

"E'er since by faith I saw the stream, Thy flowing wounds supply, Redeeming love has been my theme, and shall be 'til I die."

Now one of the women of Saint Marcos began to sing a Spanish hymn. Sarah made out the words, 'Jesus, our Rock, who is our safety in the storm.' The harmony was perfect as voices from two different congregations sang their praises to God.

"When this poor lisping, stammering tongue, lies silent in the grave," Global Missionary people sang, led by Cory.

"Our Jesus will carry us through to the very end," Saint Marcos members rose in answer.

"Then in a nobler sweeter song, I'll sing Thy power to save."

"Jesus, our Rock and Redeemer will carry us home."

Just then the side door opened, and the ones who had stayed in the chapel room filed into the sanctuary joining in the singing.

This continued in a beautiful harmony so close and united, it captivated everyone. It was not just a group of people singing, it was a spiritual event of significant importance orchestrated by the Holy Spirit. No one needed to be told it was unique. Without a word spoken each knew in their hearts the Lord was preparing them for what they would face that day - and what they must do. The singing ceased, and a holy hush fell on the church. Everyone just looked at each other as if fixing images and faces in their minds.

"Where is Father Angeles?" one of the men asked.

This question made them face the sobering fact that they must brace for what lie outside the walls of the church. A gasp rippled through the crowd, and some of the men began unblocking the entrance doors. A shock jolted the survivors as they made their way outside. The brief sunshine disappeared, and rain was falling again. Twisted trees, limbs, leaves and debris were thrust in all directions. Lugar de Paraiso was not visible from their position on the mountain.

Those making their way around to the rear of the church building found Father Junta's house a tangled mass of brick and boards. Women began to moan and wail while the men frantically dug into the wreckage. Caleb, Sarah and their people joined in the search. Parts of the roof they pulled away. Chunks of wall and pieces of plaster were cast aside, but there was no sign of Father Angeles or the ones he had taken into the house.

"Maybe they went somewhere else," someone offered.

"But where? Are they all perished?"

"No," Caleb responded firmly, "No one would be lost here. God promised!"

A knocking could be heard on the floor, accompanied by muffled voices. There was renewed frenzy of hands clearing away remaining parts of the house to reach the tapping sound. A small door was found and opened. Up popped a beaming Father Angeles. He and the others with him climbed out of where they spent the night.

"Praise be to God, the ones who built this humble house thought to put a wine cellar here instead of under the church. I believed in my heart that the house would stand. I was soon made to understand that it could not. So we went below to take communion," Junta smiled. "We were lacking bread, but we had the wine."

"I should have been with you," Tazada muttered.

"My child, this is not a day for feasting and drinking. We are safe, but many are injured and even dead I fear. We have never seen such a storm. I heard my house falling on top of us and feared the church might also fall." Junto spoke without a smile. "We prayed in the night for the walls to stand."

"It held, Father," one of his people pointed.

"By the Hand of the Omnipotent!" Cory shouted.

"Let's join hands to thank God for protecting us," Caleb suggested. Sarah took his hand and squeezed it.

"And for the others not with us," Bomba spoke up with emotion. "We have friends - and family."

Caleb led the prayer. Father Junta came to him after.

"We can never thank you enough for taking us in," Caleb spoke before the aging priest could say anything.

"We are one, covered by the precious blood of Christ. We of Saint Marcos could do no other." Then the old man's expression grew very grave, and his face saddened.

"The people of Vera Cielo are simple - and poor. Many did not come into the safety of the church, and I fear are lost. We have much work, my brother. We must labor here in Vera Cielo. You, and your people are needed below in Lugar de Paraiso. My prayers go with you, my son. I hope your boy found shelter and safety," Father Junta concluded, as Caleb turned to leave.

"Oh, God, yes!" Sarah breathed a prayer.

# Chapter 37

# Destruction and Death

Sarah knew it had to be bad, but never imagined the magnitude of the devastation. The road down the mountain was strewn with uprooted trees and broken shrubs with piles of limbs and leaves covering the roadway, making travel slow and hazardous. In several places, rivers of mud had swept across the road making passage for their truck extremely rugged.

Hank and Tulipan kept Blanca with them in Vera Cielo. They would come down later after the road was cleared.

The group was quiet, lost in their own thoughts, some reliving the nightmarish storm, others wondering what they faced next.

Cory sat up front with Caleb and Sarah. He broke the somber silence.

"I don't see the guy who told me to come with you."

Sarah suddenly remembered Sierra was not with them.

"You mean Sierra?" Caleb replied. "I hope he is okay."

"Me too. I would probably have stayed at the Casino were it not for his urging. Tell me about him."

"Don't know anything about him. We seldom see Sierra, and he hardly speaks."

"He's a strange man," Sarah injected. "I should be afraid of him - but I don't…" her voice trailed off. All she could think about was Mark.

Water was still receding back into the Gulf as they drove into the north end of Lugar de Paraiso. The city was in shambles. Buildings had been broken up and swept away. A mass clutter of trees, boards, furniture, cars, clothes - and dead bodies were in every direction they looked. The few living were hysterically, frantically going from body to body - turning them over - looking for family members or friends.

"Oh, my God!" was all Sarah could say. She felt a flood of hopelessness surge over her surely and strong as the storm surge driven in by Chantal.

"How will we find Mark?" she cried out. "Dear Lord, there are bodies everywhere. Mark could be one of them. How will - where?"

Caleb touched her hand. His face turned ashen, and Sarah felt sick!

"We'll get our people to the church first, then we'll look for Mark at the Casino and Resort. Those appear to still be standing," she heard Caleb as if in a dream.

"I should have stayed here, Caleb. I should have stayed – looked…" Sarah could not face the unspeakable, burying her face in her hands.

"We'll find him, Sarah, I promise we will."

"I can't bear to think of coming up on a body… Oh, Caleb, I'll die a thousand deaths - each one we come to - would it be - our son - I - I - can't do this!"

"I'll look, sweetheart."

"No!" she objected. "I've got - I want to be there - to hold him."

"We don't know he's dead, Sarah!"

"That's right," Cory agreed.

"Yes, he is! I know he is!" Sarah began shaking. She covered her head with her hands and buried her face in her legs. She could hear cries from the ones in the back of the truck. She knew they too had seen the carnage scattered along the way, and understood what they saw was affecting them just as deeply as her. No, how could they? This is her son missing!

She heard Caleb gasp - she sat straight up. They were in the rubble-strewn parking lot facing what was left of the church.

"Merciful God in Heaven," Caleb spoke in hushed tone, "it's gone. There's the roof over there," he pointed.

Sarah could make out pieces of the church roof, or what was left of it, in place of where two houses used to be. Only parts of the walls were left.

Everyone got out of the truck to sort through the wreckage. The group was stunned as they surveyed the damage.

"Piano is pushed over," Cory examined the instrument.

"My study is the only thing left," Caleb observed. "Still have my desk."

"We'll rebuild the church in short order," Chris tried to be optimistic.

"Can the piano be fixed?" Espolito asked.

"Lets try and turn it over," Plomo grabbed a corner. The rest of the men joined him, and with effort righted the piano. Cory played a few notes - not bad," he said smiling. "A little soggy."

Sarah shuffled through papers, rubbish, some hymn books, and she saw Bibles. She collected those and absent-mindedly walked toward Caleb's office to place them on his desk.

'All our work - destroyed in one night,' she thought sadly. When she deposited the Bibles on the desk, she glanced behind it on the floor, and let out a blood-curdling scream. Caleb came running. Sarah pointed with shaking hand to a body - face down in the muddy floor.

"Is it?" her mind and voice refused to function at this point. Maybeline took her hands and helped her out into the open. Chris was now in the office with Caleb. Caleb was bent down examining the body. Sarah felt her heart stop, her mind went numb, she held her breath - waiting for Caleb's answer.

"Do you know who he is?" she heard Caleb ask. Chris bent down for a closer look, then he stood back up.

"Yea, I know him. He hangs around the Casino, a loud mouth and a trouble maker." Chris lowered his voice, but Sarah could still make out what he was saying.

"You remember at the school meeting someone yelled - 'Shut him up!' That was this guy. I think he hit you too!"

At that moment, two Policia ran into where the group was standing. They were wild-eyed and overwhelmed.

"We have a dead body in here," Caleb told them.

"Don't you see, Amigo? Look around! There are bodies everywhere you look. See to it yourselves! Whose truck is thes?"

"Mine," Caleb answered.

"It run?"

"Yes."

"We are confiscating it."

"You can't do that. It's my truck," Caleb protested.

"We are a disaster," the officer pulled his handgun and trained it on Caleb.

"Caleb, don't argue with him," Sarah pleaded as he held up both hands and backed up.

"The keys," the officer demanded.

## Chapter 38

# Where Is Mark?

The truck gone, the group was on foot. Everyone went different directions to check on their homes, except for Caleb and Sarah who started the walk to the Casino, hoping and praying Mark was there. Cory went with them. The trio passed by numerous corpses, as they neared the Casino and Resort. They could only see the backside of the resort, which hid the casino.

"The Resort looks in pretty good shape," Caleb observed.

Sarah's sat-phone rang. She saw it was Global Missions.

"Hello."

"Sarah! Thank God you are alive! We have been trying to reach Caleb all night and worried sick. We have been in prayer." Sarah covered the mouthpiece.

"Caleb, it's Gerald at Global. They have been trying to reach us - you - he said."

"Let me talk to him," Caleb reached for the phone as they kept walking.

"Gerald - so thankful to hear your voice. Yes, yes, I know. My battery went dead keeping reports to the people. I conserved Sarah's because Mark would... Yes, we are safe, but we don't know where Mark is. Our church went up the mountain to take shelter in the Catholic Church. Only Mark and Sierra didn't come. What? Don't know yet. We are hoping Mark took refuge in the Casino and is okay."

Sarah's lip began to quiver, and her face scrunched up in pained worry. Caleb noticed and put his arm around her as they walked. Her tears mingled with the light rain.

"The church building is totaled. It will have to be rebuilt. What, Gerald? Fly us out? There's no airport! I tell you; in Vera Cielo the only building standing is the Catholic Church. In Lugar de Paraiso we are walking through rubble. The only building we can see is the Resort."

"Oh, dear God," Sarah gasped. They had passed the Sands Resort where they got their first glimpse of the Golden Sands Casino.

"Gerald," Caleb went on. "This is unbelievable! The ground floor where all the slots and gaming tables were - you remember - the glass is all broken out. You can't imagine the complete devastation. It's gutted."

Sarah steadied herself against Caleb. Hopes of Mark's survival were shredding to pieces. No one on the first floor could have lived through that horrific storm.

"Gerald, I'll call you back if I can. The situation here is desperate. Dead bodies are strewn everywhere. We must have walked past - over a dozen on the way here. We even found one behind my desk - you can't even - begin - to - oh, God - there are no words - this is horrible! Thank you, Gerald, we need that. Goodbye."

The three ran to the lower floor of the casino. Inside, they had to climb through tangled slot machines - twisted and broken - tables - chairs - bottles - monitors. The destruction was massive.

The Policia were present to prevent looting. There was an open area that had been cleared, lined up with bodies. Sarah could see that volunteers were carrying in more bodies.

Those fortunate enough to live through Chantal were trickling in looking for loved ones. She grabbed Caleb's arm!

Caleb talked to the first Policia they came to.

"What happened here," Caleb asked in Spanish.

"The Casino here was full. The wind and water took them all away," he began weeping. "My wife - is over - there."

Sarah covered her mouth, "Oh, you poor man!" Caleb put his arm around this broken officer.

"What about those in the ballroom?" asked Caleb when he felt the time was right.

The Policia began crying again. "They were trapped."

"Trapped?"

"Si. The water from the hurricane came higher as the second floor. When the sea broke the doors, it flooded. There was no way out, senior. We are bringing them down. I cannot tell you what it is like - up there."

"Oh, dear God!" Sarah shook her head in disbelief. She looked at Cory whose face was pale and grim.

"Do you know our son, Mark?" Caleb asked.

"No, senor, but you can - look - to see…" The officer could say no more and stumbled away in a daze.

Cory was shaken; he gagged, turning his back. Holding his mouth, he hastened outside. Caleb and Sarah began the gruesome task of identifying the dead.

"I think I will die if we come upon Mark," Sarah blurted out. "My stomach is churning!"

"Mine too, Sarah. This is the hardest thing we have ever had to face."

They started down the rows of bodies. None were covered, as nothing was available. No blankets - no body bags - this was raw death. Most were fully clothed - others had clothing stripped away by the surge of water.

"I saw her two weeks ago at the grocery," Sarah stood looking in a silent face.

"This young fellow worked on our car - once."

"Ohhh…" Sarah groaned, as she recognized one of Mark's schoolmates. She heard Caleb crying loudly and turned to see he had picked up a little girl, holding her to his breast.

One of the Policia came running.

"Senor, do not touch them!"

"Where are her - mommy and daddy?"

"Senor, I do not know. Please - put her down!"

"You mean she died alone?" Caleb cried through his tears.

"Senor - please - please - just put her down."

Sarah went to her distraught husband who was laying the lifeless body on the cold concrete. He was on his knees by the little girl and buried his face in his hands.

"Oh, God! What can we do? There are so many!"

Sarah joined Caleb on her knees and held him. By now she felt completely in shock and didn't even know how to pray. How could this horrible disaster have even occurred? Was God far away somewhere in Heaven on His throne watching all this - and just letting it happen? She trusted God's love and will, yet this madness could not connect to love or will. Sarah seemed isolated from her Heavenly Father and anything good or wholesome. For years she had disagreed with people who blamed God for indifference in the face of disaster. Today, in this place, she could not answer those accusations. Pain welled up and her heart questioned.

'Don't You care, Lord? Why would you let Mark die - and all the rest - and just sit there - above it all? Are you mad at us?' Immediately she knew she was wrong, but just didn't have the strength or words to make amends.

"We must keep on, Sarah," Caleb got on his feet and helped her up.

They looked upon one lifeless face after another. Caleb stopped at one and shook his head.

"It's Braci Vasquez, the manager. I can't even imagine what her last thoughts were as the sickening realization hit her that she and all the others were about to die."

Sarah looked on this woman who only the day before was so smug and confident, still in her business suit, one heel missing, hair matted and tangled around her neck and face.

She remembered the soothing words Braci spoke to the people. She believed she had it all together - Ballroom well stocked and safe, casino open for everyone's enjoyment. She was like the people of Noah's time - never believing until the water came to take them away.

Caleb halted at another body. Sarah held her breath as she reached him. She looked upon the cold form of the psychic, Destini Polovi. An expression of horror plastered on her face - burned in by images she may have seen in the last moment of her life!

One of the volunteers saw them standing over the dead psychic's body. He came to them.

"Aren't you the minister who warned at the meeting to go up the mountain?"

"Yes, I'm Caleb Hillag," he replied.

The man fell to his knees before Caleb. "I am afraid! Please save me!" he begged.

Caleb dropped to his knees and put his hands on the man's shoulders looking him in the eyes.

"I can't save you, but Jesus can."

"What must I do?" the man cried out.

"What is your name?"

"Rubin."

"Ask Jesus to forgive your sins, believe He died for you on the cross, and ask Him to come into your heart."

"Oh, I do - I do. Jesus forgive me - I am so much a bad man. I believe - I believe - come in - come in - oh!" Rubin stopped, and a strange peace settled over his face.

"Senor, He did - everything. He saved me- now!" Rubin tapped his chest. "Jesus is here!"

Sarah, who had been standing, praying for Rubin, sat down beside the two men. She touched Rubin's hand. "Welcome to God's family," she spoke softly. "Do you have - a family?"

Rubin's mouth tried to form words, but no words came. Sadness clouded his face as he stood to his feet and motioned for them to follow. Dread came over Sarah as she followed down a row of bodies. The man stopped at a young woman's corpse. She was pregnant.

"Don't she look like an angel? She was faithful to God and tried many times to get me to go to your church. I forbid it! She - begged me - to listen to your warning to go up the mountain. I was a fool! She stayed because of me. Her last words - like she knew the end was - find the minister - find his Jesus - I – I…" Rubin covered his eyes; then he crumpled to the ground next to his wife, patting her face.

Sarah looked at Caleb with deep sorrow. By now there were others holding bodies. Wails of grieving filled the room. Screams and cries could be heard every time a loved one was found. There was no victory here! There was no joy! The scene was beyond human comprehension! Her stomach heaved. She staggered through wreckage to a private place where she threw up. She bawled her heart out to God until her legs gave way, and she fell onto an overturned slot machine.

"I hate this thing!" she pushed it! "I hate this place! It's dark – black - it's full of death!"

By and by, Caleb joined her.

"All the bodies are down from the ballroom, Sarah. I've checked them all. Mark is not here, thank God. I was told they have set up an emergency hospital and shelter at the Sands. Shall we look there before we take to the streets?"

"Yes - yes - we must find him."

They hurried across the cluttered grounds to the resort. Caleb asked directions to the emergency care. Mark was not found there, but someone thought they had seen him. They hurried on to the shelter. They had no sooner stepped into the crowded room than they heard a familiar voice.

"Mom - Pops! Over here!"

# Chapter 39

# Evacuation

There couldn't have been a more welcome sight than to see Mark alive!

"Dear God, thank You!" Caleb whispered a prayer of relief and gratitude.

Sarah ran past him to embrace their son, who jumped up from a mattress. She held Mark tightly, crying, kissing and patting his face. Caleb saw bandaged wounds on his hands and arms.

"Mark, we can't tell you how worried we were about you," Caleb spoke with deep emotion as he pulled them both into his arms. He kissed his son's tears and felt the boy tremble and take a deep breath. Mark pulled away never making eye contact with his parents. He plopped down cross-legged on the mattress next to an attractive young woman.

"Oh, Mark, how did you manage to survive?" Sarah touched his hand.

"I never dreamed the hurricane would hit us that hard. I was scared out of my gourd!" Mark confessed.

"Where were you?" Caleb wanted to know. "We thought you were at the Casino."

"I was - until I met Kim and Terri. We decided to go up to their room at the Sands."

Caleb noticed the young woman cover her face and break down. She also had bandaged face, neck, arms and legs.

"Their room faced the water on the second floor. It was protected by the Casino - so we hung out - it wasn't bad - until..." Mark swallowed hard. He dropped his head, and there was a long pause.

"We never saw it coming - a huge wall of water," the girl spoke up. "I'm Kim - Terri was - was - my best..." She couldn't go on.

Mark picked it up, "The force of the water and wind shattered glass all over us, that's how we got cut up. Water flooded in, and we scrambled for the door - but - oh, God! It was too strong - Terri was - she tried to grab - we reached - it was dark - we couldn't find her in the water!"

"We were almost swept away ourselves!" Kim cried out.

"We struggled into the hall up to our chests in water, and it was rising fast. We felt along in the dark. There were others, and - and - we made it up to the third floor."

Caleb and Sarah sat down on the mattress to console the two shaken and distraught teens.

A side of his son not seen for a long time touched Caleb. Mark caught his father watching him, and anger erased that gentler spirit.

"Isn't this what you want?" Mark turned away. "So you can gloat - that you were right, and I was wrong? Go ahead! Say it! Make yourself feel good!"

"When people have died, it matters little who was right - or who was wrong. What makes me feel good, Mark, is seeing you alive! You too, Kim, but we grieve with you over the loss of your friend. We are so sorry."

"She was trying to help me," Kim broke down again. "It should have been me! Not her!"

"Kim, she was closest to the windows. She didn't stand a chance in hell," Mark put his arm around her - "there's nothing you could have done."

Kim groaned and lay down on the mattress, drawing up into a fetal position.

"Where are their parents?" Sarah asked gently.

"I don't know - from different places, I think," Mark replied. "They go to college in Boulder, Colorado. They came for a vacation and to have fun. This was pure horror!"

"In college? Do they know you are only sixteen?"

Mark gave Caleb a flash of eyes that could kill. He turned his head and refused to look at his dad or even acknowledge him. Caleb immediately recognized his blunder.

"Mark, I'm sorry! That was completely unnecessary."

"Just typical of you, Pops."

"Stop it, you two!" Sarah ordered. "Mark, has Kim called her parents?"

"Mine was dead, but we lost all our phones in the storm."

"Mine still has some charge," Sarah handed her phone to Mark to give to Kim.

"Oh, thank you," Kim murmured, as she got up and took the phone. She walked to another part of the room. Soon, Caleb could see her crying and talking. Later, she leaned against a wall, sliding down to sit against it. She returned when she finished.

"Did you get them?" Sarah asked.

"Yes, they want to know how I am getting home - I don't know how I am getting - home!" Kim covered her face with her hands again. "I called -and told - Terri's mom," she groaned. "I just want to die!" She lay back down and turned over.

A staff worker touched Caleb from behind.

"You must get any belongings and go to the roof. The government is sending helicopters to evacuate everyone to Mexico City."

"What if we choose to stay?" Caleb asked.

"No, senor. There is no medication left, no food and water. There is no electric, and soon there will be sickness. No one can stay! It is not safe!"

"When do you think we can return?" Sarah asked.

The woman shrugged her shoulders.

Caleb and Sarah took off to their house to see what could be salvaged. They stopped by what was left of the church. Sarah refused to go in. Caleb retrieved his phone charger from his desk and looked through drawers.

"Someone removed the body," he informed Sarah when he joined her. They took one last look at what once was Global Missions Christian Church. They had experienced so many traumas in the last 24 hours; Caleb couldn't feel anything anymore. His emotions were equally dead as the bodies he had looked upon. He felt that every message preached, lesson taught, decision made, times remembered, songs sung, prayers given, meals eaten, fights fought were cast into a vast ugly black cave. They were gone, leaving an indefinable sadness and loss. What if feelings of tenderness and love were also lost forever, leaving only resentment, bitterness and anger? The good must come back, or he would live as an empty shell. Caleb shook his head.

On the way to their house, they came upon Sarah's car turned on its side and partially buried in mud.

"This is unreal," Sarah muttered as Caleb tried to open a door. Suddenly, he felt totally helpless. This man who always had words to speak, a ready plan of action - was beaten –broken– spent. They walked on in silence. Hope for anything left of their home now dissolved into despair. Sarah put her arm in his and lay her head against his shoulder as they walked. They passed others picking through remains.

The whole city was gray falling rain, surreal, like a scene from the living dead!

Their home was a pile of boards and trash. Much of it wasn't even theirs. Some clothes and belongings were tangled in the clutter. They stood in disbelief.. Sarah got angry as she began digging in the rubble.

"This was our home, Caleb, for over eight years of our lives. We made memories here. It was - our home. Look at this, Caleb! How can something so warm and precious that took so long to build, be reduced to - to - this - in one day! We've lost - everything! Caleb - where is our God?" Sarah sat down, crying. "I - I - just don't feel - very - loved - right now."

Caleb climbed over the rubble to get to her - to hold her in his arms. Words wouldn't fit anywhere. He only knew that they had each other, and Mark was alive. Maybe that was enough - all that really mattered. Reaching deep into his battered faith, he stubbornly held on to the belief that God loved them and had not forsaken them in this horrible storm. He had spared the members of the church. Possessions were gone - yes - but love and its memories remained in the face of loss.

"Sarah, love, trust and the memories can never be taken from us."

"I don't care so much about the house, Caleb," Sarah commented softly, "but we've lost pictures, photos, DVD's of our family - things we can't replace."

"We have them in our heads."

"Kind of hard to show those to anyone," she murmured, and resumed moving boards, digging, looking.

Caleb searched the surrounding area to see if he could locate any of their stuff. He found a dresser - broken - remaining clothes wet and mud stained. He kept searching to no avail.

"Lord, our things could be scattered all over this mountainside," Caleb prayed aloud.

"Caleb, look! It's a miracle!"

Caleb turned to see Sarah holding up a frame, which he recognized as a picture taken of him and Sarah soon after they met. She began laughing. It had graced their home since they were married, and unmistakably Sarah's favorite. God, to show His special love for her, had preserved it through the storm.

Two days later - in the dark of the night - Caleb, Sarah, their son Mark, along with the last of the Chantal survivors, boarded a chopper. Weary, thirsty, hungry, dirty, Sarah clutching her picture, they were evacuated from the Place of Paradise - Lugar de Paraiso - to Mexico City.

# Chapter 40

# Chantal Shelter

The hurricane refugees were taken by bus from the heliport to a cafeteria on school grounds where they were given food and drink. When they finished eating they were issued a change of clothes, towels, toiletry items, blankets and a pillow each. They were escorted past several buildings on campus to a gym, which had been set up for a shelter to house the Chantal victims.

Cots covered the gym floor that was filled to capacity. The building was hot, stuffy and smelled of sweat. The lights were dim as many were sleeping - others were engaged in conversation, playing cards, passing time. The shelter worker led the group to some empty cots in the middle. Caleb felt they were on display.

"Restrooms are in the side hallways," she instructed in Spanish. "Bathing showers are in locker rooms."

"How can we locate others?" Caleb asked.

"There is bulletins in eating place - or you can just look."

"Can you tell me how many are - in here - and how many casualties?"

The woman eyed Caleb a moment as if deciding whether she would share that information.

"Senor, you are very lucky. Four hundred seventy three persons inside here."

"God spared us! How many are dead? Caleb asked again.

The woman's eyes teared up. "Three thousand thirty-nine," her voice broke, "they have found. There are still more."

"Oh, dear God!" Sarah was aghast.

"So sorry," the woman turned her head and walked away.

"I'm going to find Kim," Mark announced as he strode off down an aisle between rows of cots.

"Try and locate our church," Caleb called after him, but Mark gave no visible response.

"You want to get a shower, sweetheart?" Caleb asked Sarah. She shook her head no.

"Maybe later. Right now I feel exhausted.

Caleb located a place to charge his phone, and a luke-warm shower felt heavenly in the unbearable heat of the gym. He prayed and sang praises to God while the water poured over his head and body. He attempted to course out in his mind what he must do first thing in the morning.

Returning to Sarah, he found her talking to a young woman with two small children.

"Caleb, meet Arcy Garza, her little boy Hernando and baby girl. She just found Jesus as her Savior."

"Praise the Lord!" Caleb exclaimed with surprised gladness.

Caleb looked into the face of a young mother who was tired, sad and lonely - but he could also see a glimmer of hope there.

"She saw us and remembered you on the table giving a warning at the school meeting. She came to me, Caleb, and I was able to help her receive Christ," Sarah recounted.

"I told my husband you are a man of God, and I believed you," she spoke to Caleb. "We should go up the mountain to Vera Cielo. He got outrageous and threatened to beat me - if I did. I was frightened, but took my children and went to my cousin's house in Vera Cielo. My husband went to the Casino. Now he is dead, and I am alone. I don't know what to do or where I should go. I believe on Jesus – will He protect me?"

"Yes, He will - our hearts ache for you over the loss of your beloved husband," Caleb replied. "May Sarah and I pray for you?"

"Si, Senor," she put her cheek against the baby's face as she slept so peacefully. Her son was playing nearby.

As Caleb prayed, he was aware that someone had come up to them. Closing the prayer, he opened his eyes to see Mark with Kim. Mark had a look of disgust on his face.

"See, what did I tell you, Kim. My Pops is always trying to push his religion on someone - anyone who will listen, even at a time like this!"

Kim frowned at him with a questioning look.

"For God's sake Mark, this woman lost her husband. What's wrong with you?"

Mark turned his attention to Arcy. "I hope you didn't listen to him. He needs people to follow his nowhere path."

"That's enough, Mark," Caleb flashed in anger, "Knock it off!"

"What, Pops? Afraid I'll embarrass you?"

"Mark, that wasn't necessary," Kim protested.

"It is okay," Arcy interrupted sadly. "Your son is like my husband - big man talk in a little boy. Not a bad boy - just foolish - and stubborn - still a child."

She gathered her son and with her baby retreated to their cots. Sarah aided her.

Caleb could see Mark puff up and his face turn crimson; his son did not know how to respond to Arcy's verbal cuts, because she spoke a truth Mark did not want to face.

"Smart ass woman," Mark managed to mutter. "Come on, Kim." and the two located empty cots nearby. They sat and began talking.

Sarah returned to her place by Caleb. She reached out and touched him. Her eyes conveyed the words, 'It's alright - I love you and believe in you.' Caleb kissed her.

"I'm going to clean up. Pray I don't fall asleep in the shower."

She turned back to smile at Caleb, and their hearts met in a deepening love that had just weathered a horrific storm.

He knew for certain the Lord had not abandoned them to Chantal, but carried them through.

"I'm glad we're together and safe," he called after her.

# Chapter 41

# Getting Direction

Caleb was up early. He couldn't sleep with an over-whelming sense of responsibility on one hand for his family - for the church members on the other. He knew the church would find places to stay and work, but he wasn't sure how much Sarah could handle. Mark already made his intentions clear. He was ready to return to the states. As Caleb sat on the cot watching his wife sleep, he made up his mind to throw in the towel. He would call Atlanta and request plane tickets - home.

Yet he struggled with that decision. It seemed the Lord showed him sheep scattered without a shepherd.

"Let the Good Shepherd lead them! He can do it far better than I," Caleb argued in defeat.

Unrest drove Caleb to the restroom. When he was washing his face, he felt a hand on his shoulder. He looked up - surprised to see Sierra.

"Sierra! Thank God you are safe. Where - I mean how did you - get through?"

"I rode out the storm Preacher, you must stay here. The Lord is not finished with you yet."

"Sierra, I don't know - my family has been through so…"

At that time several men came to the washbasins. When Caleb looked again - Sierra was gone. He searched back in the gym, but this strange man was nowhere in sight. Caleb began looking down row after row of refugees to try and find his church. As he made his way past one person after another - Fina and Carmen wrapped their arms around his leg and waist from behind. They were laughing and giggling, holding on tight.

"Where is your mother?" he asked the girls.

"Over there," Carmen pointed.

He saw Espolito, and then he spotted Chris nearby waving. They all scrambled to hug him and tell him how glad they were to see him - and how was Sarah - Mark?

"Kay and I kept everybody together," Chris announced proudly. "We are all here - except Sierra and - uh…"

"Sarah is ok but worn out, Mark is with us. I just saw Sierra in the restroom, but I don't know where he disappeared to."

"What do we do now, Pastor?" Maybeline needed assurance she would be taken care of.

Some sat down, others stood, but all eyes were on him as they looked for leadership. Caleb searched each of their faces, years of memories filled his thoughts - years they labored together on this mission field. They were more than friends - they were family - how his heart swelled full of love for them. How could he leave them to fend for themselves? He began to cry!

"We love you, Pastor Senor," Blanca spoke timidly. "Please do not cry-or we will cry with you."

Caleb covered his face. They gathered around him.

"God spoke through you to save our lives," Hank patted Caleb's back.

"Si, if I had worked at the Casino, I would be body bag today," Bomba added.

"We all saw the destruction of the city," Caleb heard Kay. "We would all be - gone!"

"Thank you, Pastor," Tulipan took his hand.

"I don't know what to tell you, I don't," Caleb sniffed, "but I know we can't leave you! God will show us a way through."

Caleb returned to wake Sarah. He gently touched her.

"Sarah," he blurted out, "I don't know what you thought we might do - maybe go back to the states - but we can't leave our people - we just can't - they are - our family – it would be heartless to abandon them!"

Sarah blinked her eyes trying to wake up and to understand what Caleb was saying to her. After a moment of thought, she smiled sweetly, and wrapped her arms around his neck.

"I know," she whispered, as she tenderly kissed him. "I sure love you, honey!"

A few minutes later Caleb made the call to Global Missions.

"Rona, patch me to one of the board members. This is Caleb Hillag calling from Mexico City."

A moment later Tiffany Gong was connected.

"Caleb, I can't tell you how glad I am to hear you. We have been out of our minds waiting for a word!"

"Our sat-phones were down, and there was no power to charge them."

"I can't even imagine how awful conditions have been for you. Reports are coming in, and the death toll is staggering and still rising!"

"I can tell you, Tiffany, we went through a holacaust. We were evacuated to Mexico City, and we are in a shelter the government has provided. I need a decision from you."

There was a pause before Tiffany spoke. Caleb glanced over to see Mark and Kim asleep on separate cots.

"Do you want flights to Atlanta, Caleb? Do you need money?"

"Tiffany, by the grace of God all the church was spared, but we are displaced. It will be some time before we can return to Lugar de Paraiso - perhaps never - but I believe there is a work we can do here. I need funding in the bank here for housing and food - other needs until they find jobs. What kind of Christians would we be if we just drop these people?"

"I agree," she replied. "I'm here alone, but Gerald should be arriving in a few minutes. Oh, my, how I miss Hub's wisdom in these times."

"Me too," Caleb sighed, remembering a dear friend now gone.

"Let us call you back."

"What did they say," Sarah was anxious to know.

"They are deciding. Sarah, see that area under the basketball hoop? Our people are there. Why don't you gather them to the cafeteria for breakfast, and we'll have a meeting."

No sooner had Sarah taken off than the ring tone for Global Missions went off. It was Gerald Pullman.

"Brother, we have been sick with worry over your welfare. Tiffany relayed everything! Of course, Caleb, anything you need. We will do a wire transfer into your account within the hour. We are relieved you are staying with your people. Keep us paged up with you, and God bless! We are praying for you!"

After Caleb hung up, he went to a frightened Arcy Garza.

"Arcy, you are part of my church family and a sister in the Lord. Bring your children, and come with me."

Caleb introduced Arcy to the church members, and they immediately, lovingly took her in. Then he went searching for Rubin. "Come, join my family," he invited and led him to the cafeteria where Global Missions Christian Church was gathered.

After a hymn of praise and prayer of thanksgiving for their safety and breakfast, Caleb stood and announced, "Loved ones, we have direction from the Lord! I have exciting news!"

# Chapter 42

# A Moment in Time

L ate morning Caleb gave the assignment to locate a place where they could transfer. Everyone eagerly jumped in. Caleb sat down with Mark and Kim.

"You will be leaving soon?" he inquired of Kim.

"Yes, sir, a bus is taking us to the airport. Thank you for being here for me. Your son is - pretty special."

"Yes, we think so," Caleb could tell Mark was having a hard time saying goodbye.

"Mark, you know that Mom and I are staying here in Mexico City. I won't try to persuade you, but simply ask what you want to do. You are welcome to stay with us, or I can get you a flight - any - where." Caleb choked on his words – fearful of Mark's response.

"I've got to go," Kim stood up.

"Pops, I've thought about it. I kinda like it here, so think I'll just hang out awhile and check out the hot spots and chicks in ol' Mexico City."

"Well, be a party animal," Kim remarked coolly. "Ill be checkin' out the – MEN - in Colorado!"

As the two walked away to the outside exit, it sounded like their conversation was degenerating into an argument.

Caleb rose to find Sarah when he spied Cory approaching him. Cory waved.

"I'm glad I found you before I leave, Pastor." He offered a firm handshake, which went into a hug.

"Glad you're going home, Cory. This has been one heck of an adventure."

"I wanted to thank you for saving my life. What happened to those who thought they could ride out Chantal in the ballroom, I saw myself a hundred times in each dead body. The hours of the storm and - after - every detail - are etched in my mind. I owe you, Bro."

"Sierra sent you along," Caleb added.

"When you see him, give my thanks. I heard from Chris you're staying on here."

"Yes, I can't leave these people - yet, Cory. I feel I'm on a slippery slide going backwards. Everything is gone... I think I'm getting too tired to keep starting over."

Cory studied Caleb a moment before he commented. His demeanor and voice took on a deeper kindness that Caleb could feel.

"With some folks, it seems they were born for a special moment in time. It's like their whole life is moving towards one great incredible event - or maybe its significance isn't noticed right then because it passes quietly - only to become history, known to millions later.

"Remember the man born blind from birth whom Jesus healed. His disciples asked who had sinned - the man or his parents."

"I remember," Caleb replied thoughtfully. "Sin had nothing to do with it. It was for that moment he was born blind. That moment Jesus healed him and was glorified."

"Exactly, and remember Abraham Lincoln failed at every attempt until he was elected President, but he wasn't born for the failures; his moment came when he became America's greatest President!"

"Maybe some of us were never born to do great things."

"Everything any of us do has importance. If you weren't there - I would be dead."

"God would have warned you another way. Like I said, Sierra did it."

Now Cory took on a different seriousness both men knew the Holy Spirit was applying to their hearts.

"Caleb," Cory's voice grew husky. "I sense you have encountered a lot of disappointing setbacks in your life, but you were born for greatness - and it is coming - just like the man born blind - Jesus Christ will be glorified in you. It will be your one big Hooraw!"

Both laughed, and Caleb gave Cory a hug.

"Just the same, Pastor, I owe you. Here is my card. Call anytime if I can help you. I'll never forget you and what we went through here."

"Nor will I. God bless, Cory!"

Caleb felt sadness as he watched the young man who had touched all their lives in such a short time pass out of sight. He looked at the card. It read:

Jennifer Skye and Raintree Forest

Keyboard - Cory Atkins

"Hummm," thought Caleb. He took his phone and called Esther. She answered, "Wow, Daddy, two calls in one hour. What's up?"

"Esther, have you ever heard of Jennifer Skye and Raintree Forest?"

"Have I heard of them? They are only the hottest Christian group going! Why?"

"Well, we had this fellow, Cory Atkins..."

"You had Cory Atkins?" Esther screamed. "Dad, girls all over the world would die to see him. I wish I could have been there!"

"No, you don't, believe me. Anyway, he's coming back to the states in a few hours. Just wondering, was all. Love you!"

Caleb ended the call deep in thought, 'What's this all-mean, Lord? Has this been my moment in time?"

# Chapter 43

# Major Project

The members of Global Missions Christian Church faced impossible odds. Lost in a mass of strangers, they were homeless, without jobs and income, a band of refugees looking for a place they could settle into.

Each member had limited funds in bank accounts, which Caleb knew would soon be depleted. Only Hank's retirement money and wire transfers from Global Missions would replenish their resources - at least until work could be found.

Like going to a restaurant, those who need a table for two are seated long before a group of 15 adults and 4 children. So the pressure to separate was tremendous, bringing emotions to a raw edge. It was all Caleb and Sarah could do to keep peace and hold the line.

With each rejected proposal government officials at the shelter began to display more displeasure and some hostility. They simply could not understand the group's need to stay together! By the fourth day, one of the volunteers exploded in exasperation.

"We could have had you out of here two days ago if you would just listen and go as families!"

"We are family!" Caleb retorted.

By now, Hank and Tulipan had purchased an older solar car and were out searching for a suitable place. On the fifth day, Caleb ran into a man with a hydrogen van for sale. He promptly bought it so the group would have transportation.

Morning of the seventh day, Sarah shook Caleb on his cot. He was sleeping as one dead.

"Caleb, honey, it's nine-thirty."

"Whaa?" Caleb sat up rubbing his eyes. His wife slid her arm around him with a 'good morning' kiss. Her face carried a tone of concern.

"You were sleeping so sound - I didn't want -."

"No, no, that's fine, Sarah. I prayed so much in the night I was beat. Ummmph."

He rubbed his face, looking around. The gym was vacated except for a handful of cots. Theirs!

"Caleb, what shall we do? Everyone is gone except for our people. I think the workers are angry and ready for us to get out of here. They were rude serving us breakfast!"

"Our church family?" Caleb asked, scanning the gym floor.

"Hank and Tulipan left before I woke up. Mark took the van when he got up - said he would be back soon. Chris and Kay went for a walk, and I think Tazada is finding - well, you know. Some worker started dogging Bomba, but I ran him off. The rest are on their cots or in the cafeteria."

"While I shower, gather everyone. We need to have a meeting."

The group was waiting for Caleb when he emerged from the restroom. Plomo came into the gym right on Caleb's heels, with Chris and Kay. A few minutes later came Rubin dragging Tazada from his booze quest.

"Hank, Tulipan, Mark, and Sierra are the only ones missing," Caleb observed.

"They're out turning over stones, Preacher," Chris smiled. Caleb nodded acknowledgement. No one had seen Sierra.

They opened in prayer seeking the Lord's divine leading. "I don't know where You want us, Lord." Caleb prayed. "We feel lost and helpless. We know we can't stay here, so we must move, or let them separate us. Please show us the way - open a door, Lord," Caleb concluded.

"I'm alright with separation," Maybeline offered after they had prayed.

"I am an afraid widow," Arcy voiced her fear. "I have no one with my babies."

"I could do it - yet I also am fearful," Espolito expressed her own feelings. "Mexico City is - so big!"

"Can't we just all go to a hotel?" Blanca suggested quietly.

"We could do that," Caleb said thoughtfully. "It would be more expensive - perhaps for a few days to gain some time."

"Yeah!" many agreed.

"We have worn our welcome thin here," Kay remarked matter – of - factly. "Breakfast was - cold - and they have stopped cleaning the restrooms."

"Appears we are agreed. As soon as Mark returns, we'll transport to a hotel."

"Senor Pastor, I will now go on internet to search," Rubin volunteered.

"Find a clean one," Sarah called out, laughing.

"We can all look - save time," Chris directed.

Mark strolled in by noon.

"What's the data, cyber dorks?"

"We are trying to locate a reasonable hotel," Sarah explained.

"Hell, I saw one less than 2 miles from here."

Caleb gave a look to convey the order, 'Cut the language!' Mark ignored him.

"Mark, we can't afford a resort," Sarah knew Mark's tastes.

"Damn, Mother, I'm not dumb. Come on - let's check it out." Mark led her out the door. They were back in forty minutes.

"It's nice, Caleb," Sarah was excited over what they had found. "The rooms are comfortable and clean, they offered a lower rate to help us."

"Yeah, Mom played the sympathy gig. Give her an Oscar!"

"Oh, stop it, Mark, I just told them what happened to us in the hurricane. They were very kind."

"How much?" Caleb asked.

"Fifty-five U. S. dollars," Mark answered proudly.

"Ohla" Rubin whistled. "I discovered one cheaper. Sadly, it is on other side of Mexico City, and one must share the banjo. Is it so with this one?"

"No, each room has its own bathroom."

"Hallelujah!" shouted Maybeline, and everyone laughed.

"Anyone find a better deal?" Caleb asked. They shook their heads.

"Best I found was 60 – the rooms weren't too bad," Chris replied. "I say we take the one Mark found."

"Good! Mark, I'm putting you in charge of transporting the church over to - our temporary home," Caleb smiled, relieved.

Mark carried an air of triumph, and for once didn't challenge his father's leadership.

While Mark was driving the first vanload to the hotel, Caleb called Hank.

"Hank, where are you?"

"We are on the south side of the city. We have looked at so many dang places, our eyes have criss crossed!"

"We found a hotel not far from here. It is called El Diablo. I don't have an address, but you can track it. We'll get you and Tulipan a room. It has - a hot bath!"

Caleb could hear Tulipan squeal with delight. Hank laughed.

"We have one last place to check on, then we'll head in. Probably be late though. This traffic is crazy!"

Next Caleb reported to Global Missions. He heard Marcus Willabee's voice.

"How is your condition?" he asked.

"We have to leave the shelter, Marcus. We were the last of the hurricane survivors. We've encountered trouble finding a place because we didn't want to separate."

"Was that wise?"

"I think so. Most of the women were scared of being alone or with strangers. There definitely are places here you don't want to be!"

"Hmmm, I hear what you are saying."

"We are in a hotel at 55 dollars a room. We will keep looking."

"The expense is not a problem. Donations have been pouring in for you folks. We trust you to make reasonable use of your resources."

"Any word, Marcus, on the conditions at Lugar de Paraiso?"

"Not good! From what news is filtering in, the city is abandoned. The storm surge destroyed the airport and runway. It will take months to rebuild that alone. We saw shots from a fly-over. There is no city – it's tragic - thinking on what it was when we came down there."

"Any idea when we can go back?"

"I would say at least a year. We heard they are airlifting supplies into Vera Cielo."

"Thank God! Father Junto Angeles and his villagers are still there."

"Caleb, we heard a report there are still 380 bodies unidentified?"

"Yes. Some of us took shifts ministering to those - viewing - bodies!" Caleb paused. "Marcus, such pain and misery - very hard to take, and the visual - with the smell - is gruesome!"

"Lord, I can't imagine! Our prayers and thoughts are with you all. God bless!" Marcus closed off the call.

Next morning everyone gathered for breakfast at a small restaurant across the street from El Diablo. Hank and Tulipan appeared excited when they joined the group.

"We may have found our nest!" Tulipan announced.

"Go figure, its on Mission Street. Guess we should have checked there first," Hank laughed.

"Of course! We should be on Mission Street," Bomba clapped her hands ecstatically. "What is it?"

"Not much to look at, but lots of personality and potential," Hank explained.

After breakfast Blanca, Maybeline and Tazada rode with Hank and Tulipan while the others piled in the van. Hank led them to the far southern end of Mexico City to Mission Street. They drove out of the industrial area until the street was lined with shanties filled with women and children. Hank pulled into a wall-lined, large sprawling building and stopped. Everyone got out.

"This was built in the 30's for the rich and famous. Couldn't compete later with fancy resorts so it finally closed. Slums grew up around it. This has been empty for years. Tulipan negotiated for us - we can get it for a song," Hank explained.

"That is so - last century," Mark muttered.

They came upon an ancient faded sign near the entrance.

"Casa de Amor," Sarah read out loud. She gasped!

"House of Love! What kind of place is this?" Caleb was horrified.

"Don't ask," Hank smiled.

"It will be our place of love," Bomba giggled.

"Not like that!" Sarah corrected.

"It's not anything - right now - but an empty shell. Come inside - and see," Hank unlocked a heavy, ornate door that hinted of a once prestigious face.

Empty it was, a gutted building. Nothing remained but floor, walls and roof. Some doors were missing; broken windows defied any sense of warmth, the emptiness projected a repelling cold that argued a hasty retreat back to the comfort of their hotel. The muted band did a quiet walk through.

"I - I - don't know. This would take so much effort and money…" Caleb was not sure.

"Look beyond what you see, Pastor, to what it can be," Hank took Caleb's arm to show him. Look at all the rooms - the bathrooms - enough for all of us and then some. Sure the bathrooms are shared, but they are plentiful. Come in here. Dream big! This large room was for dining and opens onto an enclosed patio and Ball Room. We can grow plants on the patio - and the Ball Room will be our church. Did you see all those families outside? They need Jesus, Pastor, and we would be smack dab in the middle of them."

Caleb caught Hank's vision. He looked at Sarah who had come to him. She nodded. The rest stood in silent awe at the possibilities and incredible challenge God was presenting them, calling on them to attempt the impossible!

"What do you think, Chris?" Caleb trusted this man's judgment.

Chris took a harder look around before he gave his opinion. He rubbed his chin as he calculated. Then he started shaking his head up and down as he too opened his heart to what could be.

"We can fix this. It will be a major project, but we can make it work. Yes, we can do this, Preacher, together with God's help and good graces," Chris exclaimed, still shaking his head now with a growing fire inside of him. "We can do this!"

# Chapter 44

# Window of Opportunity

"When we fell in love and married, Caleb, did you ever think by July, 2026, we would be living and holding church services inside a resort of prostitution?" Sarah smiled impishly.

Sarah's question was so off the wall Caleb had to laugh. "I wouldn't go so far as to label it the 'best little ol' whorehouse in Mexico!"

"Just a high class one - in those days," Sarah snuggled against Caleb in bed. "Who knows what went on in this room."

"We don't even want to think...." Caleb's words were cut short by Sarah's kiss. He realized with surprised curiosity and excitement Sarah's playfulness was turning to passion.

Caleb awoke in the dark of night with a deep sense of satisfaction - yet, the voice of the Lord speaking to him was unsettling. He looked around the room, lit only by a flickering candle on their dresser.

This was their first night in Casa de Amor, a place of their own again, and it felt good! The bed's warmth and comfort,

Sarah sleeping against his arm, made the catastrophe of hurricane Chantal a distant part of his memory.

Two weeks of hard work by the church and other helpers converted Casa de Amor into Global Missions Christian Family Center. Remodeling had progressed far enough to allow all of them to move from El Diablo. They would miss the private baths with each room, but certainly not the expense.

Caleb reviewed events in his mind as he prayed. He was grateful to Global Missions pouring funding into this project. Without Missions' support there would have been no El Diablo or Casa de Amor. No utilities turned on and working, no fresh paint, no furnishings. The Casa would still remain a gutted shell. Instead, it was bursting alive with vibrant people. It stood a House of God where worship services would be held and the Word taught. Shanty slum folk poured into the church tripling attendance – even before renovation on the Ball Room was completed.

During those rushed two weeks, Caleb sent Mark to locate a second van for purchase and placed him in charge of driving members or running errands. The lad fit comfortably into this newly assigned responsibility. He made it quite clear, however, his church duties did not obligate him to attend services, but Caleb was confident his son would warm up to the exciting energy force driving the other members!

So with such a sweet and peaceful feeling of security and successful accomplishment, why did an old faded poster he saw two days before, in one of the slum members shack keep haunting his thoughts? Why? He tried to shake it, but it held on like a bulldog with iron jaws clamped around his mind.

The poster was of the rock group, 'Tribal Ecstasy's spring concert in the new futball stadium.

"Okay, Lord, what's going on here?" Caleb prayed softly not to awaken Sarah.

It was known the concert was a disaster. True, they filled the 127,000-seat stadium, but toward the end it developed into a disgusting orgy of drunken nudity and drug-induced sex. The Policia lost control of the rioting mob. There were reported injuries, rapes, and even deaths. Caleb couldn't understand why this terrible event should be so strong on his mind - until... Until...

Wait a minute...words shared by Cory Atkins superimposed into his searching thoughts!

'You were born for one incredible moment in time - and its coming. Just like the man born blind - Jesus Christ will be glorified in you. Your one big Hooraw!'

Caleb was so excited over the vision the Lord flashed before him; he couldn't sleep the rest of the night. He was up long before Sarah and on the phone. He must have displayed a smug look the way Sarah eyed him suspiciously upon joining him in the center's makeshift dining room.

"Alright, honey, you're up to something. I think you ate desert before breakfast."

"Ha – that I have, Sarah. You'll never believe what has happened."

"Tell me!" She was eager.

"I've been awake part of the night. All I could think about was the concert Tribal Ecstasy gave earlier this year. I couldn't understand why that dominated my thoughts - then it came to me! Why not do a Christian concert?"

Blanca came with a cup of coffee for Sarah and filled Caleb's cup.

"Thank you," Sarah murmured, caught up in what Caleb was recounting.

"Listen to this, Sarah. I called Cory Atkins, and asked if Raintree Forest could fly down here and do a concert in the futball stadium this fall. He told me he would have to check with Jennifer Skye, but was excited."

Caleb took a long sip of coffee.

"Well, has he - called back?"

"He did, and they can come Friday September 11th."

"Oh, praise the Lord!" Sarah squealed, clapping her hands. Then she grew serious.

"Can we get the stadium? Is there enough time? July is almost gone!" her face displayed a tinge of worry.

"Well, that's the hard part. The Presidente has to give permission, but the Lord opened a window to see him and his wife in two days. We are given 30 minutes between his military advisor and the Ambassador of Norway."

# Chapter 45

# El Presidente

Caleb and Sarah were treated with polite coolness at the Presidential Palace where they were escorted to a waiting room. The parts of the palace they walked through were ornate and elaborate. This waiting room was plush, but Caleb suspected it was not the nicest one. This room was available for the lesser visitors.

Caleb was in a sharp summer suit, and Sarah in her dress and heels was stunning. They both sported new outfits, still Caleb had the uneasiness they were underdressed for this meeting. He really was not sure what would be appropriate to see the Presidente of Mexico City, and truly did not know what to expect, even though he had rehearsed this meeting in his mind the better parts of two days.

Both of them were nervous when a female aide came into the room and motioned to follow her. They walked a long hallway before entering into a large room, which resembled a massive study. The woman introduced them, and the Presidente and his wife greeted them warmly.

"I am Presidente Fernando Villanueva and my wife Armelita. We have heard of you, Senor and Senora Hillag, and have been most anxious to meet you."

"You have?"

"Si, have a seat, be comfortable, and tell us about the figure of light who told you to go up the mountain."

"I - uh - that may have been a dream - I wasn't sure -" Caleb stammered.

"Still, it proved vital. You are no doubt a hero to Father Angeles and the people of Vera Cielo."

"You know Father Angeles?"

"Quite well," both Fernando and Armelita waited to hear of the messenger of light.

"This bright light filled our bedroom. It looked like a man, and he told us to go up the mountain. It seemed so very real."

"You saved the people of your parish," Senora Villanueva injected into the conversation.

"Oh, yes," Sarah replied, "but it was grievous that more didn't heed our warning."

"Ah, alas, such a tragedy - but you are here safe. Tell us now the purpose of our meeting," Presidente Fernando was more abrupt.

"We have come to ask your permission to use the futball stadium for a concert and evangelistic service. If we are able to schedule Friday, September the 11th that would be best – or the following Saturday the 12th would also work, then we can obtain Jennifer Skye and Raintree Forest to do the concert - and, I would give the message. Raintree Forest's music is heard worldwide."

Villanueva's eyes narrowed, and his face hardened.

"Why you do this? For money? To bring enlightenment? Or to entertain?"

"No, because the Bible tells us to spread God's message of Good News. This is a way to do that."

"The Bible is an ancient book of stories written by different men. Why should I believe it?"

Caleb thought for a moment, choosing his words carefully, asking the Holy Spirit how to answer, and for wisdom.

"Mr. Presidente, have you ever been to the South Pole?"

"No."

"How do you know it even exists?"

"By those who have traveled there and told of it."

"How do you know they just didn't make it up? Like some who said the first man on the moon was staged."

"We believe those who were there and documented their findings."

"That's absolutely right. Men in the Bible were there and wrote about what they saw and heard as the Holy Spirit inspired them. Senor Presidente, sometimes we just have to have faith to believe. That's the only way to approach Jesus Christ. You accept there is a South Pole because you believe someone who was there. I believe the Bible for the same reason."

The Presidente appeared annoyed that he had gotten pinned in a corner. Checkmate!

"I was most outraged by Tribal Ecstasy. They caused me grave trouble with the Prime Minister. I won't tolerate what took place at that concert to duplicate again in Mexico City."

"We won't have those problems; our people will keep order."

"Yes, they will. You are aware of the International Hate Crimes Directive? You cannot speak of any other religion nor can it be in your literature. There can be nothing derogatory spoken about one's sexual orientation. You cannot speak or read from Romans the first chapter, or recite the Ten Commandments. You are permitted to discuss Heaven and love, but not hell or sin. No teaching or singing of creation."

"I'm aware of man's law," Caleb answered.

"That is our law!" Fernando thundered. "No discussions or condemnation to any who choose abortion, and remember, no visible crosses or religious symbols. You are also forbidden to force your beliefs on anyone for conversion!" Villanueva raised his voice.

"We will have an invitation at the close. They respond of their own free will," Caleb stood his ground.

"No! No invitation!"

"Why not?" No one is coerced into coming to Christ."

"I'll not have the crowd moving about."

"I see no problem -."

El Presidente snapped his finger for silence! "Are you afraid of me, Senor Hillag?"

"No," Caleb hesitated, not sure where Fernando was going. He could see Sarah out of the corner of his eye and knew she was nervous.

"Well, you should be, Senor Hillag. Don't you understand, with a snap of my fingers – like this - I can have you thrown in prison - perhaps the rest of your lives - you and your attractive wife - or just you!" He snapped his fingers again to dramatize the point he made.

"I do not doubt you can do what you say, Senor Presidente, but you can do only what God allows you - same as me. I am not afraid of you, but I do respect your position of authority. I will make sure you and your family are seated in a high place of honor."

Presidente Villanueva took up a pc cell and scrolled something in. He studied the response a brief minute before he rose.

"Saturday is a soccer tournament: however you are lucky Senor Hillag as that Friday is dark. Whether or no there is such a concert will be up to you. The cost is 80,000 U. S. dollars, and it must be in U. S. currency, wired into my account before the event. Then there are important details to work out. I must warn you, Senor and Senora Hillag, if there is even a whisper – a tiny whisper - of civil disorder, I hold you personally responsible. I will order my guards to hunt you down, and you will rot in my prison until you forget what the day looks like. You will wish you had never lived!"

He pushed a button on the desk, and the woman who escorted them in reappeared.

"Give them instructions and contact information for scheduling an event at the stadium for September the 11th," he instructed the woman.

"By the way," Fernando stopped them as they were going out the door. "A spirit guide from the glorious age of enlightenment paid you a visit. If you did not recognize him, then you are as dense of spirit and dull of mind, as Father Angeles."

"The spirit guide came to visit physic Destini Polovi whose dead body lay on the cold floor of the Casino. An angel from God's host of Heaven came to warn me with a saving message," Caleb responded, confident in his faith and position in Christ.

"If you truly believe that, Senor Hillag, then you indeed are a fool!"

## Chapter 46

# Concert Crusade

Today was the day! Every part of their future would be determined by the unfolding of events over the next 15 hours. This marked the culmination of weeks of long, accelerated preparations. During those weeks Caleb had hurriedly challenged and organized the churches in Mexico City and surrounding areas to get behind this Concert Crusade. The response was encouraging and quickly developed into a strong growing ground swell. Now the extent of their efforts would be revealed!

The churches trained and provided workers for parking, greeting, collecting an offering, and counseling for those who wanted to receive Christ. Caleb applied concepts learned from crusades at the turn of the century, but would they still work? Caleb and Sarah were confident old ways still rang true, and the results were left in God's Hands.

Approaching this event many churches joined in a prayer vigil across the vast city. Several more weeks would have been most helpful for better preparation. Putting together an event of this magnitude in little more than one month proved exhausting and extremely stressful. Alas, time ran out, and the event must take place – ready or not, the day was here – Friday 11, 2026!

Caleb was on edge! He fought off a dull sick feeling in the pit of his stomach every time he allowed his mind to dwell on possible outcomes of the crusade, 'What if only a few thousand people come - or worse - a few hundred? I, undoubtedly, will be the laughing stock of the world. What if the power dies? What if the offering falls far short of expenses - churches and Global Missions have already invested far too much! What about the message - what if it sounds dumb and uninteresting, and the crowd leave disappointed – or worse yet – bored? That would be a humiliating disaster. Wait! This isn't about me! I can't control – the outcome! God, only you - can make this work! Oh, Father, pour out Your Spirit. Help us! Draw the people as we lift Jesus up! You promised! Anoint the music and the message - open hearts. Just let each of us - be faithful to do our part - our best - for you.'

Caleb looked up to see Sarah sitting - waiting quietly - wondering what he was thinking."

"Oh, Sarah, we have never attempted anything so – so - huge!"

"I know. Isn't it exciting?"

"I don't know – yes – it is - I am scared out of my wits!" Caleb tried to smile, but his face felt frozen, wanting to laugh hysterically, yet his mind was plagued with doubts. Part of him wanted to hide, but a stronger part forced him to stand! "There are so many things that could go wrong, Sarah! We could go belly-up – or worse - face prison, and I can't tell you how I've wrestled with that possibility."

"I know," she answered softly. "I'm prepared for whatever we must face."

"I'm not, Sarah! Not for you!" Caleb grappled with images of his sweetheart thrown in a rat-infested cell. "I can't send you to prison because of my brazen stupidity!"

"What is the Lord telling you to do?"

"I thought I knew – then I have moments of fear... I feel He wants me to do an invitation - and how can I preach a message and not discuss sin? Then I think of the consequences and - and - I don't - I'm not sure."

"You always advocate doing what the Lord says. He will show you, Caleb. We must hold fast to that, and His promise to protect us. You said yourself, they can't do anything unless God allows."

"I know - I know, Sweetheart, but I am so bombarded with worry? This is the greatest endeavor we have ever attempted for God, so is it any wonder the devil would fight? Souls, thousands of them, hang this day in the balance between Heaven and hell. We are a man and woman of faith in Jesus Christ. We must stand up for our Lord, no matter what the cost! In a few hours we will lift the Son of God up before whoever is there, whether 10 or 100 or 1,000 or 100,000. So let's spend the rest of our time until Hank and Tulipan pick us up, on our faces before God, seeking His Power to fall on us - the crusade - the city!"

# Chapter 47

# Spiritual Warfare

"Preacher, I hope you are on your way to the stadium; I think we are in big trouble!" It was Chris on the sat-phone but his face was turned away so Caleb couldn't see him.

"Dear God, don't tell me that, Chris! What is it?"

"You got any big screen remotes in your pocket?" Chris began laughing.

"Chris! What's happening there?"

"You'll never believe this, Preacher. I don't think we will have enough space the way they are coming," Chris' laughing face filled the phone screen.

"What?"

"Here, I'll hold my sat, look for yourself! They are like locusts - pouring in every entrance - filling the stadium! You should have seen the crowd outside from early morning, waiting for the gates to open. We are flat overrun in the parking lot - thank God, we have plenty of help. Call me when you get close, so we can direct you to your space."

"Praise God, Chris! Be on the lookout for Presidente Fernando and Armelita Villanueva, and seat them on the platform."

"Gotcha. You decided what to do about the invitation?"

"No, that's the toughest part, but it will come to me."

Caleb was thrilled beyond words when he saw the size of the swelling wave of humanity making their way excitedly into the stadium - having no concept of what awaited them there - just eager to be a part! Where Caleb had experienced concern over too small a crowd, a new fear took over at the enormity of this turnout. He felt his knees get wobbly when he stepped out of the car. Hank grabbed him.

"You alright, Pastor?" he asked looking into Caleb's face.

"This is overwhelming, Hank," and for the first time he sensed the furious spiritual battle that was going on in the heavens and realized it was not the size of the crowd affecting him. His eyes locked with Sarah's and her glance assured him she too sensed the battle coming against them and was right beside him all the way. He gave her hand a gentle squeeze.

"I'll be praying," Sarah whispered.

"Let's do this for the saving of souls to the Glory of God!" Caleb spoke with firm resolve.

Hank and Tulipan made their way to reserved seats in the stadium. Soon, Caleb and Sarah emerged onto the platform. The musicians were engaged in final sound checks. Caleb and Sarah had instantly fallen in love with this bunch when they met at the airport. Raintree Forest musicians were funny, engaging, high-energy people - yet a spiritual depth emerged in their words and actions that spoke of maturity that only grows from intimate time spent at the Lord's Feet.

"Let me know when you are ready to start," Caleb got Jennifer Skye's attention. A technician was hooking him up with a remote mic.

She turned her head toward him, smiled, and nodded toward the noisy, overflowing stadium.

"Look what God is sending us!"

The rest of the band acknowledged the missionary couple. Cory at his keyboard tipped his fingers off the side of his face in a hello salute. "You ready for this, Pastor?" he called out.

Caleb gave a thumbs up then he and Sarah shook hands with the diverse group of ministers and city officials who were already seated on the platform. Close to the time for the concert to begin, El Presidente, his wife and their friends arrived. Caleb, Sarah and the others rose to greet them.

As they waited to start, Sarah motioned to the few she recognized.

"Wish we could have gotten Esther here for this," she sighed. "I forgot how demanding college is."

"Me too. Sarah, look! Mark has brought in shanty people down on the soccer field. See him there - he's waving at us. Mark is here!"

"Praise the Lord! Yes, he is going to stay. Do you think this may be our Mark's night?"

"My phone - its Mark. Hi - Mark?"

"Hey, Pops, be cool, lose the suit jacket and tie. What a blowout, huh?"

"I'm floored, son. Thanks - I - I love you - I'm sorry I've not been the dad...." Caleb hung up wondering what prompted him to say those words at a time like this.

"Oh, Caleb," Sarah touched his arm. "Jennifer is ready!"

Caleb's heart was pounding in his throat when he stepped to the podium before a packed stadium. He felt lost in such an enormous audience, and prayed everyone could hear him. He stammered through the welcome and introductions followed by a lifeless prayer. He retreated, embarrassed as a stage-struck teenager in a play who had just failed miserably to say his part. To his dismay the huge stadium screens magnified every blunder.

Next, the announcer for Raintree Forest walked on the platform, waved and loudly proclaimed, "Amigos! Senors, senoras and senoritas! Ninas and ninos! Hear me. From the states - from around the world - to bless your hearts and souls! Jennifer Skye and Raintree Forest!"

With that acclamation the crowd came to life with a deafening roar, standing to their feet. The drummer started tapping the call:

"1 - 2 - 3 - "

"Here we go!" Jennifer shouted, and the rhythm took hold of the throng.

Caleb watched hands waving all over the stadium with bodies swaying in time to the music. Multitudes were dancing. The group would rock the crowd and lead them into singing along, then the tempo slowed to a mellow sound that evoked tears, memories and tender emotions. Then the sound would take off again with its driving, thumping beat that held 150,000 hearts captive.

When they came to a break, Jennifer turned the platform over to one of Mexico City's prominent and respected pastors, who led the offering appeal and prayer. Caleb was pleased at how smoothly the offering was taken, but knew time was getting closer for his message, pushing his nerves into a jangled mass as fear wrestled with his courage to dull his mind and block an invitation.

The concert resumed with two more quieting down songs concluding with Jennifer Skye and Raintree Forest's version of the timeless, "Amazing Grace."

"How sweet the sound," they sang, "that saved a wretch like me. I once was lost, but now am found, was blind but now I see."

Caleb picked up his Bible and notes when they reached the last verse.

"When we've been there 10,000 years, bright shining as the sun, we've no less days to sing God's praise, than when we first begun."

The instruments softly played as the singers murmured, "God's Grace - Amazing Grace - has brought us here - brought us home - brought us home..."

A hush fell on this enormous crowd as the music faded. Caleb turned to Sarah.

"Pray for me, sweetheart, I'm really scared." Sarah squeezed his hand as he stood and walked toward the podium, his image coming up on the stadium screens.

"They're all yours, Pastor," Jennifer whispered as he passed.

"We sang of Heaven," he opened his message, "and I got to thinking - when we get there - Jennifer and her crew will still have work to do. But I'll be out of a job."

Sounds of laughter swelled, followed by applause.

"So I better get this right while I have the chance. My message tonight will be brief, but perhaps the most important one of your life.

"People have asked me for years, what does the future hold? What does the Bible foretell? Does it predict what will happen to us?"

Caleb felt a powerful surge of the Holy Spirit filling him and directing the message.

"Yes, I declare unto you that the Bible tells the whole history of man and what will happen to us. But I must hasten to make clear that prophecy was given with a purpose - not to inform us - but to prepare us for that future.

"Listen carefully, because I'm teaching tonight on five things that speak to our future. Five crucial points, on which God would not have us to be ignorant:

"The first revolves around God's plan for Israel. When Christ returns - and He will as sure as I'm standing here - it will be to the land of Israel, and He will reign in Jerusalem.

Understand in discerning the prophecy hour, Israel is the time clock. She has been an independent nation since the 1940's, and now the temple is again a reality. It has been rebuilt! The Lord would not have us ignorant of the time.

"The second thing God doesn't want us to be ignorant of, is His plan for spiritual gifts. Those gifts are given to His children singularly or in combination by His choosing for the purpose of accomplishing ministry. We have seen as the devil manifests his power in his followers, so the Holy Spirit reveals His strength in the followers of Christ with spiritual gifts. As we are in the end times, spiritual war erupts pitting raw power against raw power: But be not afraid, for the scripture says, 'Greater is He that is in you than he that is in the world.' Peter wrote, 'Resist the devil and he will flee.'

"The third point the Lord does not want us ignorant of, is satan's devices. In Ephesians 6, Paul calls it trickery. Satan tells us there is no sin, and laws are in place to prevent me from even speaking God's Word because someone might be offended. Yet, Jesus spoke openly many times that we must repent of our sins and confess them."

Fernando Villanueva was at his side. "You must cease this direction in what you say," he demanded. He was angry.

A cry began to swell from the crowd, "Let him speak - let him speak - let him speak!"

Fernando, fearing a mob riot, conceded and returned to his seat.

Caleb held up his hands for silence before resuming his message. A holy boldness was filling his veins with a burning fire.

"Satan says there are many ways to Heaven. Jesus never said that. He said He was the way! The only way! Satan mocks, Christ has been gone over two thousand years - He's not coming back. But I say to you that Jesus Christ when he walked the earth, declared many would say that He's been gone a long time so where is His return? Ha! Over two thousand years ago the Lord heard satan's lie. The truth is that Jesus rose from the dead and is alive today living in the hearts of believers - and no country or legislation can make laws against that!

"The fourth thing the Lord would not have us ignorant about is believers who have died in the Lord. Praise God!

"As I have driven this beautiful and great city, I pass many cemeteries. Some are quite old - other graves as recent as today. Most of you have friends or loved ones buried in the ground - mothers, fathers, grandparents, aunts, uncles, cousins, brothers and sisters, maybe children, a husband... a wife.

"The Bible gives us hope, because He promises that when He comes in the air, these graves will be ripped open, and the dead in Christ will rise in glorious bodies – to unite instantly with their spirits... never to know pain or sickness again - no more suffering - no separation - no more death. They will rise to meet Jesus! A believer in Christ has the hope and gift of eternal life.

"The fifth point; Jesus did not want us to be ignorant of end time prophecy. He spoke of it. 'When you see Israel bud into a nation remember the time clock. The hour is near.

"When the world becomes wicked and evil as it was in the days of Noah - watch, for the Lord's return is near.

'Be ready because I will come as a thief in the night, and you know not the hour.'

"Maybe, tonight - maybe tomorrow - next week - but He will come and a most incredible event will take place. Some graves will rip open giving up their dead. The sea will give up her dead. Believers who are alive will disappear off the face of the earth. Those who are left will face a horrible tribulation such as the earth has never seen.

"Remember, dear ones, I started this message to say the purpose of prophecy is to prepare us. How do we prepare? By admitting we have sinned against God, trusting in Christ as our Savior, believing He became our sin on the cross and shed His blood that we could be washed clean and given a new heart.

"My heart breaks thinking multitudes of you might miss Jesus tonight. I plead with you - I beg you - open your heart to Him who loves you so much He died on a cross in your place– believe He is the Son of God - invite Him into your heart - tonight - before it's too late. Please! Don't leave this stadium without Him!

"Everyone seated, praying, if you want to receive Christ as your Lord and Savior, starting here on the platform and spreading all over this great stadium, I'm asking you to stand up wherever you are. Caring people near you are ready to talk with you and pray with you. Now is your moment; may God bless you as you stand for Him and embrace His Son, Jesus Christ."

Caleb dropped his head in prayer. When he glanced up, he could make out people all over the stadium rising to their feet.

"Oh, praise God!" he cried aloud.

He was about to continue speaking when the crusade was interrupted by loud funk music. He shook his head - where was it coming from?

Slowly, two stadium gates opened onto the playing field compressing onlookers back to make way for two revved up glistening black and chrome trucks to drive onto the field. On the truck beds were two bands shrieking in rhythm at high volume and frequency. The trucks circled back and forth until they had cleared a sizable space in front of Caleb.

Caleb looked behind him to his fellow pastors as if to say, 'Do you know what this is?' They were as bewildered as he. A sweeping glance detected a smug smile on El Presidente Villanueva's face.

The bands abruptly stopped. Their music was heralding the arrival of someone - or something. Next a silent assembly marched from both gates to fill the area before the platform. They wore black hooded robes obscuring faces.

"Satanists!" Caleb gasped. He heard a faint cry behind him and spun to see terror in Sarah's expression. As their eyes locked they communicated, 'We must trust God now as never before.'

When the satanists were positioned, by a silent command they turned in unison to face the left gate. A spotlight in an overhead bank came on and focused on that opening. The satanists raised stiff left arms in one accord, pointing to the gate. An evil sounding drum roll proceeded from the bands as a black limo emerged slowly through the gate, driving to a spot directly in front of Caleb. He felt a wave of lightheadedness wash across his mind. He prayed to fight it off.

The limo stopped, the music ceased, and for an instant there was total silence in the vast auditorium. Then the limo chauffeur jumped out to run around the vehicle to open the rear side door. There was a long pause before an elaborately dressed man in black tux, shirt, coat and top hat stepped onto the grass. He stood before Caleb, not looking up, as if waiting. Then a deep commanding voice came over the stadium sound system, which sent an icy chill creeping up Caleb's back!

"Behold, an Enlightened One. Hear him and obey."

"Well, well, well," the Enlightened One spoke. "I heard you were having a party, but you neglected to send me an invite. Shame, but I was given a most personal invitation from El Presidente."

Caleb looked back just in time to see Fernando nod in acknowledgement. Caleb felt betrayed! He turned his attention back to his enemy, who was still not looking up.

"I've not even been offered a wireless - how rude - but no matter - I will use yours." Now the Enlightened One's voice was booming all over the stadium. "I can project my voice - and I can project my thoughts."

Suddenly Caleb heard a voice in his head, 'Who is Jesus? Where is Jesus? He has been gone over 2,000 years. Jesus is dead! He is never coming back. You are stupid to believe He means anything to you.'

"Not true," Caleb countered loudly. "There is power in the name of Jesus Christ, and I stand against you in that Name. I call on everyone here who believes in that glorious Name to stand!"

All over the stadium, believers rose to join those already standing! Voices of agreement mingled with those of disbelief. Tense opposition filled the air.

"Jesus Christ said over 2,000 years ago there will be scoffers in the last days who would question, where is this Jesus? He has been gone a long time. But, I declare to this vast throng, He will return, just as He promised. This man is not light, but darkness, because his deeds are evil, and he speaks lies!"

A deep long sigh could be heard from the Enlightened One. He snapped his fingers, commanding his attendant out of the limo to hand him a shiny silver-tipped cane and take his hat.

"I had hoped we could avoid making you a fool in front of all these people; however, you pushed too far, Caleb Hillag, and I must claim what is mine and reveal you for the clown you are."

Then a force like a searing hot iron drove into his brain like it would weld the cells together in one molten blob. He prayed the Name of Jesus over and over to keep from blacking out, then the voice again.

'I will destroy you. I will have your son, your daughter and your wife, and I WILL destroy you. You said in your message it was raw power against raw power. Do you think you have that kind of power, Caleb Hillag? You are a mindless idiot!'

Now for the first time the Enlightened One looked up where Caleb could make out his face. Stoner!

Caleb spun around to see his wife shaking, pointing a trembling finger toward the Enlightened One.

"It's Stoner!" she shrieked. She flew to Caleb to stand beside him.

"Now, I will have what's mine. Mark Hillag, satan's child, come join me now."

"No, Mark!" Caleb and Sarah yelled. "Don't do it! Don't listen to him."

"Silence!" the Enlightened One thundered. "He has wanted wealth and power from the day he was born. Wealth and power you could never give him. Come to me, Mark, and I will give you everything you desire."

Caleb wanted to cry out, but he could not open his mouth, he choked for breath, and from Sarah's struggling he knew the Enlightened One had the same grip on her throat. They watched in forced silence as Mark made his way onto the field to take his place beside Stoner, whose countenance displayed his sense of glorious victory. He placed his hand on Mark's head.

"You've submerged words deep inside that you've longed to say to your pathetic father. Now is your time. You have the power, and you can project your voice like me. Go ahead, Mark, they will listen."

"I tried to tell you, Pops, so many times, I hated being a P. K. I hated the taunts I put up with at school. We never stayed in one place long enough to make friends, and I hated we were always dead broke. When it came to church and church members, I felt I always came in last - they were first. You said you loved me, but why did you never show it. I tried to tell you, Pops, this, right here, is where it's at. Sorry, you are such a loser."

"I'm proud of the decision you have made, Mark, and you have come to the light. Many here will follow your example tonight."

"Hear me, Caleb, I will have your daughter, for she is now ready!"

Sarah shook her head violently, as cheers opposed by cries of indignation arose on the field and in the stands!

"And - I'll have her mother!"

Sarah hid behind Caleb, shaken.

"Behind me are 400 of satan's high priests who have assembled to demonstrate our master's powers which will be unleashed on this unlawful gathering."

Caleb prayed over and over in the Name of Jesus Christ, against this force that had its hold on their minds and voices. He felt that searing power release its grip.

"Sarah! Run for safety!" he gasped.

"No! I won't leave your side."

"You could..."

"No!"

Caleb turned to face Stoner and brace for the onslaught to come when he noticed a stranger ambling in front of the satanists. He carried a hippie look about him, dressed in jeans, a t-shirt with a large cross, which could be seen through his open, coarse-weave jacket. He was barefoot, walking around the limo to pass in front of Stoner.

The stranger never looked at either the priests or Stoner, who suddenly appeared intrigued by this person's detached brashness.

A hush fell on the stadium - everyone seemed glued to their place - wanting to see what would happen next. This unknown man made his way up onto the platform and approached Caleb and Sarah. Caleb held her close to shield her - his heart racing in his throat. The man drew close and whispered in Caleb's ear.

"Be strong and of good courage; be not afraid, neither be thou dismayed; for the Lord thy God is with thee. You must speak to the people."

The stranger stepped to one side and folded his arms. The power of the Holy Ghost came over Caleb, and with boldness he gave a final appeal. Stoner stared in utter disbelief!

"Hear me! Time is running out. Reach out to God; He will reach out to you. He promises eternal life with Him. Embrace His Son Jesus Christ! Believe in Him! He died for you on a cross over 2,000 years ago! He shed his precious, cleansing blood, for you! He lives today, and he is calling you. Open your heart to Him and receive his life, love, and His forgiveness. Mark, Stoner, please, believe, I beg you before it's too late."

"No!" thundered Stoner. "Enough! How dare you! Burn from my master's wrath!"

With that command, all the satanist priests leveled their hands pointing toward the field and stands. Stoner aimed his cane at Caleb and Sarah.

"Feel my power and die!" Stoner exploded into a mocking, evil, hideous laugh that increased in volume until it enveloped every other sound in the stadium. Caleb recognized that laugh from their first encounter in the Juvenile Hall. A lightning bolt came out of Stoner's cane headed straight for the missionary couple. The stranger reached out and grabbed it with his hand, drawing it to his breast where he snuffed it out.

"Who are you?" Stoner was stunned.

As by unspoken command, all 400 satanist priests turned to face the stranger. Stoner again aimed his cane.

"Kill him!" Stoner sneered.

Lightning bolts burst from his cane and the fingertips of every priest. The blast threw Caleb and Sarah to the platform. The sight was incomprehensible, and he feared for their lives. He cried out to the Lord, "Save us!"

The stranger collected all of the electric charges forming them into a large glowing, flaming ball. Next, he tossed it up into the air where it burst into a shower of sparks over Stoner, the satanists and a fleeing Mark. Every spark turned into a tormenting coal burning itself through cloth into flesh. The evil priests screamed and cursed in pain, spewing smoke from their mouths. Confusion broke out as the priests, stumbled, bumping into each other as though drunk. They shot lightning bolts into the stands, whichever way their hands pointed. Pandemonium erupted with the crowds jamming toward exits. Screams of pain and horror filled the stadium!

Caleb sat in a daze, holding Sarah. What started as a victory had turned into chaos. He heard Presidente Fernando amidst Armelita's hysterical screams, call for the military.

"All hell is breaking loose! Get the militia here - immediately," he repeated the order loudly over and over. "Get us out of here!"

The priests were running wildly in every direction, ripping off their robes. Caleb noted some of them were men, others women. He looked for Mark, but for the running - pushing mob could not see him. It seemed the noise faded into a soft song, and everything stilled to slow motion before him. The unknown stranger was gone.

He saw bodies on the field and knew they could be dead - trampled to death. He watched as the chauffeur and attendant tried to drag an unconscious Stoner into the limo. The trucks had already driven off. The pastors and guests on the platform deserted them. Jennifer and her band were gathering equipment. It was everyone for themselves! Caleb helped Sarah to her feet.

"Wh - where is Mark?" she stammered. She clung to him attempting to gain her footing.

Caleb felt someone grab him from behind. He looked into the face of Sierra and was jolted back to real time.

"Quickly Preacher, you must leave at once before the soldiers arrive!" He took Caleb's arm and Sarah's hand, leading them through the frightened, screaming crowd to a shadowy, secluded corner where a cab waited.

"Get in," he instructed, and the taxi sped them off to the safety of Casa de Amor.

# Chapter 48

# The Dead of Night

The shock of seeing her stepbrother, Stoner, dredged up fears and feelings Sarah had long thought buried. The Concert Crusade, which started as a dream-come-true for her, and Caleb, was now a hideous disaster! Stoner's threats and taunts even now made her shake. It was nearing three a.m. Saturday morning, and none of their people were back at Casa de Amor. Sarah refused to watch anymore horrible news broadcasts from the futball stadium.

Caleb threw up his hands in despair.

"The death count just reached 119 and hundreds are injured. We don't know if our people are alive or dead! I should be there."

"We can't," Sarah objected. "Already, we are blamed - even for harming Stoner and the satanist priests."

"I know, Sarah. Lord, what can we do? Nothing. Nothing. Nothing!" he fumed.

They sat in silence for a long while, Caleb intent on the news broadcasts - Sarah lost in thought, sick at heart.

The entrance door opened and voices broke the silence. Sarah's heart stopped. Was it the militia? A few seconds later Hank and Tulipan entered the meeting room, followed by

Blanca, Maybeline, Bomba and Kay. They looked haggard and scared.

"Oh, thank God!" Caleb exclaimed.

Sarah ran to hug them. Relieved they were all safe.

"What of the others?" Caleb asked when the hugs and praises to God subsided.

"We lost Arcy and her kids in the stampede of the crowd," Hank spoke sadly.

"Crazy people," Bomba shook her head. "They swallowed up my dear Plomo."

"What?" Caleb was aghast.

"Plomo and Rubin were trying to quell the panic," Hank explained. "We never saw them again."

"No Espolito and her ninos," Tulipan added.

Sarah sensed a deep sorrow in Kay. "Where is Chris?" she asked.

Kay turned her head away to cry, then walked to the far side of the meeting room to be by herself. Sarah followed her.

"Tell me, Kay."

"I can't!" she buried her face in her hands.

"Please, Kay, don't carry this alone."

After a moment of tears, Kay wiped her eyes, took a breath.

"Chris went after Mark. He told us wait no longer than 15 minutes - we stalled for 25, but they never came. When we were in the line of cars trying to get through a checkpoint, we saw them. Soldiers had them handcuffed and were loading them in a truck with - others." Kay waited for Sarah's reaction.

"Oh, Kay! God help them! What shall we do? We have to get them out!"

Kay looked away and spoke quietly.

"I wanted to go with him, but he said no. I'm not a brave person. People who know us, Sarah, and watch us probably don't think we are very close - Chris - and I because we don't show a lot of affection. That's not how we really are, Sarah."

Sarah took Kay's hand, and they sat down on nearby chairs.

"I love Chris with every breath I take, every beat of my heart, every inch of my being. I can't - tell you how much I wanted to be by his side. If he was going to jail, I would go too..."

"I know," Sarah understood.

"We couldn't have children, so it was just - us - together - but we always longed for them - I know Chris did. I would watch him with other's children - Fina and Carmen - he was crazy about Arcy's little boy Hernando and her baby. He was always doing things for people, making them feel good and welcome - unplugging their toilets at that damn Casino - just doing...I knew how much he loved your family. I thought he would die - when Mark..."

"Kay, please - don't!" Sarah pleaded with trembling lips. "Please... They'll be out before..."

"I don't think so, Sarah. You know Mexican prisons' regulations. I fear they will never get out, and I don't know what I will do." Kay broke down again.

"I feel lost and alone; helpless. Chris is my life, Sarah. Oh, God - Father, help us! Oh, Sarah, I am so sorry for Mark - I am so sorry!"

The two women held each other until Caleb's gentle touch got her attention.

"Hank told me about Chris and Mark. We'll get them back somehow. Sarah, I've got to go - try to obtain their release - maybe others too."

Sarah clutched at Caleb. She could not accept losing him as well as Mark. Her mind refused to think in those terms. She refused Caleb's leaving. She shook her head in wild protest.

"Don't leave me - please! Don't, Caleb!" she begged.

"I must, Sarah, we have some of our members missing - maybe dead - Chris and Mark in jail. I can't just sit here idle - people - families are hurting. Don't you understand, Sarah, I must go."

"Then I will go with you," Sarah spoke in grim resolve, knowing full well the consequences.

Caleb was ready to object when a shout rose from the other members.

"Praise God! It's Espolito and Arcy! They have their children."

Sarah, Caleb and Kay ran to greet the latest arrivals. The women and their children were happy to be safe, but tired and dirty.

"I thought we were to be killed," Arcy emotionally told her story. "There were many people rushing – rushing like bulls. I lost little Hernando's hand and could not feel him. I cried out to God to spare my son!"

'Oh, me too,' Sarah cried silently with Arcy for her own son.

"I feared there was no hope - then this man was holding my little Hernando, and he gave him back to me."

"Sierra!" Sarah and Caleb breathed in unison.

"We were separated from Arcy and her children," Espolito excitedly broke in. Everybody had lost their senses, and we would have been trampled underfoot. The girls were being yanked from my hands by the pushing and the shoving - then we stepped into a little doorway and huddled there until - it was over. That's when I saw Arcy."

"There were soldiers and medics everywhere," Arcy described the horrible scene they saw. "They were getting the hurt to the hospital and just leaving the dead..."

At this point, both women covered their mouths and choked back the tears.

"I saw Rubin, lying in the stairway," Arcy cried. "He was dead!"

Bomba covered her ears and ran screaming to her room. Caleb looked to Espolito and Arcy to confirm if the same fate had overtaken Plomo. They nodded, and then held each other tightly in quiet grief.

It was Blanca and Sarah who went to Bomba later. She was sitting quietly on her bed. As Sarah looked into her face, she saw past the barmaid demeanor to look upon a sister - a friend.

"He is dead - si?"

Sarah and Blanca sat on each side of her and took her hands. Their silence affirmed the answer.

"I knew he was. I could feel it," she spoke softly. "I never admitted I was in love with Plomo until - now. I never told him - I loved him - goodbye - time ran out..."

The three sat without words, watching the sun come up through Bomba's window.

# Chapter 49

# Caught Up

News reports of the tragedy were streaming in. The final death count hit 142 and the injured still uncounted. The militia was arresting pastors and leaders of the crusade throwing them into jail - even Jennifer Skye and her band were detained. El Presidente Fernando Villanueva was determined to make heads roll - especially the stranger who had beaten the Enlightened One and his 400 false prophets. A sizeable reward was offered for clues leading to his arrest.

"How do you place a bounty on an angel?" Sarah heard Caleb remark under his breath.

El Presidente wanted Caleb and Sarah in the worst way. He was humiliated and they must pay! Sarah knew it was only a matter of time until authorities uncovered where the missionary couple were staying.

Global Missions urged them to flee across country hidden in a car to a border and safety.

"We can't!" Caleb countered. "We won't abandon our son in jail - maybe prison. Besides that, we can't leave our people."

"How about Sarah?" Gerald Pullman wanted Caleb to think rationally.

"We stay together!" Caleb insisted with staunch determination.

"Caleb! The Mexican government is about to lock you up. You could be lost for years - or for life! Sarah will not survive a Mexican prison, and it's doubtful you could."

"Gerald! We are not the guilty ones in this!"

"This is no time to stand on principle or demand your rights. You will die - both of you - and you are no good to us - dead!"

Sarah could tell by Caleb's movements and expressions he was buckling under the weight of the responsibility for the decision he was making. She touched his arm, and when he looked at her she mouthed, 'We stay together no matter what.'

Caleb's eyes filled with tears, and his face scrunched up with pained emotion.

"I'll call you back," he hastily told Gerald, then turning to Sarah.

"Sweetheart, I can't do this to you! I've got to get you out of here."

"I'm nothing without you, Caleb, I might as well be dead!"

"Don't say that! Think of Esther."

Soon they were in each other's arms, clinging to their love and bravely pushing away fear, so undecided what to do.

They both knew if they were arrested they would definitely be separated whether they liked it or not. At that point their decision to stick together would be irrelevant. To add to their indecision was the kids. Sarah's heart feared for Mark's welfare. He had openly denounced Christ to Caleb and publicly taken his place beside Stoner. Would he follow his monstrous uncle now? Was he doomed to prison - to hell? That possibility terrified her! How could they help him?

Sarah and Caleb had no hope to rescue their son - or win him to Christ - if they were indeed plunged into a dismal prison.

What about Esther? She might as well be parentless. Sarah's whole family in Washington was reduced to a shamble of nerves, concerned over her and Caleb's fate. Penny and her mom fell apart when they heard the news of Stoner, and his threats drove Esther to her grandparents. She needed her mother and dad right now!

Or what of their church flock? Sarah was so torn she thought her heart would just quit from the unbearable pressure. Their church family attempted to console her and Caleb.

"Running to the border like a fugitive is not the answer," Hank counseled. "After midnight, I think Tulipan and I can slip you to the American Embassy. Let them protect you and deal with Mark's release.

All of the members affirmed they wanted their pastor and his wife safe, and so the plan was agreed upon.

"We must pray the militia doesn't find you before then, and for Chris and Mark's release," Kay Fowler suggested as she got on her knees by the chair she was seated on. The rest followed and began earnest prayer intercession.

Sarah was touched and amazed at the various avenues prayer took. It began with prayer for their safety, to Chris and Mark, finally praying for the salvation of the Enlightened One, Stoner, and the 400 evil priests. Caleb was disturbed by El Presidente Fernando's blindness and deception, pleading to God that he would see and know the true Light, Jesus Christ.

Sarah believed Armelita was like Pilate's wife and receptive to the Lord. She prayed Caleb's message in the stadium found fertile soil in her heart.

Prayer and conversation later in the afternoon was interrupted when they heard the front door open. The group fell into a frightened hush and held their breath. In a moment, Tazada staggered into the dining area.

"Tazada!" Sarah gasped. In the confusion, they had completely forgotten him.

"Hey! Buenos Dias!" he shouted loudly.

"Merciful Lord, get some coffee in him," Maybeline ordered.

"Where have you been?" Caleb inquired.

"Tazada removed his shabby hat and scratched his head. He shrugged his shoulders - confused.

"Where were you at the concert?" Caleb reworded his question. "Did you see it - hear my message?"

"Si, I was at one of the bars having a beer. I could see - on the screen - except the end, El Capitan Senor, I fell asleep."

"Asleep! You didn't see all the people running and screaming?" Hank was incredulous.

"I saw nothing until the soldiers woke me. They took us out on the futball field where many others were questioned. They were asking if there was any person who knew where you - and you lived." Tazada pointed to Caleb and Sarah nearly falling over.

Sarah's heart went cold.

"How could you, Tazada," she shook her head in disbelief.

"I raised my hand - 'I know - I know,' - I tell them," he beamed a drunken, toothless grin.

"Oh, no!" the exasperated group groaned.

"I tell them you fly like birds to Heaven, and you live there," Tazada laughed.

"You impossible man!" Espolito threw up her hands.

"What did they do next?" Caleb asked.

"Put me in jail. They call me loco," he laughed jokingly again.

As nightfall approached, new members from the shanties began gathering in the church room with them. No one told them to come - they only said they were compelled by the Spirit to be there. Maybe to send them off to the Embassy- Sarah had no idea. By 10:30 Saturday evening the room was nearly full, no one understanding why they were there exactly, only that they should be.

Sarah and Caleb's eyes met, and he was uncertain as she over this unplanned gathering. Then without warning an unexplained wave of emotion took command of her actions. She rose and went to Caleb, taking his face in her hands.

"Caleb, I am so happy you married me. Thank you for our children and such wonderful memories! Our life has been good!"

"I could never have found a better wife," Caleb began to cry. "Oh, Sarah, why are we talking like this?"

"I don't know!" Sarah wailed. "If we are going to die, I want to be in your arms."

Everyone seemed moved in their own ways. Suddenly it happened. Sarah heard a sound as of a far distant trumpet.

"Did you hear that?" she exclaimed. "There! I heard it again!"

"Yes," Caleb heard it too. There were murmurs from the congregation acknowledging they also heard the sounds.

"I don't hear anything - only barking dogs on the street," Tazada spoke coarsely.

The sound again! A call loud and near - "Come!" Then a trumpet, a shaking in the room, a whirling of air around her, and Sarah was caught up so quickly it took her breath away.

# Chapter 50

# The Bridegroom Has Come

Caleb was propelled through the clouds like a rocket. Something happened to him, he was changed, but it took place so fast he didn't understand what it was. Excitement mounted wildly - he knew in his spirit he was going to meet Jesus!

He was vaguely aware of Sarah nearby and other magnificent creatures. Sarah shone with a heavenly beauty and was shouting praises to God. He joined in, singing, as never before in his life, songs and words so glorious, to match his joy-overflowing heart.

They were being drawn to a brilliantly lit place in the sky. As they came closer he was conscious of multitudes of people and angelic beings around him. The number grew and grew until the throng was in the billions. He instinctively knew Jesus was where the light was. He was eager as a little boy to see Him!

It seemed only moments before they arrived. The sky was filled with angels and music - melodies and words that reached into Caleb's soul creating the deepest devotion. In the center of the light, he could see Jesus surrounded by the vast multitudes of His church. He was so far away, the face of Christ could not be made out - just a figure - but he knew it was Him - his Lord - he couldn't take his eyes off Him. His spirit quickened! The music carried a magnificent grandeur, thrusting forth to be heard in the great expanses of the universe.

Blending with the music, a swelling of voices from those nearest Jesus spread out to the farthest edges of the gathering. It increased in volume and triumphal shouts and at first Caleb thought it was a cheer, but as it grew louder, he realized it was songs from the bride, alone. There were praises, adoring words, thanksgivings, shouts of joy and excitement, a beautiful love song from the Bride of Christ, the Redeemed, to the Bridegroom. Caleb was moved to tears as he thanked Jesus for saving him. He expressed his love for the Son of God and his exuberant longing to see Him face to face. This praise and worship continued for some time until Jesus raised His hands. The multitude became still. Then as if to signal the number of the redeemed was complete, the music faded, and all was quiet.

The scene was incredible! Angels bright shining, countless as the stars, filled the sky around them, above them, below them, as millions upon millions of believers floated around Jesus.

All the angels bowed their heads and folded their wings in respect as an angel far more magnificent than all the others came forth. Caleb sensed this was the one who had called them up. He took his place near the Lord Jesus.

"The bride has been waiting," the angel cried with a loud voice. "All things are ready. Behold! The Bridegroom has come!"

A thrill went through Caleb of such force he couldn't restrain himself from shouting and laughing with a freedom and happiness he had never experienced on earth. No consideration of what had taken place, nor wonder of the future, he was totally focused on Christ!

A deafening cheer arose, and praises from the Heavenly Host filled the air as Jesus turned to lead His bride, the church, to the place He had prepared for her.

## Chapter 51

# The Body of the Raptured

C aleb was enthralled! He was now seeing and experiencing things beyond anything he had ever tried to imagine or hope for in mortal life. The scene was gigantic and expansive in scope! He was so completely captivated with Jesus and wanting to see Him, it was difficult to focus on anything else.

The mass of Christians moved quickly through space toward a distant glow. He knew he was changed, looking at his feet and hands. His clothes were warm shades of beige and brown and fit his body perfectly. He could touch and feel his arms and chest and his skin was warm. Did he have a heart? It seemed so, because he still felt with it. He realized in the excitement he had gotten separated from Sarah, and now his heart longed for her.

Wait a minute! They were in emptiness, still he seemed to be breathing - or was he?

What amazing feelings! He touched his face - was that wind blowing? Impossible! He looked around and was quite startled by an angelic creature next to him, who was looking intently into Caleb's eyes.

"Hello, I'm Caleb Hillag," was all he managed to say to this magnificent creature.

"I know you - Caleb Hillag," was a deep baritone reply.

Caleb wondered about this being. He thought to speak a word of greeting.

"You look familiar," was what came out. That didn't make sense. "I mean who - are you?"

"I am Herculon, your guardian angel."

"Wow!" gasped Caleb. He looked more closely at this angel. "I would swear I – your voice..."

"You have," Herculon read his thoughts. "I was there to protect you from Stoner Howser."

"You were the stranger?" recognition came.

"Yes..." Herculon smiled. He was a stunning sight in his shining white robe. Caleb felt intimidated.

"Fear not, Caleb Hillag, favored one of God," Herculon again read his thoughts.

"You fought one possessed of devils in Tennessee, and I protected you, but Stoner had 400 of satan's prophets of darkness. He determined to kill you. That was his goal, and to violate your wife and daughter after he took away your son before your very eyes."

"I don't understand - that kind of - lust."

"With every breaking of God's Law, he gained more power. He had an insatiable thirst for it. Your murder plus rapes of your wife and daughter would have added to his might with more evil signs and wonders.

"Dear Lord, have mercy," Caleb moaned. "Tell me of Mark? I must know - I must pray for him! Has the darkness swallowed him?"

Sadness crossed the angel's face. "Your time for prayers is over," he spoke softly. "I cannot tell of your son, but all will be revealed in the Master's time."

A thousand thoughts and memories crowded into Caleb's mind, and he grew silent. Eventually, he became more interested in the vast congregation of people and angels surrounding him. He remembered that scriptures taught, angels were neither male nor female, yet curiously some looked like men and others women.

"We have been given the appearances and traits of one or the other," Herculon commented. "You needed a warrior guardian angel."

"And Sarah's?" Caleb asked.

"She is guarded by Portus, a gentle angel of strong courage."

What an air of celebration when the vast gathering arrived in Paradise. They first came into a beautiful valley adorned with all manner of trees, shrubs, grass, and flowers. A shimmering, clear river coursed its way past groves of trees and green meadows. Colors were in absolute harmony, striking a pleasant picture for the eye. Flowers, plants and grass appeared to wave in a gentle breeze.

'Is there wind here?' Caleb wondered. It looked so, but no air brushed his skin. This place was more than he could take in! Whatever he had ever thought about Heaven was completely lost in the scene spread out before him.

"Praise be to God!" he exclaimed in awe.

He was ready to move on with the crowd, but was held back by Herculon.

"You are to remain here to meet the Master."

"Ah!" Caleb cried aloud, and he began to hum a song he learned as a boy. Now it took on a whole new meaning, as hope wished for and held in yearning anticipation was faith turning into sight. He sang!

"What a day this will be, when my Jesus I shall see! When I look upon His face, the One who saved me by His grace. Then He'll take me by the hand and lead me to the Promised Land. What a day! Glorious day! This will be. Hallelujah!"

While he sang, he observed much of the church disappear through a far distant canyon in the mountains. He became concerned why he and many others were left behind in this valley. He ceased singing and turned to Herculon.

"Why are we not allowed to go with the others?" he anxiously inquired of his angel.

"Because their spirits were already greeted by the Master when first they arrived. All of them tasted the sting of death, but you did not. They now have glorious resurrected bodies just like you. Theirs were raised from the grave; your change came in the air. You along with the others in the valley comprise the Body of the Raptured."

# Chapter 52

# It's Jesus!

The valley filled completely with the raptured, the most amazingly beautiful people Caleb had ever witnessed. All mingled together, every nationality and background from the four corners of the earth, resplendent in their garments, eager for the appearing of the Lord.

'What an incredible sight!' he thought. Some were clustered along the river, others walked in patches of flowers, while many roamed the hills - each with a guardian angel beside. The scene was one of noisy excitement! As Caleb walked in a grove of trees, he met brothers and sisters from India, China, the Americas, Europe and Africa. It was miraculous how everyone understood each other - how conversation flowed. There was only one language and no racial or cultural barriers.

He kept looking for Sarah, Esther, and Mark, his family, anyone he had known in life, but they were nowhere to be found, so he simply wandered - searching. He suspected others were doing the same.

He became aware of a growing commotion in one end of the valley that was spreading to where he was in the trees.

It grew intensely, swelling in quickened sound until Caleb could make out shouts, "It's Jesus!"

"Where? Where?" his eyes searched through the trees to where he could see in an open meadow and beyond up a hill, but he could not see the Son of God. Then he observed angels bow their heads with folded wings and a most wondrous event happened. Everything around Caleb blurred out of sight - the trees, grass, people, angels - everything. Next, Jesus appeared, walking toward him, and he couldn't believe it! Of all the millions - Jesus was coming to him! Just to him! He ran to his Savior and took His hands.

"I wanted to see your nail-pierced hands," Caleb cried, "like Thomas did."

Jesus showed him the scars - Caleb wept and kissed them over and over.

"Would you see the wound in my side also like Thomas?" Jesus asked gently.

"No, Lord, I believe."

"Yes, you have - since your childhood."

Wave after wave of the Master's love flowed over Caleb until he collapsed on the ground. Suddenly, closely following love came an overwhelming sense of loss and failure.

"Lord Jesus!" he confessed, "My life was a loss. I failed at every ministry you gave me to do, and at the end, the mission and the crusade were disasters that caused harm and death. I tried so hard, but watched every work crumble. In my youth, everyone said I had a bold dedication that would take me far for you, Lord, but I couldn't seem to – get past college. Please forgive me - I was the man who buried his talent. I'm so sorry!" Caleb was on his knees and face before the Lord.

Jesus smiled and tenderly lifted the broken man to his feet.

"Walk with me," Jesus instructed, and they walked amongst the trees.

"I don't recall any of that," Jesus spoke kindly. "I paid for your sins on the cross, then placed them in the deepest part of the ocean to be remembered no more.

"What I do remember is that you gave me your whole life - from your childhood, Caleb Hillag. When you were little you testified of Me on a newscast that went around the world. Have you any idea how many souls believed the words of a child? You spoke from an innocent heart. They listened!"

"But I divorced, Lord, and I had no right to be a pastor."

"My call on you never changed, and I'm the One to decide if you had the right," Jesus replied firmly. "As for your divorce, my word decreed adultery a valid reason to end a marriage?"

"Yes, Lord, but we didn't..." Caleb stopped.

"That is true, you didn't."

That revelation rendered Caleb speechless as they walked out into the brightness of a field of waving lilies. Birds called from overhead. Caleb finally spoke.

"Lord, every pastorate You called me to was plagued with problems." Then a thought came to him, "Unless You didn't call me?"

Jesus laughed, placing His arm around Caleb's shoulder.

"The calling was sure for each. Yes, the enemy opposed you greatly. I used that to prepare you for the work at Lugar de Paraiso. Wasn't it at Timberdyke you met a special person and led her and her family to believe on Me?" Jesus stopped to face Caleb.

"Sarah!" Caleb whispered.

Now the Savior looked deep into Caleb's heart, soul and spirit.

"Jesus, what a friend for sinners, what a Redeemer," Caleb responded.

"My child, everywhere your feet walked you planted, watered and harvested souls. Well done."

"But there were so few…"

"I look at hearts not numbers. What is the worth of one soul, Caleb?"

Caleb began to cry. "It just always seemed to fall far short of what I hoped to do for You, Lord."

They began walking again. Jesus reached down and picked a beautiful lily.

"Lord, what good came out of the crusade? People got trampled to death!"

Jesus gave Caleb a sad, knowing glance.

"I didn't even get to give an invitation, and Herculon had to rescue us. Brothers and sisters were thrown in jail. Lord, I don't even know if Mark is here - is Mark here? Is Esther - the rest of my family?"

"All will be revealed, my child; you will see."

They walked in silence for a ways before Jesus spoke again.

"It was tragic, what occurred at the stadium. Satan sent one of his powers to oppose and destroy you and My work. What you did not know is that everyone there, including Stoner Howser, heard My message - yes, even the 400 evil prophets heard it on the speakers. Everyone there saw the power of the Most High defeat and confound the powers of darkness. My son, an invitation to come to Me was not restricted to that moment. Many fled the stadium, but found Me. I used what you call a disaster to broadcast My message and proclamation about the saving power of the cross, around the world. Right now, the part of your message about believers being caught up and graves ripped open is heard in homes in every country, as the world tries to make sense of the disappearance of millions. For that purpose you were born and prepared, Caleb. That truly was your moment in time!

Caleb stood amazed as the impact of God's Plan hit him.

"I am deeply humbled, Lord, that You even considered and found me worthy of Your call!"

Jesus hugged Caleb and held him close, then stepped back. He handed Caleb the lily He was holding.

"Give this to Sarah when you see her," He said lovingly.

# Chapter 53

# Sent

Caleb blinked, and Jesus was gone. Herculon was again hovering near, and the people around him in the flower field came back into focus and were all at once in motion and exuberant!

"I just saw Jesus!" a man, close by, of Arab descent shouted.

"Be golly, I spoke to Him I did!" an Irish sister exclaimed.

"Hey, mate, so did I!"

"I walked and talked with Him only a moment ago. We came from those trees out into this field. I didn't see any of you!" Caleb exclaimed dumbfounded.

"I never laid eyes on you either, mate, but I say I talked with the Lord - right in this field. He told me my whole life, He did!"

"A miracle!" they all acknowledged.

"With God, nothing is impossible," a Chinese man quoted scripture in a low voice.

Their conversations were interrupted by the gentle beatings of multitudes of angels' wings. It was like an invasion, but Caleb knew it couldn't be that. He looked to Herculon. His spirit quickened as angels descended all over the valley.

"They are gathering angels coming to take you to the place the Master has prepared for you," Herculon answered his question.

In the next instant, a beautiful angel softly lit in front of him.

"Caleb Hillag," she bowed in respect, "I have come to escort you to your home."

"I couldn't be more ready," Caleb laughed excitedly.

Raptured believers, along with their angels, streamed towards a canyon opening in the far end of the valley. His feet were moving, but they did not touch the ground. The pace was incredibly fast, and Caleb discovered he could speed up or slow down with just a thought. "Wow! This is fantastic, and I can do this - forever. Amazing!"

The canyon in the mountains was vividly picturesque. The river tumbled over rocks and formed deep pools. It was nestled between varieties of trees on each side, many of which bore delicious looking fruit. Caleb would have dallied and picked some; however, the angel hastened him on.

The canyon emptied into a valley so huge, one could not see the far ends of it. All he knew was that which he now beheld was so awesome and delightfully spectacular it completely captured his heart! He understood instantly why the writers of scripture could not describe it.

The beauty of Yosemite, the wonder of Yellowstone, the grandeur of snow-capped Rockies, blue waves washing on white sand at Lugar de Paraiso, any spot on earth that Caleb had ever seen or heard about, bowed in reverence to the majesty of this place. Many believers just stood and gazed. A man near Caleb tearfully exclaimed, "I was born blind and saw only in my spirit. Now I see with my eyes!"

The valley was teeming with life. Flocks of birds peppered the sky. All species of animals added motion to the valley floor. People were evidenced everywhere, and situated across the expanse of the valley as far as Caleb could see, shown cities of intricate design, detail and splendor.

"No two alike," Caleb marveled.

Streams of water, rivers and lakes were scattered in dazzling array, surrounded by trees, plants of many varieties, flowers of rich colors. Walkways invited exploration. Everything blended in perfect harmony. Looking up, Caleb discovered it was not sky but some kind of dome that constantly changed soft colors casting different hues on the valley. Mountains in the far distance rose in rustic magnitude outlined against the dome sky.

"Paradise," Caleb breathed in awe. He glanced at the lily he held in his hand, then studied it closer. The beauty of the lily, the beauty of the valley – was one and the same to a loving God. "He made them both for us."

The gathering angel waited patiently for Caleb, giving him the opportunity to drink in the wonder of God's creation. Caleb nodded he was ready, and they proceeded swiftly into the valley.

People along the way greeted them. Caleb was impressed by every person's stunning appearance. No homely person graced this place. They may have been so on earth, but the Lord brought out an indescribable look of expression and charm in every face Caleb saw. He wondered what his looked like.

Herculon knew his thoughts, "There are no reflections or mirrors in Paradise."

A magnificent city loomed before them. Tier upon tier of precious gems were stacked giving the city a building block look. Stately towers rose high gleaming into the light. A wide cobblestone path led to an entrance, and the bricks making up the road glittered crimson like rubies. Caleb reached down to touch them.

"They are rubies," Herculon smiled.

Two angels greeted them when they reached the city. Both bowed to Caleb.

"Welcome to the city of Sent. We will escort you to your dwelling place," they said in unison.

The gathering angel excused herself and left. Caleb and Herculon followed the escort angels through winding streets. Wide stairs made of jade went to higher levels. Caleb wondered why they were there since they weren't needed. People lined the streets giving warm welcomes, all anxious to get acquainted. The two angels rounded a corner and stopped in front of an elegant house displaying three gold-crested doors. He read his name stamped into the crest of the door he faced.

"This is the place the Master has prepared for you," the angels motioned to the house.

Caleb stepped back to look over the outside. It was the most perfect Spanish-style house he had ever seen. This building; which had three doors, seemed three homes together. The houses sat back from the street about thirty feet. A flower-lined circular walkway led to each door. His home exceeded his highest hopes and wildest dreams! He was about to go inside when his door flew open, and a woman of radiant beauty ran into his arms. Even though her appearance had changed, the manner in which she came to meet him had not, and he recognized Sarah.

"Caleb, oh, Caleb, it's me! We made it! We made it!"

They kissed and hugged, holding each other tight – they were ecstatic - their joy overflowed! They wept, patting each other's faces.

Cheers, laughter, shouts and clapping came from the gathering curious crowd. Caleb should have been embarrassed, but he was so happy to see Sarah, he didn't care who saw them. This was love that now found completion in Paradise. They both gave a shy little wave and slipped into Caleb's place. They had so much to talk about – they could go on for a century over what had already happened to them. They wanted to share, but where to start?

"Heaven is so - what can I say, Sarah. I could never have imagined - this." He motioned around the large room lined with comfortable, colorful sofas, chairs and thick, plushy pillows. The matching furniture was rich.

"Where did we get the idea we would be living in something that resembled an ice palace?" Sarah laughed.

"Our guardian angels will think we are going crazy," Caleb teased, seeing the curiosity on their faces.

"Why? They have been with us our whole lives. Mine is named Portus."

"Mine is Herculon."

"You got a strong one; I got the gentle one, dear. Caleb, I'm so glad to see you - be with you. I got panicky out in space when I couldn't find you. There were so many people – and – and – angels! Portus helped me. Then to see – Jesus…face to face," Sarah spoke reverently.

"Yes, Sarah, that alone, those moments with Him, made everything we went through on earth, worth it."

"Oh, Caleb," Sarah pointed to a wall, "You must see all your pictures!"

For the first time, Caleb took notice of his dwelling and the pictures on his walls. He tried to remove one to see it better. It would not budge.

"Gosh, look here, Sarah. These are people at Timberdyke - hey, here's one of when I came to your house that first night. Wonder who took it - I didn't see anyone with a camera."

"There wasn't," Sarah smiled, and Caleb realized what he was saying.

"Here's one when we were in Tennessee, and look - the mission - oh my, the meeting at the school when Chantal was coming in. Why would that be here?"

Sarah shrugged her shoulders. There was a knock on the door.

"Come on in," Caleb hollered. They were surprised when a woman stepped through the door without opening it. Sarah gasped.

"Don't be alarmed," she spoke graciously. "You can do it also; you just haven't tried. Anyway, I have come to welcome you to Sent. I was informed you just arrived, and you were raptured."

"True."

"Ah, good. That means the end is near. Now tell me where you were missionaries - what country?"

"How do you know we were missionaries?" Sarah asked.

"Child," the woman laughed heartily, "everyone in Sent was a missionary. That's where the name came from - we were all sent. David Livingston's place is close to me. Hudson Taylor and Mother Teresa, 'course she hasn't been here near as long, is just down your street."

"But who are you?" Caleb was curious as to her identity.

The woman appeared embarrassed, smiled, and then collected her self. "There are so many interesting missionaries with fantastic stories from every country on the globe we could just stay right here in Sent forever, listening and telling of it. Anyway, I'm no one you ever heard of, Lottie Moon."

Caleb and Sarah both caught their breath.

"Of course, we've heard of you, Ms. Moon, you were a missionary to China."

"Don't need the 'miss' title; just call me Lottie. Now where did you serve?"

"A resort town on the Mexican Coast called Lugar de Paraiso."

"I want to hear all about it. I'll be back to visit, and then you can tell me. I have a trunk full of questions. That's what I packed everything in when I sailed on those freighters. Pleased to make you welcome. You must have been wonderful and loving to your people." With a warm 'goodbye' she disappeared through the door.

"Wow! Caleb scratched his head.

"That was our first visit," Sarah spoke, deep in thought.

"And what a visit!" Caleb replied as he began to search the pictures.

"Do you remember Zipper and her children in Oregon?" Sarah asked. One of my pictures had them in it."

"Where?" Caleb started searching.

"Not here, silly man, in my house."

"Your house? You mean you aren't living here?"

"I'm next door."

"Humph, we coulda saved the Lord the space and just shared this one." Caleb laughed, but grew serious when he saw a deeper concern cross Sarah's face. She dropped her eyes.

"There are three houses - together," she said quietly.

"I saw that. Who has the third one?"

"Esther."

"Esther! Is she here?"

"Somewhere, but a gathering angel has not brought her to her house yet."

"Do you think something's wrong?" Caleb asked.

"I can't imagine what it would be - in a place like this."

"What about Mark?"

Sarah's face revealed the grief she bore.

"Caleb, there are only three houses!"

# Chapter 54

# The Grand Reunion of the Ages

Esther burst through the doorway! "Mom - Dad!" she screamed, running to them.

"I'm so glad to see you!" Those last few days on earth were horrible. I was so scared!"

"It's alright - it's alright now," Caleb and Sarah comforted their daughter. "We are home and safe now."

Esther wept out her feelings. "The evening of the Concert Crusade an evil black as midnight formed around me. Knocks on our door frightened both my roommate and me but there was never anyone in the hall. She called security, but the knocking persisted. I felt some evil force, something monstrous, was trying to get in the room."

"Stoner!" Caleb and Sarah agreed knowingly.

"When you told me about him, and what he said..." Esther cried, "that's when I went to Grandfather's and Grandmother's, but..."Esther broke down again. "This evil – Stoner - attacked me in my sleep. He was touching my body. All over! It was so real I woke up screaming! I'm just glad Jesus came for us! The world had gotten so ugly I wanted to leave... Where's Mark?"

"We don't think he made it," Sarah answered gravely.

"Oh, no! Not Mark! It can't be!" A look of horror filled Esther's eyes. "We must search Heaven for him!"

Portus, seeing their concern and fear, offered to help. "We can search for you."

"You can?" Sarah was surprised. "Oh, yes, please do."

All three guardian angels sang the most beautiful song. As the small angelic choir raised their voices, they lifted off the floor with unfurled wing, louder and upward their song soared. In a moment, they touched down, their wings furled, and the singing quieted. They folded their wings, and a sorrow clouded their faces.

"Mark Hillag is not in Paradise," Herculon spoke gently with steadfast gaze.

Shock and grief struck the family deeper than any Caleb had ever experienced. He and Sarah shed tears of anguish over their lost son, and wondered how such deep anguish could ever follow them into a place like they were in now. Esther cried for the little brother she loved and had always tried to protect. There was no protecting him now, but they took comfort in the possibility Mark would trust Christ during the Tribulation.

"He will pay with his life for his faith," Caleb commented solemnly.

They sat in silent thought before discussing memories of the past, renewed by viewing life pictures in all three of their homes.

"I don't have as many pictures as you do," Esther observed.

"You didn't live as long as we did, dear," Sarah reminded her.

"But mine seems so frivolous."

"Not so;" Caleb answered, "each one has its meaning. We have to believe that."

They were in lively conversation when a gathering angel appeared in their midst.

"Come," he instructed, "your family awaits."

The angel led them along a riverbank, then across the valley to another beautiful city. He stopped in front of what anyone would have called a dream home. It had a yard of rich green grass surrounded by a rose garden of vibrant colors. Butterflies fluttered through the blossoms. Large trees swayed in a gentle breeze that filled the air with an angelic sound of music. An inviting rock walkway led across the yard to the front door.

"What a cute house!" exclaimed Sarah.

"Only thing missing is a lamp post and mailbox," mused Caleb under his breath.

"Cool space!" Esther's voice was charged with excitement. "Who lives here?"

The gathering angel motioned for them to come and find out.

A woman opened the door to Caleb's knock.

"Penny!" Sarah screamed, and the two squealed, thrilled to see each other.

Inside the house was T. J. and their two girls. Standing to one side was Hannah, and Esther ran to her grandmother. Tears, cries, chatter and unbridled laughter blended into one happy reunion! Caleb heard Sarah say, "Penny, your home is so beautiful!"

"Oh, this is Mom's, but you should see mine! An angel gathered us here. Where is Mark?"

"He's not here!" Sarah lamented. "We're heartbroken."

When Caleb had the chance to speak to Hannah, he inquired about Gary Howser.

"He was a stubborn, prideful, bitter man," she answered softly. "He was hateful and cruel, rejecting Christ until the very end. I know he will be mad when he can't find the children or me. If he is here, he hasn't shown up yet."

"Do you know our angels can search Heaven for us?"

"No!" Hannah could scarcely believe Caleb.

"Herculon?" Caleb turned to his guardian. "Would you search Heaven for Gary Howser - and Stoner Howser too, please?"

"Heaven is where the Most High sits on His throne. This is Paradise where you dwell," Herculon corrected Caleb respectfully. "Yes, we will search for your loved one."

All the angels rose in song, expanding even to the far reaches of Paradise. Hope upon hope, Caleb knew in his spirit it was futile to think either of these hardhearted men had trusted the Lord at sometime during their lives - yet, there was always the possibility - at the last moment... The angel's drooped wings and downcast eyes confirmed the absence of Gary and Stoner Howser. With each realization of an absent loved one, the hurt and pain drove deeper into all of their hearts. They discussed at length the dark transition to an Enlightened One Stoner made early in his life, and the hideous demon that possessed him. They speculated about what might have started him on this evil course to the ultimate possession of satanic power. Gary's rejection of Christ was willful disbelief; however Stoner embraced the darkness. What began as curious dabbling in the occult eventually consumed his spirit, mind, soul and heart in evil obedience to his underworld master.

Later, Hannah shared her sorrow over her parents, grandparents and family, too busy to listen to her pleas to receive Jesus as their Savior.

"Now we've all disappeared and they are left," she shook her head, wondering if she couldn't have done more to persuade them to believe.

Caleb had no idea how long they had spent at his place nor now at Grandmother Hannah's, for concept of time in Paradise carried no reference point - no passing of day into night to show a progression of 24 hours. Certainly, no clocks hung on any walls or were displayed in city squares. No church steeples chimed the hour. No Sat phones with time display.

On earth there always grew a sense of urgency due to the lateness of the hour, an unforgiving bite into one's day by an overtaxed schedule. Ah, but here, there was a never ending unhurried peace. Time would not run out; it had no end - make it long or short, whatever suited you. Forever is a long, long, long…forever!

Therefore, Caleb, Sarah and Esther were not in the least upset when the gathering angel returned to lead them to more reunions. They could come back to Hannah's again and again, as the passing of time was insignificant.

"Come," the angel invited, "you have more family eagerly waiting for you."

Caleb felt a thrill of excitement for he knew this meant his side of the family. He was thankful they were taken to Sarah's first, but now he couldn't wait to see his loved ones.

The angel took them into the mountains where tall and stately timber filled the landscape. This area carried a charm and beauty different from the other parts of Paradise, one that reminded Caleb of the great northwest, only a far greater grandeur than any spot on earth.

Caleb recognized spruce, aspen, pine, fir and redwood trees - healthy and thick on both sides of a road they were walking on. Open light filled meadows were alive with animals. In a juniper and cedar patch of trees, Esther pointed out a herd of deer - or was it antelope? Different kinds of birds flew in abundance.

They passed homes nestled in the trees, and Caleb thought each one would be their destination, but the angel led on, higher, higher up a canyon that yielded a fast running, spar-kling stream. The sound was so inviting and restful, they had to stop and drink in the scene before them.

Crystal clear water spilled over rocks and rushed down the canyon. Tall trees formed a canopy over the water, and far above stood majestic mountain peaks in magnificent splendor. Caleb, Sarah and Esther could only bow their heads in quiet reverence to God who created such a place. There was a feeling inside that wanted to linger and bask in the awesomeness of this spot for ages, but they knew they must continue on.

The gathering angel led them along the creek to a place that opened into a spacious meadow. Caleb laughed out loud.

"A log house!" Sarah cried out.

"And what a house," Caleb exclaimed. "Look at the size of it!"

"I love it!" Esther clapped her hands.

As they neared the log house, they saw a waiting crowd of people on the huge porch surrounded by angels.

"Family is coming!" someone shouted.

"Who is it?" another asked.

"Can't tell. It's a man and two women."

"Dear Lord, I think its Caleb!"

"I see Grandmama," Esther cried and took off running.

In an instant, Caleb and Sarah were engulfed with hugs, warm words, pats and kisses. He found his way to his Mother Morgan and Father Joseph's embrace and blubbered like a child.

After Joseph concluded hugging and speaking to his granddaughter Esther, his penetrating gaze at Caleb gave away his stricken heart.

"Mark is not with you?"

"No, sir, he rejected Jesus."

Remorse rippled through the family welling up in a mournful cry for one of their own. The angels not under-standing the feelings, but knowing the dreaded place where Mark would go, grieved in their own way along with the family. Though they never experienced these same emotions as humans, they certainly were aware of the effects on men and women. They bowed in humble respect as the family sorrowed over those who were lost. Each member was reminded of someone they knew and loved who was not in Paradise.

Caleb wiped tears from his eyes. Looking up, he saw his Grandfather Clifton and Grandmother Rachel waiting to greet him.

"We are thrilled to see you, Caleb! It has seemed such a long time," they both said, giving him a happy welcome.

"Sarah, you are so beautiful! I wish we could have known each other on earth." Rachel exclaimed, "and Esther, my great-granddaughter all grown up and here – forever – together!"

"Remember me? I'm your Uncle David, and this is your Aunt Cynthia and Cousin Mary."

"Yes, of course," Caleb recognized them. Waves of compassion swept over him. "I heard of your tragic deaths in that terrible storm in Alaska. Mary, weren't you engaged to – ah…?"

"To Kasha. He's not here either," Mary spoke remorsefully.

"I'm so glad to finally meet all of you," Sarah took Mary's hands. "Caleb spoke of you often and missed you so. We had your pictures."

"Come in the house, Caleb, Sarah, Esther - come! There are others you must meet!" Mother Morgan held out her hand and called them inside the enormous, rustic, log house.

Family who were on the porch followed the new arrivals into the living area. It resembled a huge resort lodge - only bigger and grander in its Northwood's charm.

A tall lanky man approached Caleb with outstretched hand and broad grin.

"So you are my niece's boy? Last I saw ya - ya was a mere lad," he shook Caleb's hand.

"Yes, sir," Caleb was puzzled.

"I'm Walter Trevor," and taking Sarah's hand he kissed it gallantly. "Welcome to the Trevor log house in the woods. This be your daughter?" He asked, pulling Esther close to give her a hug.

"Yes, I didn't know you well, but I heard stories about you," Caleb replied.

"Better been decent ones!" Walter laughed, "Or I won't claim 'em, an there's nothen but the truth in Paradise."

"I was told you were a pilot, and that you never married, and were killed in a plane crash."

"Humph," Walter scratched his chin. "Have to admit to all o' those."

"Stop hoggin' all the lad's time. You never talked that much to the rest of us your whole life, Walter." a woman interrupted.

"Making up for lost time - 'sides there ain't no time, so stop yer complaining."

All the family laughed heartily.

The woman carried brashness, but commanded an unspoken elegance that caused her to be noticed and stand apart from the other family members. She put one arm around Caleb and one around Sarah. "I saw you when you were a little boy. You know you upstaged me on a newscast?"

"Janee Stemper," Caleb breathed aloud. Sarah gasped!

"I saw your movies!" she gushed.

"I'm glad, but I'm here to tell you kids, the movies - the Oscar – the fame – the fortune - just doesn't stack up to this. Isn't Paradise glorious? Isn't it? The future Jesus planned for us?"

"It's true," they both agreed with Janee.

"My husband, Bernard, brought me to Jesus, and I can never thank the big bozo enough. You were at my wedding, Caleb. You came with your Mother. Remember? Anyway, Bernard isn't here right now - some of his family were caught up - he is with them, and I'll join him - but had to welcome you all first."

Now Janee stepped close to Caleb. Her expression conveyed that all joking was laid aside. She spoke in a coarse whisper charged with emotion.

"Caleb, child, I never had the chance to tell you this, and I couldn't wait 'til you arrived to say what I've held in my heart for so long. Do you remember at Grandmother Emile's house when we were there for her funeral?"

"Yes."

"She had told you to ask - "tears filled the actress' eyes. "You asked how long I was going to be mad at God for taking my Grandfather, and was I still mad at God?"

Caleb searched his mind to recall the incident. He mostly remembered playing in the house with Mary, and the encounter Janee spoke of was dim, but he sensed the impact on her.

"Your childish way and words was the beginning of a long road back to Jesus, and I am so happy, Caleb; you were faithful as a child to deliver the message I needed to hear. I can never thank you enough!" Janee hugged Caleb and kissed his cheek.

"Alright, Janee, who's hoggin' now?"

"Oh, Mother, you always were one to cut a scene! Father, can't you do anything with her even now?"

"Too late!" a man Caleb couldn't recall apart from some pictures, laughed.

"Oh, if I must! Caleb, Sarah, Esther - this is my Mother Leah and Father Harold." Janee introduced them.

Caleb remembered seeing Janee's parents on rare visits, which seemed to end upon Janee's untimely death.

Leah and Harold asked questions. They wanted to know what had been taking place on earth, what it was like to be raptured, and what happened after that?

"You never experienced death," Leah said reverently. "What a blessed generation."

Janee brought a man eager to get acquainted.

"My son, Seth," Janee spoke softly.

"A son?" Caleb questioned. He didn't recall Janee having a child.

"I had a secret abortion," Janee explained, but look at him now - isn't he - so handsome? My son...."

"Oh!" Sarah began to cry and took Janee in her arms. Caleb took Seth's hand and shook it. He wasn't quite sure what to say.

"Welcome - to our family," Seth spoke awkwardly.

Caleb had to laugh!

"Amen, Brother, we're in this together!" Caleb's warm words told Seth he was accepted.

Walter, Clifton and Rachel, escorted them across the room where much of the family were gathered around couples seated on sofas. The family members moved away for Caleb, Sarah and Esther to approach. The noisy chatter softened, and the room grew still. A man and woman rose to their feet. They smiled, and the man spoke in a cheerful, gentle manner that portrayed the love he held in his heart.

"I reckon with all the commotion thet's been a'happenin', these be some folks we best git acquainted with. Come over here, an' tell us yer names."

"I'm Caleb Hillag; Sarah my Wife, and our Daughter Esther. We had a Son, Mark, but - but - he didn't - make it - here."

"Right sorry to hear thet distressin' piece o news. Had a Sister Stella what didn't make it neither, so's I know o' yer pain. But we be powerful glad you all air here. Hillag, ya say? Ya air Morgan's Son?"

"Yes, sir." Caleb kept trying to place this couple. Then it hit him. This must be his Great-grandparents Farmer and Emile Trevor!

"We saw your log house!" he blurted out.

"Ya did?" Farmer laughed. "Come tell us how it be," he and Emile gathered them in their arms in a warm welcome. They sat down.

"It stood solid - and in good shape," Caleb went on.

"We built a fire in the fireplace and everything," Esther was eager to tell.

"I found your bedroom," Sarah spoke up, "I knew it was yours."

Emile smiled and took Sarah's hand.

"What year it be when ya saw the ranch house?" Farmer asked.

"Uh - it was - was -."

"2017," Sarah helped Caleb.

"What!" Farmer exclaimed. "Thet log house be near a hundred years old."

"Ha!" Caleb laughed. "It would be now!" Then he grew serious.

"It stood solid, like it was waiting for you, or someone, to return."

"Your parents also just arrived and told us you were missionaries?" Emile shifted the subject, and with that Caleb, Sarah and Esther shared their life stories. They also met Great-Great-Grandparents Franklin and Allison Jane, Farmer's Brothers and Sisters-in-law, Nephew Sidney Dean and the Holts and Neilsons on Emile's side.

It struck Caleb as he watched different family members talking, laughing, making their points with animated hands and arms and giving happy expressions with their eyes and faces - this had to be the grand reunion of the ages!

"Look at this!" he got Sarah's attention. "We are seeing generations, sitting in this - this - giant log house - all together. This could never have happened on earth! We could never have attained this kind of fellowship and bond of love - or known this degree of joy.

"Praise God!" Caleb shouted. "This is glorious! Praises be to Jesus Christ!"

"And we've only just begun!" Sarah declared, clapping her hands in girlish glee.

# Chapter 55

# Judgment Seat of Christ

A strange shift was reported to have occurred since the Rapture. Caleb was not aware of it because he had not experienced it like those who had gone before. Great grandfather Farmer told him of it when he queried Caleb on what it was like to be raptured.

"We heard the trumpet sound and then a commanding voice shouting to 'Come.' We went flying up into the air as fast as - uh –a..."

"Lightning bolt?"

"Yes, sir."

"Well, I reckon thet ta be a thrill greater than one of those roller coaster rides. We was called to go with the Lord Jesus ta meet ya all in the air. We was everone spirits ta thet point - then our bodies joined up with us in the sky. It be so swift we never knew when it happened. Thet's was bout the time ya all appeared, I reckon."

"An incredible event I'll never forget!"

"Nor I, son, but there be one thing I be missin'."

"What's that, Greatgrandfather?" Caleb asked.

"Well now, before thet resurrection, Jesus would speak ta us - in our heads ya know. Oft times He appeared in our homes or walked with us along the road or in the trees. Since we be back, He up and quit. I jus reckoned He didn't hev anything ta talk ta me 'bout, 'til I finds out no one else was seein' Him or hearin' from Him either. Now thet struck me as a mite odd."

"Jesus appeared and spoke to me when I was in the valley beyond the mountains after we first arrived, but now that you mention it - nothing since."

"The Lord be doin' somethin'," Farmer concluded. "We'll know when He be ready ta let us in on it."

Caleb was content, at peace, and he enjoyed countless unhurried visits with family and friends. The city of Sent revealed many park-like areas and was situated on the shore of a huge lake - or sea - Caleb was unsure which. All Caleb knew was how much he and Sarah loved walking the waters' edge when the sky turned a darker hue of blue reminding them of an early evening.

It was on one of those walks their angels informed them there was a sudden strong stirring in Paradise and to get ready.

"Ready for what?" Caleb and Sarah questioned.

The next instant the far reaches of Paradise were filled with peals of countless trumpets. The sound was a call and an announcement.

"You must return to your dwelling and gather your life pictures," Herculon instructed Caleb "You will appear before the Righteous One."

Caleb didn't question, and he and Sarah hurried to their houses, wondering how they could pull their pictures off the wall – they were fastened tight before.

Esther was standing outside her house already holding a bag.

"Mom, Dad, there was this bag in my house, and all my pictures came off the wall. What are we doing?" She wasn't sure whether to be apprehensive or excited.

Caleb also found a bag in his house. It was of the most elegant weave and design with the feel of luxurious richness.

To his amazement his life pictures came easily off the wall, and he placed them with care in his bag. He thought them to be heavy until he shouldered the bag to step outside and discovered the load indeed to be light.

He joined Sarah and Esther outside their houses.

"Wait," the angels instructed.

Another loud peal of the trumpets broke into what seemed a long pause, followed by a loud cry that could be heard all over Paradise.

"The Judgment Seat of Christ."

# Chapter 56

# Getting Things Right

Caleb felt no sense of dread as the whole of Paradise was ushered into the presence of Jesus Christ who would now be Judge. Instead, he had the excited feelings of anticipation. He had believed God's Word all his life that, yes; his works were to be judged, but Praise the Lord, not his salvation. Those sins were judged by Christ's death on the cross and gone forever.

He was uncertain though about what was to happen. 'How were his works to be judged? Paradise was filled with millions of people. If each of God's children stood before the Judge alone - this could take forever,' Caleb mused. 'Oh, well, what is time. No! Wait! This has to be done in 7 earth years. Hmm...and how does this bag of pictures figure into the judgment?'

A hand took hold of his clothing. He looked back to see Sarah had a firm grip on his shirt and Esther in her other hand, just like she used to do when they were in a crowd of people on earth.

This heavenly throng converged into a massive open valley filled with the redeemed as far as the eye could see.

"This is momentous!" Sarah exclaimed in awe.

"This is one humongous field of grass!" Esther gasped. "Look at how many are here!"

"Makes our Crusade Concert pretty puny!" Caleb laughed.

The sky overhead that had been a darker shade of blue began to lighten. As the sky grew lighter a quieting of the noisy chatter took hold. A stunning royal throne that had not been noticed before became prominent to the view of everyone, as it seemed to increase in size. The sky was now a bright white, which penetrated every area of Paradise and displayed the brilliance of the Judgment Seat! It was like white granite, perfect, without any flaw and adorned in gold and silver. A collective praise cheer of amazed wonder rose from the lips of millions. They couldn't wait to see Jesus!

Again, the trumpets sounded, and Heaven's host began to sing the most beautiful chorus. Never had an overture like this been heard by human ears. The words and music reverberated throughout Paradise filling it with moving and inspiring sounds! It contained a tremendous power to open hearts and stir emotion.

"Worthy is the Lamb that was slain to receive Power - Honor - Glory!"

Angels with instruments joined in, and Caleb's heart and mind soared with the songs. He became aware that millions were singing in harmony with the angels. Not the same song, each with a different one that swelled from the heart, but they all blended together perfectly. Caleb heard Sarah's beautiful voice ringing out praises to God. His own voice joined hers as they sang, 'Holy, Holy, Holy, Lord God Almighty!'

Then the music score became a triumphal entry that thrilled and inspired Caleb to the very depths of his soul. His spirit quickened! Jesus was coming!

Instantly, the music ceased, angels' wings folded, instruments in hand, heads bowed in deep reverence for the Lord of Lords - a hush fell on the vast multitude.

Jesus appeared beside the Judgment Seat, not as they had seen Him before, but resplendent in His Glory! Not as Friend and Savior, but as King, Lord and Judge. Cries of worship swept amidst the throng, as one after another fell to their knees and faces before the Mighty God.

Jesus took His place on the throne, and the angels sang! Jesus called for everyone to stand before Him with the spreading of his arms wide.

"Dearly beloved," He spoke with great love. "All things are now judged and made right."

The brilliance of Christ's countenance illuminated every part of each person's life. There were no covered parts, no secret places, and no shadow of turning, hidden closet doors swung open. Sins, committed as Christians and not confessed in life must be dealt with now. The Light, Jesus Christ, shone on every wicked and evil action, thought, word –now exposed in all its black ugliness.

Caleb began to hear cries of repentance from those around him.

"Oh, Lord, forgive me for doing that!" Sarah wailed.

Jesus took Caleb back to the moment he trusted Christ and replayed his life to the last instant when he was caught up. Incidents he had never considered as sinful were now revealed in their true nature from the Lord's perspective. Every motive was analyzed. Wrongs and grievances he had suffered leaving him with an unforgiving heart must be confessed. A life Caleb had thought pretty clean and righteous was full of dirty smudges, and although all his sins were paid in full, they still must be acknowledged before the Righteous Judge, Jesus Christ. Caleb was on his face - weeping confessions - asking forgiveness!

At this point, it didn't matter what anyone else had done or hadn't done. This was strictly between him and the Son of God. Caleb watched in horror as he viewed his life revealed in the all-penetrating, exposing Light of Christ. He wondered if he did any good on earth at all. His sins and failures eclipsed any positive part of his life. The thoughts of his mind were blighted with dark images he was ashamed for Jesus to see.

Every second of his Christian life was reviewed. Caleb remembered blatant sins, which were never mentioned here and wondered why. Then in his spirit he remembered asking forgiveness on earth. He heard Jesus say, "They are remembered no more."

"Thank you, Lord!" Caleb cried out, and thought, 'If I would have known this, I would have been quicker and more thorough in seeking forgiveness on earth.'

Next, Jesus Christ, revealed the perfect plan He had for Caleb's life compared to how Caleb actually lived it. Some parts were on target, but mostly he was shocked at the differences and grieved over the areas he had widely missed the mark. Realizing what could have been, how could he have been disgustingly blind and at other times – just plain – indifferent?

# Chapter 57

# Going to Others

C aleb was taught in seminary that there were occasions in a congregation when feelings needed to be cleared. Words of appreciation or requests for forgiveness were exchanged among the people. He had not only been a part of such services, but had afforded that opportunity numerous times to the members of the churches he pastored, as well as at Global Missions Christian Church. Caleb sensed the Lord was moving upon this vast multitude to do that very thing. Words that longing hearts wished to speak over decades of centuries, hindered, held back, never said or written could now be expressed. A stirring began that broke into vast movement!

Who should Caleb speak to? Without a second thought he turned to Sarah.

"Sweetheart, I remember the first day I met you and will never cease to thank God for it - and for you."

"I believe I fell in love with you the moment I laid eyes on you," Sarah softly responded.

"Sweetheart, I always tried to be honest with you over all things, but there was something I never told you. I meant to, but just never got around to it – then so much time passed."

"What was it, Caleb?"

"I went to the Juvenile Hall right after I first came to your home. I confronted Stoner, we fought, and he attempted to escape. I was the reason he ended up in lock down. I felt your family would be upset with me, so I..."

Sarah covered a laugh with her hand. "Oh Caleb, we knew that. A deputy told us. We realized you felt badly, so we just never mentioned it." They laughed and hugged!

"Despite the hard times, didn't we have a good life together?"

"Yes," she agreed.

"I'm sorry my love seemed stiff and unbending."

"You made me happy, Caleb, I felt loved."

"You were a true helpmate - a loving wife."

They both felt a tug on their arms. It was Esther.

"Mom - Dad! I never told you enough how much I loved you and appreciated all you did for me!"

"Oh, Esther," Sarah drew their daughter close, and sadness and regret flooded Caleb's heart.

"I'm just sorry I never got the chance to walk you down the aisle at your wedding!"

"But, Daddy, we are going to be part of the grandest wedding ever!" Esther smiled through her tears and patted his face. "You can walk with me to that."

The next instant a man threw himself at Sarah's feet.

"Sarah, for the love of Jesus, forgive me - forgive me!" the man cried.

Caleb gave Sarah a questioning look, as he had no idea who the man was. He wouldn't look up where they could see his face. Sarah shook her head - she did not know him.

"Sarah, please forgive all the hurt and pain I put on you! The loss I made you suffer!"

"Who are you? I don't...!"

It was then the man lifted his eyes to meet hers with the shocking revelation, "Sarah, I'm your Father."

Caleb saw a jolt hit Sarah. He knew she had just taken for granted this man was lost to her forever.

"I abandoned you and your Mother. I was a coward - selfish! I left the ones most dear and ran away. I wrote a drawer full of letters, but never mailed a one. Sarah, in life I died so many times I didn't care anymore. I see now I missed out on so much - and I hurt you deeply. I am so sorry!"

At that moment, Hannah joined them. Caleb could tell by the look on her face that Sarah's dad had gone to his wife first.

"I never stopped loving him, Sarah," was all she said.

Sarah's demeanor changed to one of a child as she slipped to the grass to face her father.

"Oh, Daddy," she cried as she studied each feature of his face. "I surely do forgive you. I'm so happy to find you! I kept your letter all those years!"

While this was happening, a woman approached Caleb.

"Caleb?" She held out her hands to him. He recognized his ex-wife Tammy.

"Tammy!" Caleb gasped as he took her hands.

She looked intently into his eyes.

"I couldn't wait for my guardian angel to locate you. I have a confession I harbored inside from the time we were married."

"I know, Tammy, you don't need to say any more. I already forgive you, but you need to forgive me for being such a boring husband that made you go looking for someone else."

"It wasn't you, Caleb; it was me! We were both busy with studies, and what started as a casual friendship with another man who listened and made me feel – special - became something more. I got in too deep and sinned against God, and against you. I told you I couldn't be a pastor's wife because I knew you would never leave the Lord's call on your life. The truth was, Caleb, I wanted out of our marriage to marry - him. I've wanted to tell you this for so long - and to hear you say you forgive me. Thank you, Caleb!"

"Did I know your - er - husband?"

"No."

"Did he make you happy? Did you have a good life?"

"Yes," Tammy answered softly, releasing Caleb's hands.

"For that, I am glad. Is he here?"

"Yes."

"You must come and spend time with Sarah and me. Promise! You know I forgive you both if I welcome you into my house."

Tammy's face and eyes conveyed her gratitude and release. She smiled, touched his face, and left.

Another woman had been waiting to speak to him.

"Do you recognize me, Pastor Caleb Hillag? I am Armelita Villanueva. I thank our Lord, Jesus Christ, for the message you spoke in the stadium that so touched my heart. Because of it, I am standing here talking to you! I praise our Father you stood firm in your faith and in my husband's face, speaking the truth of God's Word."

"Praise the Lord, Armelita, that Jesus saved you! Is Fernando here?" Caleb looked around.

"No...he was a raging bull right up to the moment I disappeared from our bed."

Members of Global Missions Christian Church gathered around Caleb and Sarah, who had just finished reconciliation with her Dad. They all welcomed Armelita, and wanted to talk at once.

Chris Fowler was the first to express what they all wanted to say.

"We can never say in words how dear you both were - and are to us."

"Thank you for leaving your home in the States to come to us," Kay Fowler added.

"You gave me hope," Maybeline shared.

"You were a refuge in the storm for me and my girls," Espolito murmured through her tears.

"You were my Momma and Papa," Blanca cried.

"You taught Jesus; I am here now!" Plomo spoke with bold conviction.

Hank and Tulipan gave them both hugs.

"What can I say, Preacher - Sarah," Hank displayed his love and respect in his voice.

Bomba was last.

"Thank you for introducing me to the greatest man of my life - Jesus Christ, my Savior. I could so easily not be here with you - but left behind. She kissed them both on their cheeks.

Rubin joined the group.

"Caleb, I owe you big time, Senor! You took the time in the darkest hour of my life to make sure I received Jesus, the Christ."

"So did you, Sarah," cried Arcy Garza, who came running up. She threw her arms around Sarah's neck. "I am here today along with my children, because of what Jesus did on the cross, and you shared Him from your heart. Thank you, my sister!"

The group went into animated conversation, then stopped as if taking a head count.

"I was with Mark in a prison cell," Chris remembered. "Where is he?"

"He didn't make it," Caleb and Sarah answered in unison.

"Tazada was with us at the church when we were raptured," Sarah gasped.

Caleb looked to Herculon, and the group's angels searched Paradise. It soon became evident Tazada was not there.

"That leaves Sierra."

"I am with you," a familiar voice came from behind. They all spun around to face a brightly illuminated angel in splendid raiment.

"You are an angel!" they exclaimed aloud.

"The same one who led Paul and Silas from the prison," the angel declared. "You knew me as Sierra - I am Articus!"

"Well, as I live and breathe forever, we entertained an angel unaware," Hank laughed.

At this juncture, the Global Missions fellowship scattered as each had other contacts. For the first time, Caleb observed those around him and deducted that families appeared in clusters. He spied his and Sarah's parents, with a few individuals talking to them. Near, also, were his grandparents and other family members. His great-grandparents, Farmer and Emile, were surrounded by a host of people. Janee Stemper caught his eye and attention with her strong melodic laugh. He noted with concern and sadness, Seth, standing alone near his mother. He thought to go to him when a woman grabbed his arm.

"Caleb, I'm so glad you lived a life that reflected your faith. I watched you closely, and admired a man who had given his heart to a Jesus he loved more than life itself. Your loving kindness led me to find that Jesus for myself!"

Caleb searched the woman's face, but recognition refused to surface in his mind. His puzzled look prompted her to continue.

"I'm Symphony. We worked together at DeLamo's Pizza."

"Oh my gosh, Symphony!" Caleb was genuine in his joy that she was a Christian and in Paradise.

"You thought you delivered pizza to help support your family, but it was for me! I will praise God for eternity for saving me - and for sending you."

Caleb turned to Sarah.

"You remember Symphony I worked with? She's here too!"

"Oh! Symphony, I'm so excited you made your decision for Christ," Sarah reached over to give her a hug.

"And Caleb, I was just getting reacquainted with Zipper Drake and her two sons from Douglas Landing."

"Ah, we knew you would be here - and these boys of yours, but tell us of your husband - ah – uh…"

"Taget? He ran off with a woman young enough to be his daughter. Never saw the likes o' him again, but he ain't here - we done searched. He broke all our hearts then - and again - here…" Zipper bravely fought back the tears.

There was a continuing flurry of activity spread out before the Judgment Seat of Christ. What a sight it must have been for the Lord to watch, and how well pleased He was - finally, the church coming together in perfect peace, harmony, joy, unity and great love. Without realizing it the church was being conformed into a Bride without spot or wrinkle, and it would go on until every last contact was made, forgiveness given and word spoken.

Caleb wanted to see the greatest missionary of all time, the Apostle Paul. Herculon assured him humorously it might take a million years or so to get an appointment.

Caleb next contacted Global Missions' board members to express his deep appreciation for their sensitivity to the Lord's leading, and their faith in him and Sarah. He also conveyed his affection for these brothers and sisters.

"Did you bring your successions of Ronas?" Caleb teased.

Hub got a kick out of the joke, and they all laughed together.

"We left them to fight the anti-christ and his army," Tiffany Gong tittered.

"We programmed them to do that you know, Caleb, and to self-destruct if they were forced to take the mark of the beast," Gerald Pullman added.

Others Caleb had led to the Lord in the churches he pastured crowded around him as well as many who trusted Christ because of his testimony on Network News. A large throng of people from many countries followed these brothers and sisters. He was made to understand they accounted for every offering Caleb had ever given which was used to reach out to them with the Good News of the Gospel. Some of it helped finance mission work or national pastors. Other portions provided Bibles and literature. Caleb was overwhelmed at how extensive and massive the work of God's Kingdom had been.

One by one the process of going to others continued until all were finished, and each one resumed their places by their bags of life pictures.

# Chapter 58

# Judgment of Works

Have you ever experienced a peaceful excitement over an upcoming event? That's what Caleb felt now as the Lord announced the Judgment of Works.

He remembered scripture, which told that his works would be tested as by fire. The Word taught that some would reap reward and others would suffer loss.

He did not approach this test with dread, like every misdeed or wicked thought would be played on a huge screen for the whole assembly to see. Jesus had personally dealt with that.

He was not sure about the suffering loss part. There was no competition or envy in this blessed place - no sense that if others had greater reward than he, Jesus would love them more. He had already experienced the Lord's love. Jesus loved each of them equally, but differently, just like Caleb did his own children.

Nor was he threatened if Sarah received more reward than he did. He embraced this deep feeling that he would be thrilled and truly satisfied with whatever he was awarded, and a longing overflowed his heart with the desire to lay it all at the feet of the Master.

Strong anticipation gripped the massive assembly gathered before the Judgment Seat. Jesus spread His arms open wide, taking in the people standing before Him.

"Beloved!" His voice sent waves of His unending love into every heart.

"Take one 'Life Picture' at a time from your bag," He instructed. "They are in the order you lived them. Look deep into each one, and your works will be revealed. Each will be tried by fire, but fear not, children, for it is a refining fire and will not harm you."

A rustling noise stirred as each person reached in their bag and produced their first 'Life Picture.' Caleb looked at his picture, and it was when he was very young going to church. He was amazed, as he looked into it; the picture came to life, like a mini-television or I-pod.

It revealed his faithful church attendance while other children wanted to just play. It made clear Caleb's desire to be there along with his childlike eagerness to learn.

When the scene played out, a burning coal descended on the picture, and it immediately burst into flame in Caleb's hands. His first instinct was to drop the flaming picture, but he remembered Jesus' Words and held tightly to his 'Life Picture.' To his amazement, his hands or garment were not burned.

The flame burned with intensity like a sparkler. It went out just as abruptly, leaving a smooth piece of polished gold in his hand. Caleb was surprised and thrilled as he rolled it around with his fingers. Since his clothing was without any pockets, Caleb laid his nugget carefully at his feet.

The next 'Life Picture' was of Caleb with playmates in school. He told them of his newfound faith, and the older ones ridiculed him. The picture noted the opportunities he had to share Christ with his friends - even the teachers, but he was too afraid to open his mouth.

An acceptable image won out over sharing Christ, and when the fire fell, the picture burned quickly, leaving ashes in Caleb's hands.

He regretted being too timid to speak out, but took comfort he had learned a valuable lesson back then, so when he stood before news cameras at great-grandmother Emile Trevor's funeral, which was his next 'Life Picture', he spoke boldly for Christ. When the flame burned out on this picture, Caleb beheld a beautiful diamond sparkling in his hand.

The discovery of each work held new insight for Caleb. For the first time in his life it became clear, those things he thought really mattered, some were fluff. Much of what Caleb considered important turned out not to be - and little, insignificant events or encounters that Caleb had even forgotten, produced the most adorning gems.

For instance, when Caleb worked hard at the pizza place, he thought the sacrifice to provide for his family was a noble and a good work. That scene burned into a tiny piece of silver, while the few words of witness and the testimony of his life before Symphony yielded a precious sapphire. Still others, such as blocks of time spent watching movies, television, idle talk or worthless arguments burned up as wood, hay, and stubble, leaving only a residue of ashes.

Caleb now understood what it meant to suffer loss. It was shame! He was ashamed how he had mismanaged his time - wasted it! It wasn't guilt he felt! No, it was shame for not doing more of what was really building treasures in Heaven. His eyes were open now; if only he could have known then, he would have done things differently - more time in prayer, God's Word, witnessing, serving, giving - these were the gold, silver, and precious stones.

An incredible thrilling discovery of the good works covered over the bad ones. Caleb couldn't wait to pull out the next 'Life Picture' to see what it would be. It was akin to a fantastic opening of Christmas presents.

One picture played out a brief encounter Caleb had forgotten about. One day while driving to college, he passed a man on the side of the road carrying a gas can. Caleb gave the man a ride to his stranded car, which was some distance, making Caleb late for class. The man thanked him over and over. In parting, Caleb gave him a little Gospel tract. There was no indication this man ever believed, but Caleb's heart and intentions were honored before the Lord Jesus. This work and many others became precious stones.

The two confrontations with enlightened ones burned into large rubies. Everyone who Caleb had prayed with to receive Christ was a pearl of great price in Caleb's growing collection of good works. Many emeralds were added from the ones who trusted Christ from the Concert Crusade.

This large cluster of gold, silver and precious gems glistened in the wetness of Caleb's tears of praise, adoration, joy and shame, which washed away the ashes. He took out the last picture and was puzzled why this one and why last? It was a portrait of him, Sarah, Esther and Mark.

So much emotion filled his heart as this one played out. It started with the first time he saw Sarah. It recalled every detail of their falling in love - their marriage - beginning their journey in life together. Sarah's pregnancy with each of their children came up. He saw the births of Esther and Mark. Through it all how Caleb and Sarah pulled together as a team - as partners - as one, and at those explosive times when hot, unkind words were hurled, and they made mistakes - with each other - with their kids - with those around them - tears and laughter, defeats and victories, they walked faithfully the path the Lord set them on - staying the course. The good times burned warm in his heart - the bad stabbed pain. He could see no more, he held the 'Life Picture' before Jesus. This was the most precious thing in all his life - his family

- and he offered them to his Lord Jesus. Flames of mercy came down to burn it up. When it was over, Caleb's hands were full of many little precious gems of all kinds, mingled with ashes.

## Chapter 59

# Rewards

Caleb saw his grandpa Clifton weeping and realized he was suffering loss. The fragments of his earthly life, which were fused into gems, he clutched in one hand. Clifton dropped to his knees and wailed. Rachel, whose pile of precious stones far exceeded her husband's, tried to console him.

Cries of anguish and lament rose all around Caleb.

"Oh, dear!" Sarah was deeply moved. "I feel so sorry for all of them!"

"I come to my Lord empty-handed," a man's voice in the crowd could be heard.

A pitiful moan of a woman behind Caleb sobbed out, "My life was wasted – wasted - wasted."

"I was a fool!" spoke another.

"Oh, God, what could have been!" Caleb recognized Janee Stemper's voice. She had a sizeable number of gems, but still suffered loss from years of selfish living.

Caleb looked at Sarah, and her eyes met his.

"Oh, Caleb! What can we do? We have so many - of these. Do you think we can share ours with others? Look at poor T. J. and Penny!"

"I know," Caleb replied. "Some of my family too, and Esther has only a few. Let's just give all ours away, Sarah, we can do without. Just being here is enough!"

"Oh, yes!" and Sarah bent down and scooped up two handfuls of her own jewels.

"You cannot," both angels gently halted the couple's unselfish intentions.

The anguished cries of grief, sorrow and shame grew to a deafening roar. To those who suffered loss, and now understood what they could have done in their lives, their regret was heart wrenching. Many of them, no doubt, devoted their whole lives to that which was only wood, hay, and stubble. They watched it all burn up before their eyes, leaving only a pile of ashes.

Others, who built on gold, silver, and precious stones, were dismayed not knowing how to help their grieving family and friends, then Jesus' love began to spill out of His Heart to everyone who stood before His Judgment Seat. His Word was recalled into every mind, "For by grace are ye saved through faith; and that not of yourselves; it is the gift of God; not of works, lest any man should boast."

That joyful revelation fell on the assembly - salvation is a gift of God - rewards are according to the works of each believer. They remembered what Jesus had told them, "Rejoice that your name is written in the Book of Life."

Suddenly, the whole of Paradise was filled with adoring, thankful praises of God's people - coming before their Lord, Jesus Christ, seated on His Judgment Seat – heard into the very throne room of God, the Father.

# Chapter 60

# Crowns

"Dearly beloved," Jesus spoke to His quieted people. "The moment I spoke of in my Word has now arrived. Your works have been tried, and now I am pleased to give you my rewards. There are five judgments to pass in the course of mankind, occurring at different times. I am the Judge of each one of them. This is the third judgment, and its purpose is for rewards. As there are five judgments, so are there five rewards. Crowns I give to you - your rewards!"

Five angels, giving forth-brilliant light reflected from the Lord Jesus Christ, took their place at the foot of the Judgment Seat. The first angel shouted for the multitudes to hear.

"The Crown of Life! For those who loved God and found strength to overcome temptations and endure trials."

There followed a loud whooshing sound of millions of angels descending on the children of God. Each carried a Crown of Life. An angel alighted in front of Caleb, knelt on one knee, and bowed his head as he held up the beautiful crown to Caleb.

"Caleb Hillag," the angel spoke with the utmost respect, "for your faithful love of the Father."

Caleb received his crown, and through tear-filled eyes saw Sarah hugging her crown.

"The Crown Incorruptible!" the second angel at the Judgment Seat declared, "for those who denied self and ran the race to win."

Again, there were the sounds of angels' wings as millions of the creatures arrived, bearing stunning crowns. One set down before Caleb, knelt and spoke with reverence, holding up the crown.

"For denying self, keeping your eyes fixed on the Christ, finding strength to run the race, and placing your all on the altar of the Lord."

Caleb received his second crown humbly. With his messed up life, he never dreamed he would receive two crowns. Weeping even more, he glanced over to see his great-grandparents Farmer and Emile holding high their crowns in praise to the King!

The third angel stepped forth to announce, "The Crown of Rejoicing! The soul-winners' crown!"

This crown was true to its name, as rejoicing broke forth, not just from those who had won souls to Christ, but from everyone, remembering with grateful hearts, those who had been a part of their coming to Jesus. The rejoicing turned to praises to the Lamb that was slain, and ended in profound worship.

Each crown was breathtaking in the design, workmanship and material used. No human hands or angelic beings had assembled these exquisite crowns. No! The Lord Himself had been busy forming, molding and making each one with His own Hands. A humble carpenter now a glorious crown maker - each a prize that would endure forever.

"Caleb Hillag," the angel spoke, lifting up a Crown of Rejoicing, "for your faithful witness with your life - words you spoke – and cheerful giving that led many to faith in your Savior."

For an instant, when Caleb took hold of this precious crown, images of people's faces came before his mind. Those he reached with the Gospel message of salvation. He lifted his voice rejoicing over each one he saw. He heard Sarah doing the same next to him.

"The Crown of Righteousness!" pealed the voice of the fourth angel loudly. Her voice was strong and melodic, "for those who looked and longed for the return of the Son of God, Jesus Christ."

Caleb was not sure about this crown. He had thought about the return of Christ while on earth, but got caught up in business - not in Christ. In fact, there were times he prayed for the Lord to delay His return so he could reach more souls. His idea of someone to be given this reward was that person totally consumed in Christ's return. He couldn't think of enough to qualify him for this crown. He was flabbergasted to see an angel float down in front of him, holding a brilliant crown. She knelt on one knee, holding up Caleb's crown as the other angels had done. He heard Sarah beside him cry as she also received her crown.

"I didn't believe I would get this crown; I was fearful sometimes of Jesus coming back - that I wouldn't be ready!"

"Caleb Hillag," the angel spoke softly, "because you believed in the return of your Lord and lovingly looked for Him, you fought a good fight, you finished your course, and you kept the faith. Your Crown of Righteousness."

Many of Caleb and Sarah's families were also given the crown. The whole assembly began chanting as they sang, "Hallelujah! Hallelujah! Hallelujah! You kept Your promise and returned for us! Hallelujah! Hallelujah! Hallelujah!"

This worship commenced for a long – long while. Finally, the praise singing and shouts of glory subsided, and stillness fell upon the congregation. It was time for the fifth and final crown. The last of the five angels stepped forth.

"The Crown of Glory!" the angel's proclamation energized the Body of Christ with eager anticipation! "That
fadeth not away!"

Everyone waited for the angel to give the explanation
of this reward; however, it was the Lord Jesus Himself who
spoke.

"This crown is for my faithful pastors who fed my lambs
and sheep without compromise, and were responsible for
their care and spiritual oversight. You preached the Word as
I instructed you, in season and out of season, without fear, or
to please man, or for money. Many of you endured hardships
and rejection. Others gave your lives. You did so because
you loved my people as you loved Me."

Caleb could no longer hold back tears that now freely
flowed in a stream that carried away all the heartaches, diffi-
culties, disappointments, and mostly those painful ministry
wounds inflected in the line of service! He wept unasham-
edly before the Lord, as an angel descended before him with
a magnificent crown. The angel bowed with humility and
great respect.

"Your Crown of Glory, Caleb Hillag, favored one, called
of God."

Caleb nodded; taking the glorious crown in his arms with
the other four he had received. He was surprised and curious
that Sarah also was given this last crown. He figured it was
because she was his wife, until he heard her presenting angel
speak.

"They that receive a prophet in the name of a prophet
receive a prophet's reward. Your Crown of Glory, Sarah
Hillag, for uplifting the Lord's ministers by prayer and
encouragement, giving freely of your time and offerings."

Sarah was also weeping now as she looked at Caleb.

"Oh, Lord," Caleb cried out, "how much my wife was a
part of what we did. Thank you, Sarah!"

They hugged each other, and then turned to see how many of their family had also received this precious crown. Caleb and Sarah's parents beamed, holding up their crowns - Grandparents Clifton and Rachel had theirs - Leah and Harold - Walter. Janee was dancing with hers. All these and countless others had under girded the work of their pastors. Caleb's mind drifted to the ones he had served with in his pastorates and at Global Missions. How each of them in their own ways had encouraged and lifted him up, shouldering a share of the load, becoming such a vital part of his ministry – some in a great way while others in smaller – all demonstrating their gift of helps. One by one, he pictured them and knew beyond any doubt they held their own Crown of Glory right now.

"Oh, Caleb, look at Seth," Sarah pointed. "He has nothing!"

Caleb's eyes sought out the man in the crowd. He looked so left out and dejected.

"He and millions like him who were aborted had no life experiences. They were never given a chance!" Caleb spoke softly to Sarah.

"I know," she whispered. "How sad - oh, look, Caleb!"

Before their eyes, Seth's Mother Janee, and his Great-grandparents Farmer and Emile gathered around him and joyfully placed their crowns on Seth's head. He was thrilled, and Janee spun him in happy circles.

Then an awesome thing occurred. The Lord Jesus Christ rose from His Judgment Seat to stand before His people. All eyes were intently on their Savior and Lord. A tremendous sense of gratitude came over everyone assembled in this vast valley, and it just seemed a natural thing to do. People fell on their knees – with an adoration of depths Caleb had never experienced in mortal life. With thankful praise and song - each in their own way of expression – one by one all laid out their crowns - with loving and grateful hearts for what He had done on the cross. It was an incredible moment! Every heart, mind, spirit and soul were totally in tune and united in worship of the Lamb that was Slain, the Lion of Judah, the Door, the Way, the Bread of Life, the Good Shepherd, the Rose of Sharon, the Bright and Morning Star, the Resurrected Lord, King of Kings and Rewarder of those who diligently sought Him, the Alpha and the Omega, their Savior and Bridegroom!

The Glory of the Son of God became so brilliant in splendor that lasers of white light shot out reaching into every corner. People sat up in surprised wonder. The beams of light appeared focused on the piles of works' gems. Then the Lord did an amazing feat! One at a time, the precious stones were fused into the crowns.

Caleb watched in astonishment as his pieces of gold and silver were first attached, then diamonds, emeralds, rubies, pearls, amethysts, topaz, turquoise, jade, opals, sapphires and many other beautiful varieties that Caleb had never even heard of, adorned and crested his crowns. The design and placement were perfect, and he realized now his crowns were not complete before. A thrill raced through Caleb and Sarah as they beheld this wonder. The works of their lives were now a part of their crowns - resplendent - lasting forever!

Jesus showered His rich blessings on all His people, spreading wide His arms, He spoke with great pleasure and unfathomed love, "Well done, My good and faithful servants! Well done!"

# Chapter 61

# Wedding Jitters

S arah was taken by surprise to find a shiny silver robe hanging in her house. She hurriedly laid her crowns on a table; she couldn't wait to try on her new garment. It fit perfectly! She selected one of her crowns and fit it on her head. She hurried next door to show Caleb. He was studying a robe identical to Sarah's.

"This has to be for the marriage feast," he commented.

"Oh, how exciting! I can't wait! Look at me, Caleb!" Sarah spun around in girlish glee.

"Sarah, you are gorgeous," Caleb complimented her beauty.

"Try yours on! You will be so handsome!"

"Sure, a handsome bride," Caleb remarked dryly. "The Lord Jesus will have to help me with this bride thing. I was a groom on earth."

"Oh, funny man, Jesus will make it a perfectly wonderful wedding. Okay, think of it this way," Sarah laughed. "We are the whole church as one body before the Lord. We make up the bride - together."

"Yes, I know you are right," Caleb sighed.

"Hurry, try your robe on!"

Caleb had no sooner donned his robe than Esther burst into the house in her robe and her Crown of Life seated atop her head.

"Hey! Aren't we cool or what?" she bubbled over.

Sarah grabbed Esther's hand, and they swung in circles, laughing exuberantly, "We're going to a wedding - we are the bride of Christ - the Son of God!"

Caleb frowned, then had to smile at their antics.

"Let's visit our parents," he suggested.

"Oh, yes, let's," Sarah agreed, "and let them see our robes -." She hesitated – sensing a check in her spirit that these were not to be worn yet. A look in Caleb's face told her he felt the same.

"Have you noticed, Sarah," Caleb spoke as he removed his robe, "since the Judgment Seat, a continuing increase in knowledge and understanding?"

"Yes, I think it just dawned on me."

"Me too! For the first time, geometry makes sense."

"Oh, shush, Esther," Sarah pushed her and all three laughed.

"We are pleased to see you happy," Sarah's angel Portus smiled. "We observed you in such anguish and pain frequently on earth."

"Those struggles are over, so you can truly laugh from a joyful heart," Herculon added, and Esther's angel agreed.

"Let's go visit anyway," Esther tugged at Sarah's sleeve, and through the door they flew.

A curious thing left them puzzled when they made their visits. Hannah, Penny, T. J. - their robes were silver. So also were the robes of Caleb's parents, but Caleb's Grandparents Clifton and Rachel had robes of golden brown. So were Harold's, Leah's, Walter's and Janee's.

Since no one seemed to understand the reason for the difference, the trio decided to go ask Great-grandfather Farmer.

"Beats me ta pieces," he declared, "didn't even know there was a variety 'til ya jus' now tol' me. Ya all jus' sit tight, an' I'll be right back."

While Farmer was gone, Emile showed them their crowns.

"How do you tell them apart?" Sarah asked. "You have them all mixed up."

"Oh, we know. Farmer's head is much too big for mine," Emile smiled.

"I only have one crown," Esther said sadly.

Emile took Esther in her arms. "That's such an accomplishment for you in such a short time. Think what you could have done had you lived more years. Why, I declare, child, when I was your age, I doubt I had any crowns won. Jewels - ha! I would have held a handful of gravel. So don't you fret. Thank God, you are here!"

"My Mom and Step-sister were rewarded two. Penny's husband T. J. received only one," Sarah reflected.

"There is no envy in this place - no counting - no comparing," Emile hastened to remind them. "I'm as proud of you with one crown as if you had five. Think of Seth along with countless others. They have no crowns."

Just then Farmer appeared.

"Well, a right strange thing thet's got me to do a powerful heap o' thinkin'," he stroked his chin, fishing for the words he wanted to say.

"Now, my Ma and Pa hev turquoise colorin' on their robes. Smartest I ever did see! Outshines those Indian stones we saw in New Mexico and Arizona, Emile. But what has me also a mite wondering as ta what the Lord is up ta, 'cause He don't do accidents or haphazard things, but always has Hisself a plan. Also seen my Great-grandpa and ma has robes o' light tan. Now explain thet to me. The church will be a speckled goose."

The family was engaged in lively and questioning conversation over robes and crowns, when the air split open with the sounds of thousands of trumpets pealing over all of Paradise! Everyone was instantly quiet. Was it time? The angels were alert as though waiting a command. The trumpets resounded again, then once more for the third time. Instantly, all of Paradise was alive with the most astounding heavenly instruments and choirs announcing the coming of the Bridegroom. Sarah's spirit quickened inside of her. She was experiencing the joy and excitement of anticipation in proportions she had never known as an earthly bride!

"The Bridegroom cometh," all the angels announced in unison.

Suddenly, the inside of the log house was a flurry of activity and noise!

"We must go!" Caleb urged Sarah and Esther.

"Oh my, it's been so long since I was a bride," exclaimed Emile.

"Be a first fer me an' Caleb, but I reckon we can be jus' as anxious!" Farmer laughed.

"I'm so excited, I - can't - even talk! Right!" giggled Sarah.

"I've got the jitters!" Esther blurted out.

# Chapter 62

# Marriage of The Lamb

S arah could not imagine what was in store for all of them.
That unknown factor heightened her curiosity, which, in
turn, supercharged her excitement. She felt breathless and
giddy, wondering what Caleb and the others were thinking.

"It will be a sight and experience like no other" – Caleb
seemed to read her mind.

Sarah wanted to rush, but their angels restrained them.
When Sarah glanced behind, she realized the group she was
in, with their silver robes was last. 'Well, that certainly made
sense. They were the last ones to leave earth,' she thought.

Believers were all headed in one direction, forming a
huge congregation miles upon miles wide and stretching out
before her as far as the eye could see. Sarah was able to make
out that they were coming to a far distant mountain range,
and the Christians were going up and over it. It felt like ages
drug by to Sarah's anxious spirit before they arrived at the
mountains. Then it took what seemed forever to reach the
top.

The closer they came to the high ridge line, the louder
a noise reverberated back which were assembled clamors
of shouts, cheers, whoops and exclamations of awe and

wonder. She understood what was causing the commotion the instant she crested the mountain, for spread out in the vast panoramic space below was a sight never before seen by human eyes. Millions of people who made up the church, the Bride of Christ, taking their places at rows of tables spread out before them clear across the valley. Millions of angels singing heavenly songs hovered over the bride. They formed a brilliant canopy.

"My Lord and my God!" Caleb cried out at the sight. Sarah was speechless in awe.

"Wow!" Esther exclaimed.

Sarah would have figured they would be seated at this end of the valley, most further from the Lord, but all of these tables were already filled up. Sarah could tell this puzzled Caleb, Esther and the rest in her group. 'We will be closest to Jesus, but why?' she questioned.

"From what I can tell," Caleb spoke, "is that we will follow those ahead of us down those rows between tables to the far end.

"Do you think there is a place for us?" Esther asked. "Or will we have to stand on the sides?"

"Of course we will have a place at a table. Whoever heard of a bride standing at her wedding?" quipped Sarah.

Approaching the first tables of eager, applauding believers, the arriving Christians were funneled into isles to walk between lines of tables. Happy people on both sides reached out to touch them. What a reception this was! Christ's redeemed in their robes, wearing their crowns. What a procession! Sarah's group in their silver robes surrounded on both sides by fellow Christians attired in their rich choco-late-colored robes and brilliant crowns.

"This is the last generation," Sarah heard someone on her right say. "They were caught up to meet Jesus!"

A gentle hand on her left took her arm. Sarah turned to look into a beaming smile.

"I'm Tabitha - we are overjoyed to see you!"

"Tabitha?" Sarah questioned.

"Maybe you know me as Dorcas."

"You mean the woman Peter raised from the dead?"

"Yes! Praise be to God!"

Sarah squeezed Tabitha's hand not knowing quite what to say. She moved on. This was like a dream!

"Caleb," she tugged at his robe whispering, "We are in the midst of the first century church.

He nodded - overwhelmed. About then a man reached out to him. Sarah strained to hear above the crowd.

"Hail, brother! I'm Timothy."

Sarah could see Caleb break down and weep, as they moved on.

"Why aren't we here instead of you? This is the end farthest from our Lord!"

Another man stepped in to answer.

"I'm Andrew, Peter's brother. Don't you remember Jesus' teaching, the first shall be last and the last shall be first. We are blessed by your presence, my friend."

As they made their way through the rows of tables, shouts, cheers and happy clapping greeted them. There was an overpowering urge to stop and visit, but they had to keep walking. Abruptly the robes changed from the chocolate to crimson then to yellow to green. The understanding that came to them as they proceeded between long rows of tables was how each century had a different color of garment. What they couldn't know right then was that the believers whose lives crossed over from one generation to the next had a different color also, and that each color reflected the historical events of that century. Some colors were bright, others bleak! What was seen only by the angels overhead was that the set-up of the tables formed the shape of a long, flowing wedding gown, and the robes placed a stripe of color across the width of the gown. A gorgeous dress of multi-colors could be seen looking down. Thus, the collected church as a whole made up the bride. The Raptured in their silver robes formed the neckline.

Poles covered with flowers held white streamers fluttering softly in a gentle breeze giving the entire valley the look of wavy chiffon. White doves in great abundance added their songs of love to those of the angels.

The table decorations were exquisite, carefully done in a delicate, elaborate fashion to enhance the beauty of each table with unending creativity. Sarah was dazzled and thrilled when she found her place marked by an elegant solid gold plate with her name on it.

Glancing around, she found much of the family in different locations at tables several rows away, but in eyesight. Esther sat five seats away on her right; her and Caleb's places were together for which she was thankful. It seemed her resurrected mind still carried its girlish shyness. She slipped her hand in Caleb's as they were seated.

"Can you believe we are a part of this, Sarah? Never in the course of human history has there been a banquet to compare! And here we are by the grace of God! Praise the Lord!"

Sarah wondered at the seating. She knew it wasn't random - it must have purpose. She decided to get to know the ones around her. Across the table was a woman from the West Bank, a Palestinian. Next to her was a man from Jerusalem, and on the other side a woman from Kansas. Sarah learned the woman on her left and her husband were raptured out of Peru. Caleb was engaged in conversation with a man and grandmother who were from Viet Nam.

"Sarah, this brother was a pastor in Viet Nam. His wife was murdered in a prison, but he and his grandmother were raptured along with his two children.

'This is so incredible,' Sarah's mind boggled with the enormity of this gathering. Spread across a vast valley was assembled over 2000 years of the church age. Many were standing, others seated, all engaged in excited, engrossed conversations. Just like a typical wedding that could have occurred in any century.

Trumpets sounding brought everyone to their feet! Next a shift in the angels' song as millions of voices of purest sound swelled in glorious music for the redeemed.

The angels sang, "Here we are to worship, here we are to bow down, here we are to say that You're our God."

Millions of voices of the church responded in melodious song, "You are altogether lovely, altogether worthy, altogether wonderful."

The angels, "Here we are to worship, here we are to bow down."

The church, "Light of the world, You stepped down into darkness. Opened our eyes so we could see!"

Then the voices of angels and humans rose in majestic harmony, the angels singing, "Here we are to worship, here we are to bow down," while the church chanted, "We'll never know how much it cost to see our sins upon that cross. We'll never know how much it cost to see our sins upon that cross!"

The tempo of Heaven's instruments changed, and the key dropped an octave. Every Christian felt a song of praise well up in their hearts - each different - but they blended perfectly - a sweet incense of music - as every heart sang as never before, making a sound unlike any other in all of time.

Now the angels burst forth:

"You are the Lord. Great is Your Name. The Heavens declare your Glory!"

The Christians answered:

"You are beautiful. You are our Lord!"

Now the music from the angels slowed and softened:

"Prepare - prepare the way of the Lord.

Prepare - prepare the way of the Lord."

The Bride answered:

"Jesus - Jesus - Jesus - Jesus - Jesus."

"You are the Light of the world - You are the King of the earth!"

"Jesus - Jesus - Jesus - Jesus - Jesus."

Now the two parts came together in mighty victorious singing reaching to the very Throne of Grace! Then a sudden hush... Jesus was coming! Every heart knew it! The One we love comes...Be still. No sound...Our Bridegroom comes...

Trumpets heralded over all of Paradise, followed by a multitude of shouts announcing the Lord's arrival.

"Behold, the Bridegroom cometh!"

The church bowed their heads in submissive love and adoration.

After Jesus took His Place as the Head of the Church, there was heard the voice of a great multitude, and as the voice of many waters, and the voice of mighty thunderings, saying,

"Alleluia: for the Lord God omnipotent reigneth. Let us be glad and rejoice, and give honor to Him: for the marriage of the Lamb is come, and His bride hath made herself ready!"

In one sweeping motion of His Arms, Jesus gathered His Bride to Himself and loved her. The greatest love story in the entire universe for 2,000 years had been moving toward this very moment. Now it was here!

Sarah felt Christ's Love wash over her in unbridled freedom. She was His - they all were His, and in that instant every robe - from the birth of the church to the last saint raptured - turned a spotless, pure white.

This became a time of basking in the presence of the Bridegroom. No words spoken amongst them - every eye on Him and Him alone - every heart in tune to His. Nothing else mattered; just being with Him was enough. Love so strong, words unnecessary! What needed saying was felt. Hearts - souls - spirits - as one.

# Chapter 63

# The Marriage Feast

"Let the celebration begin with the arrival of honored guests!" Jesus proclaimed to His Beloved. Mirth, gladness and delight radiated from His Face and Loving Smile!

Sarah had been so caught up in busy activities, the glorious singing and just seeing Jesus, the radiant Bridegroom, and the marriage, she had paid no attention to all the empty tables on both sides of the Bride.

"We sure are missing a lot o' folks from this here supper," Walter Trevor could be heard from two rows over.

Again, the trumpets made their brass announcement, but this time it was the beginning of a triumphal march, as scores of people clothed in garments of splendor and royal crowns on their heads made their appearances. Angels sang out their names as one by one they approached the Lord, Jesus Christ and knelt before Him. The Bride of Christ stood to their feet in respect.

"The very first man and woman, Adam and Eve, followed by their descendants who looked to the coming of the Lamb of God," the angels sang about the first guests.

A collective gasp came from the Christians as they realized the honored guests were the Old Testament saints. Caleb looked at Sarah.

"I can't believe what we are seeing!" she whispered to him, touching his arm.

She did not recognize many of the names of a numberless flow of individuals kneeling before the Christ. Who knew how long this would take, nor did it matter. There was no "tired" here, no boredom or disinterest, but every time a name was sung out by the host of angels, who were listed in scripture, a burst of excitement shot through the whole body of Christ, which prompted shouts of praise, wild applause and joyful acclamations.

After Methuselah, Lamech and their families, the number of saints dwindled over centuries until there were only eight. A subdued awestruck response came from the Bride when the angels introduced Noah and his family.

"We wouldn't be here if it were not for them," Caleb commented in appreciation of their sacrifice and long years of faithful preaching to the lost, and toilsome labor to build the ark.

Hymns of praise, shouts of Hallelujah and excited cries rose to match the angels' song when the processional of the Patriarchs and their descendents approached Jesus to drop to their knees. Abraham led them. Jesus reached down to lift the great old man of faith to his feet, and then the Son of Man folded that Patriarch into His Arms in a hug that spoke words known and understood only by Abraham.

A huge roar burst from the church, and Sarah saw tears streaming down Caleb's face, matching her own. Emotion swept through the heart and soul of the Bride, reaching a depth of unsearchable richness. Actually, seeing those read about in scripture brought an abandonment of excitement, while they were moved to weeping. There was Moses, Joshua and all of the rest, followed by the Judges and the saints of that era. Loud applause exploded for Samuel, but silence fell over the church when the angels' song introduced King David. This was a man after God's own heart, and for the second time, Jesus Christ rose from His seat to receive this guest as He had with Abraham.

David drew a sword as he approached Jesus. The king of Israel knelt before the King of Kings on one knee holding up the sword in both hands - symbolic of one king surrendering to one greater.

"I've waited ages to do this," the whole congregation heard David proclaim. Everyone went crazy when Jesus accepted the sword and raised David to his feet to stand before Him. With a grand sweep of his hand David gave attention over to Bathsheba and his other wives each with their children, led by King Solomon. Generations followed them.

Last to arrive were the Prophets of old. Their appearance also generated an enthusiastic response from the Bride of Christ.

"Wow! This is fantastic!! Esther blurted out.

One after another they marched in: Isaiah, Jeremiah, Ezekiel, Daniel, Hosea, Joel, Amos, Obadiah, Jonah, Micah, Nahum, Habakkuk, Zephaniah, Haggai, Zachariah, Malachi and many others - most Sarah had never heard of - none the less, just as important.

A meaningful awe settled on all believers when the man who called down fire from God, Elijah, was introduced by angelic song. On his heels came Elisha, and the congregation erupted once again, with profound shouts in a heavenly standing ovation!

Now Jesus stood up again, and the immense gathering slowly stilled. Jesus spoke the same words he said to his disciples over 2,000 years before.

"For I say unto you, among those that are born of women there is not a greater prophet than John the Baptist."

A most beautiful tribute to the man who only decreased that his Lord might increase, swelled until it filled the sky above the Bridegroom, His Bride and all of the Old Testament guests. John the Baptist thrilled them all with his appearance, bringing tears as John fell at his Savior's feet, kissing them.

As these prophets had marched to a different drum in life, that same stubborn, loyal, raw courage that caused them to stand apart facing ridicule, torture, prison, untold hardships, even death, was still demonstrated in the love they displayed to the Lord they had longed to see! With holy laughter they took their places.

Everyone seated, millions of ministering angels flew in to serve the savoriest delicacies ever eaten by mankind. The greatest of feasts attended on earth paled a thousand times over compared to this Marriage Supper. Pure food, true fellowship, luscious drink, stainless celebration, unblemished Bride, Holy Bridegroom, immaculate love!

"Eat your fill, my friends of old. Drink deep, my Beloved!"

# Chapter 64

# Last Things

Caleb and Sarah never figured any experience could top the Marriage Supper of the Lamb, preceded by the Victorious Processional of the Old Testament saints - that is until Jesus led all of them into the very heart of Heaven before the Throne of God the Father.

They felt the power of the Almighty as they assembled on a sea of glass mingled with fire, which did not burn. It was as stated in scripture, 'To look upon Him was like unto a jasper and sardius stone.' Surrounding the throne were thick clouds emitting lightning, thunder, an emerald rainbow and the voices of many waters. They stood in awe! They were looking into the Face of God the Father!

Before the throne were seated twenty-four elders in white raiment. Round about the throne were four beasts full of eyes, crying, "Holy, Holy, Holy, Lord God Almighty, which was, and is, and is to come!"

Then the twenty-four elders fell down in worship, and cast their crowns before God, saying, "Thou art worthy, Oh, Lord, to receive glory and honor and power: for Thou hast created all things, and for thy pleasure they are and were created."

Next, Jesus did something totally unexpected, still they should have anticipated He would walk to the throne and take His place at the Right Hand of the Father, and the Glory of the Father, Son and Holy Spirit burst forth as One God!

With a sweeping motion of His Hands, Jesus presented the Old Testament saints, and then He introduced His Bride to the Father, who gave His love, pleasure, and acceptance. Without hesitation everyone fell upon their faces before a loving Father who was Creator of the universe. He had spoken the world into existence by His Word. Caleb and Sarah could not comprehend that kind of power, and knew if the Blood of Jesus Christ did not cover them, the Brilliance and Glory of God would instantly consume them.

Yet instead of wrath, they felt a vast abiding love coming forth from the Father, and they simply wanted to love Him back. He was the One they had prayed to in the Name of Jesus Christ the Son. He was their Father, the One they constantly ran into His presence in prayer, pouring out their hearts. He was the One who knew each of them by name and numbered the hairs on their heads. He was the awesome God they sang about and above all else were anxious to please. In reverent wonder, the numberless multitude worshipped the God of Heaven and cast their crowns humbly before Him following the example of the elders.

Jesus called His children to their feet. What a sight! WHAT A SIGHT! The Old Testament saints who by faith had believed and looked toward Christ's work of redemption on the cross, standing in their regal robes, alongside the church clothed in dazzling white, shrouded by heaven's host of angels and holy creatures.

Music erupted from every side, and there grew a sense without any instruction that what was taking place was of utmost importance. It was a deeply spiritual matter and all of heaven was moved. Jesus Christ, the Son gave the Kingdom to the Father. This caused enormous victorious rejoicing from the vast throng of humans and angels.

After a time, the Lord called for every ones attention and quiet. A great multitude from all nations and kindred and people and tongues filed in to take their place in front of the Father. They were clothed in white and held palms and harps in their hands.

When they were all assembled, a loud voice cried out!

"These are they which came out of great tribulation and have washed their robes, and made them white in the blood of the Lamb. They have won victory over the beast, and over his image, and over his mark, and over the number of his name."

A collective gasp spread throughout the Bride as they realized these were Tribulation Saints who had been martyred for their faith in Christ. The gasps converted into groans of deepest grief and anguish over what these saints had endured. The groans grew stronger and increased louder and louder into cries of great indignation taking on a unified appeal to the Lord:

"How long, oh, Lord, how long will You allow this to continue? How long?" billions of hearts wailed in an agonized pleading!

Frantically, Caleb and Sarah looked for Mark, but there were simply too many assembled at the Throne to single any one person out. They looked to Herculon and Portus, who indicated that for now, only God, who would wipe away the Tribulation Saint's tears, knew who these martyrs were. Jesus alone would give them special care. For now, the latter generations were left to wonder, uncertain of their loved ones' fates.

When it was over, everyone was released to return to their places. Every heart was full, minds reeling to replay events and experiences they had just come through together. Time to think was needed, but no one wanted to be alone.

The family heeded Farmer and Emile's invitation to gather at their place.

The mood was somber in the Trevor log mansion. They had just seen and been a part of momentous events that carried them from the heights of emotional exhilaration to the depths of agonizing grief. The compelling desire for quiet reflection, to assimilate, even with their ever-expanding knowledge, the enormity of events cloaked the group in silence.

Eventually, the need to express feelings spilled over from flooded hearts, and, of course, Caleb would be the one to say what many were thinking.

"We all looked and longed to see loved ones and friends standing there that we left behind on earth, but there were so many and we weren't close enough to see their faces. For whatever reason, the Lord chose not to reveal who was there or who was not. But this fact we know for certain; the end is near. We can't conceive of the horrible conditions there right now or the terrible persecution of those still living. They are facing peril, wars, disasters, starvation, and diseases, and intense persecution everyday. Those professing Christ are subjected to cruelty and torture we never knew. The ones we saw standing before the throne resisted the beast and refused his mark. They paid dearly with their lives, and there will be more to follow – it's not over."

"Mark would never take that awful - thing!" Esther cried, throwing herself into Sarah's arms for consolation.

"We hope not, Esther. Hope is all we can hold onto now," Sarah smoothed Esther's hair.

Caleb put his arms around both of them. The words came hard. "We don't know what he will do. He could be among those standing before the throne - or - or in the place of torment - or still alive on the earth. Right now, only God knows."

Printed in the United States
213624BV00002B/2/P

9 781607 913948